Praise for Carolyn Crane's
Head Rush

"*Head Rush* is just as it should be, a perfect end to an amazing trilogy of illusions."

~ *Readaholics Anonymous*

"This final book in the trilogy offers plenty of, romance, action and adventure, and a satisfying ending. It had me in tears and cheers."

~ *La Deetda Reads*

"This series is one that has an earned a permanent spot on my keeper shelf."

~ *A Buckeye Girl Reads*

Look for these titles by
Carolyn Crane

Now Available:

The Disillusionist Trilogy
Mind Games
Double Cross
Head Rush

Head Rush

Carolyn Crane

Samhain Publishing, Ltd.
11821 Mason Montgomery Road, 4B
Cincinnati, OH 45249
www.samhainpublishing.com

Head Rush
Copyright © 2012 by Carolyn Crane
Print ISBN: 978-1-60928-808-2
Digital ISBN: 978-1-60928-625-5

Editing by Heather Osborn
Cover by Kanaxa

First Samhain Publishing, Ltd. electronic publication: December 2011
First Samhain Publishing, Ltd. print publication: September 2012

Dedication

To my readers. Your enthusiasm and support have been among the most unexpected and greatest gifts of my life.

Chapter One

Simon skids his souped-up Cutlass to a stop on the tire-strewn ridge. Below us, the Midcity impound lot stretches for miles, an ocean of cars enclosed in a razor-wire fence, and beyond that, mountains of gravel and old tires.

"Christ, Simon," I say, gently shaking my hand, trying to relax it out of the claw position it froze in from gripping the passenger door. "I am never riding with you again."

"If we find your car, you won't have to." Simon passes me a pair of binoculars, and points down at a distant section of cars. "My intelligence says that cars towed in mid-January are in the southeast quadrant."

"Your intelligence." I peer through the binoculars, adjusting the focus. "If you had any intelligence, the last half hour wouldn't have happened."

"You are such a baby when you don't zing."

"Oh, that must be it."

Getting here involved recklessly eluding my bodyguard through a maze of Midcity side streets, cutting across a mud gulley, sideswiping several concrete barriers, and speeding through a narrow gap in a high-voltage electric fence. At least the legendarily thuggish impound-lot operators haven't materialized. But hey, it's still early.

"No bodyguards. Pure freedom. Like old times," he says. "The days of kebabs and ouzo."

And with that, Simon evokes everything I've been trying to forget, or at least leave behind. Lazy dinners at the restaurant. The camaraderie of our shadowy club. Packard and me in the back booth. The candlelight, the discoveries, the lies. The intensity in Packard's gaze, as though the emotions inside him burn too hot. The aliveness I felt.

I grip the binoculars hard, willing this train of thought to stop before it hits its destination.

"You know you love this," Simon says.

"Yeah, Simon, I love this." My sarcastic tone is a lie—I *do* love it. It's been weeks since I've been off the radar and free of a bodyguard. Okay, maybe I'm not thrilled to be hanging around in Midcity's highest-crime sector, but then again, all of Midcity is a high-crime sector these days. In fact, this March is already the city's most violent month on record, and it's not even half over.

I scan for gray car tops. The last time I saw my trashed little Jetta was just before everything went to hell, and it was safe and sound in my own parking space behind my apartment building. Where is it? It's like this mystery nobody can solve—it doesn't make sense that somebody would steal it, except maybe for a joyride.

A lot doesn't make sense these days.

Simon cranks open the window and a crisp breeze flows in, carrying the mineral scent of thawing mud. I breathe deeply. A bit of a March warm-up before the blizzard tonight. It's always warm before a storm.

Simon sighs happily. "I think I'll have a special suit made, and possibly a top hat. How do you feel about top hats? Maybe all of us bridesmaids can wear top hats, to show we're a unit."

"We haven't found the car yet," I say.

"Keyword *yet*. Haven't found it *yet*."

Simon and I have made a bet: if he helps me find my car, he gets to be one of my bridesmaids for my wedding to Otto.

Simon won't win this one; Otto's had people checking every impound lot in the tri-state area—including this one—ever since my car went missing this past January. But if Simon loses, he's promised to make a genuine effort to be friends with Otto. It's pathetic of me to wager for that, but I want him to get to know

Otto better. Simon's the only disillusionist friend I have left besides Shelby; the rest have disappeared, some with Packard, probably far away by now, and I've heard other disillusionists are traveling, calling their own shots on where they go and what they do. A luxury none of us disillusionists had when we were minions.

A rattle. The cassette tape. Simon's flipping over Johnny Cash. Again.

A flash of red lights in the distance.

"Crap!" I pull away the binoculars and look with my naked eyes, but it's only a tow truck on the far side, pulling a car around the end of a gravel mountain. They're so far off, they look like toys.

"I'm on it," Simon says. "Keep looking." He's made this car thing such a priority.

I go back to my scanning, adjusting the focus for maximum crispness, but I can't tell where I'm looking in relation to the sea of cars as a whole; I'm just lurching around in oversized motions.

Lurching around in oversized motions is like a metaphor for my entire existence right now. In the last two months, I found out I wasn't a servile minion for life, I got engaged to Mayor Otto Sanchez, my building was condemned because city engineers discovered a mysterious sinkhole under it, and I was forced to move into Otto's condo because of it. And between the mysterious new wave of violent crime, the sleepwalking cannibals, and Otto's growing faction of enemies, the entire city is lurching around too. It's terrible, after Otto worked so hard to clean up the crime problem when he was police chief.

But most devastating of all, I watched Packard shoot a good man, point blank.

I thought I knew people. *I thought I knew Packard.*

Watching Packard shoot Avery—not only a good man but the man my best friend, Shelby, loved—changed everything. I haven't trusted the ground beneath me ever since.

I haven't trusted myself.

My thoughts drift back to the scene. Avery's frightened eyes. The way his body jerked when Packard shot him in the chest, then a different jerk when he shot him in the face.

A twinge in my head. *Damn.* I lower the binoculars and take a centering breath. I've been getting this stabbing pain behind my eyes whenever I think about the shooting. Shock, no doubt.

Otto says that whenever I catch myself dwelling on the shooting, I should switch my focus to the future. He doesn't understand why that won't work. How can I tell my fiancé that every time I think about his enemy Packard shooting a man, it feels like the end of the world?

"Definitely a top hat," Simon says.

I concentrate on the image of Simon in a top hat. "What color?"

"Black," Simon says.

"Oh yeah? What else."

Simon drones on, and I allow my thoughts to be hijacked by his disturbing description of what he'd wear if he gets to stand up for me at my wedding. It involves a shirt constructed from belts and chains, black pants, some sort of cape, and pirate boots. I'm laughing by the end. "Otto will be so thrilled."

I resume my scanning.

In spite of his potential bridesmaid's outfit, part of me wouldn't mind Simon's winning, because it would mean I'd have my little car back. Yes, it makes a funny noise and has a smashed taillight. And yes, Otto has repeatedly offered to buy me a new car. But having my old one back would be like having a bit of my old life back. Something of the old crimefighter Justine.

The binoculars are irritating my eye sockets. Some of the car tops seem familiar. Am I going over the same area twice? I pull the glasses away from my face. Is this bad for my head? I rub my left temple. "It's like a kaleidoscope of car tops."

"Are you being methodical?"

"No."

"Give me those." Simon grabs the binoculars, flips a hunk of black hair out of his eyes, and takes over looking. Simon fancies himself a crack investigator, though to me, the first rule of being a good sleuth is that you should not draw attention to yourself, something Simon utterly fails in. Today he's wearing a shaggy, white fake-fur coat, perfect for creating that bedraggled poodle-bear effect. No shirt of course, all the better to display the dragon tattoos covering his chest. He's finished his ensemble with black jeans and boots.

"Trashed gray Jetta," he says. "But you don't have a parking sticker on your windshield, right?"

"No. And look for the Gumby on the dash."

"Right. 'Ol' Gumby'."

"The car must be intact and operational," I remind him. "Otto says that after two months, it's sure to have been chopped up or junked."

"We'll see about that." This in a tone that's just a little too casual.

I give him a look. Simon's definitely up to something. He says he heard through his "PI grapevine" that an impound-lot employee was accidentally transposing license plate numbers, causing some cars to become invisible to the computer, and that this was happening during the stretch of time my car went missing. And he insisted on a bet. Simon can't pass up a long shot; his specialty as a disillusionist is recklessness. Gambling.

"Oooh, ooh, ooh—Jetta. Rear light smashed. Your license plate start with an H?"

I sit up. "Yeah."

Simon hands me the binoculars. "See that corner? Red car? Count twenty-four rows down and thirteen over."

I count down, then I lose my place and have to count some more, going back and forth between normal sight and the binoculars. After the fifth misfire, I take a rest, rubbing my eyes. "This back and forth is straining my vision," I say. "This is bad for me."

"You better not wig out."

"I'm not wigging out. I'm pacing myself. Excuse me if vein star runs in my family." I lift the heavy binoculars back to my eyes. "Strain on the eyes affects the whole head, you know. It strains the cranial-muscular system."

"How long has it been?"

How long have I gone without a zing, he means. "Sixty-two days."

"You're insane," he says.

"I'm free." Sixty-two days ago I zinged Otto's kidnappers. I petrified them with my fear. My last zing.

"Sixty two days," he groans.

"Which is amazing, considering all the nursing and anatomy textbooks I've been studying. Do you know how much fear that stokes up? But I haven't zinged any of it out. I couldn't have lasted this long without Otto." I feel this wave of gratitude for Otto, the one person who understands my terror, who's always there with me in my deepest pit of fear, because it's his pit too. We know the darkness of it, the sharpness of the rocky bottom. We help each other when we're down there—other people can't understand it because other people haven't been there. Nobody else fears vein-star syndrome like we do.

And of course, it doesn't hurt that Otto's considered one of the sexiest men in the city, all dusky curls and deep brown eyes. Lush, thick features and the strength of an ox. Local magazines and papers love to run his picture.

Simon says, "Sixty-two chances to feel normal. To feel that peace. Squandered."

"It's not peace if it ruins things for somebody else."

He sighs dramatically.

I give him a hard look above the binoculars. "And I'm not free if I have to zing somebody just to feel good."

He says, "The thirteen starts at a red truck, I think."

I get back to searching. Soon enough, a familiar car top. "Whoa!"

"You see it?"

Carefully, I adjust the view. I spot the smashed taillight, and my panda bumper sticker. "Holy crap! That's it!" I laugh incredulously. "You found it!"

"Good. Let's handle this. I have to pick out an outfit for your bridesmaids' dinner tomorrow. And start working on my outfit. Three days to the wedding. Can't wait!"

"I can't believe you found it."

"I *am* a PI."

"Oh really? Do you have a PI license?"

"I found your car, didn't I?" He starts up the engine.

"No bridesmaid of mine is wearing a chain-and-belt shirt."

"This one is." Simon makes a U-turn and speeds around a tire pile; ice crusts cling to its shady side like gray moss.

Simon as a bridesmaid. Otto's going to hate this. I take a deep breath, rubbing the muscles around my eyes. I wish Simon hadn't reminded me that I haven't been zinging, because it reminds me of the pain, and now I'm focusing on it again. Is it coming back? But I forgot about it before, didn't I? That shows it's not dire. *Snap out of it!* I tell myself. *It's nothing! You're just a stupid hypochondriac!*

"Look at you," Simon says. "You are building up way too much goddamned fear."

"I'm fine."

"All that potency, going to waste. With how much you have stoked right now, you could dominate anybody. Trump any weapon." He's been dying to see me strike fear into a random person, ever since we found out we can psychologically attack whomever we choose.

"Zinging isn't a superpower," I say. "It's a crutch that I don't need anymore. Because I'm free."

"I know you remember what it's like, Justine," he says smoothly, "when it all rushes out. All that darkness, overtaking them, and how light you feel. Serene, and so goddamned aware. The wind in your fingertips, the bliss. Glory hour—"

"Enough."

He turns back. "Fine. Let's talk top hats then."

We bump down a utility road, rocking over deep, mud ruts. I hang on, hoping the car doesn't slip down the hillside into the electrified fence.

Yes, zinging would feel good. Beyond good. That doesn't make it right.

"Of all things, Simon," I say. "What guy wants to be in a wedding? Most men would consider getting *out* of a wedding to be the prize. Are you sure you don't want something else? I bet Otto would pull strings to get you a PI license."

"Nah, I want to be in your wedding. I think it'll be fun...in a totally messed up way."

"Are you just trying to get back with Ez?" I ask.

He gives me a jaundiced look. "It'll take more than your wedding to pull *that* one out of the fire."

"Right," I say.

He grunts. "We're better suited for frenemies anyway."

Ez, one of my other bridesmaids, dated Simon for a few weeks. It seemed to be going well until he zinged her, infusing her with recklessness. She dumped him the day after.

So why the wedding? As he steers his mean machine around garbage and potholes, the two of us on yet another one of our weird outings, the strangest thought occurs to me: *because we're friends.* In fact, I might be his best friend in the world. Is that why he wants to be in my wedding?

"So are you thinking what I'm thinking?" he asks.

"Doubtful."

"Got your keys, right?"

"Does this involve crashing through that gate down there?"

He slams on the brakes and turns to me with a glint in his dark blue eyes. "You *are* thinking what I'm thinking," he says.

"No. I'm thinking there's no way in the world I'm stealing my own car."

He puts a hand on my wrist. "I've got something that'll help with that."

I jerk away from him. "Don't you dare."

"Just a little."

"Forget it!"

"It'll counteract your fear."

He wants to zing me with his recklessness. "It was stupid to do it to Ez, and it'll be even stupider to do it to me."

"You sure?"

I say, "The mayor's fiancée will not be going on a gate-crashing and car-stealing spree today. We're going to continue on to that little office and explain the circumstances, and they'll unlock the gate and give me my car."

"They won't see it in their system," he says. "You really think they'll come out to check?"

"That's exactly what I think."

"Because they'll recognize you?"

I snort. "You think they read the *Midcity Eagle*'s society section up here?"

This is one of the reasons I like coming to North Midcity—people don't recognize me, they don't treat me like the future first lady of Midcity. "They'll do it because they screwed up and they'll want to make it right."

"We'll see about that, Pollyanna." Simon peels out, fishtailing around another garbage pile, and then we shoot forward, mud spewing behind us.

The impound office is a small, low concrete building the size of a trailer. There's a metal door on one end, and on the other is a service window with a cage-like covering. Midcitians don't take kindly to their cars being towed and being charged to get them back.

We park and go up to the window. The scratched Plexiglas panel behind the cage covering slides to the side and a red-faced fellow glares out at us. He wears a cap with a pesticide logo on it, his lips are pierced in two places, and his shirt says Steve.

He lifts a walkie-talkie to his lips and mumbles into it, then slams the thing down. "What were you doing driving around on the access road? Were you just up on the ridge?"

"Yes we were," Simon says, managing to make it sound like the ultimate insult.

I kick him and explain to Steve about finding my car.

"No one's allowed on that ridge." Steve barks. "That entire side of the complex is restricted. Personnel only."

Simon grins.

I say. "I'm sorry we did that, but I really do need my car back, and it's out there." I push my stolen-car police report through the little slot.

Steve just folds his arms across his chest. "Do you not know the meaning of restricted access? How do we know you're not a couple of mutant freaks come to attack the place? We would've been within our rights to shoot you."

Simon grins some more.

Just then, a truck squeals up. A burly guy with a droopy moustache jumps out. "What were you doing up on the ridge?" His reflective orange safety vest gleams in the gloom.

"We were looking for my car, that's all," I say. "We had a hunch it might be entered into your system wrong, because my friend here heard of a clerical error happening to another car that went missing." According to Simon's sources, it was more than one car but I don't want to insult their operation.

The guy with the moustache looks at me like I'm crazy. "I haven't heard of any clerical errors."

I turn to Simon, who's been unusually quiet, and discover, much to my horror, that he's aggressively eyeing this new guy, who is twice his size. Eyeing him enough so that, simply put, there's a *thing* between them now.

"Look," I say pleasantly, trying to counteract Simon's insolence. "You have a little gray Jetta out there that's mine. When this lot was called, there was no record of it. But it's out there, and I just want to get it back. I have my ID here, and I know it will match the registration, which I know is in the glove compartment, and I also have the keys that go to it."

"What is this, Cinderella and her glass slipper?" Steve says from behind the window, not taking his hard-assed gaze off Simon. "If there's an error, we'll turn it up. We don't need civilians in restricted areas."

"We saw my car."

Simon crosses his arms, gaze boring even harder now into the guy with the moustache. "I think our friends don't understand who they're dealing with, Justine."

I scowl at Simon. He thinks I'm going to play the mayor's fiancée card?

Simon doesn't see my scowl; he's turned his aggressive gaze to Steve. I'm starting to worry; there's so much heat among the three of them, it's like a fight's already started.

"They don't get who they are dealing with *on any level,*" Simon amends mysteriously.

"Who would that be?" Steve disappears from the window. The metal door opens and out he stomps. "Who would that be? That we're dealing with here?" Steve goes to stand by the man with the moustache. Convenient. Simon can antagonize them both at the same time.

Finally, Simon turns to me. "Don't you think somebody needs attitude adjustment?"

My mouth falls open. Simon wants me to zing my fear into them.

"Don't like our attitude?" the one with the moustache asks Simon.

"Oh my God," I say as I come to understand his plan: he's going to put himself in danger and force me to zing them. "Ignore my friend!" I command.

Steve and the man with the moustache ignore me instead.

"He's *trying* to antagonize you," I plead. "Don't fall for it. Look—" I hold up the police report. "This car is out there. How do I get it out? What are the steps? I need your help."

Steve smirks at Simon. "It'll be a while."

"I have an idea, *Steve*," Simon says. "How about if I rip off this guy's moustache and shove it up your ass? Will that expedite things?"

"Stop," I say to Simon, hand on his chest. I turn to Steve and the other man. "Don't take the bait."

The man with the moustache steps forward, orange vest flashing. "Nothing's stopping you."

Simon takes a step forward. "The image of you, slobbering like a baby and begging me to lay off is stopping me, actually." He's now officially in the man's face. The men have the fight on; it's in their eyes. Simon will make them hurt him until I cave. "You'll be sorry," I say to Simon under my breath.

"What are you waiting for? You know you want it," Simon says silkily. Steve and the moustachioed guy think Simon's talking to them, but he's talking to me.

Yes. *I want it.* I want to zing more than anything.

Simon touches two fingers to the man's orange vest and shoves. "That's for you, baby."

"Don't." I pull him away.

Too late. The moustachioed man pushes me out of the way and shoves Simon—hard. Simon stumbles and falls backward onto the ground, laughing.

"Stop!" I yell.

"That's all you got, you pussy?" Simon grabs up a handful of slushy gravel and whips it into the moustachioed man's face. The man's vest seems tighter suddenly, like he's puffed up with rage; I gasp as he lunges for Simon. He yanks Simon up by the collar and punches him square in the nose. The force of the punch sends Simon stumbling backward, back down.

"Don't!" I grab the man's arm, but he pulls out of my grip. I could make him back off if I wanted to. One zing from me and he'd run off in fright.

Simon coughs and smiles at the same time, not bothering to wipe away the blood streaming from his nostrils. He'll let the man hurt him, and he knows I know it. He takes great joy in following through on bluffs. He grins, and then, out of nowhere, he spits at the man.

"Simon!" I say.

The spit doesn't hit; it doesn't have to. The moustachioed man's eyes turn blank. Blind rage. The eyes don't see, or more, they don't take in new information.

Steve pipes up now: "Can't let that shit stand, Hal."

I grab the moustachioed man's arm—Hal's arm—again. His nostrils flare, like he's readying to attack. I'm touching him now, and automatically—greedily, excitedly—I locate the surface of his energy dimension. All my fear and worry—I could be rid of it. I grip him harder, reminding myself I've sworn off zinging.

The man breathes in a snort, like a mad bull.

Simon gazes up at me with velvety blue eyes, nose vivid with red blood. He has the look of a brilliantly-colored tropical bird. A bad bird, staring, waiting, too far gone in recklessness, about to get badly injured. A part of him hates being there, but it's where he always goes. I know. I do the same thing with fear, careening into the pit of it, over and over.

The man jerks away from me and stalks toward Simon, who starts scrambling backward, laughing, taunting. Simon saw how close I came and he thinks I'll give in now. He's the most warped and brilliant student of human nature you will ever see.

Besides Packard.

One second is all I'd need to unload my fear into Hal; I have enough in me to turn both Hal and Steve into quivering bundles of terror. My fabulous skill, taught to me by Packard during his despot days. The fear builds higher in me—hot, jagged. One zing and I'd be free of it.

Hal hauls Simon up by the jacket sleeve. "You think that's funny? Spitting at me?"

Bad question. I wince.

"No. I think it's fucking hilarious." Simon says.

The man cracks Simon on the side of the head.

"Stop it!" I scream.

Simon's down again, crawling dazedly on all fours, on fire with his recklessness.

"The spit didn't even hit you, you jerk!" Oh, I want to zing this guy. I hate myself for it, but that doesn't stop the wanting. I storm over to him.

Steve's laughing. "Christ, Hal."

Simon will go to the hospital. Simon. My friend.

Hal pulls Simon up for more hurt.

"No, you don't," I say.

Simon turns his gaze to me. I expect to see a look of triumph, but there's just pain. I start stoking it higher. It will be wonderful, delicious. We're both sick. And I'm going to help him. I grip Hal's shoulder. I can get to his energy dimension through fabric as easily as I can through skin.

A loud *honk! honk!* stops everything, including Hal, who freezes, fist cocked in the air, like a cartoon man.

A big, shiny, black car screeches to a stop. A back door swings open. A big black boot is planted in the mud. Black velvet pants.

Otto.

Chapter Two

I step back from Hal, mortified. I was about to zing a man!

Otto rises upward, out of the car, surveying the scene. A dark expression plays across his sumptuously large features.

A whisper behind me. "Oops." Steve.

Hal relinquishes his hold on Simon, who falls back to the ground like a grinning sack of stones.

I walk over to Otto, circle my arms around him. I have a million things to say, and nothing to say, and then he kisses me. The press of his lips on my forehead is like a sigh, his fingertips are whisper-light tingles in my hair. I breathe in the familiar rosemary scent of his hair—thick, dark curls that just graze his collar.

"I was so worried, my love," he searches my face with his big, soulful eyes.

"It's okay. We're okay."

Simon addresses Otto from the ground—casually, like we're at a dinner party. "We found her car."

Otto raises his black-as-coal brows. "You did?"

"Spotted it, anyway," I say.

He takes a moment to digest this. He seems unhappy about it. "You're sure you're all right?" he asks me.

"I am now," I say, though I wanted to zing that man so badly I'm still trembling with anticipation. I'm so glad I didn't—for my own integrity, but also, I'd feel as if I were abandoning Otto, leaving him alone in our secret pit of fear. I glare over at Simon.

Otto's new driver, Smitty, leans casually against the car, but I happen to know he's working, gathering impressions from the future. Smitty's a short-term prognosticator, just like Otto's old driver.

Otto is doing the opposite of what Smitty's doing: he's in detective mode, looking at the past, assessing what happened.

He pulls away and takes a step toward the guys, hands clasped behind his back. Before he was mayor, he was a superstar sleuth, and that's still a big part of him. His jacket is cut long, like an old-west sheriff's jacket; he favors old-timey stuff like that, always black. I remember staring at his picture years before I met him, marveling, imagining. Being ravished by Detective Otto Sanchez was one of my go-to fantasies back then.

"There's no trouble here," Steve says. He's got his coworker by the coat sleeve and collar. "Those two were sneaking around on restricted public property, and we're just doing our jobs. Coulda been mutants for all we knew." By mutants, he means highcaps—humans with mutations that produce different powers. I think how surprised he'd be if he knew Otto was a mutant. A highcap.

Hal grumbles.

Steve jerks him, growls a word or two, then turns back to Otto and continues: "If we'd've known this was some official capacity..."

Otto's got a hand up. He doesn't want to hear it. Otto sees everything, and his harsh and accusing gaze is now turned to Simon.

Steven continues. "Reacting to a legal form of assault's all he was doing—spitting is a legal form of assault—"

"Are we all okay?" Otto interrupts.

"We're okay," Steve releases Hal.

Simon grunts. Hal grunts.

"Then let's see that it stops here." Otto extends a hand to Steve and they shake.

"It's an honor, Sir," Steve says. "We really meant no harm. And I have to tell you, all us guys here are behind you all the way, for all what you've done. The curfew and all the rest. Don't listen to the whiners—let's get this job done. Let's yank the criminal element out by the root." Steve goes on to repeat different iterations of this message as Otto listens with keen and noble interest.

The female citizens of Midcity have mostly approved of Otto and his flamboyant ways for years, but men like Steve didn't warm up to Otto until he almost single-handedly ended the eight-year crime wave, first as a detective, then as police captain, performing many feats of strength and cunning, like when he personally chased down and captured the Brick Slinger, one of Midcity's most notorious serial killers. Then, during his first month as mayor, Otto survived a brutal kidnapping by a gang of killers, participated in their arrest, and got elevated to beloved Midcity action hero.

The inexplicable new crime wave has cast Otto in the role of the embattled yet charismatic new mayor who dared to take a stand, whereas any other politician would be seen as ineffective and weak. That's the magic of Otto. Though his latest strong-against-crime policies, especially the curfew and enhanced police powers, have turned some against him. Not everybody wants to trade rights for safety, even temporarily.

Hal pulls himself together enough now to shake Otto's hand, apologizing for the scuffle and assuring Otto that everybody at the lot knows he's doing what it takes to "put the boot down". Otto converses with them in low, confiding tones. Hal and Steve seem enthralled.

Sometimes I watch Otto and just marvel that we're together. I most enjoy looking at him from the point of view of my former self, the self who so idolized him as Detective Sanchez. I like to call him Detective Sanchez when we're having sex, and he plays along. It's very exciting. Actually, we've developed a whole slew of X-rated Detective-Sanchez games. Sometimes I think it's probably not the healthiest thing in the world for a couple to pretty much only have role-playing sex, but there's nothing like the dirty fun of role-playing sex to take a girl's mind off of that.

Simon groans. I go over and take his arm, help him up. He stands unsteadily. I keep hold. "Don't you ever do that again," I whisper. "Ever."

He touches his bloody nose. "You were going to do it. You'd be glorying right now."

"You need to respect my choices."

He wiggles a tooth, and his breathing seems weird. Labored, somehow. Wheezy.

"Hey," I say. "Are you okay? Do you need medical attention?"

"I'm fine."

"You sure?"

"Of course I'm sure."

I glance over at Otto, who seems to feel my stare, and he turns his eyes slyly toward me, head tilted, as he asks the men some question. I don't hear the question but I sure hear the voice. It's his gravelly Detective-Otto-Sanchez voice—the one he uses when we have sex. This shot goes through me.

Simon follows my gaze over to Otto, then he wrenches his arm from mine, like he's really angry all of a sudden. "You were stupid not to do it," he says.

"You were a jerk to back me into a corner."

Otto comes over and kisses me on the cheek. "We're going to straighten out this business of your car," he says.

Simon smiles, like he's not in pain, like blood isn't dripping all over his face and coat and chest. "Excellent."

Otto frowns. "For God's sake, Simon."

I flinch as Otto slides his hand inside the breast pocket of his coat and pulls out a handkerchief.

Quickly I look away, hoping nobody noticed my fearful reaction. Even two months after I witnessed that killing I flinch when Otto reaches into his breast pocket. It makes no sense—Packard's the one who killed Avery, not Otto.

"What led you two to check here?" Otto asks me.

I say, "Simon got the idea there was a clerical error. I guess there was."

"Except we don't make clerical errors," Steve puts in.

I give Steve a look. "Yet lo and behold, the car was there."

Otto turns to Steve. "I don't care about any of that. What happens now? Do you have a process for releasing a car like this?" Otto would never ask for special treatment. He doesn't have to.

Steve straightens up, all business, and asks me if I can point it out on a lot map.

"I can," Simon says.

Steve heads to the truck and Simon follows, slowly, listing a bit to the right. With a huff, Hal retreats to the office.

"How'd you find me?" I ask Otto.

He comes back with a question: "Why did you and Simon shake Max?"

"It was just a crazy, stupid thing..." I watch a car pull in across the way. More Midcitians with towed vehicles. I tell him about the intensity of the ride, going through the electrified fence. He doesn't like it, but he needs to accept my friends, just as my friends need to accept him.

"You're smiling," Otto says.

I realize I am. "It felt exhilarating. Being off the radar. Free. It just feels confining, sometimes, that a bodyguard is always there...and everybody recognizes me and expects me to act upstanding. It felt good to, you know..."

"To bust loose?"

I put a hand on his arm. "I love being your fiancée, and I love that you want to make sure I'm safe, but it's stifling."

"Justine. I know you prize your freedom, but highcap crime has gone up a thousand percent. Cannibal gangs are roaming the streets at night. It won't always be like this."

"How'd you find me?"

"Honey—"

It all becomes clear: *I was never off the radar.* "You're tracking me!"

"It's a dangerous time."

My face goes hot and I step back. "I won't be tracked. I'm not a pet you can put a locator chip into."

"No," Otto agrees, brushing my hair from my forehead. "You're my fiancée who I love so much, sometimes I think my heart might explode."

A lump forms in my throat. I should be happy with this. It's the life I wanted, I remind myself.

He moves closer. "Just two months ago—"

I fling up a hand, cutting him off right there. I don't need a reminder of how close we both came to being killed, and I especially don't need a reminder of how it feels to be alone and helpless, surrounded by sleepwalking cannibals, or how sharp human teeth feel when they're piercing the tender skin of your belly. "I don't care. No trackers."

"Justine—"

"I mean it."

Otto looks distressed. I should've said "I love you" back, but it's too late—the timing's weird and it'll feel like a lie, as it so often does. Sometimes I wonder if witnessing so much violence has eroded my ability to love. I used to think Otto and I were soul mates. And I know in my mind that we fit perfectly, and that I'd be insane to let him go. And we understand each other, and we need each other in ways other people can't comprehend.

Still.

I brush back a curl, careful not to disturb his beret, which he wears as a protective layer. Like me, he worries a vein in his head could bulge and burst at any time. The beret is mostly psychological, but in some cases, it really could help against vein star syndrome.

"Let's get rolling." Steve calls, waiting by the open back door of his giant extended-cab truck.

I touch Otto's arm. We head over as one and get in.

Steve watches warily as Simon climbs in after me, probably worried about blood getting on the upholstery.

The truck sounds like a huge semi when he starts it up, but it bounces a lot less than Simon's car. I sit between the two men, hating the tension. Why won't Simon just accept Otto?

From the top of the ridge, you can see thick snow clouds floating in from the west. To the southeast, the tall buildings of downtown gleam pale yellow. Just beyond that stands the dark, hulking highway interchange known as the Tangle, looking like a skyscraper made from a snarled Slinky, encircled by misshapen buildings.

Otto watches black smoke trailing up in the distance. "Lord help us if that's the river on fire again," he says softly, pulling out his mobile and scrolling. The winter before last, the Midcity River went up in flames. It never freezes because of all the pollution.

Simon wipes his chin with Otto's now-bloody handkerchief, though it's more like he's smearing the blood around his face. He blows his nose. "I'm going to look hideous for the bridesmaids' dinner tomorrow."

"You're not a bridesmaid," Otto says.

Simon smiles. "I understand you're having blue crab flown in from the coast. That's going to be delicious."

"Simon," I warn.

"We have a deal," he says, offering Otto the handkerchief back. Otto shakes his head and pockets his phone.

"Behavior unbecoming a bridesmaid will nix that deal," I say.

"What deal?" Otto asks.

I plop my head back and stare forward as we bump past razor-wire fencing. "I told Simon that if he located my car"—I turn back to Simon—"in good working condition—then he can be a bridesmaid."

Otto is silent a beat, likely coming to terms with the fact that he can do nothing about this. He looks at me admonishingly, out the side of his big, brown eyes. "How delightful."

"Isn't it?" Simon says from my other side.

And then Otto laughs his warm laugh. "Oh, Justine." His laugh makes me smile. He takes my hand and brings it to his mouth, kisses it.

When I look over at Simon, his lip is curled in disgust. Quickly he pastes on a grin and touches his tooth. "I really wanted to keep this one," he says. "It's my third-favorite tooth." He turns to look out his window, wiggling the tooth.

I stare at the back of his head, baffled. When Simon has an opinion, he always offers it; the more upsetting, the better. Why is he holding back?

Up front, Steve grunts something about section D-13 and passes a clipboard back to Simon. "Just so you know, Mayor Sanchez, this is irregular. Civilians never ride along like this."

"I thank you for making this exception, Steve," Otto says.

"And for what it's worth, this is the first I've heard of clerical errors. I'll be damned surprised if that car's out there." Steve seems sincere in this.

Otto nods. "All that's important is getting it back, if it is indeed there."

I can't get over Simon's disgusted look. What did it mean? But if my friends didn't like Otto, they'd tell me. Shelby used to dislike him—she used to tell me so all the time, but she's long since changed her mind.

Ten minutes later we're all standing around my little gray car. So it was towed after all. "Why would it have gotten towed?" I ask nobody in particular. "I left in it my own space behind my building where I've parked it for years."

"You sure?" Steve asks. "No offense, but lots of people forget where they left their cars. You'd be surprised."

"I'm 100 percent sure." I look at Otto. "I remember very specifically—it was when Francis picked me up, on our way to, you know—" I give him a significant look. I mean when Francis and I and some guys went to find him. Back when he was kidnapped.

"Could be some kids took it out for a joyride, and then it got towed. If it was in our system, we'd know where and why it was towed."

Simon says, "Maybe we should search the car. Maybe there are clues for what happened."

Otto pulls on his leather gloves. "Don't touch. I'll have crime scene come out and dust it first."

"I want to drive it home," I say. "Look—" I pull my mittens from my pocket. "Okay? I really want it back. More than I want answers."

Otto gives me a warning look.

"I'll hardly touch anything." Before he can stop me, I unlock the door and get in.

Otto comes over and crouches between me and my open car door, scanning the interior. "Wasn't hot-wired. Are the mirrors and seat adjusted correctly?" he asks.

"Yeah," I say. "And this is the only key." I start it up and the engine growls to life. Through my windshield, I see Simon gesture like he's lifting a top hat from his head.

"Hold up," Steve says, "got some things for you to sign." He goes back to his truck.

I get an idea. "What about the thieves who robbed me the day you were kidnapped? Maybe they took my car at the same time."

Otto stands, winds a gloved finger into my hair. "And made a copy of your key, leaving you with the original?" The featherlight brush of his glove on my ear makes a whisper sound, and gives me shivers. "Unlikely. Nevertheless"—this now in his rumbly and commanding, sexy detective voice—"we need to treat this seriously. *Don't* touch the glove compartment. *Don't* touch the trunk. We'll see what we find."

"But I'm still driving it home. Anyways, I already touched the wheel with my mittens."

Otto smiles down at me. "Yes, you've already compromised that bit of evidence, haven't you?"

I inhale sharply; this is something he sometimes says when we're playing X-rated Detective Sanchez. He's the stern detective, and I'm the unrepentant criminal.

"Yeah, yeah, yeah," I say in my saucy gangster-moll voice. "Too goddamned late for the steering wheel, I guess."

"But not too late for the glove compartment and certainly not the trunk," Otto says slowly. "I'll be mercilessly thorough there."

I make a supreme effort to keep my expression neutral.

"I won't rest," he grumbles, "until I'm completely and one hundred percent satisfied that there's nothing more to be yielded."

I widen my eyes minutely at Otto, shocked that he's bringing our secret detective-sex game so fully to this level.

Simon's there, suddenly. "Well, we know what Packard would say, huh?"

I give him a hard look. For once I wasn't thinking about that horrible scene, Packard shooting Avery. Pulling the rug out from under my entire world.

Otto holds up a finger. "Ah, yes, our friend Packard." He turns a cool gaze to Simon, "Our dear friend Packard, who would have us believe that the day after the kidnapping, Justine drove around on some mysterious errand while some *other* person shot Avery." He turns back to me. "And then Sophia brought you to the lake parklands, marched you up to the crime scene, erased your memory, and implanted the false one of Packard killing him. And your car languished until towed."

Sophia is Otto's assistant, and a powerful memory revisionist.

"The day I'd ever let Sophia look into my eyes," I say, "I'd gouge them out first."

Simon inspects his fingernails with strange ferocity, like he's struggling to stay out of the conversation. It's so unlike him! Back in the old days, Simon was always the first to condemn Packard. He and I used to bond over our hatred of being Packard's minions, trying to think of ways to get free. Of course, neither of us thought Packard had it in him to shoot a man.

And Packard's explanation of what really happened—that somebody else shot Avery, and Sophia revised my memory to make me think I saw him do it—it's just the sort of outlandish claim Simon would make fun of. But he doesn't.

Something's not adding up.

Just then I feel the warning tingle of pain again and I clap my hand to my head, willing myself to think of something else...anything else. Otto catches my eye. He gets it. He puts a hand on my shoulder. He's with me.

Thank goodness for Otto.

Steve comes back with a clipboard. "Some items before I can let you go."

I get out of my still-running car, and he hands the clipboard over, points out the blanks he wants me to fill in. I try to concentrate wholeheartedly on this little task while the guys talk—something about Steve giving Simon a lift back to his car at the little trailer office. Otto and I will be along shortly. Otto wants to check a few things.

I pray the warning tingle doesn't turn into full-fledged pain. Maybe it's a vein degrading. But it was never like this—so frequent, so scary. Tension seems to bring it on, especially the tension of thinking about the shooting.

Carolyn Crane

Steve and Simon take off in the truck, bumping between the rows of cars toward the distant edge of the lot, where they'll skirt the perimeter until they hit the outer gate.

I stand by my open passenger door. "Ready?"

Otto shakes his head sternly. He walks to the front of the car and points to the hood.

"What?"

"Come around the car," he says. "To the front of the car."

Traffic Stop. My favorite Detective-Sanchez game. Is he kidding?

"Otto—"

"Come around to the front of the car, with your hands where I can see them."

My mouth falls open.

Otto waits, all rumbly and detective-y.

In the distance, Steve's truck has reached the outer gate. They'll be out of sight soon.

"Otto, I have that weird thing—that pain tingle." I touch my head. "I have to concentrate on not thinking about it. Or the shooting. Or anything."

"Now."

I smile, disbelievingly. "Seriously. I have to concentrate."

Otto smiles slyly.

A fluttery feeling in the pit of my pelvis, like feathers inside me. "Jesus, Otto."

He points to a spot on the hood of the car. "Right here."

Is he bluffing? There's nobody here, just acres of cars; Simon and Steve are too far away to see us, and they'll soon disappear. Still, it's a public place. It's kind of exciting. I cross my arms. "You want me to compromise more evidence? By sitting on the car?"

"You'd like that, wouldn't you?" he says. "Are you going to comply?"

"Hell, no." I stroll over with a sassy smile, and I laugh as he lifts me onto the hood of the car. "Hey!" The hood is warm beneath my coat, and the vibrations of the motor touch the center of me. "You have *got* to be kidding, Otto."

A lock of hair has fallen over one of his eyes, but he makes no effort to remove it. "Why don't you tell me what you're wearing under that skirt?"

Unaccountably, my mouth waters. I put on my gangster-moll voice. "You really think I'll tell you?"

He holds my gaze with his. "Yes."

"Dream on, copper." I bite my lip to keep back a smile. "You don't know nuthin'"

"Maybe I do."

I press my thighs together, which feels sort of delicious. My head is feeling normal again, and the air is mild and misty. "Oh yeah?" I glance around, searching for Steve's truck, or any other sign of human life. Nothing.

"Don't look around, look at me." He takes my mittened hands in his and positions them behind me.

I leave them like that. The car engine vibrates, warm beneath me. He draws in close, between my thighs, cheek brushing against my cheek. My breath speeds as I feel his warmth, his energy. He whispers into my ear: "You know I always find out."

I love how unlike himself he is in this game. It's dizzying, and suddenly I really want to fuck.

He puts a gloved hand on my knee, bare above my boot. Nearby, a crow caws.

"Ignore it," he whispers.

I watch his eyes, the irises are lines of cocoa alternating with burnt sienna. His lashes are thick, and the olive skin below his cheekbones is baby smooth.

"Maybe I want to see what the crow is doing," I whisper saucily.

"Maybe you should've thought of that before you compromised all that evidence."

"What're you gonna do about it?" I ask as he slides his hands onto my bare legs. He's never worn gloves before. I like it, on a sort of dirty level. He presses his fingers onto my knees and firmly pushes them apart. Then he pushes his hands up under my skirt, up my thighs. There are little ridges around his gloved fingers that drag lightly along the skin of my inner thighs. I gasp. It's all quite exciting.

"Shhh," he says. He stops and takes off the gloves, slowly, face stern and serious, or as serious as he can consciously make it. When he's truly feeling serious, his jaw is more defined, and his lips are tight, not pillowy like they are now. His lips always give him away.

He pockets his gloves and continues up toward my panties with ungloved hands. My heart beats wildly as he pushes his fingertips under the elastic, grazes my tender center.

"Take them off," he whispers.

I narrow my eyes. "Or what?" I say it slow and mean, lingering over the *w* and the *t*. "Or *what?*"

With a happy smile he pulls back, totally breaking the role—the detective in this game isn't supposed to smile. And then he leans in to kiss me, passionately.

He's not supposed to kiss me passionately either. I don't like when Otto ruins the Detective Sanchez game.

I thump a mittened hand onto his chest and push him back. "What do think you're doing, Detective? You want them? Fine." I pull off my mittens and set them aside. He steps back as I wiggle out of my panties and present them to him on one finger with my best unrepentant-bandit-girl smile.

He pockets then without expression. Then he pulls a condom from his pants pocket.

I snatch it away. "I don't know about your methods, Detective," I say.

"You don't?" His delivery is lackluster, almost melancholy.

I wait for him to say something more; when he doesn't, I feel this jolt of annoyance. He shouldn't have started the Detective-Otto-Sanchez-traffic-stop game if he didn't want to play the part.

"You know what I think?" I snap. "I think you've crossed a line!"

He regards me thoughtfully.

I tip the sharp corner of the foil package onto the tender skin of his throat. "I *know* it. I know you've crossed a line."

He closes his fingers around my wrist. Then, "I don't cross lines; I make hard choices."

"Hard choices. *Rrrrrright.*"

"Yes. Right. I make the choices that have to be made. The choices nobody else has the guts to make." He pulls my hand away from his neck, condom and all. "I see what needs to be done and I do that thing." He rests his other hand back on my thigh, heavy now. He's even managing a serious mouth, which surprises me. He looks like he's actually being serious. "I handle business and I accept the consequences. I take the hit. Your choices are easy. You only have to comply." He comes closer, whispers hot into my ear. "Compliance is your only remaining option."

He's silent for a while and I wait, unsure where he's going with this. Is it a prisoner thing? That could be exciting, though we might need props.

I pull away. "If you think compliance is my only remaining option, you're crazy, mister."

He gets this strange look. "You should be glad. It's making things easy on you. It's a kind of gift when things are made easy like that." Suddenly he seems to remember himself. He releases my hand and tilts his head, giving me the Detective-Sanchez eagle eye. Then he undoes his belt buckle. "Now. Are you going to put it on me?" He holds my gaze as he unzips his pants. "Or am I going to have to put it on myself?"

I rip open the little foil package. "Guess you're going to have to wait and see."

"Put it on me," he says in the rumbly voice.

I unroll the condom over his hard cock.

"Come here, you," he whispers, but he's the one who comes to me, snaking a hand around my waist, touching me gently with the other, in all the ways I like, and eventually he guides himself into me. I rest my hands on his shoulders as he fills me slowly, being sort of tender, which *really* isn't the game—I'm the felony girl and Detective Otto Sanchez is supposed to be all action and say dirty, demeaning things, preferably using the word *fuck* a lot by this point.

Instead, he holds me tightly, presses his cheek to mine, makes love to me slowly, with emotion. Even if I didn't sense it from the desperate cadence of his breath, I'd feel it in the way he moves, the way he holds me.

If he hadn't ruined the game already, this would've definitely done it. And really, why did he pull off the gloves? The gloves were good.

This intensity—this rawness I feel from him—is suddenly dizzying. Is it passion? Grief? Distress? And then it hits me: it's love. They say love is a kind of wound. That's what I'm feeling from him. It's as though his heart hurts with it. He's being real.

I suddenly feel inadequate, unable to match his level of emotion.

He wraps his coat around us like a cocoon, and I try to lose myself in his scent, his warmth. I push up his shirt and run my hands over his chest, wanting to enjoy him for just him. All his familiar Otto sounds. My fiancé.

After we're done, Otto stays in me, holding me tightly, face buried in my breast. He stays there for a long time, panting, overwrought.

I wait for him to let me go and pull out of me, but he doesn't. It starts to feel a little uncomfortable—not physically, but emotionally. Like there's too much truth here.

I don't want him to think I don't love him! If he could maybe just wait, I know I have love inside me, but it's as if I can't locate it. Like it's hidden away. Like love is a thought from inside a long-forgotten dream.

He kisses my neck. "I'm so sorry," he says right up against my skin.

I stiffen. "You? For what?"

"I'm just sorry." He holds me, like he doesn't want it to be over.

Is he sorry he ruined the game? I close my fingers tightly on his shoulders and straighten up, and he finally pulls out of me. "You have nothing to be sorry for," I tell him.

He looks at me so strangely. I'm starting to feel nervous.

"I'm going to be a better man," he says, pulling off the condom.

I tilt my head with a *you're-crazy* look. "Otto, I don't need you to be different or better in any way whatsoever."

"Justine—"

I press two fingers to his lips. He seems so serious. "You have nothing to apologize for or be better for. Nothing. Got it?"

I watch his eyes with the sense that many grave thoughts pass behind them.

"Okay?" I remove my fingers, resisting the temptation to make a joke, like he only has to apologize for screwing up the game. This isn't the moment.

There's a fast-food bag on the ground nearby. He puts the condom inside it and pulls up his gloves from his pockets.

The wind has shifted: the air feels drier; sweat chills on my skin. I can hear the steely whine of a jet in the distance.

Otto's jaw is tight; lips in a grim frown. He looks around, seeming remote now, disgusted, even.

Disgusted? Is he disgusted that we had sex in the middle of the impound lot? That he ruined the game? That he gave me so much, when I gave him so little?

Carolyn Crane

I jump down off the hood and put out my hand. "I believe you have something of mine." Meaning my panties.

He hands them to me and pulls his gloves back on. "Let's get out of here."

Chapter Three

I decide to demand the tracker later, given Otto's strange mood. I crank the heat and drive us out, enjoying the familiarity of my car and its quirks. As we pass the impound trailer-office, Smitty joins us, following in the limo.

Just as I'm turning onto the main road, I notice that somebody has messed with dashboard Gumby.

"What the hell?" I gape at his rubbery green arms, raised up high. Happy arms. "Somebody changed dashboard Gumby."

"Mmm?" Otto scowls at his mobile.

I bend Gumby's arms down—his glum position. "I always adjust dashboard Gumby when I drive. To reflect my mood. The last time I drove, I specifically remember adjusting Gumby so his hands were over his eyes. Because I was worried. About *you*."

I have Otto's attention now.

"That's when I last drove," I say. "The moment we knew the Dorks had you, but we didn't know if you were okay, or if we'd be able to rescue you. I left my car behind at my apartment when we went to find you. But when we got in just now, Gumby was set on happy Gumby. Arms up is happy Gumby. It's not how I left him! I never put him like that."

"Does anybody else know you do that?"

"Everyone," I say. There's this awkward silence where I realize that doesn't include Otto. "—who's ever driven with me," I add, feeling weird that Otto doesn't know about dashboard Gumby.

"How about people who knew about Gumby and had access to your apartment?"

"Who would drive my car somewhere, leave it, tweak Gumby, and put the key back?"

Otto gazes at me, still with that grim edge. "Who indeed?"

It takes me a moment to get who he means. "You think it's Packard? You think this is part of his trying to make me think my memory was revised? Changing dashboard Gumby?"

"It would be smart. He obviously wants you to distrust your memories." Otto points at Gumby. "Superficial wrinkles, is what that's called."

"What?"

"Superficial wrinkles are small, random details that don't prove the larger picture, but match it. Any kind of frame job or con is most effective when the superficial wrinkles are right. Juries love them. If that's what this is...well, it would be quite masterful."

"You think Packard engineered this."

"I didn't say that."

"To make me doubt what I saw."

Otto's silent.

Would Packard really mess with my mind? Stupid question. Packard's highcap mutation gives him awesome powers of psychological insight; he can get people to think and do almost anything. This is the man, after all, who had more than a dozen of us believing we were his minions, and if we didn't do his bidding, our brains would fry. I replay Packard's words: *You love to remind me that I'm a villain, but when I actually do something the least bit villainous, you act outraged.*

But to make me doubt my own memory? I drive us past the bleak factories and empty warehouses of North Midcity, trying desperately to sort out Packard's possible motivations.

"My sweet?"

I straighten. Otto's been talking. "What?"

"What is Gumby now?"

"What do you mean?"

"You adjusted Gumby. What's his mood?" Otto asks.

"Glum," I say.

"Oh."

I slow as we hit the traffic crowding the Midcity River bridge, heading toward the nice side of town. I'm feeling pretty shitty about making Gumby glum. After all, I have my car back, we're getting married in three days, and we just had sex.

"Gumby's not feeling so good about the tracker, that's all."

"What if you got kidnapped? Wouldn't you want to be found? You're the mayor's fiancée."

"I have a bodyguard. Isn't that enough?"

"It wasn't enough today."

"I just got done with being a minion. I won't have a tracker on me. I just won't."

Otto's phone buzzes. He frowns at it, then answers, scowling as he listens, all swarthy and stormy. From what I can gather, an old factory by the river is on fire. Probably the source of the smoke we saw on the horizon. Otto seems upset.

My thoughts go back to Packard. Why would Packard kill Avery right in front of me and then concoct an elaborate scheme to make me think I was revised? Why not kill Avery in secret?

And with that, I'm at the shooting again: Packard, aiming the gun. Avery, backing up, hands raised. The jerk of his body.

Pain behind my eyes—it's as if the shock of the memory physically stabs at my veins. *I have to stop remembering the past!*

I focus on Otto's phone call. He wants to go out to the scene. Whoever's on the other end protests, because Otto repeats himself, a bit thickly. "I'm coming out. I need to see." He ends the call and turns to me. "Fire marshal. Mind if we take a quick detour?"

"Not at all."

He directs me to turn off and we head west along the river instead of going over the bridge; soon we hit a stretch of road lined with emergency vehicles, some with flashing lights. Police officers strut about, submachine guns strapped to their backs; firefighters seem to be packing up. I pull over and we get out.

Camera crews spot us immediately and start moving toward us. *Shit.*

Otto puts an arm around me and kisses my cheek and suddenly we're on: lights, microphones.

There are questions about our wedding plans. As usual, I refer people to the old photos of the last time a sitting Midcity mayor got married, which was in 1943. Even the plumes on the horses pulling the wedding carriage will be the same. Our wedding will be fabulous, and it's fun to talk about it. My dress will be a close copy of the one that the 1943 mayor's glamour-puss bride wore—with some modifications, like fake fur instead of white ermine. And, now there might be a top-hatted, belt-and-chain-shirt-wearing bridesmaid, but I don't go into that with the reporters.

Somebody asks Otto how he feels about the Felix Five holding an emergency session to recall him as mayor. The Felix Five is five council members headed up by Henry Felix. If Packard is Otto's number-one enemy, Henry Felix is his number-two enemy, and the rest of the Felix Five would be three through six.

Otto smiles and informs reporters that nobody is more interested in ending martial law than he is, but the right way to end it is when safety is restored. "Mayoral recalls won't make citizens safe again," he says. "But if working on a recall will keep Henry Felix and his pals out of the way of the police, I'm all in favor of it. However, if their sessions stretch past the ten o'clock curfew, I'd advise them to pack pajamas, plenty of snacks, and board games. A bit of advice: Park Place and Boardwalk are always excellent values."

Some of the TV crew members snicker. Henry Felix and his allies will not think that's funny. They've accused Otto of exploiting his popularity and the dangerous situation to create his own personal police state. I might agree if I didn't know Otto was operating from goodwill, and making extreme sacrifices to keep violent highcaps sealed behind force fields. I do question the need for a curfew—if people want to risk getting caught by cannibals or violent highcaps by going out at night, isn't that their right?

His popularity has slipped a few points, but he's not worried. *The citizens have been frightened for years*, he told me once. *They want desperately to trust, to believe.*

This is something I understand all too well. I've been frightened for years myself, and it feels good to trust, to believe, to think there's an end. To think that if Otto and I can just work hard enough together, we can conquer our fear together, and be this happy couple in love. I'm aware of the fear even now: a low hum, like a beehive inside me. I've gotten so used to it I barely hear it anymore.

"What do you say to people who are tired of the curfew?" Somebody asks Otto.

Otto looks straight into the camera. "I say, I'm tired of it too. But you know what? We Midcitians, we're fighters, scrappers. No other people in the land have our guts, or our vision, and we're coming out of this stronger. Smarter. It's already happening. They say it's darkest before the dawn. Well, I see a future so bright, it's blinding."

The swell of energy in the air is electric.

Otto continues: "I see businesses flocking here to become part of our success story. I see Midcitians back at work. I see our schools outpacing the nation. I see a Midcity on the verge of greatness. And most of all, happiness." He looks over at me and puts out his hand and I rest mine atop it, conscious that I'm playing the part of Midcity, taking Otto's hand, but I'm also playing the part of me. We can achieve so much together, Otto and I. He closes his fingers around mine. From somewhere off to the side, there's clapping, and then the clapping spreads.

Eventually the cameras stop. The fire marshal, a portly man in a puffy gray coat, accompanies us up the walk to the building. He lifts the crime-scene tape; the news crews stay behind. The fire marshal tells Otto that there's accelerant present, but it could be for the purpose of cooking. This factory once made pogo sticks and stilts, but it's been empty for decades—children don't play with pogo sticks or stilts anymore, and the factory never updated its products, an all-too-common Midcity story. "It'll probably have to come down now," the man says.

Otto wants to be taken inside; the fire marshal complies, though I get the feeling he'd rather not.

The place is dark and dank; a sharp smell hangs in the air; rusted-out machinery looks strangely sculptural amid piles of rubble and beams.

Otto glances at me significantly as he touches the wall.

I get it: he needs a moment to commune with the building, to use his highcap power on it. I turn to the fire marshal. "Let me ask you something that's been bugging me forever. Why do firefighters sometimes use foam, and sometimes use water?"

I listen intently to his answer, as though it's the most crucial information in the world, then distract him with some follow-up questions.

Packard used to say Otto and I are like fear junkies, enabling each other, pulling each other down. *We're not pulling each other down now,* I think defiantly.

Otto acts like he's listening, but all his attention will be on the place where his hand meets the worn, gray stone. Thanks to his force-fields power, Otto can interface with structures on an atomic level. When he wants to imprison somebody inside a building, he uses his power to harden and extend walls invisibly across every opening, keying it just to that prisoner. He can modify the shapes of walls, too—which accounts for the gorgeous and ornate woodwork in his condo—or push his hand right through. He can also *gather impressions*, which is what he's doing now. Gathering impressions is a more unreliable use of his power—the way he explained it to me once is that when extreme, high-emotion events take place inside a building, they can leave impressions in its atoms. He picks up those impressions in the form of glimpses. Pretty handy when he was a homicide detective; killings are such extreme, high-emotion events, he could usually get a quick image—the weapon, if nothing else.

He pulls his hand off the wall. There's a heaviness in his demeanor.

"Homeless?" Otto asks.

"That'd be my initial guess," the marshal says.

Otto nods. "Seeking shelter."

"Amount of refuse would suggest it," the man says. "Cans and such."

"Thanks for all your good work." Otto smiles a smile that doesn't quite reach his eyes and the men shake. "Keep me in the loop on this. Investigation plans and any demo plans. I want to be directly in the loop."

"Will do."

Otto takes my hand and we walk out.

"You felt something," I say.

"No. Nothing spiked for me." He helps me over a gap in the floor. "I think he's right. Homeless. Human error."

When we get to the front, he stops and puts his hand on the wall. "Sorry old boy," he whispers.

I wait, mildly baffled. Did he just talk to the building? With human speech?

We continue in silence.

"Do you think it hears you?" I ask after a while.

"No," he says. "But it feels me. All matter is alive."

"Do you think the building is sad? Because it will be torn down?"

"The building isn't sad." A pause, then, "It doesn't have an attachment to one form or another. It's all matter." I get the feeling he says this as much for his benefit as for mine.

I link my arm in his. "Are you sad?"

"Yes," he whispers, "I'm sad. We used to play here. I spent my happiest hours here."

It's only now that I put it together: less than a mile down, on this side of the river, was where Riverside Elementary once stood, the abandoned, crumbling old school building where he and Packard and the other discarded highcap kids lived. There are probably paths between here and there. Or were paths. There are condos now where the school stood.

His happiest hours. I always imagine that time as a dark one: all those children out alone, using their fledgling powers to keep themselves fed and clothed, and to escape the hunters who kidnapped and supposedly sold them to a lab. Many of Otto's little friends disappeared from there, including his beloved foster sister, Fawna. And he killed for the first time there—more than once. He and Packard turned from friends to bitter enemies there. I never thought of his being happy back then. But he was happy playing here, in the abandoned pogo stick and stilt factory. And now it will be torn down.

Finally we reach the car. The wind has shifted, bringing with it a sulphury-sweet river smell. In the space beyond the old warehouses, you can see clusters of garbage, bobbing in the river; *garbage flotillas*, they call them.

He tips his head toward it. "The Pentagon was here. Testing the water."

"What?"

"Taking samples. The Pentagon and the CDC. That's not a fact for public consumption, of course."

I unlock the doors. "Because of the highcap connection?"

Otto nods. "The highcap question's made it to the national news."

"I thought it was more like, news of the weird." We get into my car and I start it up.

"The Pentagon takes news of the weird seriously. Telekinetic highcaps stole half their equipment on the first day. Not while they were watching, luckily. I have to get this under control before they decide we're real and devise a test or something. It would be highcaps against humans. That must never happen."

I maneuver around a sinkhole marker in the road.

"The researchers put an ad in the *Eagle*," he continues. "For highcaps to come forward for study."

I smile. "Like any highcaps in their right mind would come forward."

"Plenty of fake ones will," he says with a sparkle in his eye. I'm pleased to see it.

The traffic's loosened near the bridge; I spot Smitty, ahead of us in the limo. I follow him to the underground garage. Another car pulls in behind us—a pair of bodyguards.

Otto points out an area to the side. "Take one of those spots," he says. "We'll get you an assigned place. Maybe a double-wide."

"Are you impugning my driving?" I joke. Of course he is.

"We've got more than enough spaces available, my sweet."

That's for sure. He's taken over the entire floor below our penthouse condo. I'm not supposed to go down there; I suspect he's creating a wedding present—a lower wing of our home, in a sense, just for me. He knows how distraught I was to lose my apartment—and my solitude and independence along with it.

I turn off the car. Otto unbuckles his seatbelt.

"Wait." I put a hand on his arm. "Where's the tracker? I don't want one on me."

"It's for your safety," Otto says. "What if you'd gotten in serious trouble back there?"

There's this awkward pause where we both think of the answer. I would've zinged those guys. I would've filled them with my terror.

"Zinging won't stop bullets," he says.

"Who would shoot at me?" The sound of car doors slamming echoes through the parking garage.

"Zinging won't stop a telekinetic attack. Or sleepwalking cannibals," he says. "Even the police feel nervous, and *they're* carrying submachine guns."

I nod. It's a well-known fact that single gunshots don't stop sleepwalking cannibals; Stuart, the highcap dream invader who controls the cannibals, can't feel their pain. You have to shoot the cannibals over and over, physically disabling them.

"I already agreed to a bodyguard." I stare into his eyes. "No tracker. It's too much like a leash. Anyway, it's not like Stuart's cannibals come out during the day."

"All powers grow, my love, just as yours did."

He's talking about the way I can zing anybody I want now. "A tracker is a leash."

"You know I would do anything for you—give you anything..."

I look into his eyes. There's not much I'm sure of anymore, but I'm sure of his honesty at this moment. He would do anything for me. He needs me desperately. It gives me a strange sense of security, but it also sometimes scares me. "Then show me the tracker."

He tightens his lips. His serious lips.

I push a dark curl behind his ear. "Baby, we're both fear-driven people, but our lives can't be just about staying safe. We have to grow bigger than our fear." I stop, wanting so badly not to cry. This is something Packard once said: that I have to be *bigger than my fear.* I want that so badly, and it feels so far away.

"Hey," Otto says. "Don't worry, Justine—we're getting there. We're making each other stronger—can't you feel it? We can conquer it together."

I want to believe. I almost can.

Another car door slams. Chauffer Smitty and the bodyguards are out there, waiting.

"We need trust, not trackers," I say.

"I can't let anything happen to you."

"Where is it?"

I can see in his expression when he decides to give in. He touches my purse. "May I?"

"My purse?"

He reaches under it and peels a little square sticker off the bottom. It looks like a hologram.

"Thank you." I throw my keys in. "Ready?"

He stays, looking troubled.

"What?"

He holds out a beefy hand. "Give me your dollar coin."

"What?"

"There's a dollar coin in your coat pocket."

I smile. "How'd you know?" Then, "Oh." I slip my hand in and pull it out, a cool weight on my palm. I'd found it in with my change recently and had put it in my pocket. You never see dollar coins, and it seemed lucky. "What if I'd spent it?"

"I knew you wouldn't. You like the little things."

I stare at it, feeling betrayed.

"It's part of what I love about you," he says. "I can't lose you."

I hand it to him. "You won't."

We get out and stroll arm in arm through the dim garage and into the condo building's warm, elegant lobby. This place was a grand hotel in the 1920s, one of the architectural jewels of Midcity's prosperous era.

Norman, a thick-set, Swedish-looking man in beat-cop blues, waits next to the elevator. "King's penthouse, I presume?" He punches the top button. The golden doors *thunk* open and we get in.

He's being funny—people have been calling Otto "King Otto"— not out of sarcasm, but out of adoration.

I smile at Otto. "Lord help you if the Felix Five hears that one."

Otto stares grimly at the blinking lights: two, three, four, five, six, seven, eight. "Let them," he says finally. "Let them."

Chapter Four

I push away my nursing textbook and stare out the window of Maurice's, a Midcity institution for French cuisine. I come here in the dead hours after lunch to study my anatomy textbooks. Otto's back at work at the government center on the next block.

My window table has a view of the entrance of Otto's condo—Otto's and mine—across the street. A cop with a submachine gun is hunched underneath the green awning. Snow has begun to fall in big, lazy flakes.

At first I was surprised by how readily people embraced the police getting more weaponry and power, but along with the surge in highcap crime, there's been a surge in the number of citizens who believe in highcaps—and fear them. Even Midcity's mainstream media accepts the idea that highcaps may exist, a big change from when they treated highcap stories the way they treated Big Foot sightings.

A couple and their little boy dine at a table near mine, and all three of them wear gloves and long-sleeved shirts...*inside*. Like many citizens, they're fearful of Stuart the dream invader, the main highcap boogeyman. Nobody knows what Stuart looks like these days, but he has only to touch you to get control of your dreams and force you to do horrible things in your sleep. As soon as his hold is strong enough, he adds you to his band of sleepwalkers who lumber around at night, attacking and cannibalizing citizens. I've heard rumors that just before dawn, he has his sleepwalkers wash their faces, hands, and feet— some say they even wash their clothes—so that they don't wake up in their beds all dirty or bloody and know they've been dream-invaded. I can't imagine the logistics of that, but the stories have added to people's paranoia; lots of people could be dream-invaded and not know it. I don't wear gloves, but I'm careful who I touch.

I flip idly through my textbook. Otto believes I'm ready to fulfill my dream of being a nurse, and he pulled strings to get me into nursing school next quarter, but studying anatomy and pathology is just disturbing. Every new piece of information gives me new ideas for things to worry about.

I take a break to page through the *Midcity Eagle,* and I find Pentagon researchers' ad Otto told me about on the back page.

Do you identify as a high-capacity human being or "highcap"? Do you believe you have one and only one of the following powers: telekinesis, telepathy, dream invasion, structural interface, psychological insight, memory revision, short-term prognostication? Have you possessed this power since childhood? Do you believe it is a genetic mutation or genetically based? If so, you may be eligible for a study involving a confidential interview and a quick and easy cheek swab test and skills test. We'll pay $100 for one-half hour of your time.

So the Pentagon found the highcap conspiracy websites. I snap on the cap of my yellow highlighter. I could see a truly desperate highcap coming forward for more money, but it would have to be *a lot* more. Hell, I'm just an overwrought human with the power to zing, and I wouldn't want the Pentagon knowing about that. But if I were a highcap? You couldn't pay me enough to get tested. Because what happens when the powers turn out to be real? What would the scientists want next? Where would you hide?

Needless to say, Otto hasn't revealed his highcap status, and he won't be going in for tests.

Again I think about Otto's foster sister Fawna, the gentle little telepath, taken so long ago from that abandoned school where they were living as children, presumably to a lab for horrible tests. Are kids like her even still alive?

I pack up and leave a five-dollar bill for my coffee. On the way out, I catch sight of a couple sitting across from each other in a booth, heads bent, lingering over coffees...there's something about the way they sit, with all that fierce focus on each other that hits me in the gut—it reminds me of the way Packard and I used to sit, back at the Mongolian Delites, the restaurant where Otto had him trapped. The two of us spent so much time in that one stupid booth, talking, laughing. Later fighting. Eight years he was imprisoned there. Until we struck the deal that got him out.

And then he killed Avery.

A numbness in my head. Shit! I shouldn't have thought of him. I close my eyes. Is a vein weakening? I can't find pain, but my fear of the pain surges, and fear of the fear that it causes.

"Miss Jones?"

I open my eyes. The waiter waits, hand outstretched with money. My change.

"No, it's for you. Thanks." I head out into the snow. A police helicopter *chop-chop*s overhead.

My bodyguard Max falls into step behind me. He has Brillo-like brown hair and the biggest Adam's apple ever, and he puts lotion on his hands a lot. Antibacterial. *Good luck with that*, I always think. *Antibacterial won't save you.*

Otto says to ignore Max, but we end up waiting for the light at the same time, and it's too weird, so I say *hi*, and he says it back, but his attention is on the top of the Maurice building behind us. When I look up there, I catch a glint.

I point. "Something's up there."

"Don't point." He pushes my arm down. "It's nothing. It's us."

"Like a lookout?"

The light changes.

"Go on," he says. "I'm not here."

"Like a lookout?" I press.

"Yeah," he says dismissively. "Go ahead of me."

"Why be so secretive? Don't you think my obviously having a bodyguard would make me safer than my seeming to wander the streets alone?"

"I think you should do your job and let me do mine."

I give him a look that says I know I'm right and cross the street, feeling like I'm confined to a very small box. Even my thoughts are confined to a box, because every time I think of the shooting or Packard my head tingles or hurts. This isn't how it was supposed to be. My whole goal has always been freedom.

Nordic Norman is in the elevator as usual, all spiffy in his street-cop blues. He punches the top button in his military way, standing ramrod straight, seeming to concentrate on distant, pleasant thoughts. The door *thumps* closed and the old elevator lurches up. Live shots of Max heading up the stairwell feed into a mobile phone clipped to Norman's belt.

"You're not highcap, are you?"

"Human," he says.

"How long have you been a cop?"

"Couple months," he says.

"Really." This surprises me; he looks like he's at least 40. "What were you before that?"

"Navy Seal. Military contractor. Combat operative. South America consultant and so forth."

"Oh." Otto's security arrangements are getting curiouser and curiouser.

Up in the condo foyer I set my hat and gloves down on the table under the chandelier with the strangest thought; is Midcity's social order breaking down? Isn't this what it would look like? Bodyguards, curfews, cops with machine guns, a mercenary running our elevator.

Max strolls out from the interior of the place, having arrived ahead of me and checked everything. All clear.

"Thanks, Max."

Max joins Norman in the elevator and the doors *thunk* shut.

Alone. Sort of.

I hang my coat on the hook and wander through the big, empty living room, with its ornately carved panels and bookcases—ornately carved by Otto's mind. I light a fire in the fireplace and sit in front of it, hoping to feel cozy. I don't.

It's not just all this security; for the first time in years I don't have my own job or my own place, and that makes me feel weak. But after the wedding, I'll have my own space again— surely that's what's going on down on the seventh floor. Otto and I even had a conversation recently about the how the perfect home for a couple would be arranged—it would feature parts that we share, and private spaces where we can each enjoy our respective solitude.

I wander to the corner where I keep my books. I pull one out, but it has a vampire—that reminds me too much of the cannibal attack. I put it back and take another, but the girl is kidnapped in it. I grab a third, a fourth, rejecting them all. Finally, I choose a romantic comedy that I've read twice, hating myself.

Just as I'm settling in with it, there's this weird squeak in the far corner, like metal on metal. I spring to my feet, gripping my book.

Another squeak. Prickles spike across my skin.

Somebody's opened the back window.

The heavy, velvet curtains move and shift, like somebody's trying to find the opening.

Crap.

No way can I run for the elevator—I'd have to pass within grabbing distance of the curtains. I stand there, frozen, like if I don't move or scream, I'll be invisible. The strategy of a rabbit, I think with disdain. What would old Justine have done? The brave disillusionist? Then again, when I was a disillusionist, I wasn't so full of fear—I got to zing it out all the time.

A dirty, brown hiking boot appears under the curtain. Another boot. Folds of fabric shudder, then fly aside. Out steps Packard.

Packard.

"Oh my God!" I sigh in relief. I don't know what I expected— cannibals, machete-wielding killers, rabid zombies. Not Packard. I'm so stunned I can't think.

He regards me with that burning gaze of his, though it strikes me that this burning gaze is somehow sadder than his old burning gaze.

"Justine," he whispers. Snowflakes glisten on his long, black coat, his cinnamon hair.

Wait a minute... I stiffen as the memory floods back— Packard pulling the gun from his pocket and shooting Avery. The blood.

A few long strides and he's in front of me, clasping my upper arms. He smells of the cold.

"You know me, Justine."

I shake him off. "The hell I do."

He searches my face, like he might find something hidden there. "I saw it, Justine—you were relieved when you realized it was me. Weren't you?"

"I was glad you weren't a cannibal!" Dimly, I think I should call somebody.

"Trust yourself. Trust that instant where your heart knew me."

"Knew you? You killed Avery! I don't know you at all!" I push him, hard. He doesn't move. "How could you?"

His pale green eyes glisten with anguish. "Those are *Sophia's* images."

"Don't." But it's too late. The pain is back. "Damn." I squeeze my eyes shut.

"Oh, Justine, come here."

I put up a *stop* hand. "You have two seconds until I call the bodyguard."

Silence.

How long was he out on the ledge? "Packard, shit!" I open my eyes. "There are security lookouts all around on the rooftops. Turn yourself in—let this be over!"

"Those aren't lookouts; they're snipers," he says. "It's handled."

"Jesus!"

"You've been revised. Can't you feel it? Just a little?" he pleads.

"You killed a man. You don't get to undo that by messing with my mind."

"I'm not the one—"

"God, would you just stop? How many times have you tricked me? How gullible do you think I am? Plus, I happen to know that if you really thought I was revised, you wouldn't be here. Because according to you, a revision is permanent. Remember telling me that? You're obviously here to *convince* me I was revised. It won't work."

He seems about to say something, still watching me with that searching gaze. I remember thinking once that if I became blind, his would be an easy face to recognize by touch—rough-hewn nose and lips. The way his cheekbones jut out too harshly. It's a strong, crudely-made face.

But when he smiles, there's this lightness to him, like when you crack a rock and a gem shines out.

Now he just looks lost.

And he shot Avery. I close my eyes as the sound of the shot rings in my head.

"I saw you shoot him." Rage wells up in me as I see Avery lying wrong and broken on the shoreline. Dying. "I'm in love with Otto too," I tell him. "I love him." Saying I love Otto still feels like a lie. Even that is Packard's fault—he made me second guess everything, even my own feelings.

The pressure in my head builds. "Uh!" I press the heel of my palm to my forehead.

"It's the revise," he says. "It's too deep an internal contradiction. Zing me. You'll feel better."

"*That's* why you're here? To get me to zing?" I pull my hand from my head, shocked. "Do you know how hard I've struggled with it? And you come here to upset me, then offer to let me zing you?"

"No!"

"Stop lying!" I push him with all my might, and he stumbles back this time. "When will you stop messing with me? You think I'm so stupid!"

"You've been revised."

"And you yourself said that when a person is revised, the one who would *know* the truth is gone. Or was I revised to imagine that conversation, too?"

"We had that conversation."

"Then why are you here?"

He looks at me wildly, eyes shining, face flushed.

"Why?" I demand.

"I *know* nobody comes back from a revise," he says. "I know it's impossible. Of course I know that." This, like he's talking to some part of himself. "You can't remember. The *you* who knows the truth is dead. Yes, Justine, I couldn't be more aware of these things!" He clutches the thick, soggy lapels of his long black coat. "Of course you can't remember."

He comes nearer, gaze intense.

I back up.

"You asked me if I think you're stupid. No, Justine, I don't think you're stupid at all." Lapels in hand, he pounds his fists to his chest, once. Hard. The sound of the pound reverberates through my own chest. "*I'm* stupid. Me. *I'm* stupid," he says. "I know it's impossible to come back from a revise, but I want you to come back anyway. I want you to remember what really happened. I want you to know I could never kill a man. I want you to remember us."

I watch him through the haze of pain. He seems so genuine. But he always has.

His voice softens, like the air is going out of him a little. "I *need* you to remember us..."

"Stop it." Still I don't call out for Max. Where is this urge to protect him coming from?

"I was stupid to lie to you. Stupid to betray you and to use you. I was stupid to believe you when you said Otto made you happy. To send you to him, to think he might have a shred of decency where your free will is concerned. I was *stupid* to let you out of my sight that last day. I regret so much of what I did. And I keep hoping things will be right again. It's stupid, of course I know that. And I'll keep being stupid, Justine. I'll keep being stupid because I love you."

I back away with a sob trapped in my chest. "You love me? How could you say that?" It's so twisted that he'd say that *now*, after all that he's done. For the first time I wonder if he might be going crazy. I picture his face when he shot Avery...the pain in my head sharpens, and I get this lurch of fear—I think it might consume me. "Just get out."

He doesn't move. Is this what a vein-star blowout feels like? Even zinging can't cure a ruptured vein.

"In one second I'll yell. I mean it."

"I love you. I won't stop waiting—"

"I mean it. I shouldn't even warn you."

I hold the back of the couch and lower myself to the floor, sitting cross-legged. I close my eyes. He's saying something, but I barely hear him. I feel like I might pass out from the pain. Things go dim—a very bad sign! I warn him again to get out. And, though it goes against every fiber of my being, I push through my urge to protect him. Because I have to protect myself. "Max!" I yell.

Banging, screeches, footsteps. I regret it instantly as I sink deeper into the pain. What have I done? I feel like I've betrayed him. More sounds.

"Miss Jones?"

Is it a second later? Two minutes later? I look up.

Max rests a hand on my shoulder. "Are you okay? What's going on?" Norman's behind him. Max asks again: "Are you okay?"

"No—yes." I feel like I don't understand the question. "Call Otto. Tell him to get over here. Hurry. Please."

He pulls out his phone. Only then do I look over at the curtain. It's still. Was he even here? But foot-sized puddles are drying on the floor.

I feel sick that the killer of Avery said he loves me; it feels like a perversion of something good and true. I should tell them Packard was here. Point out the puddles. They could still catch him. I keep silent.

The old Justine always knew what to do. Well, most of the time.

I reach up and Max gives me the phone. "I really think it's something," I say to Otto.

A door squeaks on Otto's end of the line. "I'm on my way," he says.

Elevator bell. He's on the move. Luckily, the government center is just a block away.

"It's too much," I whisper. "It's different this time. A surge of stress—"

"Relax your face. Try that."

"I can't."

"Breathe. Can you do that?" He launches into the reminding technique, where we remind each other how past episodes turned out to be nothing. Max and Norman retreat to give me privacy. Otto asks me to relate my symptoms. We always do that because if you pass out and you're taken to the hospital unconscious, it helps with the diagnosis. I relate them with total precision.

If I'd been revised, I'm sure I'd know it. Simon and Shelby don't believe it either, or surely they'd say something.

Another wave of pain. "This feels wrong," I say. "Even with 'The Boy Who Cried Wolf', the wolf came at the end."

"I know," Otto says. "Just wait." It sounds like he's running. "I'm already halfway down the block. Breathe."

I lie down on the floor and breathe. It's all very ignoble.

"Slow, deep breaths. You need your autonomic nervous system to slow down."

"That's my line," I say weakly.

The *thunk* of the elevator doors through the phone. He's already downstairs?

"I'm scared," I say, the only true thing I can think of.

Another *thunk*. Eventually I feel the vibrations of his footsteps on the floor beneath my head. "That was fast," I whisper as his shadow darkens the world beyond my closed eyes.

He sits on the floor, shifts me gently to cradle my head on his lap.

Unbidden, I picture Avery's eyes. Again I feel the fear. A wave of rage roars through me. "Packard was here," I blurt out. "Goddamn him. Why does he keep—"

"Packard? What?"

"He came in the window. To tell me I'm revised. Ahh!" I cry as the pain turns pinpoint.

Otto's muttering something into his phone. I barely realized he made a call. Again I'm seasick with this regret, deep in my gut, as though I betrayed Packard. Why should I have allegiance to Avery's killer? Am I going crazy?

"You should've told me earlier," Otto says. "We'll never find him now."

"I called out to Max," I protest. "Excuse me if I got blindsided by pain! It's gone pinpoint!"

"Pinpoint? You're sure?"

"Of course!"

"Just breathe. I didn't mean to snap."

"It's the tension that's worsening it."

"There's nothing for you to worry about." But I can tell he's worried.

He says the calming things we usually say to each other. I latch onto his voice, rich and deep, like a song.

I look up. "Too bad we don't have our own CT scanner," I say. We often say this.

He nods, and I have this thought that maybe he's installing one in the condo below. Maybe that's the wedding surprise. It makes me feel strange.

Sad.

"Close your eyes." He brushes his fingertips over my forehead. "Try to soften here."

I close my eyes, so grateful he's come.

"Soften. Breathe. Let me take care of you."

It feels good to put myself in his hands, because he understands. I make my thoughts simple. Just him. A feathery touch to the side of my forehead. The light changes as he leans his face nearer, touches his lips to mine.

I open my eyes. Is it better? I don't know, but I feel less alone in my misery now that he's here.

He smiles. Sooty curls frame his face. "It's better. I can tell."

"You can't tell."

"Yes I can. And the fact that it's even a little better proves it's a tension phenomenon unrelated to internal physicality, therefore benign."

I smile wanly. We always try to sound like we know what we're talking about. "That was pretty good."

He strokes my forehead. "I'll keep you safe," he says. "You're not alone."

Chapter Five

I wander out of our bedroom the following evening, all set for my bridesmaids to arrive for our grand dinner. Miss Erma Saunders, the woman who married the mayor of Midcity back in 1943, held a bridesmaids' dinner instead of a bachelorette party too. And with the ten o'clock curfew, it's not as if my friends and I can go out dancing. Our party will break up well after ten, but Otto has arranged for police officers to drive my guests home.

My dress is a red-and-black satin affair with red-jewel sparkles, and my shoes are black satin with black sparkles. I think I look good, but I feel completely off balance. One moment I feel angry at myself for not sending Max straight after Packard—doesn't Avery deserve justice?—and the next, I feel like a cretin for turning Packard in at all, half-assed as it was.

I head down another hall and spy Otto in the kitchen with Kenzakuro, his new personal chef. Kenzo has a shaved head—he looks like a Sumo wrestler, and probably was one once too, considering that everyone working around here seems to have extreme pugilistic abilities. Kenzo also runs a gay-themed cooking show on a cable access channel that he thinks nobody ever watches.

Otto gives me a rosy-cheeked smile from behind the steamer. One of the things I love about Otto is that I never doubt how he feels about me. With all the men I've ever dated, I was always the one who loved the most, fretted the most, and got dumped. But not Otto. We fit like that.

With a flourish, he puts a pinch of spice into the large pot on the stove.

Kenzo glances up from his chopping. "You look good enough to eat."

"Don't tell that to Stu's sleepwalkers," I say.

Otto casts a dark look into the pot.

Kenzakuro's cheeks fatten with a smile as he tips the cutting board piled with peppers into a silver bowl.

The stony set to Otto's face tells me he's struggling to hold his prisoners in today. We often worry that the way he's using his force fields to hold Midcity's worst criminals in secret locations around town might be weakening his head's vascular structure...and making him more vulnerable to vein star. Their will to be free creates an awful pressure on his brain.

But what's the alternative? Letting them all loose would endanger the city even more.

Otto sniffs the steam and adds another pinch of spice. "Does it seem unusually dark in here?" he asks.

Kenzo shakes his head.

Uh oh. We recently watched a sad Bette Davis movie where her vision went dark right before she died of some horrible head problem. It gave us both the dangerous idea that vision issues precipitate cranial issues.

I flip on a lamp. "Does this help?"

Otto squints, seemingly unsure. He's definitely feeling his prisoners.

Kenzo and I exchange glances; Kenzo knows too. He heads around to my side of the room and pulls a bottle from the refrigerator. "Champagne?"

I nod, grateful for this distraction.

"Georges Fancher '73," Kenzo says, filling the glasses. The champagne sparkles as if it has its very own light source. He hands me a glass and goes around to give Otto his. "To both you nuts."

I sip. "So, so wonderful."

Otto puts the glass to his generous lips and, gazing at me from under thick dark lashes, he takes a sip. Probably his last

65

sip, because the alcohol will dilate his blood vessels—very bad for vein star.

"Thank you. Both of you. For all this," I say. "For helping to make my dinner perfect." I go over and put my hand on Otto's arm, remembering what it was like to zing all my fear into him, and the sense of peace afterwards. I wish Otto could feel that glorious relief right now. Not that Otto could ever zing; he doesn't generate the volume of fear I do. But I wish I could give him the feeling of it as a gift.

Chimes. Someone's coming up in the elevator.

Otto raises his dusky brows.

I smile and take off down the hall and to the foyer, startled for a split second at the red roses bursting from the vase on the marble table. So many! A surprise from Otto. I breathe in their scent and flip on the monitor that shows who's in the elevator.

Norman's in there, as usual, along with my best friend, Shelby.

Shelby's disillusionist specialty is a grim outlook on life—she thinks there's no such thing as happiness, and she's really good at convincing people of that.

We find each other's specialties amusing; our dark natures click, like disillusionist puzzle pieces. What's more, we read the same books, and we love eating and shopping together, and she's a hoot at movies, especially if you trick her into going to a life-affirming one.

I wait, hoping she's still okay with all this. I'd told Otto that having our wedding just two months after Avery's death was too soon, but it was Shelby who talked me into it—literally out in the car after Avery's funeral. It shocked the stuffing out of me.

"You must grab happiness while you can," she'd said.

"You don't even believe in happiness," I'd reminded her.

She'd gazed over at the funeral home. "Of course, I do not. Is all doomed. But for a little while we can pretend it is not so." And then she'd turned to me, there on that gray January day, and she'd said, "What is wrong with feeling safe and good?"

My line.

My line when she'd criticized my engagement to Otto just a week before that. She'd accused me of wanting to marry him out of fear, as a reaction to the shooting. And I'd said, *What's wrong with feeling safe and good?*

I watch the numbers above the elevator door flash, one after another, thinking about that bizarre conversation. It was as if we'd switched places, philosophically.

"Will be Camelot wedding," she'd told me.

Camelot wedding. This from the woman who says all celebrations are useless and empty. She'd insisted on being my maid of honor. She'd pressed me until I'd consented.

I'm startled out of my memory by the *ding* and the doors, and Shelby steps out, lush and lovely in her luxurious black curls and black outfit.

"Hello, Justine," she says in her usual monotone.

"Hi, honey." I go to her and squeeze her hands. She's not a big hugger. She's barely a toucher these days.

I take her black coat, missing the garish, clashing colors she used to wear. "How are you? What did you do today?"

She sighs. "Mooned around apartment."

"Ah. Mooning. But no starring? No sunning?"

She doesn't think that's funny. We go into the living room and sit close to the fire. I serve us a glass of champagne from a bucket and tell her about getting back my car. She doesn't seem surprised or unhappy about Simon being a bridesmaid, and even weirder, she isn't angry about Packard's visit or my failure to turn him in quickly.

Instead, she's philosophical. "Why would he do this, Justine?" she asks. "Why should he take such a risk? To see you?" She asks this pointedly, as though she really wants me to come up with an answer. She waits, lips parted, revealing her chipped front tooth, which makes her look like a beautiful thug.

I snort. "Who knows? Otto always says you can only understand Packard's motivations in hindsight."

She frowns, disappointed with my answer. "Killer of Avery will pay and pay and pay," she hisses; then she stands and strolls across the bright oriental rugs to the far wall, touches a large oil painting Otto recently acquired. Otto tends toward magical realism in his art tastes. Forests and winged beasts.

My heart breaks to look at her there, so fiercely isolated. During the short weeks they were together, she and Avery had become a unit in every way, and instead of softening her grim view the world, Avery brought his own fiery brand of it to her, and they challenged and enlivened each other.

And she'd loved him.

Shelby speaks without facing me. "Did you check it? Check car?"

"What do you mean, check it?"

"If anything is gone? Anything unusual?"

"I'm not messing with the trunk or glove compartment until it gets dusted for fingerprints. Except, one weird thing—Gumby was different."

She turns. "How?"

"In a happy position. I guarantee you, I didn't leave him like that."

"Really!" She comes and sits back down with me, her gaze boring into mine. "What do you imagine might explain that?"

"Either the tow truck driver changed Gumby, or a certain somebody's trying to make me think I'm crazy..." I raise my eyebrows. Meaning Packard.

She sits there looking intense.

"What?" I ask.

"Must be another explanation," she says.

"Like what?"

She wrings her hands. "You always see your way to truth, Justine. You will figure it out."

"It seems like you have an idea."

She stays silent.

"What?" I ask.

"Nothing."

Something's up with her. "Have you zinged lately?"

She meets my eyes. "I zinged Midcity Mavens fan on street yesterday. Hooting at night. Waking up neighborhood."

"Oh, Shelby." Now that we disillusionists aren't assigned to criminals, it's a zinging free-for-all. Except for me, since I'm trying to walk the high road.

"Was good for him. He had too much drunken joy." She crosses her arms. "One zing. Does not hurt anybody. Justine, you should pick person with too little fear and give them yours. You could try Simon."

"I want to get over my fear the right way. By overcoming it. I want to earn it."

"Shelby!" Otto strolls in with a tray of cheese and crackers. "Welcome!"

Shelby stands, startled, then seems to gather herself. She hasn't seen much of Otto in the two months since the funeral.

"How lovely you look," Otto says.

"Thank you," Shelby says brightly. Her tone stops me; she never speaks brightly. She sits back down on the couch. "What are citizens of Midcity to think," she says, "to see you act as waiter?"

Otto hands us each a napkin. He's donned a dapper suit with a midnight blue shirt; he's one of those men who look perfectly at home in finery. "Maybe they would think I'm in love with your friend."

"Perhaps so." Again brightly. Shelby takes a cracker and dips it into a soft cheese as we both look on. Surely Otto's picking up on her weirdness.

Her attention drifts back to the magical beast painting. "Is lovely," she waves her hand toward it. "In the style of Dutch Masters. Yet subject is quite unexpected."

We discuss the painting a bit, then he returns to the kitchen.

"What's up?" I ask once he's gone.

"What?"

"The cheery act."

"You do not want me to be cheery for your dinner?"

"I want you to be normal for my dinner."

"Pfft." Again she stands. "Perhaps you should put up your Japanese prints here."

"I can't redecorate."

"Is half yours soon," she says.

"I'm holding off until I know what I'm working with." She knows my suspicions about the floor below being turned into more space for us.

"Have you seen yet? Downstairs?"

"Of course not. Why would I want to spoil Otto's surprise?"

"They continue to work down there?"

I nod.

She lowers her head conspiratorially. "Like what?"

"Remodeling sounds." I'd told her all this before. Why is she so interested? "Hammering. Drilling."

"How many workers?"

"I'm on the floor above; how would I see them? What's up with you?"

"I am curious. Tell me, if he makes new wing below, how do you get from here to there?" She looks around. "Are they joined?"

"Right now, it's just the elevator, but I'd think they'd blast through."

"Or perhaps the fire escape."

"Use the fire escape to go between floors of our own home?" I laugh. "I hope not."

"Do they work nights and weekends?" she asks, then adds, "In preparation for wedding?"

"God, Shelby, stop it." I sit back. "I want it to be a surprise. I want it to be..." I want it to be lots of things. I want it to blot out the confusion inside me. The sense of being empty. Of Packard with snowflakes melting in his hair. I feel like crying, suddenly, and I close my eyes. "I need to turn off my brain for a few days."

"Do not," she whispers. "You must not."

"I was kidding." I sip my champagne. "So guess what? My pop says he might come."

Her mouth falls open. "No!"

"Yes." I smile. Dad hasn't gone anywhere for decades. "You'll recognize him by his biohazard suit and level-four respirator."

"He would not."

"Oh, he would," I say. "He's an airborne pathogens guy of the first degree. I don't know how I feel about him giving me away in all that gear, but I'll be grateful if he even comes." I inspect my manicure. "I think he won't, though. Fear is a powerful thing."

She looks at me sadly. Then, "You must not let Simon wear a dress."

I snort. "I'd prefer it over the leather and chain shirt and top hat he has planned."

Chimes. A minute later, Kenzo escorts Simon and Ez in. Ez wears a lovely forest green dress. Simon's a study in contrasts, a fine white suit setting off the glowingly dark bruises on his mouth and eyes. Intentional, of course.

Ez hugs me, looking around at the lavish living room. "Bet you're glad you got evicted."

Otto enters, saving me from having to answer.

"Ez, Simon, welcome," he says warmly, drawing near to them, taking Ez's hands. My heart swells with pride. Like Stuart, Ez is a dream invader, and all she needs is skin-to-skin contact to forge a link. But my fiancé risks shaking her hand, to show his trust. "Justine is so lucky to have such friends. We both are."

Ez smiles her elfin smile. "Thanks for having us."

Otto moves to Simon.

"Twice in a week," Simon says as they shake.

Kenzo has brought out more champagne. Simon and Shelby talk in the corner while Ez entertains Otto and Kenzo and me with anecdotes about her new role in the Midcity Rep— she's Hedda in *Hedda Gabler*. Ez shows us five different ways a person can angrily hold her tongue during another actor's monologue, which amounts to four hard stares at a couch, and one blank expression.

I sometimes wonder if Otto pulled strings to help her get the part. I know he feels badly about wrongly imprisoning her for three years—he'd used his force fields to seal her inside a coat check booth.

Shelby and Simon have moved farther away, deep in conversation. It's strange to see them being friendly after so many years of despising each other. Then again, we're the only three disillusionists who haven't gone to the dark side with Packard. It makes sense we'd pull together.

Kenzo and Otto want to know if I think the rest of the hors d'oeuvres should be put out, even though my last bridesmaid, Ally, is running late. I decide yes on that.

Otto and Kenzo leave; I spin around just in time to catch Ez exchanging meaningful glances with Simon and Shelby.

"What's up?" I ask.

"Ez hopes to see your night garden," Simon says, sauntering toward me.

"What? Did she just communicate that silently?"

"No," Simon says. "She told me before."

"Famed night garden. Ez has never seen it," Shelby adds.

Why are they acting so weird?

I take them out to the humid rooftop patio full of the tropical plants that Otto tends obsessively. I do my best to replicate the botany tour I've heard Otto give other guests.

"How the hell do they get this dome thing on here in winter?" Ez asks.

"Helicopters and workmen." I cross my arms. "So you all think you're all off the hook? Something's going on. Not about the garden."

Simon says, "I'm sorry, are the bridesmaids not allowed to have awesome secret surprises for the bride?"

"Where is the girl Ally?" Shelby asks.

"The girl Ally is late. She called." Yet another change in subject. I watch their eyes. "What's the surprise?"

"We will not tell you," Shelby says.

I think they're lying. Am I being paranoid?

"Will the king be joining us?" Simon asks.

"Don't call him that. His prisoners are putting a lot of pressure on his head today."

"I thought that was all in his imagination," Simon says.

"It's not, and it's an enormous strain to keep those people confined. It's not as if he can put someone like the Belmont Butcher or the Brick Slinger in a human jail—they'd escape in a minute."

"If it's such a strain, maybe he should lay off the personal force field of his," Ez says. "Must take a truckload of energy to power that thing."

I spin around. "What? A personal force field?"

She gets this blank look. An *oops* look.

"Like a force field around himself?" I say. "Otto doesn't have that power. His power is only with buildings."

"Oh, okay." Ez shakes her head. "Brain fart."

But I can tell she believes it. "Why would you think he has a personal force field?"

"Never mind," she says.

Simon gives her the eagle eye. "You mean his personal magnetism, Ez? Is that what you meant?"

Simon's covering for Ez's misstep. Why?

"Does not matter what she meant," Shelby says. "Is all the same, anyway. Is all the same utterance in the end."

I focus on Ez. "Even if it was within his power to do that—to somehow secretly have this personal force field I don't know about—he wouldn't. If you recall, Otto walked around in the public even at the height of the Dorks, exposing himself to enormous danger."

Ez doesn't reply, but she clearly differs. This, of course, is not the kind of conversation we can have around Ally, who is a normal human and completely in the dark about us.

Ez shrugs. "Forget I said it."

"Yet you won't retract it."

"Brain fart," she says again, like that explains everything.

"Look, it's obvious you think he's fielded himself," I say, "And I want you to understand that I touch his energy dimension, and his skin, all the time. He just couldn't, and wouldn't."

Ez's gaze turns diamond bright. "Just because *you* don't detect it, doesn't mean it's not there."

"Actually, it does mean that," I snap.

"Excuse me," Ez says hotly, "but I was imprisoned inside an Otto Sanchez force field for three years. I think I know what one feels like."

"Kids, kids," Simon says.

"Otto would tell me if he's developed an entirely new branch of power, like he's in a walking protective field," I say. "And I touch his energy dimension all the time."

"A highcap power isn't like a jacket you put on; it's more like a secret skin," Ez says. "The only way you could tell it's there is if you tried to penetrate it."

"Then how would you know he has one?" I ask.

Ez gets the look of an elf in headlights.

"Unless you tried to penetrate it?"

The awkward silence confirms it.

Ez tried to penetrate Otto's energy dimension. I feel sick. "Were you trying to dream-invade my fiancé?"

Simon puts his hands on her shoulders. "Lay off her, Justine. Of course she reaches out."

"Penetrating is more than reaching out. There's only one reason Ez would try to penetrate..."

"She was cut off from all touch for years," Simon interrupts. "Can you blame her for wanting to know she can fight Otto if she has to?"

"He trusted you enough to take your hand, and you tried to punch through and dream-invade him?"

"He only took my hand because he knew I couldn't penetrate."

"It was Stu who framed you for that crime, Ez, not Otto. Otto made an honest mistake."

She twists up her lips. "I know. I know Stu framed me."

"Then why?"

"Justine," Shelby says, "Ez is dining in home of man who imprisoned her for three years. She needed to know she could link to him. Like sighting person with rifle."

My heart pounds. "And you're telling me Otto's fielded himself, with a field so deep and so subtle that I can't detect it?"

Ez turns up her palms. "Hey, I could be wrong."

Except she doesn't think she's wrong. And Simon and Shelby don't seem surprised.

I swallow down a pang of grief in the silence that follows, feeling suddenly and strangely alone.

"Justine, if you're so curious, you could try penetrating him," Simon says. "You don't have to zing him. Just poke in and spelunk him again."

I spin around, glaring. "How can you even suggest that?" Spelunking is a maneuver where you punch down inside another person's dimension and actually merge into them.

"He'd never know. Just get in and out."

"*I'd* know."

"So?"

"It would be a violation of...everything." Specifically, it would be like pulling a thread that would unravel our whole relationship, just when I need to trust again. I think back to how he felt inside when I spelunked him last year: cool, orderly, solid. But it was such a violation.

"Don't you want to trust him fully?" Simon asks.

"Trust is a state of mind, but it's also an *activity*," I say. "A choice that you make. Trust is my choice."

Just then, the door opens and Otto strolls in with a beaming Ally on his arm. "Look who I found coming off the elevator."

Ally's my jock friend—my rollerblading buddy and former coworker at the dress shop. She's a big, blonde tomboy, and like most Midcitians, she idolizes Otto.

Otto. Secretly fielded. Could it be true?

I go to her and we hug in a big, jolly way. But then I meet Otto's eyes over her shoulder, and I get this flash of unease that cuts clear to the bone.

He escorts us to a candlelit table, bantering with Ally, who's on a tirade about the Felix Five.

Am I being paranoid? It wouldn't be the craziest thing in the world for Otto to figure out how to wrap himself in a secret personal force field—he does have powerful enemies, and the city *is* under siege, after all. He'd be protected from bullets as well as a highcap attack. Or disillusionist attack, for that matter. But why not tell me? And it's not as if I can bring it up to him.

I slam a glass of champagne. Somebody's not being honest.

Distractedly, I play the hostess as Otto and Kenzo deliver the crab. I exhort Otto to dine with us, but he reminds me he's no bridesmaid. The crab is a huge hit. People praise Otto and Kenzo's chefly genius.

My unease stays.

I try to focus on my party. Ez and Ally get along surprisingly well. Simon's pushing it, as usual; his stories are starting to shock Ally, and I have to kick him under the table after one too-extreme anecdote about his losing everything he owns and then getting beaten up so badly he gets hospitalized. The last thing we need is for Ally to start looking at the bunch of us too hard.

I'm mostly worried about Shelby. She seems more sullen than normal.

Basically, I'm overwrought throughout the whole dinner. But then, I *am* getting married in two days! Maybe overwrought is natural.

Otto comes in later and takes the chair at the far end of the table, looking suave and sexy in the candlelight.

Ally asks him about the crime wave, and he pronounces it nearly handled. "Things always look messiest while you're in the middle of cleaning." He has lots of grand plans for the city after the curfew is over, and he updates us on one of his favorites: the new port that will replace the blighted docks up around Sailor's Sweep. He paints his vision of how it will revitalize the north side, and he wants it to be a rich site of public art and interaction. My friends have fun making suggestions; even Shelby gets into it, though her jagged-glass park idea will probably not be implemented. Ez declares that there should be people acting like citizens from different historical periods of the city, mingling with the park-goers and having conversations about the leading concerns of their various eras.

Ally, who's quite drunk now, thinks the Sailor's Sweep tragedy of 1849 should be represented. In the Sailor's Sweep tragedy, an empty ship crashed into the shore after a storm— it's believed that a rogue wave swept all the men away into the ocean, though their bodies were never found. "We should have guys pose as the dead sailors in period sailor suits, crawling around on the boulders and scaring people." Then she claps a hand over her mouth and turns to Shelby. "Oh my God. I'm sorry. Your man—I didn't mean to remind you of—"

"Is only reminding when one forgets," Shelby says.

It was on those lakeshore rocks that Avery died.

"I'm still sorry," Ally says.

"Be sorry for killer of Avery," Shelby says. "Because I will kill him slowly. And painfully."

A hush falls, heavy as a sledgehammer.

"And I shall saw off his tongue with dull, serrated knife," Shelby continues. "Then I will pierce his brains with ice pick through his eye. Then I will remove his heart and throw it to crows. He will wish he never lived, I promise you."

Her hatred feels strangely intimate—an uncouth article of grief.

"Do you know where Packard is, Shelby?" Otto asks.

Shelby grits her teeth, hate flaring in her eyes. "Would I be here, do you imagine?" She tilts her head as she addresses him. "Do you think I would dedicate my life to destroying killer of Avery, as I have indeed done, and then squander opportunity to make him pay, just to dress up and have dinner?"

"He'll be brought to justice," Otto says. "Mark my words."

"Do *you* know where he is?" she asks Otto.

I shoot her a warning look she doesn't acknowledge.

"Not yet," Otto says.

Shelby pushes wild rice around on her plate, fork clinking on the china.

Ally drains her wine and slams down the glass with such force I'm shocked it doesn't break. "Well, if Police Chief Sanchez was still..." she looks confused. "I mean, if you were still Chief Sanchez, instead of Mayor Sanchez, you'da got the guy." She squints at Otto. "Am I right, or am I right?"

"I can assure you," Otto says, "Chief Sanchez is most definitely on this case."

Ally nods. "There we go."

Shelby's fixated on the candle.

"Well, Shelby, we're all glad you're here," Simon says.

She glowers up at this sentimental utterance.

"Because really," Simon continues, "it's gauche for the maid of honor to go on a murderous rampage in lieu of attending the bridesmaids' dinner."

Shelby snorts, eyes on the candle.

"And I should warn you," Simon continues, "killers' severed heads on posts are not acceptable as reception décor this season."

Ez raises a finger and says, "Nor their intestines as streamers."

"Nor fingers as finger food," Simon adds.

"Yuck!" Ally's waving her hands. "Yuck!"

Shelby wears a mysterious smile. Though she claims there's no such thing as happiness, she does delight in this sort of talk.

I'm not finding it amusing. Sure, I saw him kill Avery, but the idea of Packard hurt or dead upsets me deeply. I know that's why I called out when it was too little and too late yesterday—just enough to scare him, but not enough to get him caught. Why should I feel so protective of him?

I feel Otto observing me and I give him a quick smile. What does my detective see? I reach across and take his hand, smoothing my fingers over his. It really is outrageous that Ez thinks he has a secret personal force field.

"The crab was so delicious, so exquisite."

"You said that already, my dear," Otto says.

"And I might say it again." I squeeze. His skin feels normal. His energy dimension feels normal. It would be easy to punch in and test him, but I won't.

I shouldn't!

Kenzo arrives with a carafe of coffee, plus creams and sugars, then he retreats. I make my coffee *cow brown*, as Packard used to say. Thinking of him saying that gives me a good feeling in my heart, and then I force myself to remember what he did. And then I tense up in fear, waiting for the cranial pain. *God! I'm so sick of myself.* My mind is like one of those snakes trying to eat their own tails.

"Justine!" Ally pokes me and I look where everyone else is looking—Kenzo is back, now with a pyramid of chocolate truffles on a tray.

"Oh my goodness!" I say. "Kenzo, will you marry me?"

"Oh no you don't." Otto comes over and stands behind me, gently places his hands on my shoulders, and kisses the top of my head. I put my hands over his.

Again I glide across his energy dimension. I could settle the whole question right this instant. Simon's right—I could spelunk him. Really fast. In and out, though it's a dangerous maneuver, because you risk getting trapped. Simon developed the technique, needless to say.

I trail my pale fingers over Otto's dark knuckles. I could just burn a hole and slide in. Otto would never know.

I try to shake the idea out of my mind, but I can't. Hell, maybe it would be better if I tested it. Just to remove the suspicion!

"We are so going rollerblading tomorrow," Ally says. "The whole circuit. Bring your goggles; it's going to snow more. Cleatskates."

I nod. "Sounds like a plan." I rub the backs of Otto's hands, pressing them to my shoulders. I touch his energy dimension, the dimension that surrounds and pervades a person's physical body; it's cool, orderly. Could he really have fielded himself underneath? Right there, I decide I have to know. I tell myself it's because of the way Packard abused my trust. But that's just an excuse—I have to know, and before thinking about it any further, I use my focus to burn a tiny hole, just to see if I can. I'm gratified to burn through easily. Unfortunately, the fact I can burn a hole in his energy dimension doesn't mean he doesn't have a force field under there. I could make a hole in somebody's sweater; it doesn't mean they're not wearing a bulletproof vest.

Ally's talking about the last time we went rollerblading, how Max the bodyguard grumbled.

I push my awareness over the hole, readying myself to spelunk. You have to trick yourself into spelunking a person because it goes against human nature to join so deeply with another. It's wrong on every level, what I'm about to do, and certainly not what a loving, trusting fiancée does. Nevertheless, I take a deep breath and start easing down into him, letting the separation between us dissolve.

But I just slip sideways over the surface.

I try again, with more intention this time, allowing myself to freefall.

Nothing.

I attempt to plunge in, outright, the way you might jump from a high dive into icy water, shoving aside all hesitation and simply going for it. Much to my shock, I'm blocked. I can't jump in, punch in, plunge in, nothing.

My friends are right: my fiancé has surrounded himself with a powerful, protective field.

Ally extols the greatness of girl's hockey. Otto chuckles warmly at some smart-alecky comment Ez makes. I rub his hands less tenderly.

Why wouldn't he tell me? Generating a personal force field is a surprising and newsworthy enhancement of his powers.

I catch Simon watching from across the table. He knows what I just did—I can tell from his smug smile.

I look away. It's all I can do not to tell him to go to hell, to send everybody home. How could Otto keep me in the dark?

Simon stands, raising his glass. "I want to thank our host and hostess for this wonderful dinner." He grins at me, then at Otto, who is still standing behind me, still with his hands on my shoulders. "I've heard it said that trust is both a state of mind, and an activity."

I bore into him with my eyes. I'm going to kill him.

He continues: "Or wait. Is it that trust is a state of mind? Whereas, the *lack* of trust is an activity?"

I swallow, betraying no emotion.

"Or is it that trust, like love, is a state of the heart? Yes, that's it. And love is a state of the heart, but also, an *activity*. And quite an awesome one." Ally and Ez snicker. Otto chuckles behind me. Simon continues: "With these wise words in mind, I want to wish our hosts, Otto and Justine, a happy future full of love and trust, and the right kind of activity."

"Here, here," Ally says. People clink glasses.

I look up at Otto and give him a smile I don't feel. Then I level my smile at Simon, and this smile is one I do feel, and it's definitely an activity, too—the activity of fist suppression.

Chapter Six

Soon after we finish our coffees, four police escorts arrive and suddenly everybody's saying good-bye. I'd wanted to talk privately with Shelby, but apparently the police can't wait around.

"Tomorrow," she says.

I watch the elevator doors *clunk* shut. Otto comes up and stands beside me. "I think people had a nice time," he says, winding his fingers in my hair.

"I hope." I really want to confront him about this force field thing, but how? *Hey, Otto, my bridesmaid tried to penetrate your energy dimension and was blocked by a force field, and then I tried to spelunk you, and I couldn't. What's up with that?*

"You're lucky to have such friends," he says.

We head into the kitchen, where I spot Otto's coffee cup on the counter, mostly full, and his truffle barely touched. Avoiding a caffeine and sugar spike. He's more concerned about his head than he let on. Could that be what the force field secrecy is all about? That he doesn't want to worry me?

"I'm going to revitalize a while in my office," he says.

"Okay, honey," I say. Revitalizing is Otto's way to center himself; he uses his fields to create a cone of complete silence for a couple of hours.

I watch him disappear down the hall, still feeling angry, but tonight is not the time to talk to him about this force field issue. And in the end, it's all so stupid—silent cones and protective fields don't help a person feel safe.

I think back on Packard's words: *You're bigger than your fear, stronger than your fear, and you can outshine it with what you have inside you."* It seems like an impossible dream.

And there's nothing I want more.

Back in the living room, I find the coffee-table book we were looking at—*Lost Midcity*—open to a spread about the 1943 wedding. I slam it shut and shove it back onto the shelf next to the fireplace, where the embers still pulse and glow, and then I cast around for a book to read in bed. What I really want is *Mrs. Archer and the Golden Plume*, but it was taken when my apartment was robbed, the same day my car disappeared.

To walk in and find my place ransacked and my stuff gone, it was the last straw after all that violence and chaos. They took my passport and other hard-to-replace identity stuff, and all my favorite clothes and jewelry, almost as if they were trying to collect my most prized possessions—they even took the *Mrs. Archer* book, which I was in the middle of reading, an especially cruel touch. Otto told me that burglars take weird stuff sometimes. *They panic. Grab what they can and run.*

Now I'm wondering if they took it at all. Could I have left it in my car? I do sometimes carry books around with me, and I was really excited about this one. Two months and I still remember where it left off. Surely if I wear gloves I can search the car for the book and not disturb the prints. It's the only book I feel like reading.

I grab my gloves and keys, slip on my little booties under my cocktail gown, and stab the button for the elevator. Norman's surprised I'm going down so late. I explain that I left something in my car.

"Be careful," he says. "Make sure Sammy knows you're in there so he can watch."

I laugh. "Lord knows what might happen in the most secure garage in Midcity." But I promise to be careful as I step off the elevator and the doors close. I just stand there for a second, wondering what it's like having your workplace be an elevator. Just this tiny box. What does he do in there when nobody is riding? Does he even sleep?

I head around the corner to the front lobby, where Sammy is deep in conversation with a cop. Sammy rests his hand on the officer's shoulder, as if to comfort him. As I draw closer, I realize the officer is crying.

"...no such thing as happiness," the officer sobs. "Nothing gets better, it just changes into new permutations of unhappiness."

I stop dead in my tracks. *That sounds familiar.*

Sammy casts me a helpless look.

"Nothing matters," the officer continues. "It's all hopeless."

I stroll over and address the officer. "Have you spoken to my friend Shelby recently? By any chance?"

"Shelby Shavoyavich?" The officer huffs out a grim laugh. "Right, I was assigned to drive her home, but look. Here I am, and where is she? I should be there...drive her home, sit on the place..." He stares into the depths of a potted plant. "Oh well. Doing my job, not doing my job, it won't change anything. Nothing matters, you know?"

Oh yes, I know. I know that he's been zinged. And what's this stuff about sitting on her place?

"Did you see where she went?"

He gives me a blank look. Cocks his head at the street.

I look out the window into the snowy night, feeling worried about my friend. Why would she ditch the cop assigned to drive her home?

Sammy looks a little guilty. He was probably on twitter during the whole thing.

The officer seems to jerk to attention, horror stricken. "Mayor Sanchez can't know! Please, don't tell the mayor!"

"I won't." I settle a hand on his arm. "Otto has enough to worry about. Shelby probably just wanted to walk home on her own."

"You think?"

No, I don't. Not in a cocktail dress, heels, and feather-light coat, not when it's snowing like this. "She's a very eccentric girl," I assure him. "This isn't something to bother Otto with."

I glance at Sammy, who looks relieved too.

The officer sighs. "People slipping away. Time slipping. All coming to nothing. Like that miserable stub of a weed out there."

"Stub of a weed?"

"It pushed up through a crack in the sidewalk back in summer...now it's just a small, snow-covered stalk. I looked at that dead little stubby thing and everything became clear. There is no such thing as happiness. No such thing."

I nod. So Shelby pointed out the weed stalk to him, and in the next moment, the intense awareness of the pointlessness of life and the impossibility of happiness descended on him like a fog, and it's all he can see now. In other words, Shelby zinged him.

And disappeared into the night.

What is she up to? The idea of her out there alone in the cold worries me; she *did* seem more distressed than normal. Whatever she's doing, she doesn't want an audience. But why not ask me to help? I'd do anything for her.

"I promise, you'll feel better in the morning."

"Better is an illusion," he says.

He was supposed to drive her home and *sit on her place.* Spy on her. On whose orders? Otto's?

The officer's car waits out on the dark street, a plume of exhaust rising from the tailpipe against a background of falling snow. I wonder if Shelby was offended by being spied on. But then, why not take the ride home, change clothes and sneak out of her apartment? That way, she wouldn't have had to zing him. Why shake the tail here? It makes no sense.

Unless she was already where she wanted to be.

I recall her interest in the seventh floor—the sounds, the workmen. The number of workmen. How to get in...

"You stay here; I'm going to peek my head outside." I head for the door.

"No—I can't let you go alone." The officer fights his way out of his torpor, enough to rush to my side just in time to open the door. *Damn.*

"I'm just peeking," I say.

He stays at my side. *Great.*

I step out and he comes out with me. Cold air whooshes over my bare arms. We spy Shelby's footprints in the snow at the exact same time. "Oh!" he says. "Where's my mind? I could at least have followed. Not that it would mean anything in the larger scheme."

The footsteps are dull impressions, leading south from a brushed-off spot where the sidewalk meets the building—the spot where they must've found the dead weed.

"Looks like she wanted to walk home," I say.

Like a zombie, he starts following her footprints up the sidewalk.

Double damn.

I follow. I didn't want to get her busted, I'd just wanted to see where she'd gone. The tracks lead around the corner. The trail is fainter on this side, because of the wind. "These probably aren't even hers," I try.

He grunts, plods. We follow them around another corner, along Steven Street at the back of the building. A whoosh of wind lifts my hair and my skirt. I rub my arms, wishing for a coat, and something more than fuzzy little boots, but at least I don't still have kitten heels on.

The wind has all but erased the footprints back here. Up ahead, I spot a mountain bike chained to the base of the fire escape—it's too covered with snow to tell for sure, but it looks a lot like Shelby's. Shelby *does* winter ride, but why would her bike be here?

The officer sighs.

"I've seen enough," I say. "Clearly she took a cab."

"No cabs run during curfew."

"Some other ride then. It doesn't matter anyway, right? It's all just meaningless, right?" I turn and bolt back the way we came. The listless officer follows, thank goodness.

She could've left the bike here ages ago, though it didn't have quite enough snow piled on it for that. Or maybe it's not hers. Or she could be in the building, and she's planning to ride it home. But in a cocktail dress during a curfew?

Back inside, I shake the snow off my hair and clothes. "She'll be fine," I say to Sammy.

I head back around to the elevator.

"Find it?" Norman asks when the doors open.

I step in, wondering what he's talking about. Then I remember. The book. "No."

He hits the top button. "Snowing in the garage?"

"No." I shake my head. "I popped outside for a sec. Just needed a bit of fresh air."

He's silent a bit, then, "Shouldn't do that."

"I know, but..." I place a hand on my stomach and stick out my tongue.

He nods. I watch the numbers flit from five to six to seven. We stop at eight and I bid him a good night.

Back inside, I grab my phone and call Shelby, hardly surprised when she doesn't answer. I head into the living room and put my forehead to the back window.

Shelby's main mission these days seems to be revenge on *Killer of Avery*. Packard, in other words. I think about her strange interest in the seventh floor—is it possible she thinks Packard is sealed down there? If Otto had caught Packard, the seventh floor would be the last place he'd put him. Is it possible Shelby's not thinking straight?

Kenzo's in the kitchen. And the sliver of light under Otto's office door tells me he's still busy revitalizing.

Quietly I grab the little fireplace broom. I creep back to the window, slide it open, and lean out into the biting wind to

88

brush some snow off our fire-escape landing so I can see through the metal slats to the seventh floor fire-escape landing.

And I don't like what I find. Though the snow's pretty well windswept, I can tell somebody was up there recently. Is she in there?

I set down the little broom and tuck my dress into my panties, making it a kind of poofy minidress, and swing my legs out.

The wind blows harder and colder up here; I lower the window and sneak down the steps.

The seventh floor window is partly open. I creep closer. Strains of music from inside. Something old. Jethro Tull? The large room is littered with tools, tarps, and two-by-fours. Nothing but a construction zone, just as I told her. But apparently that wasn't good enough, because I spot small puddles leading into the interior. Great.

I push the window all the way open, and climb over the sill. With icy fingers, I lower the window back to its original position, grateful for the warmth and the cover of the music, which is actually pretty loud.

I sneak along the puddle path, trying to stay generally inside it and not make new puddles. Part of me wants to call out and confront her, but there's always the chance she really did tear off into the night. And that this is somebody else.

The music comes from the first door down the hallway. Slowly I sneak up, then I tip my head forward and peer in. The walls are lined with steel utility shelving and wooden crates.

I freeze at the sound of rattling from across the hall, like somebody trying to open a locker. Then footsteps. They seem to be heading my way. I rush into the room, and only then do I see it's occupied—a man—a guard—with his head on the desk. Sleeping. *Shit!*

I slip behind the open door and hide, heart beating like crazy, hoping to hell the guard doesn't wake up. He has black, frizzy hair. His green suit coat hangs open to reveal a gun in a holster.

The footsteps stop, then start again, head down the hall, past me. I wait, staring at the six or so computer monitors that are arranged on the shelves in front of the sleeping guard, like a wall of TVs. They flash black-and-white images. Exterior surveillance. The table in front him is scattered with papers, mobile devices, and laptops.

A Peter Frampton song comes on; the music seems to be emanating from one of his laptops. What is this place? This has nothing to do with remodeling. Is Otto letting the police use this as a base of operations while the remodelers work? Is this why he comes down here? And why the secrecy? Again I feel that flash of unease. And anger. Otto...my friends...all these secrets!

The man hasn't moved. Is he okay? I watch the back of his chest and satisfy myself that he's breathing, at least. I study the monitors; shots of downtown, a few houses and buildings. I recognize a shot of our old HQ. Another image looks like the front of Shelby's place. What the hell?

Footsteps. I melt back behind the door as far as I can. A person in a black ski jacket and ski mask enters and nudges the guard, who is unresponsive, then bends over one of the laptops. Shelby? The intruder is her height, but totally covered, with a black canvas bag slung over a shoulder. Thirty minutes ago, Shelby wore a cocktail dress and carried only a tiny purse. Where and how would she have changed?

The intruder's pant leg is cinched, like a biker's. But the jacket's not wet. This tells me this person didn't come by bike, but is probably leaving by bike.

This intruder moves like Shelby, and stands a few inches taller than me, just like Shelby. I'm 95 percent sure it's her, but that 5 percent makes me hesitate. He or she opens a crate and pulls out a gun. It's a submachine gun—a Scorpion, like my bodyguard Max carries—I can tell by the weird curl thing on the end.

The person fusses around with the gun, snapping something back and forth, so comfortable and familiar with it. No way would Shelby know how to handle a gun like that. A surge of panic pushes me farther behind the door as the person pulls more guns out of the crate. I hear a crisp *zip*, and clunks of metal on metal. He's loading guns into the canvas bag. Sounds of paper. Computer keyboard. *Clicks. Snaps.*

A grunt. A *Shelby* grunt. It *is* her! I release a breath, and I'm about to say something when curiosity overtakes me, and I decide to stay hidden just a little while longer.

She goes back to the man, brushes the hair around on the back of his head, then pulls something out of his neck and holds it up, pinched between her fingers. I can't see it, but I'm sure it's one of the tiny knockout darts from Avery's blow gun. The man will probably never know he's been hit. Or that she was here. I wonder what other stuff of Avery's she has.

She retreats now, light footsteps, past me, out the door, down the hall. In my mind, I follow her to the window. The first squeak is the window opening; a second squeak and it's shut. Since when does she know how to click a machine gun like a guy in a movie? What is she thinking, running off with a bag of urban-warfare guns? Has she found Packard?

I rush out and hoist the window back open. Leaning over the rail; I can just make her out, whipping down the fire escape. Going for the bike.

I think to call out to her, but that would alert Max and Norman, and lord knows who else, and get her into a world of trouble. I stuff down my rising panic and decide to follow her. A car's no good—not only would I get pulled over for violating curfew but, with a bike, Shelby can ride places cars can't. A car is useless.

But rollerblades aren't.

I scramble back up to the condo, grateful nobody's about, and do a record-fast change into my ten layers of winter exercise gear, including face mask, goggles, and helmet. I throw my reflective jacket on, inside out—I don't want to be bright tonight. Then I shove on my boots, grab my rollerblades, and haul out the window, climbing down as quickly as I can, dropping the last few feet.

Her bike tracks lead east. I pull off my boots and hide them next to the building and put on my rollerblades.

At the beginning of winter, Ally and I sank sheet-metal screws into the wheels of our shit pairs of rollerblades; the screws bite into the ice for superior winter traction. *Cleatskates*, we call them. I feel confident I can catch up—I'm fast and sure on cleatskates, and that heavy bag's got to be slowing her down.

I take off, skating against the biting wind and falling snow, hoping to hell Otto stays in his office revitalizing as long as he usually does.

Shelby's bike tracks snake around the building, turn north, then west along the promenade path, the bike-and-walking path that runs alongside the river. I skate like crazy, trying to make sense of this all. Is she stockpiling weapons? How many guns does it take to kill Packard?

I'm going so fast on the straightaway, and it's snowing so hard, I can barely see. I pull off my goggles and just squint against the furious flakes. I push harder, crouched low for speed—and low visibility to cops. Or sleepwalking cannibals. Or other criminals. I pump my legs and arms, breathing so hard that my lungs feel dry, even through my face mask. Are the membranes drying out? That can't be good. It would weaken them.

Stop it!

The tips of my eyelashes freeze. I round a bend. I catch sight of an oil-drum fire up ahead, but no people. Who made the fire? And who—or what—scared them off?

Otto says he and his men have been catching a lot of criminals with outstanding warrants simply by sweeping up people who are out past curfew. That's nice for the city, I suppose, but the idea that cannibals and wanted criminals make up the majority of people roaming around at night isn't comforting to me at the moment. Shelby's tracks go past, so I follow, cringing, feeling like I'm in one of those postapocalyptic movies where the place is empty, but you know people are hiding.

I pass the fire without incident.

Shelby's path continues along the promenade and goes under the Midcity Bridge—a postcard-perfect ambush spot. I brace myself and skate; if Shelby did it, so can I. Though Shelby's armed to the teeth. And she's so far ahead, I doubt she'd hear me if I screamed.

I make it under. The wind's stronger on the other side of the bridge, and the blowing snow has obscured her path in places. I skate faster. Things feel bright. Am I hyperventilating? This is a lot of exertion after a big meal.

Stop it!

Eventually the tracks veer left, back to the city streets. I slow up and scramble over a curb, heart pounding. We're nearing her neighborhood. I wonder if Otto's demoralized cop has pulled himself together enough to get going. And what the hell is up with that? And Otto's force field, and the operation on the floor below? The arsenal?

I go over a bumpy sidewalk, nearly losing my balance. The part of my face mask that covers my mouth and nostrils is stiff with ice. The tracks wind around a corner, up the next street, and there she is again, maybe five blocks ahead.

She's obviously taking the guns home. And then what? Is it possible she's become unbalanced in her obsession with hunting Packard? I'm thinking about her eagerness for my wedding to happen in such a speedy fashion. Was it all about Packard? And most of all, why couldn't she have come to me with all this? Does she not get that I'd do almost anything for her? I pull up my face mask and wipe my nose and eyes with my mitten, feeling upset and worried for my friend.

And for Packard. She's gunning for him. Literally.

I pass a hospital and some run-down shops, and then there's a block of ramshackle houses chopped up into apartments. I brace as I skate through the dark stretches, thinking I see movement inside every nook and doorway. Worse, though, is when I pass under a streetlamp, because I feel like I'm on display.

Suddenly my left foot catches on something and I'm hurtling forward, arms outstretched. I slam head-first into a light post. Blinding pain in my head and forearm.

I lay in a snow bank, on my side, perfectly still, the sound of the impact echoing inside my mind: *thuuuung.*

I hit my head. On a metal post. *Super hard.*

I can't believe it. Was the crack really loud? Panic comes over me like a quivery cloud as I analyze the sound in my memory. Yes, it was really, really loud, and a massive blow to the head is exactly what you don't want when you're predisposed to vein star. There's no way to tell if you have vein-star syndrome, but it is thought to be hereditary, and it's what my mother died of. A doctor once told me that for a lot of diseases, genetics cocks the gun, lifestyle pulls the trigger.

Or, smashing your head on a metal post pulls the trigger.

I stay there in the snow bank, weirdly baffled that it finally happened. Am I in shock? I pull off my gloves and face mask and touch the area. Ow.

I try to tell myself it's just a concussion. People get concussions all the time.

But the pain is different, and intense. *Real.*

The eerie warmth seems to flow through the injured area in a warm, throbbing cascade of sensation. Dimly I try to think of the term for it. Internal cranial bleeding? Is that it? I know I know the term. How can I not think of it? That's a bad sign!

If this is a classic vein-star bleed out, even the ER couldn't help me now. Not that I brought a phone or anything. I rest my head back on the snow bank and look up at the sky. Things seem darker. Another bad sign. Panic thickens my throat.

This is it.

I pull myself up to a sitting position. It's like an out-of-body experience, the idea that after all my freak-outs, I really am in medical trouble.

My extremities feel unusually cold. It's my circulation slowing with the plummet in my blood pressure. I splay my hands in front of my eyes. It's too soon.

Keep going. Stop her from hurting Packard, hurting herself.

I don't know where the thought comes from, but I find I'm levering myself up, almost reeling, steadying myself against the post again. I push off and skate on toward Shelby's, trying not to bump too much, wishing I'd brought my boots, so I could shuffle along instead of skate.

My heartbeat whooshes in my ears. Everything seems unreal. With a lurch of emotion, I'm remembering the restaurant, Mongolian Delites. All of us together, the best of friends. I skate on, madly wishing I could skate right into the past, when anything was possible, right into the back booth, with Packard. I think back on the long days of Shelby and me, knocking around town. All my old comrades-in-crime-fighting. A family.

I turn onto her street, which is lined with more decrepit homes and boarded-up stores. At the very end, some eight blocks ahead, next to Shelby's building, rises the notorious Tangle, Midcity's highway interchange, haunting the night like a flashing, screeching, snarling death star. It almost hurts my head to look at it.

Parts of the Tangle's twenty-some stories of curlicues are still open in spite of the curfew—it's how people bypass Midcity. The Tangle is also the number-one place for people to throw themselves to their deaths; sometimes their bodies aren't ever found in the mazelike dungeon of concrete and rebar below. The *Tanglelands*, they call it. So many die there. Strange comfort.

As I draw nearer, the roar of traffic heightens, a heavy-metal ocean of sound. Shelby's building, at the very foot of the Tangle, is the most undesirable real estate in the city. *I don't wish for pretty lies out my window. Only truth,* she'd once said of the view.

Things seem strangely simple now. She's my friend, and I need her, and she needs me.

I finally catch sight of her again. She's too close to the Tangle to hear me if I call, so I speed up, trying to close the six blocks or so between us before I pass out. She's locking her bike outside the door to her apartment—I think. I squint. It could be a newspaper box.

My head feels light. I can probably function a few minutes more. If only I can make it to her.

Suddenly, a figure pops out of nowhere, just a block ahead of me.

I'm so shocked, I almost fall again. He doesn't seem to see me, though; he's trundling away from me—in Shelby's direction. But then he disappears around a corner.

I keep going, relieved, until the figure pops out farther ahead and again trundles in the direction of Shelby and the Tangle. Cannibal sleepwalker? But usually the sleepwalkers are in packs. He goes another block and disappears, but not before I catch the glint of metal. An axe. Shit! Is he stalking Shelby?

I have no weapons that will work against an axe. I have no weapons whatsoever, unless you count zinging, which definitely won't work against an axe.

I speed up. It's bad for my head, but I have to stop him, or somehow warn Shelby, and then I'll hold him off until she can get one of her guns out. I have to stay conscious. Take a hit from an axe—it doesn't matter. I'll go down protecting my friend.

A focus, a purpose. I'm feeling like my old self again. Clearer in the head. Or maybe I'm delirious.

I veer off the sidewalk and start skating down the middle of the street. The axe guy ducked in somewhere, two blocks up—is he running up a parallel street? Closing in on her?

A form rushes out into the intersection in front of me—it's him.

But he's heading toward me now! I startle, lose my balance. Wheels whip out from under me—seemingly in slow motion. My feet fly up into the air, just before I slam down on my ass, with a major tremor to my head.

He's laughing, loping toward me.

Crap! I scramble backward, hitting the curb.

Lights. I think I see fireflies.

He slows to a walk as he nears me, swinging his giant black axe in a figure-eight. "Such a loyal friend," he says.

I stare in horror. He knows us?

His axe blade flashes in the night. "Holding me off, whatever it takes, while your poor brain bleeds. Or is it your imagination? Don't worry, we'll get that sorted out."

A telepath. I immediately skunk my thoughts with a song— "Skyrockets in Flight, Afternoon Delight". Telepaths can't hear thoughts over repetitive, stuck-in-your-head songs.

"Just for that, I'll kill you slow," he growls.

I scramble sideways along the curb, head throbbing, knee white hot with pain. Around and around the man circles the axe, which is almost double the size of a normal axe, with the handle painted black.

Only one person uses an axe like that: the Belmont Butcher, the insane telepath who enjoyed tuning into his victims' fear and horror as he hacked them up. But Otto caught the Belmont Butcher last year. The man's been sealed away in a force field prison ever since.

I'm being attacked by a Belmont-Butcher copycat?

My head pounds blindingly as I run my song, loudly and as distinctly as possible, trying to recollect the stuff Packard's right-hand man Francis taught us disillusionists about large, blunt weapons. Get out of range—that was one thing he always said. Getting out of range of something long like a bat or axe means running away fast...or getting up close. A guy can't chop you with an axe when you're right in his face.

And up close I could touch him.

I could zing him.

My heart beats like crazy. Even if I have to take a hit to get there, a strong zing would incapacitate him.

And it would feel so, so wonderful.

With a dark rush of eagerness, I decide that I don't have a choice—I have to zing him. I concentrate on the song to cover my thoughts. I'll be free from the fear for whatever time I have. I'll finally feel good.

I pull off my mittens, watching the axe as he comes closer, just as Francis taught. I roll away as it slams down onto the pavement. That's my chance: I hurl myself at him, hugging him, trying to keep my hand on one spot long enough to burn a hole in his energy dimension. He tries to shove me off him with the axe handle, smooth wood pushing against my jaw, my ear, but somehow I keep hold.

A *clatter*. He's discarded the axe. He wraps his bare hands around my neck now, choking me, jerking my head back and forth. I grab his bare wrists, trying to get a breath—I can't tell if he's trying to shake me off or kill me, but I've burnt the hole. I call my fear to the surface and the flow starts instantly.

My fingers heat up as a tsunami of pure terror rushes into him, all to the soundtrack of "Afternoon Delight". Things get fuzzy but I keep hold of his wrist, determined not to break the connection.

Just a little longer.

Darkness. Wind in my fingers. Falling, holding. Knuckles burning. The term *death grip* floats through my mind. The sense of release.

Chapter Seven

I wake up to something rough on my cheek.

Icy pavement.

It's night. My toes are so numb they burn. Something hard under my ribs. I lift myself off it and find that it's an axe. My fingers are burning with cold, too. My head throbs.

And it's all perfectly fine. Wonderful even. Because I'm free of fear.

I grab the axe and sit up, smiling, surprised to see the Butcher on the other side of the sidewalk, back flattened against a brick wall, eyes wide. Does he think I'm going to try to chop him up? Why didn't he take the axe while I was out?

Was I out?

"Did I pass out?" I ask him.

He just gapes at me, like I might go crazy on him at any second.

"Come on. Was I out? It seems like I was..."

"I know you were pretending," he says.

"Mmm." Irrational. But I just zinged him with all the fear I'd built up over the past sixty-four days. Most people can't handle what I accumulate from one day.

I put my hand to the place where my cheek burns. Maybe I scraped it, but I can move my jaw just fine. My knee is killing me, but I decide it's just bruised. I wiggle my toes to get the blood back in them. This could be the beginnings of frostbite. "Skyrockets in Flight" is still running through my mind, because that's the kind of song it is. Sharp pain in my head. I recall falling and bumping my head. It seems ridiculous to me now, how worked up I got over a bump on the head.

I am a ridiculous person.

The Butcher copycat watches me mutely. Was he sitting there the whole time, thinking I was toying with him? Fear makes people stupid; I know that better than anyone. I look around for Shelby. I have to keep going. I have to stop her.

"Okay, how long was I pretending?"

No answer.

"So you're supposed to be the Belmont Butcher? Is that your thing?"

He nods.

"Where's your black apron?"

"Underneath my coat," he whispers. His eyes go wide as I stand unsteadily with the help of a sign pole and the axe, which I use as a kind of crutch. I narrow my eyes, breathing in the cool, fresh air.

"Why were you following her? Were you specifically following her, or was it random?"

He draws back, panicked.

"Come on," I say. "I want an answer." I shift a bit, and my knee buckles under me; I hold the pole, unsteady on my skates, and that's when the Butcher explodes up from the sidewalk, tearing away from me in the direction of the river. He trips and falls at one point, then scrambles up and continues, like I might be chasing him. He runs willy-nilly, away from Shelby. Away from the Tangle.

Works for me.

I turn and squint into the distance, toward Shelby's place. No sign of her, though I can make out what I think is her bike. And I'm betting there are tracks leading from the bike into her building, if the snow hasn't covered them. Luckily, it's tapered off into small, icy flakes. Cold-weather snow.

I start off. Every stride hurts, not that I care. Pain is just pain, cold is just cold, and it's idiotic to think I have a vein-star blowout. People hit their heads every day!

I clear one block, skating carefully. Two to go. Shelby's faint tire tracks look like soft snakes twining in the snow.

Another block. The Tangle looms large and loud.

Maybe I should feel bad for giving in and zinging, but I'm far too exhilarated. When you dump out the heavy, dark emotions that weigh you down, your mind gets strong, and your senses heighten—taste, smell, touch—you get more information from the world around you. And you feel so so wonderful! Because you're free.

The extreme version of this freedom lasts for up to an hour. *Glory hour,* we call it. After that, the darkness starts building back up, slowly dulling your senses and your mind.

The Tangle noise grows louder as I reach her bike, which is chained to a sign pole. Her boot prints lead away from it, but not to the door of her apartment building. They lead in the direction of the Tangle.

Why? Is she stashing the guns down in the Tanglelands instead of in her apartment? It makes some sense if she knows her place is being watched, though it doesn't seem incredibly secure—for her or for the guns. The Tanglelands, the vast wasteland below the Tangle's coil of highway curlicues, is a wellspring of scary urban legends for a reason.

I follow her boot prints beyond where the street dead-ends, then through the wasteland that encircles the Tanglelands—a realm of garbage, blocky concrete boulders, and junked shopping carts. Not the best place to be on rollerblades. But the pain in my knee and head has become its own thing, not good or bad, just intense.

Shelby's tracks lead around the perimeter of the Tangle, and I follow them, half skating and half walking, thankful for the long-handled axe, which makes a handy, though heavy, balancing aid. I move past hulking rubble chunks, over the snow-covered section of a broken-down highway, and around a concrete pillar, fat as a silo. Finally the tracks turn in through a slim opening concealed by twisted guardrails. I torque my body to squeeze through, knee protesting, and find myself in a dim cave whose low ceiling is formed by the underbelly of a highway long out of use.

The sound is different inside here—it has more of a vibrational quality, like sound inside a skull. The rubble and garbage on the floor obscure her boot prints, but I pick them up farther in, leading to a tunnel just big enough for a train to go through, if a train could run along a V-shaped gulley.

I follow, moving deeper in, picking around the debris as best as I can. What is she thinking, taking crazy chances, stashing weapons in the Tanglelands? And she probably didn't even know she was being pursued by a killer. I shudder to recall the horrible things she has in store for Packard. *Killer of Avery*, as she calls him, unable to even say his name. Killing Packard would destroy her. Even Avery would see a quest for vengeance as a form of oppression.

How could Shelby have gone off the edge like this, and I didn't even know it? I've been an oblivious friend, that's how. No more.

Her tracks fade out in a minichamber that's composed of concrete and twisted metal. The hum of the vehicles above sounds throatier here.

I pick up her prints on the other side of a slimy puddle and crawl through a small, rocky space that angles upward. Everything I touch is cold, gross, or sharp. I curse myself for not grabbing my mittens off the street where I fought the fake Butcher.

I follow her trail onward, into a smaller underhighway cavern, a space that would be totally dark if it weren't for a storm lantern, hanging mysteriously and somewhat ominously from a rebar arm poking out of broken concrete. Did I scare somebody off? Is somebody lurking? I grip my axe, straining to hear anything above the thrumming of vehicles. If nothing else, surely rats, bats, and cannibals are roaming around in here.

Okay, glory hour is definitely fading.

In the distance is a steep incline, like a rocky mountainside. I ramble over and climb it, pushing with the edges of my rollerblade wheels and my axe, dislodging rubble. I reach the tip-top, panting. In front of me stretches a stadium-sized space, except in place of a ceiling, there are crisscrosses of highway, soaring above like the heavenly dome of a dystopian world.

You can even see bits of sky between the twisting highways, some of which are dimly strobed with car headlights. I turn my gaze downward; below is a dark expanse of something—liquid? Ambient light from above pulses off it. It has its own kind of beauty, this strange cavernous place.

A dim flash draws my attention to the ledge that encircles the huge space. Another flash—it's a person carrying a flashlight. I squint, making out the figure's dark hair, large bag. It's Shelby, walking around the space, staying close to the edge, trying to avoid the dark lake in the middle

A glint of metal—she has one of the machine guns out. She carries it in front of her chest, like a mercenary. It's strange, almost comical, like seeing your cat driving a car. I call out, but the hum is too loud, and she's too far away.

I make my way down, nearly losing my footing. At one point, my axe slips from my grip and tumbles on ahead of me, but I grab onto stuff and manage a controlled slide, albeit with a hard landing. I find my axe again and survey the area. Up close, the slime lake smells, and it's full of debris that I don't want to think about. A trail leads off to my right—the one Shelby followed. In the distance across the slime expanse, I spy a kind of platform atop a hill of boulders. There are people up there, huddled by a dim fire. Two figures. Is Shelby going to join them?

The figure whose back is to me pokes at the embers, and flames rise, casting a glow on the face and cinnamon hair of the figure oriented toward me.

Packard.

I know him even from this distance. I'd know him anywhere. I watch him, stunned. Relieved. Then I realize Shelby is approaching them unseen...with a gun.

She's going to kill him.

"Packard!" I yell. "Packard!" He can't hear me, of course. Every molecule of my being screams to get to him, save him, a kind of blind primal urge. "Packard!"

Shelby continues stalking around the edge of the space. But I'm closer—if I go through the lake.

I grip my axe and take off, wading right into the slime, or more, through it, through the viscous, oily fluid. It's deeper than I thought—up to my knees in areas. I try not to splash or get any in my mouth. I hit something big and fall right onto it, or more like through it—my hands plunge into something soft and lumpy. I tell myself it's a submerged sack of garbage, and I just get back up and keep on, shaking the slime off my hands and arms, rubbing it on my lycra outer layer, moving forward on the rollerblades. There's no way this fluid isn't toxic. Virulent. Bacteria-laden. My knee's screaming again—white hot with pain, but nothing matters except stopping Shelby. She's distraught. Vengeful.

And she's found Packard.

A waving light in the distance—it's Shelby's flashlight beam—she's jerking it around. No—she's running. She's seen me! She's trying to beat me to Packard's perch!

"No!" I scream, trying to wade faster, arms out, legs fighting through the sludge. On the other side I smash into a boulder and start climbing up, axe in hand. I have to beat Shelby. I scramble right to the top.

"Packard!" I call.

He springs up from where he sits. "Justine?"

I practically fall right onto him.

He grabs my arm. "Justine!"

"Shelby's coming! She has a gun!"

I recognize the other person by the fire now: Jordan the crazy therapist, the second-most dangerous disillusionist. She makes people feel really screwed up. Is Shelby gunning for Jordan, too?

I look around for an exit. "We have to get out—"

Shelby appears on the other side, black, winter face mask pulled up to reveal blazing eyes.

I step in front of Packard, clutching him behind me with one hand, axe in the other. "Drop it, Shelby!"

Shelby points her gun at me. "No." The traffic hum seems to louden. "Away from him, Justine. Now."

"Justine—" Packard says, laying his hands on my shoulders, tentatively, like he doesn't want to startle me. "Shelby—"

"Now!" Shelby yells.

I say, "It won't solve anything or make you feel better, and it won't bring Avery back."

Shelby straightens. "What won't?"

Packard says my name again in my ear and I feel his hand curving round my waist. I begin to feel really strange. My knee screams in pain.

Shelby laughs.

"What?"

"You are protecting him." Shelby says.

I straighten. She's right—I'm protecting him. A killer. The memory of his killing Avery hits me, blindingly, like needles in my head. My legs feel weak. *Not now!*

Strong arms fasten around me, keeping me upright, holding me so tightly the breath goes out of me. "Justine. It's okay," he murmurs. Warm words on my neck.

"Stay behind me! Nobody's shooting anyone here." I pull myself together, wriggle to force him back behind me, legs still wobbling. It's pathetic to think I can save him when I can barely stand.

He pulls me right up against him, supporting me, helping me save him. "It's okay," he says again. "She's okay."

"Justine, you think I will kill him?" Shelby snorts. "I thought *you* were here to kill him."

I regard her dimly. We thought each other was here to kill Packard?

Shelby grins.

Packard grabs my axe, pulls me around to face him, close enough to kiss him. "Justine." His face is shadowed, but his gaze is fierce, and I stare into his green eyes with their pale ruffle of lashes, feeling suspended in time, in place. It's like the feeling you get on a swing set when you've swung as far forward as physics will allow, and there's this one blank moment where the world stops. Yet somehow, everything is in motion.

Packard.

Yes, I was protecting him. And I'd do it again. It doesn't make sense, because I saw him kill...the pain stabs at my head as I flash on the memory.

And then he kisses me.

And we're in freefall. The delicious sensation of him takes me by surprise. I grab on, pull him to me. I'm feeling him with my heart, and I know I've never felt anything so good—so true— as his lips crushed against mine, the gritty rub of his stubble on my cheek, my fingers in his hair. I forget about Jordan, Shelby; the momentum is too delicious, too smooth. I kiss him, soak in the warmth of him.

And then something strange happens: it's as though a layer is peeling away, and I'm discovering my heart again. The more I know my heart, the more I know Packard.

And I know that he didn't kill Avery.

The memory of it strikes me now as strangely two-dimensional, disembodied, like a deeply troubling dream. The stabbing pain in my head fades as the reality drains from the memory.

The memory isn't real.

I pull away, shocked. "Packard!" I exclaim. My mouth falls open. He didn't do it. "Packard," I say, this time in recognition.

He whooshes out a breath, gaze bright. "Oh God, Justine," he breathes, relieved, kissing my cheek, my neck.

I want to laugh, to cry. I *know* Packard. I know he hates the smell of curry, and that he loves bossing people, and swimming in the ocean. He loves dry humor and kicking snow clumps off the bottoms of cars. And I know he didn't kill Avery. It's as if my knowing got covered over, and now I'm pulling off the layers.

Up above, car lights bounce dimly off the highway undersides that stretch up into the night. I want to stay with him in this humming hideaway forever, peeling everything away until it's just us.

I hear Shelby groan, but I don't care. Shamelessly, happily, I drink in his lips, his body. Feelings roar through me as powerfully as the thousands of cars above.

I pull away and look up at him, at the unsure smile hidden inside his big, boyish lips, as the thinness of the memory becomes even more apparent. "I was revised!" I exclaim. "That whole memory—it's made of nothing! You didn't kill him."

"No, I didn't." He keeps his hands on my arms. I'm none too steady. "Justine—"

I'm outraged I'd ever believed it. "You're innocent, and I falsely accused you!"

And *I love him.*

The realization is stunning, terrifying. I look into his green eyes, feeling as if I've stepped into a wildly extravagant reality, but at the same time, the love feels like it's an ancient part of me.

"You were revised," Packard says.

"How—" Even in the face of the truth, I can barely believe it. "A fake memory was in me this whole time. I should've known!"

"You couldn't help it."

"I should've."

Packard shakes his head. "You couldn't." Even so, his gaze shifts away; it's the minutest of flickers, lasting a bare moment. Most people wouldn't catch it, but I do.

Hurt.

How could he not be hurt that I would believe such a thing?

"I don't know what to say…" I spin around. "Shelby…you knew?"

"Of course."

"And you didn't tell me?"

"You cannot tell revised person they are revised," Shelby says.

"You could've tried! I would've told *you*. I rely on you. Christ, there was even this one time when I even thought, *well, if my friends thought I was revised, they'd say something.*"

"So we would simply say something?" Shelby glares. There's a new hard edge to my friend.

"Yeah. You would say something. *Hey Justine. We think you were revised.* It's not that complicated."

"For us, is very complicated," Shelby says. "Very much. When she killed your memory, she killed the Justine who might have recognized revise."

"Well, obviously *this Justine* recognized the revise."

Packard pushes my hair back. "It's not something you can tell a person."

I turn to him. "*You* tried."

"I had nothing to lose. And it didn't work so well, did it?"

I say, "We have to tell Otto you're innocent. We have to make this right."

His face darkens. "No—"

"What? I falsely accused you!" I'm also thinking about the wedding. How can I marry Otto after I had this surge of feeling for Packard? After I kissed him like that? "I have to tell Otto."

Shelby and Packard exchange glances.

"Don't be an idiot," Jordan says, coming at me with a wand-like device. "Yuck. You're covered in sludge."

"Take it easy," Packard snatches the wand from her. "You might be tracked," he says to me. "You mind?" He touches my hand, lifts it so my palm rests on his.

"Oh." I lift my arms out to the side, and he waves the wand around. "I got sludge all over you."

"I don't care."

He didn't do it. He's innocent. I wonder vaguely why they'd focus on trackers when we need to make this right, and for the twentieth time, I wish for boots instead of skates.

"They were smart not to tell you about the revise," Jordan says to me. "Sophia obliterated the truth from your head, and no amount of reasoning or new information could ever trump what she put in there. And a planted memory like that grows roots, links up with genuine memories. It could only be trumped from inside, because nobody can revise emotions. That's likely the source of all that pain in your head too. Internal conflict. Head versus heart."

Jordan sits down, opens a laptop. Shelby takes something out of her pocket and hands it to her. Flash drive. Data from the computers on the seventh floor.

Packard snaps off the wand. "Clean." Again I get that hit of hurt off him. I believed he killed a man. How could I?

"Simon said you were tracked," Shelby says.

"*All* of you were in on this? And I'm walking around like an idiot?" I feel this spark of shame.

"Not like an idiot." Packard puts a hand on my arm. "You had your head messed with. You're going to be reeling from it, feeling crazy, feeling angry. But you came back, Justine. That's what's important."

I do feel crazy and angry.

Shelby grabs his sleeve, telling him about the seventh floor. He converses with her, but stays looking at me until she pulls him over to look at her bag of weapons.

My mind races. All this time they all knew I was revised. They let me tell this preposterous story, and I had no idea it was false. But my heart knew it was false. Because if I'd seen Packard kill, I wouldn't love him like I do.

He looks over at me from across the fire where he's listening to Shelby's report, and the breath goes out of me. I just want to go to him, and for things to be simple, but they're not simple. I'm getting married the day after tomorrow, becoming Midcity's first lady. I've dedicated myself to a nursing career, to Otto. Horses and carriages have been rented. My accusations put Packard on the run.

What have I done?

I say, "You guys, if Sophia revised me, it means she knows who the real killer is!"

Shelby and Packard say nothing. Across the fire, Jordan taps away at the computer.

"We have to tell Otto so he can question Sophia," I say. "Oh no, wait," I say. "Could *Sophia* have killed Avery?"

Jordan snickers: "Getting warmer."

"You think this is funny?" I catch Packard exchanging glances with Shelby. I know that look—they're keeping things from me. Why are they treating me like an outsider?

But then again, I accused Packard, betrayed him. A new thought comes to me: what if that's all Packard wanted? For me to help clear his name? Was that what the kiss was for? My heart sinks as I remember all the times he's taken advantage of my feelings for him to get what he wants. He seemed relieved, but wouldn't anybody be relieved when their accuser recants? I ruined his life!

"I'll make an official statement at the police station. Whatever you need."

Shelby says, "We think you saw the killer."

"And Sophia blanked out my memory," I say.

"Yes, yes," Shelby says impatiently. "I mean, we think you were *with* killer and Avery."

"What do you mean?"

"Come here," Packard says. "Sit."

"I don't want to sit." I fight back the tears. "Otto's going to be upset if I'm gone." *Otto.* Our life seems a world away. How can I marry him now?

"What do you remember of the day after the kidnapping?" Packard asks. "Anything special? You see the falseness of the memory. Does anything else..." he pauses, and my heart fills the space with pounding. "Does anything...feel different?"

"Just everything." I move nearer to the fire, balancing tentatively on my wheels, hoping to warm my slime-drenched, winter workout clothes. The warmth, at least, is true. It withholds nothing. Unlike my friends. Not that I can blame them. I've become untrustworthy.

I rub my arms, feeling so foolish. But why should I begrudge Packard for wanting to clear his name?

Packard touches my arm. "Are you okay?"

"Of course," I say cheerfully.

"You knew the memory of me killing Avery was fake," he tries, "on an emotional level. But is there anything else? From that day? That you remember or...feel anything about? Anything significant?"

I sigh and launch into what I recall of the day. "When I woke up, Otto was still sleeping. I went down to the hotel lobby. I was having coffee in the hotel lobby by myself, killing time. I decided to go for a walk, and I ran into Avery. And we walked..." I try to remember things from the walk. "We walked along the lakeshore. Some city blocks." I try to recall what we talked about. We were walking, looking at Midcity sights. It seemed perfectly normal, but why would Avery and I take such a long walk? "We had a burger at the McDonald's on 4th and Maxbert."

"With *Avery?*" Shelby says. "Avery would stab pin into his eye before he would go to McDonald's."

I stiffen. She's right. I think back on the walk, trying to remember what we talked about. Avery was a fascinating, fiery thinker, and we would've talked about interesting things, but all I can recall are streetscape images and random stuff about the shops. The walk doesn't feel false in my heart, the way the Packard killing did—I guess there's no emotional conflict—but it's definitely out of character. Could it, too, be a revise?

I recall something else: "I was wearing those flimsy clothes from the hospital free box," I say. "It was all I had with me. And it was so cold...I wouldn't have wanted to walk so far in those clothes! And if I woke up at around nine, and Avery..."

"Death was four-eighteen," Shelby says flatly. "You walked for six hours? Seven?"

More revision? I'm feeling double crazy. Is there anything I can trust?

Jordan says, "Hmm," at something on the computer, mumbling about country roads in Iowa. Surveillance.

I try to focus. "Avery and I wouldn't take a seven-hour walk in the cold, or stop at McDonald's." I start to feel sick. "Did she take the whole day? Oh God—coffee. She likes to erase back to the first cup of coffee." I look around, frantic. "If she erased back to when I drank coffee, that means she took a whole day from me. What did I do that day? What the hell did she take?"

Packard casts a dark look in the direction of the fire. "You have no idea what she took."

"You know?"

"You weren't on a walk all morning."

"Where was I? What happened?"

"It's not something I can just *tell...*"

"Why not?"

He gets this strange look. "Can you—there's nothing—" he looks at me, pleadingly almost. "Anything you can recall? Emotions..."

I feel this surge of anger "No, Packard. It's all gone. G-O-N-E, gone."

He looks away.

My heart sinks. *It's something horrible.*

Shelby watches Packard; they seem to be communing. Like they're deciding between themselves if it's okay to let me in on the big secret.

"Hey," Jordan says from across the fire.

"*Why* can't you just tell it? Why not?" I demand, ignoring Jordan. I feel like such an idiot! And I still love him. I feel the tears sprout, but I refuse to cry. "Nothing ever changes, does it?" Sure, Packard wouldn't kill, but he's always been out for himself. I point at him. "You'll never be up front with me. This is almost comical. Almost." I turn to Shelby. "And my BFF."

She turns to Packard. Like he gets to say what I'm allowed to know.

"Great," I say.

"It's not so simple, Justine," Packard says. "To tell…"

"Hey," Jordan interrupts. "Who's Fawna?"

Shelby stills. Packard goes pale. It's as if everything drains out of the moment.

Fawna.

"What did you just say?" he asks hoarsely.

Jordan straightens, startled by Packard's tone. "Fawna," she repeats softly. "You know her?"

There's only one Fawna I know: the powerful little telepath who lived in the old school ruins with Otto and Packard and the rest of the kids. Taken in the night some twenty years ago.

"What *about* Fawna?" he says.

Jordan taps some more. "There's all this stuff about Fawna in Otto's private account. This e-mail from a Fawna, forwarded a million times. Emails *about* Fawna. 'Re: Fawna. Re: Re: Fawna.' Several files about Fawna. Norman, Smitty. All his guys. They're obsessed with this Fawna." She hits some buttons. "Even the surveillance seems connected to Fawna."

113

Otto's private account?

Packard stalks around the fire and leans in behind Jordan, peering at the screen. "Open the emails from Fawna. Whatever's from Fawna."

Jordan hits some keys. "Only one is actually *from* Fawna."

Shelby goes over and stands by Packard.

"Scroll down." He points. "Try another."

"The little girl kidnapped from abandoned school," Shelby says.

"Yes," Packard says.

So Shelby's heard the story now, too. Otto and Packard once had a solemn pact to keep that boyhood episode a secret—how the two of them fought back against the men who'd kidnapped their friends, and it ended with Otto basically massacring the men. Otto didn't fully understand what he was doing, but Packard did.

I stay. "I don't feel right about you guys reading Otto's email," I say.

Nobody answers me. Like it doesn't matter.

"Seriously. Breaking into Otto's private e-mail?"

"Here's the original one from her—see?" Jordan says. "Just a few weeks ago. This started it. 'Dear Henji, I am bringing you your coon hand. You need the coon hand, because there is danger. The danger comes from your inner circle, and the ground will run red'."

Silence. Their faces look eerie in the light of the screen.

Packard stands, stares into the fire. "She's back. And she's prognosticating."

"I thought she was a telepath," I say.

"Long-term prognosticators always start as telepaths. From reading the minds of people to reading the mind of the future. Of fate. She used to get visions of the future, even as a child, though sometimes she confused them with daydreams. But then they'd come true." Packard gets this distant look. "And the coon hand, God. That's a bit of raccoon skeleton Otto decorated with ribbons—a gift for Fawna, a good luck charm. And now she's bringing it back to him."

"Well," Jordan says, "she never contacted Otto again. The rest of the emails are from Otto asking about the meaning of the prediction, or him asking her to revisit the prediction. To recheck. He wants her to define inner circle. In some of these he offers to go get her and give her a ride. She never says where she is." Jordan looks up at Packard. "His downfall. Can we trust this? Are we sure she's not crazy?"

Packard says. "Even if she's crazy, she's probably right. Wherever she's been, this vision has inspired her to emerge or escape. This is clearly a death prediction."

Otto must be freaked out of his wits.

Shelby says, "We have to get the others out first. And then I hope he dies painfully, and I will spit on his body."

"What?" Heat rises to my face. "*What?*"

"You heard," she says.

"You'll be happy to see him die and spit on him?"

Shelby's eyes blaze. "Wake up, Justine! Is Otto who killed Avery. And he is holding Carter, Helmut—"

"Shelby," Packard says in a low voice. "Not like this."

Shelby flings up her hand. "She says she wants to know. Do you want to know, Justine? Well, I am telling you."

I'm stunned by her bizarre accusation. "You're being insane."

Shelby pulls off her cap, stalks over to me, hair wild. "You feel sorry for Otto? Think, Justine. He killed Avery, and told Sophia to revise you."

"He would never do that!"

"Who does Sophia work for? Tell me! Who?"

"That doesn't mean he killed Avery. Why would he?"

"You know why," she says. "Avery's glasses allowed Otto to be recognized as highcap. They rendered him powerless. Him and all other highcaps—powerless. These glasses, they allowed him to be taken, terrorized. Otto sent people to destroy Avery's factory that day you freed him. Did you know? They destroyed everything. Otto's people, they hunted down every pair ordered. We know this. Otto wanted to erase glasses from this earth. But Avery kept formula in his mind," she slaps her head. "Last highcap glasses left on planet, these were in Avery's mind. For that, Otto killed him."

"But he knew Avery helped us," I protest. "I told him so."

"He does not care!"

Packard grabs Shelby's wrist. "She's had enough." He turns to me. "Justine..."

"Oh God." I feel sick. "You believe it too."

Shelby yanks away from Packard. "Of course he believes it."

It's too much. *Otto*. My safe harbor. A man who selflessly puts the happiness and safety of citizens above his own. "It's not true."

Softly, Packard says, "He did it, Justine."

"You didn't see him kill Avery," I say. "You just need a culprit."

Jordan sniffs. "Somebody had to hold you for Sophia. Somebody you know."

"And since I know Otto, it has to be him? You've got him killing Avery, then holding me for Sophia to revise?" I shake my head. "This is a man who is destroying himself to keep dangerous highcaps sealed up, so that the city is safe. Yeah, you're right. I *have* had enough. And you, Shelby, my fabulous maid of honor? All the time thinking this?"

"Oh, I am sorry. Otto is such an honest man," Shelby bites out. "Otto would never have secret headquarters below your condo full of weapons. Otto would never hide your car from you, or put tracker on you, or secretly make new powers which he keeps hidden from you."

"Shelby," Packard growls.

She yanks away, lost in her private storm. "Otto would never force city engineers to fake sinkhole under your apartment building so that you must move in with him. Tell me, has building sunk? Have they torn it down? And why the curfew?"

"To protect people from the cannibals and criminals!"

"No! To smoke out Packard. Where is Carter? Enrique? Vesuvius? All our people? He has them!"

I back away, bewildered.

Packard comes to my side

"Don't touch me!" I yell.

He raises his hands, to show he won't touch me. "Come and sit. Let's ratchet down. Shelby should never have…"

"I don't want to ratchet down!" The roar of cars above us seems to heighten. "I don't know what's worse, that you all…that you all would think Otto, my *fiancé*, killed Avery? And had me revised? That's horrible just right there. But then, that you would think something like that, something so *monstrous*, and not tell me? You'd just allow me to marry somebody you believe to be a deranged psycho?" I turn to Shelby. "And you hope he dies?"

"No, I hope I can kill him. We will retake city from him, and I hope I will have chance to kill him slowly."

I don't know what's real anymore. I don't know *who's* real. "I'm done with all of you." I look around, discern the path Shelby took, start toward it, impervious to the pain in my knee. I'm moving on pure adrenaline. "And you're all uninvited to the wedding."

"Justine, wait," Packard says.

I hear him behind me. I grab the machine gun Shelby put down and spin around.

He stops. "Please." He raises his arms. "The revise is making the world seem crazy, out of control. You're reacting without thinking, and you're going to go where you feel safe but you're not safe—"

"Don't you psycho-screw me!"

"If he realizes you know about the revise, you *will* be in danger," Packard says.

117

I jerk at the lever on the gun and something inside it shifts. Shelby and Jordan drop to the ground.

Packard stays standing. "You get overwhelmed with emotion, but afterwards, you always think things through and make smart decisions. Let yourself do that now."

"Tell me one more thing about myself and I'll shoot you."

A pause. Then, "You won't shoot me."

I stand there in disbelief. God! That old arrogance—it rips me up. I grip the gun. "I'm going home," I announce in a weird, calm voice. "Don't try to stop me." The weird calm voice comes from this desperate spot deep inside, and it scares me. It seems to scare Packard, too, because he doesn't move. Pushing people to their breaking points is Packard's game, but I'm sure he prefers that a person doesn't hold a gun when he gets them there.

"We won't follow," he says. "I know you'll think this through."

"Give me my axe."

Jordan gets it and hands it to Packard, who hands it on to me, handle first. I'm freezing, and covered with Tanglelands muck, and everything has been turned upside down. I just need my safe, warm life back. "You'd *better* not follow me."

I turn and skate like hell out of there, taking Shelby's path back, the ridge around the edge, which turns out to be a slightly tilted, sunken fragment of a highway that dead-ends into a rubble pile, then continues. I ditch the gun but I keep the axe, using it for balance as I climb to the next section of sunken highway, which stretches brokenly, like a chopped snake, around the edge of the space. Finally I reach the crawl hole and make my way down the rubble pile, and back to where the storm lantern was, my mind spinning at a high, strange frequency all the while. On and on I backtrack, and soon I'm out in the cold, cold night.

Chapter Eight

The heavy axe gives me extra momentum as I pump my arms, skating fast down the dark streets, trying to concentrate on my balance and not on the outrageousness of my supposed friends' thinking Otto would shoot Avery and then have me revised.

Or that they would think such a thing about him and be okay with my marrying him. I feel just stunned, and so very alone.

Maybe I shouldn't be surprised. It's always been Packard against Otto, and when I crossed over and consented to marry Otto, I became an enemy too. But Shelby? My dearest friend? *Will be like Camelot wedding*, she'd said.

My face burns in the bitter cold. I've always been able to trust her. Maybe the death of Avery made her vulnerable to these wild ideas. And I could see Packard thinking the worst of Otto. And Jordan thinks everybody is deranged.

God, I feel like such a fool for that kiss. Packard must have sensed it would help snap me out of the revise and clear his name. He keys into me like that. Is he washing his lips right now? I can just hear him gloating to Shelby and Jordan: *She loves me—that's the one thing they didn't count on when they tried to revise her.* Laughing about it.

Worse, my love for Otto seems anemic now. How can I marry Otto when I fell headlong into Packard's arms? Maybe it wasn't real for Packard, but it was real for me. It's hardly fair to Otto.

You got what you wanted, asshole, I say to Packard in my mind. *Your eyewitness will recant her story.*

I skate along, passing where the Butcher copycat attacked. Let somebody try to attack me now.

Hope you're satisfied, I think at Packard.

And then I slow, picturing that *whoosh* of relief, and the happiness in his eyes when I said he wasn't a killer. That wasn't the look of triumph, or of a point won. Packard was happy, as though my realization meant something to him. Or am I imagining that? And it hurt him that I ever thought it—I saw that, too, much as he tried to cover it up. Surely I didn't imagine that.

This pathetic little hope that he really does care flares up in me. I hate that little flare, and I pick up speed, as if I'll outrun it.

Another flare: this time, Shelby and Simon, and how they were about my car. Simon went through a pretty elaborate charade so we could seem to discover it together in the lot. I must have been the one who drove it during my lost day. *I* must have left it somewhere. And I'm the one who put Gumby in the happy pose. What made me do that? What made me happy on that day? What aren't they telling me?

I think about the way Shelby was about Gumby—over and over she'd insisted there must be an explanation for how Gumby got in the happy mode. *You always find your way to truth, Justine*, she'd said. It had seemed odd, how desperately she was fishing, like a schoolteacher, wanting me to find the right answer on my own, doing everything short of telling it to me.

When I do the thought experiment, it's pretty obvious that if they'd told me outright I was revised, I wouldn't have believed them. Yes, I'd taken their silence as part of the proof that I *wasn't* revised, but if they'd told me I was revised, would I have used different things as proof? Nobody wants to believe that even a day of their experience is fake—it's too upsetting. I still don't want it to be true.

I near the river, recalling how Simon had suggested we search the car. And Shelby had asked about the trunk. Clearly, they both thought something inside that trunk might be significant. What? I wish I'd looked, but of course Otto didn't want me to touch anything until the car got dusted for prints.

A twinge in my gut.

Yes, I suppose that *does* look bad, as if Otto didn't want me opening the trunk. And yes, there's the secret operation on the seventh floor, and his secret personal force field. Strange, too, that Otto's people wouldn't have turned up the car. He'd had them searching for it; he told me so himself, and it was right there in Midcity's central impound lot. How could they have not found it? And yes, Sophia, the only known revisionist, does work for Otto.

A chill comes over me as I recall Jordan's words: *Somebody had to hold you.*

Just then, the street lights up in red flashes. I slow, disoriented, unsure where the lights are coming from, until a loudspeaker blares behind me: "Police! Drop the weapon and put your hands in the air!"

I slow and turn—I just passed a parked cop car, but I didn't see it. I'm confused about the weapon bit until I get that they're talking about the axe. I throw it down like it's on fire.

More lights; another squad car barrels out of the alley to my left. I could get away if my knee wasn't injured, I think. But, running from the police? What is that?

Two officers emerge from the first car, guns drawn. One of them is a woman about my age. She squints. "Miss Jones?"

"Hi," I say. "Yeah."

"Are you okay?"

"My knee's hurt." It's the only thing I can think to say.

She helps me to the car. Her partner questions me, and I explain that somebody pretending to be the Belmont Butcher attacked me, though this version doesn't involve Shelby, and features the man spooking and running off rather than being zinged by me. Somebody mentions Otto. It turns out that he's in a cruiser nearby. I get the feeling they've been looking for me for a while.

Another officer gives me a blanket, and I pull it around myself, repeating my description of the Butcher copycat, insisting I don't need medical attention.

More cars and lights. I sit halfway in the back of a cruiser, feet on the street, paralyzed by two competing realities. One, Otto wouldn't kill Avery and have me revised. The other: Packard, Simon, Jordan, and Shelby wouldn't all simultaneously believe something so farfetched without a reason.

I flash back in time to January, to the scene right after we rescued Otto from his kidnappers. They'd been holding Otto prisoner and terrorizing the city for days, thanks largely to the power of the antihighcap glasses Avery'd invented, and I suddenly remember the violence with which Otto crushed those glasses under his boot—lips taut, eyes bright with anger. *Never again*, he'd said. His intensity had surprised me at the time. It had seemed out of character.

"Justine! Thank goodness!"

My heart pounds as Otto strides toward me, a dark commanding figure against a background of flashing red. I stand and he wraps his arms around my cocoon of a blanket. "I've been out of my mind with worry. You're hurt? They said your knee? And an attack?"

"I'm mostly just upset," I say.

One of the officers brings over the big axe and Otto's eyes grow wide.

"It was the assailant's," I say, telling them the story of the attack, the way the man spooked and ran off.

I see it in Otto's eyes the instant he figures out how that spooking happened. "Give us a moment," he says to the officer.

"I had to," I say. "The guy was insane, and I'd hit my head. I thought I was having a bleed out. I thought I had nothing to lose..."

"Do you think I care about that?" Otto whispers forcefully. "Do you think I care if you zinged?" He furrows his brow. "You're okay, that's all that matters. How hard did you hit your head?"

"Hard, but I think I'm okay."

"You're sure?"

I put my hand to the bump. "There's a goose egg."

He touches where I do. "Jesus! We need to ice that." He rubs my arms through the blanket. "I'd be lost if anything happened to you, Justine. Lost." Otto's such a strong, tough man, but there's a level of distress in him I've never seen. "I'll never let anything happen to you." He says it like a vow.

"I'm okay," I say. "Totally unoriginal to copy the Belmont Butcher, though, don't you think? Get your own identity, dude, you know?" I'm trying for a lightness I don't feel. "Or at least a variation. How about changing it to Belmont Baker, and he could do a rolling-pin thing?"

Otto's jaw is set grimly. "That should never have happened to you," he mutters.

I thought he'd be more upset about my zinging. If Otto and I are like two addicts, two fear junkies, then I went off the wagon—my fear won't consume me for a while, and he'll be alone fighting his.

"I'm sorry," I say.

"Don't say that! You did what you had to do. But what possessed you to go rollerblading alone after curfew? To sneak out?"

"Oh, Otto, I just...I don't know..." I don't know a lot, I realize. Too much. "It's just been so overwhelming, all this life change—losing my home, my job, becoming first lady. And everyone knows me, and those nursing textbooks are freaking me out..." All true, but not why I went rollerblading.

"Oh, Justine." He rubs my shoulders some more. Paramedics appear just then, and I let them look at my pupils and prod my knee, bending it for them and then promising to get an X ray in the morning if it doesn't feel better.

Otto's limo pulls up and stops, a sleek snake in the night. Chauffer Smitty emerges from his door and opens the back door.

Otto picks me up.

I gasp. "Otto, you don't have to—"

"Nonsense," he says, carrying me to the limo.

Everything's happening too fast, and there's too much I don't know. But here I am, moving inexorably toward the limo. Otto sets me in back and I scoot over to give him room, like it's any other night. Smitty slams the door after us and I jump. Was it an unusually hard slam? It seemed loud.

"You felt overwhelmed?"

"I don't know what possessed me." I stare out the window, heart pounding as I picture him violently smashing Avery's antihighcap glasses. He hated those glasses, and for good reason: they endangered highcaps. But to kill the man who invented them?

I turn to him and lay a hand on his arm, look into his brown eyes. This man, this good man—could fear really have pushed him so far? I believe in his goodness, but I believe in the power of fear even more. The power of fear trumps everything. This is one of the few things I know for sure. It's a law of life.

"What, my sweet?"

"I think I'm a little in shock."

"I can imagine." He brushes my hair off my forehead. "Good God, you're full of muck too."

"I skated near the river," I say. True, but not where the muck is from. It's that memory of his smashing the glasses that makes me lie. I still recall the sick feeling I had, deep down, watching him. I hadn't paid much attention to it at the time—after all, this was Otto, my knight in shining armor. His losing control, consumed with fear and rage, that didn't fit in with my idea of him.

Smitty pulls out. Just like that, we're on our way home. I stare at the privacy panel that separates Otto and me from the front seat.

"You fell in the river?"

"Not exactly in it, but apparently..." I touch my hair and start babbling about toxins.

"Oh, Justine." He reaches into his breast pocket and I flinch, struck by this overwhelming terror. I wait, frozen, as he pulls something out of his pocket.

Just a handkerchief. He hands it to me.

"Thank you," I whisper, wiping my face, thinking about the flinch thing I've been getting whenever Otto reaches into his breast pocket.

Of course, the breast pocket is where he keeps his gun when he's carrying. I'd chalked it up to witnessing the killing. Like a side effect. But then again, a lot of people carry guns in their breast pockets, and I don't freak out when *they* put their hands in their breast pockets. Why do I only have it with Otto? Over and over, ever since the shooting, it's as if I think my life is in danger on some gut level whenever he slides his hand into that pocket.

Some gut level.

Again I wipe my face. Jordan said a revisionist can erase memories, but not emotions. Whenever Otto reaches into that pocket, I get that flood of terror, like some form of knowing—something beyond thought, beyond memory—is imprinted in my cells.

Something like emotion.

That flinch, that fear, it feels like it comes from the same place as the instinct to protect Packard. And it's telling me something that I've never bothered to listen to before.

But I'm listening now. I get it now.

Chills come over me as he takes the handkerchief from my hand. I avoid his eyes. Instead, I'm fixated on this new sense of knowing.

"You've had quite a night," Otto says.

"Yes," I say.

He wants me to repeat my description of the Butcher copycat, and he asks questions about the attack: did the Butcher seem to be following me? Did I fall by the river before or after? And did the Butcher say anything? And why do I think he attacked me?

"I don't know!" I say, finally, fighting to maintain a mask of calm, and especially not look at the car door—he once told me that people who feel guilty or trapped look at doors during interrogation. The Tanglelands smell, horrible in this small space, makes me feel even more nervous. Does he know I lied? Can he tell the Tanglelands smell from the river smell? "I was too busy getting away and skunking my thoughts to be hugely observant."

"If you skunked your thoughts, you knew he was a telepath. How did you know? What did he read off you? What did he say?"

"Jesus!" I say. "I was flipped out, Otto. He picked up on my fear."

"I'm sorry," he says. "No more questions." He won't stop looking at me. I turn away. I feel like he senses I'm hiding something.

And I am.

I'm hiding this terrible new certainty, deep in my heart, that he killed Avery.

And of course he'd have Sophia revise me if he'd killed Avery. It's the obvious thing to do! I think of Packard's words: *You'll be in danger if he knows you know about the revise.*

"You're overwhelmed, my sweet, and I understand that bodyguards make you feel caged up, but you should've had Max along if you wanted to blade. I don't understand why Norman didn't see you leave."

"I climbed down the fire escape."

"Justine! Why?"

"I guess I wanted to be alone."

"Why Justine? It was such a lovely party, and you seemed so happy..."

I shiver. "I think I was temporarily insane. I never thought I'd be one of those crazy mood-swing brides, but—"

"You're not getting cold feet, are you?"

"Don't worry." I look up at him. "I'm one hundred percent sure about the wedding." *Sure it's a mistake.*

He pulls me close. My pulse pounds, and I pray he can't feel it. "I'm sorry. That was more questions," he says.

"It's okay." I stare out the window, thinking about his personal force field. I couldn't even zing him if I needed to!

"But Justine," he says, turning to me. "No more nightly excursions until the curfew is lifted. It's so important. I promised not to track you, but I need to know you're safe. That curfew is there for a reason. Things will only get more dangerous, but they'll settle very soon, I promise."

"I've learned my lesson," I say.

He looks at me a beat too long.

I try a smile.

He frowns. "There's something else," he observes.

My heart flip-flops. "Yeah. I would trade my soul for a hot bath."

His tilts his head, still watching me. Detective mode.

"The longest, hottest bath on the planet," I add. "In fact, I want to take three baths in a row. One to get clean, one to scrub this toxin-infused layer of my skin off, and one to soak in forever. Extreme bathing."

"Hmm." He turns away.

Hmm?

I have this urge to get away from him. I imagine turning to him, simply telling him I can't marry him. *Sorry Otto, there is something else—it won't work out. This whole marriage.* Then I'd lean forward and rap on the privacy panel. Smitty would open it, and I'd tell him to drop me at the Midcity Arms Hotel. People break off engagements every day, don't they? But Otto's suspicious already; I feel like breaking off our engagement would change the game. It could even put my friends in danger.

A killer! I can't get my head around it—I'm engaged to a killer! I tell myself I'm not in actual, immediate danger here in the limo, but it doesn't help. I stare at the door handle, picturing myself leaping out and making a run for it. Absurd as it is, I start planning it. I still have my skates on; I could use the alleys to elude the cop cars. But it's madness. Even if I didn't break both my legs jumping out of a moving limo, I'd be tracked down in minutes—there are so many cops out right now.

Yet it's still tempting.

The silence goes too long. "I'm a total basket case," I say.

He turns his brown eyes to me, bright and hard. Something's off. "This is a dangerous time, my love. This is a war."

"Right." I swallow, recalling my amusement at Shelby's ability to work a machine gun—I'd likened her to a pet learning an impressive new trick. How naïve! Because Otto's right—this is a war. There is a curfew. Police officers carry machine guns. If they even *are* police—how many of them are members of Otto's private army? And what happened during those lost hours of mine, the ones Packard won't tell me about?

"We'll come out better than ever, Justine. This is going to be our time—you and me. There's so much to look forward to. You've been through a lot, but just wait. You'll see what I mean."

"Right. Good," I say.

The car stops in front of our condo. Otto gets out and extends his hand. I force myself to take it, to let him help me out; I even let him keep my arm as we head in through the grand entrance of the condo building, still hobbling on my skates. Otto nods at Sammy, the doorman. "You're off the hook, Sammy." He tips his head at me. "Fire escape."

Sammy nods coldly.

"Sorry, Sammy. I didn't mean to cause you trouble." I sit on a lobby chair and unlace my rollerblades. Has Otto discovered the situation on the seventh floor yet? No way—I remind myself there's nothing to discover; Shelby would have been careful to leave everything looking the way she found it. And the darts from Avery's gun are so tiny, people never know they've been hit. They just think they dozed off. Avery was proud of that. I pull off the blades. It feels a lot better to have them off, even though the slime has soaked clear into my socks.

We cross the lobby to the elevator and Otto stabs the Up button. I can slip away tonight, I think, when I have my clothes and a head start. I have to get away.

"Are you hungry, my sweet?"

"Just tired. Looking for that bath." The elevator doors open, and there's Norman with his usual contented expression. We get in.

"King's penthouse?"

Otto gives him a weary look. Norman punches floor eight. "Interesting scent you're wearing tonight, Miss Jones," he says. "Is that eau de Tanglelands tea?"

My heart *thwack*s at my rib cage. "I had a very bad rollerblading experience," I say. "Near Midcity River."

"So I hear," Norman says.

I fix my gaze on the elevator lights. Surely there's no way a man can tell Tanglelands tea from the Midcity River smell.

"We'll run you a nice warm bath." Otto says.

"Excellent."

How would Norman even know the Tanglelands smell? Has he even been there? And anyway, *Tanglelands tea* is a common Midcity term for something yucky—people use the term the way you might use "pond scum" or "dumpster juice". I wonder if Packard and the others are still down there. Would they have cleared out? Or trusted that I would come to my senses?

Otto rubs my arms and it's all I can do not to pull away. My skin feels so sensitive, nerve endings too exposed, and I'm chilled to the bone in every sense.

Once we get inside, I head to the bedroom and straight into the walk-in closet, and I just stand there trying to collect my thoughts. *I'm not in danger,* I tell myself. *Nothing is different from yesterday, except in my mind.*

Not exactly helpful.

A crash of water into the tub. I grab my big, wool bathrobe, shake off my slimy clothes, and stuff them into the far hamper, then I put the robe around me and tighten the belt.

Out in the bedroom I sink into one of the armchairs that look out over the street, thinking about Packard. I need him to know that I know. And Shelby claimed Otto is holding Carter and "the others". So is that true too? *He cannot die until we find Carter and the others and free them from his prisons,* she'd said. Enrique, Helmut, Vesuvius. Where would Otto have put them?

I realize that I haven't seen Sophia for at least a week or two. She used to come around every day.

"Milk and cookies."

"Oh!" I startle at his voice. Then, "Thanks!"

He sets the plate on the table in front of me. We've gotten into the habit of bringing each other comfort food: cookies, mashed potatoes, chicken soup. God, our whole lifestyle has been about insulating each other. A cocoon of false ease.

I eye the plate. Even comfort food is suddenly looking sinister.

He leaves and comes back with an ice pack for my head.

I press it to my lump. "Thanks. Don't want things getting crowded in there."

"Certainly not." He takes the other chair. "How's the knee?"

I stick it out of the robe; it's red and swollen, with a dark bruise starting on the side of it. "Hurts like hell. I can't believe I was able to skate on it at all." I reiterate the details of the fight, my shock at waking up and finding the guy sitting there, thinking I was faking. The incident makes a good story, even twice told, and it keeps the focus on anything but the here and now.

Otto shakes his head darkly. "What am I going to do with you?"

"Um..." I don't know how to answer this. How would I have answered it yesterday? "Get me a home gym? Now that I can't rollerblade anymore?"

Just then his mobile phone buzzes and he pulls it from his pocket. I realize I should call Shelby, let her and Packard know I've rethought things. But what exactly would I say? Would they even believe me? How can I be sure it wouldn't be monitored?

I head into the bathroom where I quickly locate my lavender bubble-bath, thankful I'd brought it from home. I dump it in, and soon the big, old claw-foot tub is overflowing with white bubbles. After rinsing the worst of the gunk out of my hair in the sink, I slip into the tub, making a little hollow for my face so the bubbles don't get on my nose. The warmth feels good, in spite of my terror.

Terror, my old friend...it's building again. But nobody hides it like I do.

I settle the ice pack onto the side of my head.

Otto comes in. "A bubble bath," he observes.

"For relaxation." I smile wanly. "I'm hoping my parasympathetic nervous system gets the memo."

He hands me another pack. "For your knee."

"Thanks." I raise my knee just above the bubbles and fold the pack over it. "Two-pack night."

He sits on the marble edge of the tub, seemingly waiting for something. Maybe testing to see what I'll fill the silence with. He does that with criminals—it's a way to get them to divulge things. I'm feeling thankful for all that I've learned from my super detective.

When the silence between us gets too weird and uncomfortable, I say, "I'm sorry I scared you."

"No, I'm sorry," he says. "The idea that...that man," his voice shakes a bit. Lips serious. "That you would be attacked by him."

Wouldn't want that! I imagine myself saying. *Nobody attacks your precious Justine except Sophia, huh?* Instead, I say, "It's over."

Otto nods.

He killed Avery. Avery was a good man, an innocent man. Hell, without Avery's help, we wouldn't have located Otto's kidnappers so fast. Surely Otto knew that! But he killed him. I feel sick that I ever let Otto touch me. I turn the ice packs. The silence builds uncomfortably. Or is it just my imagination? "You know what I just realized?" I say. "I haven't seen Sophia for a while."

"She left for vacation last week," Otto says.

"Really? Where?"

"Countryside, it seems."

I lay the pack over the side of the tub and lower my knee into the water, thinking about Fawna's prediction that the danger will come from Otto's inner circle. If anybody is Otto's inner circle, it's Sophia. Could he have sealed her up? Killed her? Surely she'd know where Carter and the others are. Then a horrifying thought comes to me: could Otto have killed them?

Otto dips a finger into a bubble hill, comes out with a bearded finger, then blows off the suds.

No, I think. He would keep them alive and hidden as insurance; he knows Packard and my fellow disillusionists would never kill him as long as he's holding our people. But Sophia?

Another horrifying thought comes to me: I'm Otto's inner circle too. Or am I? Does a fiancée qualify as inner circle? Is a significant other the circle, or more at the center of the circle?

"Will she be back in time for the wedding?" I ask.

"Don't tell me you want to add her as a bridesmaid," Otto jokes.

"No, no but she *is* your close associate. She accompanies you to all the functions—"

"Not anymore," Otto says. "Now that you'll be first lady."

"But, you know, it seems like she should at least be there. You don't have family, but your people should be there. I would think Sophia should be there." Am I pressing too hard?

"Why the change of heart? You've always had a problem with her, with what she does."

I swish my foot in the water. Is it weird I'm pursuing it? Otto's looking at me strangely. "I still have a problem with what she does. She steals the experiences a person had, things they can never get back. She steals what they have become. Still," I add, "it's not that different from what we disillusionists did. We forced transformation. We robbed people too." I'd never thought of it this way, but it seems right. "Sophia takes what a person went through; we take what a person should've or would've gone through.

"Oh, Justine." He touches my hair, smoothing it, then pulls his hand back and looks at his fingers. They're a greenish-gray. Tanglelands tea. "Look at this." He stands and gets the shampoo.

"No, Otto, I can do it."

"Let me," he says.

I bite my tongue. Usually I love it when he shampoos my hair, and he loves when I do his; touching each other's heads is this special trust thing we have, an act of intimacy between fellow hypochondriacs who freak out about vein star. It's the last thing I want right now. Well, not quite the last thing.

Handle it, I tell myself, dunking my head in the bubbly water. He moves to the stool behind me. I hear him squirt out the shampoo and rub it between his palms—*swick, swick, swick*. I try not to cringe as his hands cup my head. He begins to massage—slow, languorous motions that don't relax me whatsoever.

Does he sense my nervousness? Is he testing me?

"You shouldn't feel bad about disillusionment," he says. "You don't steal potential experience. You shouldn't think that way."

"I can't help it," I say.

"If you give a man a pack of matches, are you interfering with his experience of discovering fire?"

"That doesn't seem the same," I say, relieved for this abstract, thinky turn in our conversation. "What we did as disillusionists was more like messing with their evolution—their personal evolution," I add. "Like in outer space shows where space travelers aren't supposed to give primitive planets advanced technologies."

"Shady Ben Foley was a despicable man, and your gang disillusioned him about his old ways, helped him turn over a new leaf much faster than he would've on his own. What's wrong with that?"

"We robbed him of the chance to do it on his own. Maybe he needed to bottom out first. Maybe he was never going to change. Maybe he needed the experience of being hated and alone."

"Even better then, that he was disillusioned." He rubs the back of my head.

"It's wrong," I say, "because nothing can replace coming to something on your own, to take a hard, important journey, to reach deep into yourself and trust your heart. Isn't that what it's all about?" I'm thinking of seeing Packard in the Tanglelands, and knowing and trusting what was real. I think about listening to my heart tonight with Otto. I've never been one to reach deep down and trust myself—I get too buffeted around by ideas and opinions and shoulds. But I want to be that person who reaches down and knows things. Deep down, I don't trust myself and I desperately want that to change. Maybe it is changing. "Stealing the chance to realize something for yourself, or the chance to evolve on your own, that is a horrible crime."

He presses his fingertips to the sides of my head, making little circles. "By that reasoning, we should outlaw school."

"No, because good teachers don't just inject knowledge into your brain." I dunk my head partly under the water to wash off the shampoo.

Otto's got the conditioner. One more round.

I focus back on our conversation. I'm doing really well, letting him touch my head. Thank goodness I had a zing earlier, though considering the night's events, no doubt I've achieved a world record in building back my fear. "Jordan once asked me, when is good not good? I think it's when a person is forced to be good."

"Nobody exists in a vacuum. We're all knocking against each other, changing each other's paths," he says. "All human interaction is a kind of interference, Justine."

I think about *his* brand of interference: killing a man. Having me revised. Making me distrust Packard. Hell, I agreed to marry him as a result of all that interference. And all the strings he pulled to get me into nursing school—is it supportiveness...or a convenient way to keep me in a constant state of fear, a constant state of needing him, just like he needs me?

Need. Fear. It's as if all the falsehoods are falling away. I look up into his eyes as he massages my head. Otto, so big and strong and flamboyant. In love with power. Does he resent needing me?

It seems like he's using a little too much pressure—or is that my imagination?

"If there's one wish I have for you," he says, "it's that you don't feel guilty. It's not a productive feeling. As a member of the force, I've shot people, arrested them, had them revised. I've fought the good fight to keep the city safe. We both have, Justine. The good fight can be bloody and messy and unpleasant. You can't fight it, and then feel bad about it afterwards. And it's not one-sided. The life Shady Ben chose led him to cross paths with disillusionists. What you did to him, that was the path he created for himself. He was creating his own reality."

"He was asking for it?"

"Yes. He was ruining lives at a time and place when the disillusionists were operating. He brought you disillusionists to him."

"Did all of Sophia's victims bring a revision on themselves?"

He stops rubbing, seems to think about this. Then he says, "Everybody she ever revised attracted that to themselves in some way. Created their own reality." He resumes the scalp massage.

"Asked for it?"

A beat. Then, "In a sense."

My anger grows as he rubs my neck. It's the most unrelaxing massage ever. "Everything that happens to a person, they asked for it?"

"Mostly. Though maybe they didn't consciously ask for it. But they created it."

"Mmm." It's all I can say through my clenched jaw. My mind roils over his words, the injustice of it. *Avery asked to be killed? I asked to be revised? All crime victims ask for it?* I sit in my warm bath, but all I can feel is this cold, cold rage. And it's here I realize: I can't go. Otto has to be stopped.

I have to stop him.

He says, "Standing up for a vision of something better is never easy."

"Too true," I whisper, moving forward, out of his hands, effectively ending the massage. I sit up and look him in the eye. "This water is getting really gross and soapy. I'm going to shower all this off, and then I'm going to crash." Meaning, get out of the bathroom and don't expect to have sex.

He stands, cheeks rosy from the steam, one lock of hair curling fetchingly over one eye. I've never hated him more. "Do you want any more cookies?" he asks.

"No," I say.

Hell no.

Chapter Nine

The next morning, I keep my eyes shut and my breathing steady as Otto climbs out of bed. I listen to his wash-up routine—the killer, casually brushing his teeth, spitting out his spearmint toothpaste. *Tap-tap-tap*—hitting his toothbrush against the sink edge. The water goes on again: washing his face—the face I've kissed over and over. I wonder if he'll scrub in his ears as he sometimes does. Water on, water off. On, off. I shudder. Otto's morning wash-up routine used to seem so simple and domestic. Now it seems vile. Insidious.

Silence.

My heart beats like crazy as I hear him come back over to the bed. Silence. Is he standing there? Does he know I'm faking? Then I hear him head on out into the hall and I open my eyes. I follow his footsteps across the apartment. Office door. Going to check his e-mail. *Clank*s from the kitchen. Kenzo, probably, starting breakfast.

Yesterday, I woke up in this bed happy with Otto and excited for my bridesmaids' dinner. Today, I'm in the same bed, but it's enemy territory. And my knee is screaming. As a test, I bend it. Bad, but not broken. My head bump is almost gone.

I plot my moves. I'll throw on clothes, and then what?

I hop up and dig my phone out of my robe pocket. No calls. I pull on my most comfortable brown cords and a big, old, red sweater, and then I wash up and make my way to the kitchen.

Kenzo and Otto are in there, and Otto's chewing something, which gives me an excuse to forego a kiss on the lips and just give him a peck on the cheek. I grab a cup of coffee and settle across from him at the breakfast nook, trying to seem normal, which is surprisingly hard. How do I usually act in the morning?

Kenzo smiles at me. "Illegal excursions and a Butcher attack, but her hair looks fabulous."

"Thanks," I say, surprised at how high my voice sounds. "I slept on it wet. It always turns out when I'm not trying."

"Mine, too," Kenzo says, smiling. Why is he smiling at me? Oh, a joke—he has a shaved head. I chuckle, and then prattle on about sleeping with wet hair, how it's a gamble. One side can end up flat, and there's no coming back from that, unless you wet it again and pin it up, but that's its own problem. I go on and on until I realize I'm talking too much about something insignificant, which is what guilty perps do, Otto once told me.

I turn to find his cool, steady eyes fixed on mine.

My stomach leaps into my throat. I pick up the creamer and dash a bit of cream into my coffee, quickly, because I think that my hand might shake. Cow brown.

But hell, why shouldn't I be acting weird? I was attacked last night, and I have a wedding tomorrow. I stir my coffee, watching the surface swirl that drags behind the spoon, as if this is the most sensitive operation in the world.

I have to see Packard and Shelby today. They need to know that I'm with them, that I'm the double agent on the inside. The disillusionists are back as a gang and we need to coordinate, now. And beyond that, I just plain old want to see Packard.

I love him.

I don't care that he doesn't love me back. Or that he's duped me over and over. Used me. It doesn't change the fact that I plain old love him. Maybe it's pathetic. No, it *is* pathetic. I put down my spoon with a clatter that seems garishly loud.

"Lemon scones," Otto says, eyeing me.

My heart pounds. He's in a dark, silk-brocade robe that I usually find dashing, but now it seems like a dangerous artifice, like one of the bug-eating flowers in his night garden, all lush, exotic petals and a sweet scent, drawing the flies and bees in close, only to be trapped and eaten alive. "Your favorite," he says.

"What?" I ask.

"Lemon scones."

"Sometimes." I take one and break it apart, thinking about a squirming bug I once watched in the gluey center of one of the flowers; the more it struggled, the more caught it got. I wanted to rescue it, but its little wings were too damaged by the time I had the impulse to do it.

I take a bite. "Yum." There's this weird silence until I think to ask him how he slept—a question we ask each other a lot, code for "how's your head," without directly asking. If there are no head issues, then it's just a sleeping question.

He raises an eyebrow. "Rather well, considering the active and dramatic night. You? I take it the knee's okay? And so forth…"

"Okay enough." I reach across the table and grab the copy of the *Midcity Eagle* that's folded next to him. Henry Felix is pictured on the front page, lifting a copy of the Midcity Charter above his head, peering victoriously through his little, round, silver glasses at the crowd around him. It's another one of his Rights Rallies where he outlines all the ways Otto is robbing citizens of their rights.

"Forty people," I observe.

Otto shrugs, but I can't imagine he's that indifferent. The crowds around Henry Felix are growing, and most of all, Henry Felix has a point.

"At least they're not running a photo of me from last night."

"And they won't," he says.

Of course. It was only police involved, and the police are keenly loyal to Otto. Not the most comforting thought at the moment.

"Have they caught the copycat yet?" I know they haven't, but I need to get the spotlight off me.

"Not yet," Otto says. "But we will."

"I'm more than happy to identify him in a lineup, you know, if…"

"We'll see." He spreads butter on his scone. The knife flashes and shines.

Of course, the man won't make it to a lineup. He won't make it into the system at all. "Just what you need," I say. "Another prisoner."

Otto grunts. His noncommittal but significant *mmph*. What is he not saying? Does the Butcher copycat have importance I'm not aware of?

I get a new, disturbing thought as I watch him eat: if Otto was so willing to kill Avery, why not just kill all his highcap prisoners? That would certainly release pressure on his head. *I make the choices nobody else has the guts to make,* he said the other day. Is it possible he's become judge and executioner?

Carter and the others would be valuable alive, as life insurance, in case his personal force fields fail—if Otto dies, everybody he's imprisoned is trapped forever. But somebody like the Butcher or the Butcher copycat wouldn't be anything but a drain. I think about Fawna's prediction of danger. Would that spur him to kill his prisoners?

Otto turns to me. "You seem so preoccupied."

"I was just going to say that to you!" I smile. "Jinx."

"I suppose so." He stands up, touches my chin, and takes his leave—he has to handle a few e-mails in his office before he goes into work. I'm relieved, though needless to say, I would've preferred that he head directly off to the government building.

Kenzo grins. "You climbed down the fire escape?" He *tsks*. Like he thinks it's amusing.

"The bride was feeling a bit wild last night," I say. "A bit off the chain."

Kenzo bustles around and I sip my coffee. I'm the spy now. The double agent. *I'm* the dangerous flower, goddammit.

Back when I was a disillusionist, my agenda was simple: infiltrate somebody's existence, and zing them enough times to leave them destabilized for the next disillusionist. My agenda now is less specific—I have to find a way to free my comrades, not an easy task considering we don't even know where they are. And considering that Packard, a brilliant mastermind, was imprisoned for eight years before he got free. And we *knew* where he was.

And then there's item number two on my agenda: destroy Otto. A man with an impenetrable personal force field.

Both tasks require information; his office would be the place to start if he weren't in it. My mind goes to my car. Otto didn't want me searching my car. Simon and Shelby did.

"I have to go down and get something from my car," I say to Kenzo.

He smiles and continues on with his work.

I ride the elevator down with Norman and find my bodyguard Max in the lobby. "Just getting something out of my car," I say to him.

"Okay." He turns a page of his newspaper.

My excitement rises as I enter the cool, dim garage—will I find clues to my lost hours? Do I even want to? Why was Packard so reluctant to tell me what happened that day? *It's not something I can just tell*, he'd said. Why not?

I approach, keys in hand, feeling this sense of dread. It's like another self put things in there. As I draw nearer, my heart sinks. A section of the back of the car shines, as though it's been washed. The car was covered in grime when I picked it up. Who would come and wash part of it? Then I realize: fingerprint dust. Otto's people have been here, and they dusted for fingerprints, and then wiped up their mess. I shove my key in the trunk and open it up and my heart sinks. The trunk is nearly empty. In fact, it seems emptier than before, like some of the junk I had in there is gone—I'm pretty sure a couple of old plant pots were in here. And it's cleaner. I run my hand over the carpet that lines the trunk. Vacuumed recently.

I go around and unlock the passenger door and slip in. The dashboard is clean too. Dusted. Inside the glove compartment

142

there's nothing but the old change, papers, and my emergency Chap Stick.

I feel so angry! Something in here might have connected me to what I lost that day. Maybe other awful things happened that day. Maybe I'm better off not knowing—obviously Packard thought so—but still, something more of mine that was taken away and it makes me mad. I twist Gumby around, bend his arms to his hips, putting him in the maddest possible Gumby position.

What did I lose? On science fiction shows, when you change one feature of a timeline, everything after it is altered. That would go for memory too—you change one memory and everything reconstructs wrong. Tears begin to cloud my vision. My memory was violated, cleaned. And now my car.

I sink back into the seat. Can I even do this? Stay? Fight? What am I even fighting for? Angrily I scrub the tears from my eyes.

"My sweet?"

Otto's just outside the open door, briefcase in hand. "Oh," I say.

"What is it, Justine? What's wrong? Sammy said you were out here..."

I get out of the seat and slam the door. "I wanted something," I say. "I had this idea it might be in the car."

"Is this your book again? You've been looking for that book for weeks. Let's get you a new copy. I'll get you fifty new copies. I'll track down the author and see if I can get an advanced copy of her next release. None of this is a problem."

"I don't want a new one. I want the one I had!" I straighten my hair, trying to put a lid on my distress. "I liked that one. It was mine."

Silence.

"Your guys dusted. Did you find anything? Any clues?"

"Nothing. I'm sorry." He tilts his head. "This isn't really about the book, is it?" He comes near, rests a hand on my shoulder. "It's okay to feel traumatized."

"I'm not traumatized." I shake him off, cross my arms. "I'm mad. Just about the wrongness of it."

"We'll make it right," he says.

Damn right we'll make it right. I force a smile. "Fifty copies?"

"As many as you please, okay? I have to go." I try not to be too wooden when he kisses me. "I'm looking forward to tonight," he says. "See you at five."

I paint on a smile and watch him stroll up the parking garage incline toward the wintry morning sunlight.

Tonight. Good lord, I'd almost forgotten. We're taking the limo the hour out of town to pick up my dad and bring him back for a private dinner at the penthouse; then we're putting him up at the Midcity Arms Hotel, right down the street from our building. It's not much of a wedding dinner, but my dad is the only relative we have between us, aside from my brother, who is unreachable in Bolivia. Otto and I plan to have a grand banquet after the wedding, and several hundred people are coming to that.

I lean against the car trunk and try Shelby. Voice mail. "Me again," I say. "I might come over to your place later. We need to talk." Then I try Simon. Voice mail. "I don't know if you know about my...er...disagreement with Shelby last night, but if you see her, I was just wrong. I want us to make up." I click off. My calls probably aren't being monitored, but I'm going to err on the side of never being stupid again.

After a chat and an elevator ride with Norman, I'm back in the cool, quiet expanse of our penthouse. Alone. Kenzo must have left to do marketing. Time to look for evidence.

I try the door to Otto's office. Locked. But I happen to know we have a master key—Otto had to use it once when a party guest locked the bathroom door from the outside. I remember his going into the kitchen to get it, but I didn't see where in the kitchen. I head in. Key, key. I root through the drawers. Nothing. I even look under the silverware tray. I check the junk drawer twice, pulling stuff out, until I discover a box of utility matches that contains something more than matches. Keys.

I head to the master bath and turn on the shower and shut the door. If Kenzo comes back and needs to talk with me, he'll wait until the shower is off. Then I skulk across to Otto's office and let myself in, locking the door behind me.

Otto's office is tidy, masculine. There's a hollow, *whoosh*ing quality to the silence of it, though maybe that's the cars in the distance. Heavy, wooden furnishings and bookcases line the walls, and a closed laptop rests on his big, old wooden desk. I can see the gold-embroidered edge of his mayoral robe through the slightly ajar closet door; his police dress uniform and sash of medals probably hang in there too.

I sit in his chair and start opening drawers, searching the insides and underneath, like they do in the movies. Sometimes Otto seals people up where there are built-in food sources— Packard in the Mongolian Delites restaurant, for example. And he has the Belmont Butcher in the back room of a butcher shop. But sometimes he puts people in places with no food source, and then he has to make arrangements. Rickie the telepath was imprisoned in a low-rent apartment in northwest Midcity, and food was delivered to her weekly. When Ez was in the coat-check booth, he had some sort of agreement with the bar owner. I'm thinking he'd have Carter and the other disillusionists somewhere isolated. Watchtowers, cabins, places requiring regular food deliveries. And with dozens and dozens of prisoners out there, and now disillusionists being held, surely he's documenting things. And if he's documenting things, it's on paper, not on the computer. Otto doesn't like to do important things online—he trusts the tactile world. It comes from being a force-fields guy.

I discover bank records in the top drawer of his filing cabinet. There are monthly recurring debits with initials next to them. What do they mean? I copy them down, along with other numbers that seem related. After that, I paw through election files. Donors, promo plans. Some government and police documents. All very innocent looking. Would he keep a list or map down on the seventh floor? I'm thinking Shelby did a pretty thorough search down there.

I move to the bottom file drawer, hating that Shelby never leveled with me. Yes, I understand why; I understand it wouldn't have gone well, but I still hate it.

I think again of the kiss, of Packard's expression when I recognized the memory as a revise. And the way he'd said my name. I want to think he was happy to have my good regard and even affection back, and not just happy that the truth was finally out. Is that pathetic? Is it wishful thinking? He certainly didn't care about my regard or affection when he conned me into giving up my life to be his minion.

In back of the filing cabinet I find a folder that contains papers covered in strange squiggles and symbols, which I recognize as Vindalese, the native language of Vindahar. Vindahar is the remote, mountainous region of Asia where Otto spent all those years in a cave under the tutelage of a wise sage. Documents from that era? I'm about to stuff them back in the file, but then I stop and pause; the paper is new, high quality, maybe even linen, and there are no creases or curled corners. Hardly what you'd expect from documents written years ago, or carried across the ocean. Some of the papers look like lists. I hold a sheet up to the light and find the watermark. I pull a sheet of paper out of his printer and hold it up and find the same watermark. They were written recently. My heart starts pounding and I shuffle through the sheets. Lists, numbers. Ten sheets in all.

I pull out my camera phone and start snapping photos, then I stuff them back. Lord knows where we'll get them translated. Is there an online translator for Vindalese? That's when I hear the footsteps. I freeze, except for my heart, which smashes against my throat. A key in the door.

Quickly and quietly, I slide the two still-open drawers closed and slip into the closet, as far back as possible. A creak. Footsteps.

Otto.

The chair squeaks. He's sitting. Damn. I hear his computer go on. *Tap-tap-tap.* I cross my arms and wait, like a turtle, pulled into its shell. And then a bad thought comes to me. I pat my pockets. Empty. I left my cell phone on top of his filing cabinet. My heart beats a trillion miles an hour. It's not in his direct line of vision, but if it rings, he'll know I was there. Here. Wildly, I think he already knows.

Tap-tap. Tap-tap-tap. A sigh. *Tap.* A *ping.* E-mail. Office chair *creaks.*

No, he doesn't know. It's just fear. I steady my breath. He couldn't know. The shower is running. Though he sometimes comes in and talks to me.

"Hello?"

I freeze. Eyes wide.

"Right," he says. "Fine. Then do it over."

I nearly implode in relief. He's on his own phone. I sit there, praying it's not a conference call. Sometimes he comes home to take conference calls, and they can last for a long time. I shift uncomfortably as Otto talks about handing out leads, distributing them evenly.

"They can get their own if they're unhappy, but beggars can't be choosers, can they?"

There's a silence. He's agreeing. This doesn't sound much like a conference call. It sounds like a sales call, what with all the talk of leads.

"Maverick's stadium," he says. Then, "Yup, and the old mill."

I wait. The shower can't stay on forever.

"Add the Mav's outbuildings," he says.

The old mill? Mav's outbuildings? These are abandoned places. Is it possible he's rattling off disillusionist prison locations? It's almost too good to be true.

"No," he says, "No underground parking structures." *Grunts.* "Aboveground. Fine, right. No low ceilings. Immediate full-court press. I mean it."

Silence. *Creak.* Another *creak. Grunts.* Rocking back in his chair. "I could see him there. Put it down. Sure, the Tanglelands. I don't care—any urban ruins," he says. "Anything with some degree of openness, ideally, an open sky above." Silence. "Canine would be excellent....No, excellent. Yes, speak with Chuck." He laughs here. "Mongolian Delites? Certainly not. The only way he's going back there is feet first in a box. I don't need his sight to know that."

Shivers crawl up my spine. He's not rattling off disillusionist prisons; he's directing the Packard manhunt. Otto said that same thing to me once, that Packard would never set foot back in Mongolian Delites while he's still alive. *His sight* is Packard's power of psychological insight.

"No," he says. "Yes. Six. Thanks." A *click.*

Tap-tap-tap. Creak.

He mentioned the Tanglelands too. Is Otto having people search the Tanglelands? With canine units? I have to warn my friends.

My legs are losing their feeling; I could probably move without sound, but I don't want to chance it.

A familiar ringtone startles me. His phone. "Hello. Yes. Coliform? How much? What's the standard." Silence. "Federal side? Right. Okay." I gather it's one of the city engineers. A municipal water problem—they've shut down one of the city wells because of unacceptable levels of something. Apparently there are ten wells. Otto has a lot of questions. Somebody is going to investigate something. He got two phone calls, and only the city business one rang; the other must have vibrated, and that was anything but city business. He has a secret, second cell phone. Of course.

Otto makes another call about the water. Questions about testing. *Click.* Shuffle. Chair *creak.* Footsteps to the door. Door open and shut. Lock *snap.*

I sneak out, grab my phone, and shut it off, and then I stand there, trying to recall if I heard his footsteps *after* he shut the door. I tiptoe all the way to the door and put my ear to it.

I wait. Listen. Silence.

What if he's right on the other side, waiting quietly? I hold still, wishing for something definitive: his voice far away, or a *swish* of cloth against wood.

Nothing. I can't wait forever. I take a breath and turn the handle, easing the door open, tensed for a surprise. I'm relieved to find the hall empty. I shut the door, sneak to the master bedroom, and find it empty, too. I rush into the bathroom, rip off my clothes, get wet in the shower, and immediately get out, winding a towel around myself.

Everybody's gone when I emerge from the bedroom, dressed, but with conspicuously wet hair. When I call Shelby, I go straight to voice mail again. Maybe she's in the Tanglelands with Packard and Jordan. That's good and bad. Good because I can find them. Bad because whoever Otto has searching can find them too.

Chapter Ten

I tell Max I'm going to Shelby's to handle some last-minute girl-hairdo plans. He'll follow me, of course, and wait outside. Let him.

I'm wearing a yellow dress, my black cashmere coat, and fancy boots, but in my bag I have rugged, waterproof layers and SOREL boots, plus jeans and a normal sweater and jacket, my flashlight, my blonde Halloween wig, my stun gun, and the pearl-handled lady's revolver Otto bought me for my birthday.

I park at Shelby's and climb the stairs to her place. She doesn't answer my knock, so I use the key from under the mat to let myself in, and quickly walk across to the window to wave to Max—that's our sign that all is okay. I change into my more rugged clothes, put on my wig under my hat, and skulk out the back way of her apartment building. I don't see anybody watching. If they are, they won't recognize me. I creep behind dumpsters and go over another street, and then across the garbage-y wasteland and into the darkness of the Tanglelands.

It's scarier to go into the Tanglelands this time, because Shelby isn't nearby, and I haven't just zinged out all my fear. In fact, my fear has built up quite a bit in the last twelve hours, almost to my usual crazy levels. I trudge on, thoroughly disgusted with myself. Will I ever be free of this madness?

I take off my itchy wig and pull my hat down over my ears. Cars drone dully overhead. The place is lighter at least; shafts of pale gloom stream through the gaps between the roadways overhead, illuminating the steam, or maybe I should say noxious vapors, that rise from the puddles of slime. Voices sound out at one point and I lose time hiding in a gully while a trio of bedraggled men tromp around. I can tell by the way they move that they're not sleepwalking cannibals. But they're in the Tanglelands, which means they're trouble. My knee screams with pain.

As soon as they head off, I continue down into the gully, over the rubble hills, and in through the cave-like passageways, trying not to bend my leg much. I finally reach the giant cavern with its roadways corkscrewing madly overhead. But when I peer across the expanse of slime to where Packard and Jordan were last night, there's no fire, no sign of life whatsoever. I want to call out, just in case they're laying low, but that could attract attention of the wrong kind.

So I set off around the slime lake, navigating the tires and blocks of broken road that compose the ridge, amazed that I somehow picked over it in rollerblades last night. I have this idea that if they're not there, I'll find some indication of where they went, or maybe I'll touch the fire scar and decipher how long they've been gone. Like I'm this woodsy scout. Soon I'm hoisting myself over a concrete barrier and into the little encampment.

Deserted.

I touch a charred piece of wood. One piece seems warm, but what does that mean? It would help if I knew how long a piece of wood stays warm after a fire is out.

Something green sticks out from under a square of corrugated metal. I go grab it. A big, sturdy, green cotton glove I recognize as Packard's. Worn on the fingers. Frayed on the cuff. I sit down on a rock by the fire scar and press it to my face, breathing in his cinnamony scent. Sure, maybe he uses me, tricks me when it's convenient, but I feel this love for him all the same. And he's out there somewhere with a reward on his head, hunted by elite cops and soldiers. With dogs. I have to find him, but where do I even look?

And Otto and I have those plans to go and get my dad tonight. And the wedding tomorrow! How long can I keep up this pretense? I have to see Packard. I have to decide what to do.

"So that's where it went."

I spring up. "Packard." Reddish curls sneak out from under his black winter cap, and his beat-up canvas coat is full of dust and dirt. And he's grinning, of course, because he saw me smelling his glove.

I feel like an idiot and I throw it at him. He catches it, grinning still. I can't help but smile back, because it feels so good to see him, just plain old good. Like a simple little daisy atop a mountain of angst.

"You thought about it," he says. "You're with us."

"You know, a person gets tired of being a predictable puppet."

His eyes twinkle, green and alive. "I knew you'd come through. That hardly makes you a predictable puppet." He pulls on his glove and pauses, as if to study it. "Did anything else…" he looks up. "Did anything else come to you?"

"Like what?"

He looks thoughtful, and I can see right when he decides to tell me. "Justine," he says, super serious—like he's preparing me for the worst.

"Wait," I say, losing my nerve. I feel good for once—do I want to ruin it by learning more awful things? "Don't tell me. I don't want to know."

"You don't?"

"I think I've had enough tumult for now," I say.

"Okay," he says softly.

And then Jordan and Shelby are scrambling down from a shade-shrouded nook in the wall beyond where we stand. "Wow," I say. "It looks like pure wall."

Jordan has her tracker-finder device.

"You guys have to clear out," I say. "This place is going to be searched."

"Already been searched," Jordan says. "Now pipe down and hold out your arms."

I comply. "It'll be searched again," I say. "I overheard Otto having a conversation about it. The old stadium, the docks, all urban ruins, including this place. With dogs. Canine units, to be specific."

"Clean." Jordan sinks to a seat and looks up at Packard. "That could be effective down here. Very effective. If they give the dogs something of ours."

"Is too dangerous at night anyways," Shelby says. "With sleepwalkers."

"*You* sleep here too?"

"If I am here too late to cross back."

"Any time frame on that search?" Jordan asks.

"The term 'immediate full-court press' was used," I say. "Otto has dangerous mercenaries working for him. We're talking about a militia working on an ASAP basis. That's your time frame."

"How did you overhear this?" Packard asks. "Justine, you can't be taking chances."

"I'm not taking chances; I'm taking care of business. I was revised. A day was stolen from me and my head was filled with lies. I'm not exactly in the mood to go out and get that French manicure, you know?"

Shelby says, "But you are a bride tomorrow."

Packard shoots me a look.

"So it seems," I say.

"Let's concentrate on getting out," Jordan says. She heads to a corner and moves some cinder blocks.

"We'll go to my place," Shelby says. "Until we can think."

"Not safe," Packard says.

"It's not like we can check into a motel," Jordan says, pulling bags out of a hole in the wall. "And we're not leaving the city. Leaving our people behind."

"There's one place he won't look," I say. "Otto said so. One place"—I use quote fingers here—"*he'd* only go into feet first."

Shelby widens her eyes. "Yes of course! Are you not hungry for kebabs?"

Packard isn't amused. "No kebabs. We're splitting up. It's too dangerous to be with me."

"You don't have to split up if you go to Mongolian Delites," I say. "It's the perfect place. You can go there and be invisible."

Packard stares hard into the distance. "We're splitting up. It's me they're hunting."

"Packard, it's not like it was. The force fields are gone. It can't trap you. It's nothing but a *restaurant*."

"Nothing but a restaurant?" His gaze is diamond-like. "I spent eight long years there. Eight dark years. You don't know what one minute in that place will do to me. It was more than my prison. It was..." he looks around, as if he can't locate the fitting term. "I'm not made of steel and circuit boards, Justine. To say it's nothing but a restaurant, that's like saying, 'this operation is nothing but a lobotomy,' or that death is nothing but the end of life. There are some places a man won't go. Otto is right. I can't go back there. God forbid even feet first..."

"*Pashu!*" Shelby plows into us with violent force as something crashes loudly into the wall behind us.

"Whoa!" I fall on my ass and Packard stumbles, then the three of us crouch behind the cement girder. Jordan shimmies over and crowds in next to us.

Pashu. 'Heads up' in Shelby's native tongue?

"It looked reddish. Like a brick," Packard says.

Another projectile smashes onto a concrete support behind us. *Smashes*, as in breaks apart. "If it's a brick," I say, "It's being hurled with a hell of a lot of force."

"Telekinetic attack. We are doomed now," Shelby says.

"Is there a way out?" I ask. "That hole up there you guys came out of—where does it lead?"

"Nowhere. There's no back door," Packard says. "The good thing about this place is that it's a hill against a wall. And it's surrounded by slime. Easily defended—you have to pick around that ridge to get here, and that's more trouble than it's worth for most predators. The bad thing is that it's a hill against a wall. And our weapons are up there." He looks up at the hole.

"You must not," Shelby says.

Packard springs up and leaps to the hole.

I gasp.

Shelby grumbles.

Packard leaps back down with a duffel bag and dives onto the ground as a brick curves in, but it looks like it catches him in the arm. He scootches in and throws down the bag.

"You hit?"

He touches his bicep. "Superficial."

Jordan and Shelby pull some of those Scorpion guns out of the bag.

I take out my small revolver, and click off the safety, eyeing the blood spreading across Packard's shoulder.

"We'll handle it later," he says to me.

"Or when you pass out from blood loss," I say, "whichever comes first."

Shelby peeks up over our barrier, then ducks back as another brick whizzes overhead. We scramble apart as it curls back around and smashes into our barrier, right about where my head was. "He is in crevice by red barrels," Shelby whispers. "Peeped his head out." She turns to me, gestures, "Perhaps, five or seven lengths of car. Down there."

"He pokes his head out because he has to see to send his bricks this way," Packard says.

"Let's be ready this time." Jordan peeks out and rests her gun over the barrier. Packard, Shelby, and I do the same.

I see a movement by the red barrels—a head peeking out. Loud blasts, like cannons, ring out in my ears, and just as I squeeze my trigger, my gun jerks right out of my hand. I look up and see all our guns arcing into the air above. Our telekinetic attacker took our guns. Packard pulls me down.

"I think he broke my finger," Jordan gasps.

A splashing sound over the ringing in my ears. It's our guns, dropping into the slime lake.

"Very bad," Shelby whispers. "This is very bad."

"Don't you have more?" I ask.

"Elsewhere." Jordan pulls a piece of corrugated metal over us.

"This will not protect us," Shelby says.

"It'll do more than your pathetic predictions of gloom," Jordan snaps.

Packard helps position it. It's like we're in a lean-to now. "Just one telekinetic. It doesn't make sense. I can't imagine Otto sending a lone telekinetic."

I say, "Maybe this is just another Tanglelands character." Another brick comes in. We all brace as it smashes our flimsy shield into us.

"Ow," Jordan says.

Packard's sleeve is drenched with blood. "Now you're going to let me look at it," I say.

"You are no nurse," Shelby says.

"But I'm in nursing school." I help Packard off with his jacket and pull the sleeve of his shirt gently over his shoulder. Jordan tips the metal sheeting slightly forward so I can get more light. Packard's skin glows pale in the gloom, broken violently by an ugly, bloody gash. I try to keep my touch clinical, but it hurts me that he's hurt, and I don't know how much I can do for him without supplies. His eyes lock on mine. "You're a damned fine nurse," he says to me.

Just like him to know what to say to jog me into nurse mode. "We'll see about that." I ponder a moment, then pull off my own coat and rip a strip from the lining. "I'm going to make a field dressing," I say, winding it around his bicep.

Packard winces as I tighten the dressing. "It's a good place to attack from. Close, well-defended…"

"Very powerful telekinetic," Shelby says.

"The urge to kill tends to bring out people's greatest strengths," Jordan observes.

When I'm done, I decide the dressing is too tight, and I loosen it. Packard winces again. "Sorry," I whisper.

He says, "I've seen lots of things down here, but I've never seen bricks. Bricks are not something you find in the Tanglelands."

As if on cue, more bricks sail over us. Jordan tips the metal sheeting back to cover us and the bricks hit like a hellish blast of hailstones, smashing the sheet against our forearms and heads. Then the sheet itself flies upward. I grab at it too late. We watch it sail over and away, like a big, square Frisbee.

"Christ," Packard whispers.

I stretch out my leg and pull a garbage can lid over with my foot. "Okay," I say, gripping it hard. "I won't let go. He'll have to take me with it."

Of course, I won't be able to deflect multiple bricks. Shelby grabs a large rock and sets it in her lap.

"Where's he getting the bricks?" Packard asks. "That's what I don't understand. He brought his own bricks?"

"Another copycat?" I venture. "The Belmont Butcher following Shelby, and now, a telekinetic slinging bricks?"

A man's yell: "I don't need to kill all of you. I just need Sterling Packard's severed head."

We all look at Packard, whose expression remains perfectly neutral. "My severed head," Packard remarks, dryly. "Well, he could've just asked."

"That's not funny," I say.

He peeks out over the barrier, then ducks as a brick sails overhead. We scramble to avoid it on its return.

"Packard!" I scold.

"This guy's not a copycat," Packard announces. "He needs his killing projectiles to be of brick. It's a deep compulsion."

"You got a read?" I ask.

"Yes," Packard says. "Did any of you see him? The Brick Slinger? Back when he was caught? I know there was footage."

"Yes," I say. "He's a big guy with a brown beard. Paul-Bunyan type. That's all I remember."

"This guy would qualify," Packard says.

"This guy has beard," Shelby concurs.

"But Otto has the Brick Slinger sealed up in a soundproof toll booth on I-25."

"A toll booth?" Shelby asks. "Does he not make trouble?"

"Apparently not." I keep a frantic eye on the air overhead as I explain how Otto prefers his prisoners to be productive, if possible. Especially now that so many workers have left the city. "The Brick Slinger can't communicate with the drivers, since the force field is soundproof, but they feel watched by him, which keeps the drivers honest. At the same time, the Brick Slinger is watched by the cars around him every hour, so if he escaped, or decided to strip his clothes off and make a spectacle of himself, there'd be consequences."

"But is he still there?" Packard asks.

"Once they're in, you know they don't get out," I say. "Unless Otto experienced some kind of breakdown. Which I'd know about."

Another brick flies overhead. We scramble apart as it curves and smashes into the space where Jordan was. My blood races. They're coming so fast, it's pure luck one of us hasn't gotten seriously hurt.

"What I saw in this guy...the compulsion," Packard says. "He's not the type to be a copycat. The bricks are likely from a specific source, or at least they resemble bricks from a specific source, one that is significant to him. This man's all about the bricks." He stares into the distance, thinking. "Either we have two sociopathic telekinetics who have deep, highly personal compulsions to kill with bricks, both appearing in this city in the same year, or, more likely, the Brick Slinger got out of that toll booth."

"Meanwhile, let's make a plan," Jordan says.

"He will never let us get close enough to zing or zap him," Shelby says.

"I've got nothing," I whisper, cold with fear. I reach out to touch Packard and he takes my hand in his. We're cornered by a powerful killer, and we have no weapons. I have the awful thought that most deaths in real life probably are just like this. Nonheroic. Just people up against a wall.

"Okay," I say, trying to think, "this hill we're on has some old rusted barrels mixed in with the rocks. Maybe we can get those barrels and construct some sort of suit of armor. Then one of use will wear it and get to him that way."

"How?" Shelby bites out. "Do you have suit of armor to help you retrieve these barrels so that you might create your suit of armor? Do you have blow torch to assemble your suit?"

"At least I'm trying to come up with something constructive," I say. The pulse in my ears is deafening, or maybe it's the roar of cars, or the ringing from the shots. "Maybe he's running out of bricks," I try.

Packard shakes his head. "Doesn't matter. He's capable of hitting us with other things, though he'll want the killing blow to be bricks." He seems distracted. Lost in thought. "Killing us will feel like a release to him, a discharge of duty. Bricks represent duty to him."

"Lovely," Jordan says.

The moments tick tensely on. Why isn't anything happening? I'm thinking about my dad, suddenly, the dinner Otto and I are supposed to have with him tonight. Will I see my dad again? "Back where I grew up, my dad..." I start laughing— it's the seriousness of our situation hitting me sideways. "He would have the perfect suit. He has this hazmat suit—the kind you'd use in biohazard scenarios, and he attached this level- four respirator and armored the whole thing up. The "hazmat exoskeleton," we used to call it. Designed for a societal breakdown caused by a pandemic. You wear it to forage for food and stuff."

Another brick flies in. I deflect it with my garbage lid, but the impact smashes my knuckle. "Crap!" I say.

Jordan takes the lid from me. Will we die here? Will Packard?

Packard looks thoughtful, and suddenly I just know he's going to try something. He says, "Loose bricks would likely obsess and disturb him. Enough of them piled together would put him off his game, representing overwhelming duty. Dark demand. That's how it is for him."

Shelby snorts. "Why should we care, Packard, what kind of man he is?"

"What kind of man he is *always* matters."

I think how much I don't know about what kind of man Packard is. I know a lot, but not everything, because he seems endless to me, like it would take a lifetime to delve into him. That thing he used to say strikes me in a new way now: *You love to remind me that I'm a villain, but when I do something villainous, you act outraged.*

I took him as a villain who was always ready to use me, but deep down, I knew that wasn't so. That's why I was always outraged when he'd act the villain. Now I *want* him to act the villain—anything but the hero. I have a bad feeling.

Shelby says, "You feared he will wear this suit to wedding?"

"What?" I ask.

"Hazmat exoskeleton—you feared your father will wear it to wedding?"

"No, he would've worn the everyday hazmat suit with a level-one respirator. No need to insult the other guests."

She and Jordan chuckle.

"We don't have much time now." Packard gazes upward, staring hard into the gloom, looking all rebel fighter with his beat-up clothes and black hat smushing down his curls. "In a minute, he'll figure out he got all our weapons and come at us big," he grumbles. "He's a careful man, but not a patient man. We need to buy enough time to get to him. We need to cross that tundra."

Shelby looks worried.

"You'll be hit." I say. "Don't be a hero." I can't believe I'd say that, after months of complaining he's only out for himself.

Packard wrestles off his jacket and shirt.

"What are you doing?"

He takes off his hat too, so that all he's wearing is jeans and the arm bandage, dark green silk gone black from blood. There are smears of dirt over his broad chest, his lean stomach—he has the look of a tiger.

"Put these back on!" I shove his shirt and jacket at him.

He ignores me, leaning far over to the side, reaching down into the rocks. He comes back with a handful of slime, which he swipes across his chest, smearing it over the solid planes of his muscles.

"What the hell are you doing?"

"Interfering with his concentration. Vulnerability and a lack of logic will disturb him. And the bricks exert a pull..." He turns to me, and there's a forlorn light in his eyes. "I have to do this thing, Justine."

"What?"

He pulls me to him, kisses me hard.

"Packard!" I push him away. The last time he kissed me like that he was sending me off. "No you don't."

"There's no time." He leaps over the concrete barrier and starts loping quickly toward the ridge. "Hold up!" he calls out. "I have to tell you something! Midcity is purchasing the Great Wall of China!"

What? Has he gone insane?

"Midcity is importing the wall, brick by brick, right *now!*" He strides, totally unprotected, toward where the Brick Slinger hides. "They're bringing it here on a boat, in its raw brick form, to be deposited in the Maverick's stadium!"

I gasp. He's nearly there.

A brick flies out from behind the red barrel, but Packard ducks in time; the brick hadn't picked up enough speed. It sails out and circles back, but Packard's storming the crevice. There's a scuffle and he yanks a burly, bearded figure from between the barrels. Shelby and Jordan and I scramble over our barrier and run toward them. The brick is coming back for Packard, but at the last second, he spins the man around, using him as a human shield. The brick stops, feet from them and starts back our way. *Shit!* I flop to the ground. Shelby and Jordan run back toward our protective little wall.

Packard hauls off and punches the man in the face, again and again. The man crumples to the ground. There's a splash as the brick drops into the slime lake.

Still clutching his shirt and jacket, I scrabble along the ridge to where Packard stands over the man.

The Brick Slinger is splayed out sideways in a way that would be terribly uncomfortable if he were awake. He has a thick beard and a gray camouflage suit. Urban warfare outfit, perfect for the Tanglelands. Probably why I didn't see him when I passed. A wheelbarrow full of bricks is hidden behind another set of barrels.

Packard just stares down at the man, trancelike, muscles pumped, dirty chest rising and falling. I get the sense that he's trying to recover.

I am too. I'm shaking, I realize. Packard's the one who went at the man, but I feel as though it was my heart—exposed and vulnerable—my life that almost ended a minute ago.

"My severed head indeed." Packard sweeps the area with a glance, not meeting any of our eyes, then he looks back down at the crumpled man. "Shelby, how much of that knockout stuff do we have back there?"

"Five pins."

"He needs one. Now."

Shelby heads off.

I glare at Packard, resisting the urge to shake him. "That was so risky. It was too goddamned risky."

"Was it really?" Jordan prods the man with her toe. "A highcap needs to concentrate to do his deed. Packard read the man and saw how to break his concentration, just enough to get to him and punch the daylights out of him." She beams at Packard. Jordan has dimples. I never noticed that before. "That was the weirdest thing you said. Just *weird* enough."

Packard simply stares at the man.

Shelby's back. She presses what looks like a modified staple gun to the man's arm. *Click.* Then she stands. "Midcity is going to buy Great Wall of China?"

"It was just weird enough," Jordan says again.

"The Great Wall of China has bricks of some sort, right?" Packard says casually. "Ten seconds of hesitation—that's all I needed."

"We've got to get out of here," I say.

"Damn straight." Jordan grabs Shelby. "Let's get the rest of the stuff." They march back to the little encampment.

Packard finally looks at me, and that's when I see it—a kind of animal wildness, like the muscles around his eyes won't untense, like the emotion is too high. And it's here I know—he wasn't at all sure it would work.

He tries a smile. It's not convincing.

"Oh, Packard." I wipe his chest with my sleeve, but it just smears the oily slime around. "That was so stupid!" Again our eyes meet. I want to hug him and hit him all at once.

"Sometimes stupid's all you have."

"We could've found another way."

"There wasn't another way. We were running out of time."

I wipe some more. "This stuff is highly toxic, you know."

He grips my arm, eyes soft. "I'm okay now." But he won't continue to be okay if he's suddenly acting heroic. And what's up with the severed head thing? I feel deeply frightened for him.

He's talking to me. "Justine?"

"Huh?"

He takes his shirt from my hands. "You were attacked by a Belmont-Butcher copycat, right? Who you thought was following Shelby?"

"Yeah," I say.

"Are you sure he was a copycat?"

"I never saw the real one." I straighten, trying to focus. "This one had a big black axe, and he was a telepath. I said, *You're supposed to be the Belmont Butcher?* And he didn't object to the *supposed-to-be* part. And I was like, *Where's your black apron?* And he said it was under his coat."

"That said copycat to you?"

"Yeah," I say. "That, and the fact that the real one is in a force-field prison for eternity. Sealed up in the back room of the Wholesale Butchery by the railroad yards."

"Is he? Or is he out now? Here's the thing—this is the Slinger and that was the Butcher. I'm convinced of it. Think— who in this world would most want my severed head?"

I see now where he's going with this. "But, to unleash criminals to hunt you down? Otto's struggling to keep these people locked up. Everything he does is about safety. Why would a safety-minded mayor free dangerous criminals?"

Packard waits.

"And, I'll tell you how else it doesn't add up. Somebody like the Brick Slinger or the Belmont Butcher, if they got out of their prisons, the only severed head they'd want would be Otto's."

"Why?" he asks. "They don't know Otto was keeping them in there. They don't know he can wield force fields. They don't even know that he's a highcap."

"They know he's the mayor. He's *the man.* He was the police chief. Especially the Brick Slinger—Otto chased him down on foot and caught him, remember? That arrest was half of how he got into office. Remember the way he milked it? There's no way the Brick Slinger would be out there doing Otto any favors."

Packard looks down at the supposed Brick Slinger. "Why, buddy? You've got the answers, don't you?"

Jordan and Shelby come up with duffel bags.

"He will not have answers for two or three hours, I think," Shelby says.

Packard nods. "Let's see who's sitting in that toll booth out on I-25."

Jordan says, "How much time do you have?"

"What do you mean?"

"Before you and Otto have to pick up your dad."

"Oh, right! It's not until tonight. But I don't think I want my dad coming into this. I'm going to call him, get him to pull out. If the criminals of Midcity have all gone loose, I don't like the idea of bringing Dad into town."

Jordan says, "If your dad's suddenly not coming, it could raise a few red flags."

"It's not as if there's going to be a wedding tomorrow anyway," Packard says.

Jordan looks at him like he's crazy. "The minute she stops playing along, we lose our element of surprise, our access. We can't expose Otto and prove your innocence without somebody on the inside. Not to mention free our people and get the city right again."

"Do we have a plan for all this?" I ask.

"It's multipronged," Packard says.

"Yes, multipronged," Shelby says sarcastically.

"We've been trying to find some weakness or damning proof that will give us leverage over Otto," Packard says, "or some way to destroy his personal force field so he can be zinged or dream-invaded." He turns to glare at Jordan. "We don't need her to marry Otto to accomplish that."

"But it would be easier," I say. "Right?"

"For you to marry him?" Packard's jaw sets hard as stone. "Hell no." Then he straightens up, seeming to realize he needs a better reason than that. "He's not stupid. He needs you, but eventually he'll see through you. There's a time to pull up stakes, and your uneasiness might be a sign that it's now."

"I feel uneasy about my dad, not myself."

"Sometimes you don't heed your instinct."

"Look, the wedding's not happening today. I'll keep going like everything's normal, and investigate from the inside. I guess if I make Dad stay in his hotel room, he'll be safe. It's not like he'll want to go out into the germ-infested streets anyway."

"He will be fine then, I think," Shelby says.

"That long car ride to get him. You and Otto..." Packard says.

"It'll be fine," I say.

Packard doesn't look convinced.

"Brides are traditionally crazy and nervous before their wedding," I add.

Now he looks even less convinced.

"Can we get out of here?" Jordan asks.

Shelby dumps the bricks out of the Brick Slinger's wheelbarrow and wheels it over. "Load him up," she says.

The three of us heave the unconscious Brick Slinger into it. I avoid Packard's gaze. I don't want to marry Otto either, but we have to expose him, and free our friends, prove Packard's innocence. Get the city back.

Chapter Eleven

Packard and I squeeze next to each other in the back seat of Shelby's little car. It's wonderful to be together again, doing a normalish thing like riding in a car. It might even be romantic if the burly Brick Slinger wasn't stuffed unconscious on the other side of Packard, head lolling on the window, and if there wasn't a duffel bag of weapons crushing my feet. And if Shelby and Jordan weren't up front, telling me about the harrowing existence they've led for the past two months.

"We have to talk," Packard says at one point, low so only I can hear.

I nod, reveling in the press of his thigh against mine, the heat of his breath on my hair, the feel of his thick forearm under his sleeve when I shift against him. Sometimes he catches my eye as Shelby or Jordan tell an anecdote, and we have this secret moment of enjoying each other. It's as if we're drawing closer together. It feels good. New, but not.

I even enjoy the way he lowers his voice when he gives directions—still the old, imperious Packard. Like a favorite song I haven't heard for too long.

Of course, I keep replaying that kiss. And I'm also gratified by how tormented he seemed by the idea of my being anywhere near Otto. I suppose it's not right to enjoy that. It's the sort of thing an insecure girl would enjoy.

Most of all, though, I'm feeling worried for him, due to his Brick-Slinger heroics. Out-for-himself Packard played it a lot safer than heroic-gesture Packard. When did he turn over this new leaf?

"Toll booth two miles," Shelby reads. Jordan scans around for radio stations, settling on a Monkees song. "Hey, Hey, We're the Monkees". Not at all fitting.

It's been over an hour since we knocked out the Brick Slinger—it took a while to wheel him and the guns out of the Tanglelands, and longer for Shelby to sneak back to her place, steal away with her car and come get us. Which means we have another hour to get the Brick Slinger into a projectile-free environment before he wakes up.

I learn they have allies—old friends and cohorts of Packard. And there's also bespectacled Councilperson Henry Felix, the man who's leading the charge to bring Otto down legally. Shelby and Jordan met with him to discuss Packard's case, but Henry Felix can't do anything without proof. Apparently, he and his comrades, the Felix Five, feel like they're in danger. Shelby said he was exhausted and distressed.

"They seemed downright paranoid, actually," Jordan turns around to face us, resting her chin on the seat back. "Worn out. Not right. Of course, any sane person has a reason to be paranoid in the best of circumstances..."

"Then when Carter, Helmut, and Vesuvius disappeared," Shelby says, "was like horror movie. Then Enrique. Jay. Every time one of us goes out alone, that person does not come back. Is because of curfew—this curfew makes it much too easy for Otto to hunt disillusionists. I wonder sometimes if that is true reason for curfew. I wonder, are cannibals really out there? But this—you will be surprised"—Shelby points at me—"last week, we had most interesting interaction with Sophia. She could not talk at that time, but she said that she wanted meeting with us."

"Sophia?"

"We think she was going to defect," Packard says. "She had something important to tell us."

"Sophia? *Defecting?*"

Packard says, "Sophia loves getting behind a vision, working with powerful people. And she loves having a reason to ply her craft, but she's not without morals."

I snort.

"Even she has her limits. Maybe revising you pushed those limits, or maybe it was something else; Lord knows what kind of revisions Otto's been having her do. Deep down, she wants to do the right thing. We thought she might help us expose Otto, but she never showed up. And we can't find her."

"Otto said she was on vacation."

"I'm guessing it's not any kind of vacation I'd want to take," Jordan says grimly.

There's a long silence. We pass another sign announcing the toll booths. Over on the other side of Packard, the Brick Slinger drools onto his coat.

"After that," Jordan continues, "well, we thought maybe we could get some kind of intelligence down on the seventh floor. Shelby drew the short stick for that. All we got was the Fawna e-mail, though, and those guns. The Brick Slinger wasn't the only telekinetic attack."

Shelby slows the car as we near the knot of traffic around the toll booth area.

Jordan says, "We're looking for a bearded man in the far toll booth? That's the thinking?"

"Yes," Packard says.

We come around the bend, and there it is. The row of booths, some automated, some designed for people. And one booth is empty. The far booth. That's where he was. In fact, there are no bearded men in any of the booths. We're silent as Shelby maneuvers into one of the open lanes.

"You're sure it was this toll area?" Jordan finally asks.

"Absolutely," I say. "Otto's talked about it."

"He was here," Packard says. "It was a poorly kept secret."

Shelby frowns in the rearview mirror. "So this is the real Brick Slinger."

After we pay our money and come out the other side, we loop back across town to check the Wholesale Butchery. There's no Belmont Butcher inside. Up on Highway 390, the weigh station monitor's booth is empty too—Jordan remembered she was assigned to disillusion a short-term prognosticator in there, before everything went to hell.

So Otto's let out all the violent highcaps. Set them on Packard. I sigh. Otto's unattackable, and he's holding our friends as insurance, so he's double unattackable. And the city loves him.

"We'll find them," Packard says.

It doesn't seem very likely. Otto has everything buttoned up, including me—he stole a day of my life and it altered everything for months. I sit back, feeling angry and hopeless.

The way Packard glances at me just then, I know he gets it. It has nothing to do with his highcap powers and everything to do with us, and how we've always been attuned. It's here, in this silent sharing, rather than the kiss or the torment or any of the fireworks, where I feel like we truly click into place. Packard speaks low, almost a whisper. "We'll get our lives back. We'll get it all back. I promise."

"We'd better," I say.

"Hey," Jordan twists around. "Think one of you can hop to and see if the Slinger's got a phone on him?"

"I checked," Packard says. "Just some cash."

"Hold on!" I pull out my phone. "I can't believe I forgot about this! I might have clues..." I flip through to find the list-like document while I tell them how I snuck into Otto's office, and that I suspect he's using Vindalese for writing secret documents. Packard scolds me for sneaking around like that.

I give him a look. "I'm the girl on the inside, Packard."

We examine the photos, and one of the docs, in addition to the cramped rows of squiggles and shapes that form the Vindalese alphabet, you can make out a few numbers mixed in, including 390, suggesting Highway 390.

"E-mail it to me and I'll enlarge it on my tablet," says Jordan.

"Hell no," Packard says. "No transmission." Jordan ends up passing the tablet back, and Packard painstakingly types Vindalese letters into an online translator. It's not easy to make out Otto's circles and squiggles, and a lot of the words Packard types come up as nonsense, but one item seems extra promising—it has five hash marks by it, and five of our disillusionist friends are missing, so we go at it hard. We finally get something: "tan foolishness happy house". We rack our brains for a tan house that would be significant to Otto. Finally, Shelby puts it together—a fun house—the ruins of the fun house on the abandoned fairgrounds at Tandy Folly.

Tandy Folly is north of the city, on a bluff overlooking the old port. We use one of Avery's pin darts to knock out a security guard, and then Packard and Shelby and I crawl under the chain-link fence and head in on foot, leaving Jordan in the car to watch the Brick Slinger.

It's like skulking through the lunatic version of a ghost town—all giant, peeling clown faces and weathered stripes on every flat surface. Once-bright shacks that housed crazy-making games sit broken and shuttered. We head around a garbage-strewn bumper-car pit and past a toppled ferris wheel, which is surrounded by a confetti of mirror shards.

The wind off the lake is strong up here. Things creak. Bright wrappers blow back and forth—the fairground version of tumbleweeds.

Up ahead stands the fun house, which you enter through a clown's smiling mouth.

"I would kill myself if I was prisoner here," Shelby says.

"No, you wouldn't, just out of courtesy," I say, "because your body would be trapped in there after you die, and your friends would have to watch your corpse rot."

"Hmm," Shelby says. "Smell it too."

"Well, now we're looking on the bright side," Packard says. We draw near. A loose shutter bangs. "I'm thinking we can walk right in there," he says.

"Me too," I say.

We're both thinking Otto probably created a force field that holds our friends in, but doesn't keep others out. It's the sort of force field he created around Packard when he had him imprisoned in the restaurant—the public could pass in and out, but not Packard. It's the easiest on Otto—it doesn't take as much power to maintain, and it's the most convenient for food deliveries. Only the really dangerous highcaps get isolated inside impenetrable force fields.

We cross a wide, wooden plank over a dried-up moat.

"Hello?" Packard calls. A face appears at a window above. Dark hair. Beard. It's Helmut! He pounds on the glass, and looks like he's yelling sort of maniacally. Which is quite unlike him. His yells can't be heard, and he'll never break that glass, but he keeps on, pounding and yelling; I'm reminded, horribly, of a gorilla I once saw at a zoo, enclosed in a Plexiglas cage. Kids would taunt him, and he'd pound on the glass and roar. What's going on with him? Helmut's disillusionist power is worry, not rage. Rage is Carter.

Packard pushes open the door.

"Oh boy. Visitors." Vesuvius stands there in the dark.

I go in after Packard. It takes a while for my eyes to get used to the darkness; when they do, I see Packard pulling Vesuvius into a bear hug. "So good to see you! So goddamned good," Packard says. "You're okay?"

"Well, Helmut hasn't killed any of us—yet," Vesuvius says.

"What's wrong with Helmut?" I ask.

"He and Carter have been zinging each other," Vesuvius says. "Carter's not being himself either."

Just then Carter comes out looking haunted. "This is terrible," he says. "We can't last."

Helmut and Jay barrel down the crazy staircase, shouts of greeting. Helmut's usually robust, opera-singer physique has diminished, and his dark beard, always so short and precise, looks as if it's been trimmed by dull scissors.

"Are you getting us out of here?" Jay asks. "Tell me you are!"

"Sorry," Shelby says, staring into a wavy mirror.

Enrique emerges from a door shaped like a mushroom and saunters up behind Shelby. "Somebody smashes that thing every day, and every day it repairs itself. This place is evil."

Shelby turns. "Oh, Rico Suave." She hugs him.

"They send the food in on a fucking trolley," Helmut bites out. "And we've been having to zing each other."

Carter glares at me. "What're *you* doing here?"

"Helping," I say.

Packard catches Carter's arm. "We wouldn't have found you without her," he says.

Wearily, Vesuvius rolls his eyes. *Ennui.* Did he and Enrique zing each other? I can only imagine what it's been like for the five of them in here—they're disillusionists because of a crazy surplus of obsessions and emotions, and they've been zinging each other? Like five bees, stinging each other? The fun house surroundings take on a horrible new dimension.

Shelby and I fill the other guys in on what's been happening, and we start making a list of things to bring them, beyond the survival provisions they're getting. It's good that we've found them, but knowing where a person is and getting him out are, of course, two very different things.

There are only three ways to break somebody out of one of Otto's force field prisons. One is for Otto to make a descrambler, and for the person inside to get hold of it. No way would he have made one for the fun house. The second is to get Otto to change his mind about keeping the person sealed up. That's how we got Packard out. The third way is to break Otto's will enough so that he just lets up all his force fields.

Disillusionment would do it. In fact, we're pretty sure that if I zinged Otto hard, that alone would probably break his will enough to get him to let them out. If Shelby and Jordan joined in, all the better.

Unfortunately, thanks to Otto's new personal force field, he's unzingable.

We can't zing him, Ez the dream invader can't get into his dreams to control him, telepaths probably can't read him, and bullets likely can't harm him either. Not that anybody wants that—if Otto dies, his force fields become eternal.

Shelby is staring at the wavy mirror again. She moves her head from side to side.

After getting everybody's requests and promises to return, we head out of there. Time is running out; not only do I have to meet Otto in several hours but the Brick Slinger will be rousing soon.

We scramble back into the car and speed off, arguing about where to question him. The backup walk-in cooler at Mongolian Delites is the obvious place—it's made of metal and you can lock it, and best of all, it's usually empty, so the Brick Slinger won't have anything to sling.

"No Mongolian Delites," Packard says.

I give him a look. It's dangerous that Packard's out in public this much already. Where will he go if not Mongolian Delites? Where will he sleep? When did he last sleep?

Time is running out. The Brick Slinger is waking up. We end up pulling him into one of the empty railcars in the yards near our old headquarters. We lay him inside and open up the vent in the ceiling for light.

Shelby stays outside with a machine gun—having a gun inside there with him would be suicide, of course, because he'd take it away. We also tie up his hands and feet before we wake him. He's a pretty big man. If he telekinetically gets his bindings off, the plan is that Packard will subdue him and I'll stoke up some terror to zing him with, but that's a last resort. Terrified people don't give the best information.

When we're ready, Jordan flicks water in his face, and the man rouses. She and I jump back. He swears a lot and struggles against his ropes.

"Hey," Packard speaks to him reassuringly, tells him we have some questions, that he needs to work with us.

The Brick Slinger looks out from under bushy, brown eyebrows that match his beard. He has the look of a hunted man. "What day is it?"

"Friday, March 19," I say.

"No!"

"Why is that significant?" Packard asks. "Why is the date significant?"

The man tips his head back against the wall and looks around. A creaking sound. I look up—the corner of an old, rusted ceiling panel moves back and forth, back and forth. Packard watches it too.

"You better let me out of here or I'll bust up this whole car and impale you with the parts."

Packard smiles. "No you won't, or you would've. You go ahead and bend that corner all you want." There's something regal about the way he settles down onto a crate, legs crossed, leaning back against the corrugated metal side—a sultan on beach holiday, amused for the moment. Thoroughly confident.

Packard once told us that he looks at people the way a demolition expert looks at a building—he can see the cracks, the lines of strength and weakness. Is he doing that now?

The man keeps bending the corner. *Creak. Creak.* It seems like it's loosening. I hold my breath, tense all over. But then it stops.

Packard says, "So, you want my severed head; let's start there."

The Brick Slinger frowns. "I'm not telling you anything."

Packard shrugs. "Maybe, maybe not."

"You can't hold me," he says. "Just a matter of time before I get something loose."

"No you won't." Packard crosses his arms. "I've got my own force fields guy coming over later. My guy's been holding up the Tangle for ten years."

The Brick Slinger harrumphs back, like it's all quite ridiculous, but he seems worried.

Packard presses him on the severed-head bit, and then he takes a different angle, painting a picture of himself as the outsider rebel. The rising threat. The man you'd be crazy not to ally with. The way he talks, I feel crazy not to be allied with him, but then I remember that I am.

The Brick Slinger looks away, face stubborn. "Doesn't matter."

"Of course it matters!" Packard talks about the severed-head job some more. "Who does that? Somebody desperate, and not all there," he says. "It will end badly for you even if you deliver, I guarantee. I'll tell you also, that you have about five minutes until we leave and get somebody else to give me the details."

"In exchange for what?"

Packard tilts his head. "You think I'm here to bargain?"

The Brick Slinger touches the back of his neck. "Get this thing out of my neck. Tonight. I'll tell you everything. Everything. But it has to be out tonight."

I stare at him. "What do you have in your neck?"

"I want a bargain first."

There's new energy in Packard's gaze. The Brick Slinger has some sort of ticking clock, counting down on him. They go back and forth some more.

I'm getting worried about our own ticking clock—we only have a few hours until I have to show up at the condo. And is Max still waiting outside Shelby's apartment? I've supposedly been in there for like five hours. I'm also stressing about Dad's being safe, and what happens after dinner. Otto will expect me to stay with him. No way will I do that.

Things are shifting. The Brick Slinger will tell Packard everything if only Packard will consider helping him. He *wants* to help Packard—to be allowed to help Packard, in exchange for some amorphous goodwill.

And just like that, the Brick Slinger is talking about life in the toll booth. Apparently, a man came with water and energy bars every week. "Got a toilet right in the floor. Like living in a goddamned latrine." His beard jerks when he makes *eeee* sounds, like in the word *latrine*. He goes on about the boredom of the toll-booth prison. And then it all changed.

"A week ago, they come to let me out. I thought I was in heaven, but the next thing I know, I wake up on an operating table in some form of hospital. I'm lying face down and I can't move a muscle. It's some form of circular room with lights all around. Greenish lights, and there are other tables with other people—I can't see any of them, but doctors are operating while they're awake—I can tell by their screams. I couldn't move, I couldn't use my powers. I don't know what they gave me. All these doctors with face masks. And the lights are green. The mayor is there. Watching."

"Mayor Sanchez?" I ask. "Was there?"

"He was there. Across the room, watching. He's in on it."

I straighten. Otto? Watching people screaming and getting operated on? It's so out of character...the last thing he'd ever do.

"So after that, two surgeons in masks come over to where I am," the man continues. "One holds down the back of my head, and the other cuts into the back of my neck—got a knife of some sort. Scalpel, I suppose, and it's this sharp pain, and I'm screaming and trying to move, but I can't. And then they've got some laser thing going, like pins and needles. It sounds like a dentist's drill, but it's a laser. I'm begging for them to stop. And then I can feel something cold going in, on the back of my neck. Sharp edges. They seal it all up and it's warm again."

He goes silent for a while, staring vacantly at the light coming through the vent. Packard's attention is focused on the

Brick Slinger, but I exchange glances with Jordan. It's all so bizarre.

"I feel this hot laser after that. The thing is still in my neck—I can feel it." He goes on about the pain, the horror, and how the green lights played tricks on his eyes, and made everything that wasn't black seem neon green.

I lean back against the cold boxcar wall. It's all so science-fictiony. And really, Otto watching an operation? But why make it up?

"The next thing I know, I'm waking up in this seat in some kind of theater. Maybe thirty other guys and a few women are in the other seats. None of us can get out of the theater seating. Fielded in. There's loose stuff all around the room—books, stools. I'm trying to get some projectiles going, cause I'm in the mood to wreck something, but it's a no-go. The fields. We get to talking, turns out we're all highcaps and we've all had this operation."

"Had you all been arrested at some point?"

"Oh yeah. It was a who's who in terms of Midcity criminals. Lots of us thought each other was dead." He rambles on about the criminals, and how deferential they were to him; he's clearly proud of being near the top of the Midcity criminal totem pole. I suppose he was pretty famous in his day.

"So the bunch of us, we're stewing there, and finally some guy in a white coat walks in through a side door, up to this podium. Man just stands at the podium and tells us we all got a chip at the base of our brain. And on Saturday, March 20, at exactly three in the afternoon, every one of our chips will explode. One week."

"The twentieth is tomorrow," I say. I should know; it's my wedding day.

"That was a week ago," he continues. "The deal was, if any one of us deposits your severed head on the steps of the government building, all the chips get deactivated."

Packard crosses his arms. "My head for all yours."

"That would be..." The Brick Slinger nods, "...yup. Yup. They showed us slides of you. PowerPoint about you and your powers." He points to Jordan. "Of you too. You're a known accomplice. A few other guys. They tell us it's okay to take out anybody defending you or keeping us from you, but no regular citizens. Any of us go and start up with attacking normal citizens, our chip will explode. One week to deliver your head." He nods at Packard. "Your head or ours. One day left now. After the speech, the doc, he walks back to the door and opens it and he says, *You are free to go.* Well, he didn't have to tell us twice. When we felt the field lift, we were crawling over each other to get out of there. Except Mangler. You know who that is?"

"Wish I didn't," Jordan says.

"Next thing I know, the podium is floating in the air above the doc. Mangler's doing it. He says to the doc, *How about you get that thing outta my head or I kill you?* The doc turns around, calm as day, and looks at the Mangler. Then, right there, Mangler's head explodes. Some of it goes on me. On my face. Warm. His goddamned brain on my face." The Brick Slinger's lips curl, and his expression stays like that for a few beats, as if the memory takes time to re-process. "It was like nothing I ever saw. So fast. Like a cartoon, but fast. His head *exploded* in front of us. And the sound..." he makes a popping sound with his lips. "Well, I would tell you that was a very motivational demonstration. We get the fuck outta there, the rest of us. You're a lucky man, Packard, lasting as long as you have."

This hush falls over the boxcar. It's all so horrible. And now there are maybe forty violent, powerful highcap criminals after his head? To be delivered to Otto by three on my wedding day? Like a twisted wedding present?

"Any of them working together?" Packard asks.

The Brick Slinger shrugs. "Nah. But yesterday we started getting suggestions where to look. Guess you're better at hiding than they thought."

"The Tanglelands?" I say, recalling Otto's phone conversation. "Was that a suggestion?"

"Yeah," he says.

Something's not right. "Was Mayor Sanchez standing close enough to be watching these operations?"

"Oh yeah," the Brick Slinger says. "Yup."

Packard looks at me. He sees where I'm going with this.

I say, "I can't imagine him watching a surgical procedure of any kind. Especially one around the head."

"Are you calling me a liar?" The Brick Slinger demands.

"And a circular medical facility. Implants that explode. As a nurse, or almost-nurse, I just have to say, that technology isn't here. Especially not in Midcity."

"Head implants that explode unless a certain high-stakes mission is completed..." Jordan's laughing. "Yeah, I saw that movie years ago. When it was called *Escape from New York*."

I straighten. She's right. It's almost the same plot.

"I'm not making it up!" the Brick Slinger says.

"Yeah, *you're* not making it up." Jordan plants her hands on her hips. "Kurt Russell starred in it. Guess who's the biggest Kurt Russell fan in town?"

My heart flips over. *Sophia*. Sophia loves Kurt Russell. He's her screen saver.

"Kurt Russell? Who is that?" Shelby asks.

"He's an actor," Jordan says. "In a movie that has a suspiciously similar plot."

"What are you talking about?" The Brick Slinger asks.

Jordan turns to the Brick Slinger. "You said *they* let you out. Was one of them a pretty redhead?" Jordan points to Packard. "Hair much redder than his, but with Cruella de Vil eyebrows?"

"Yes, yes!" he says.

"And was she there at other times? Was she there when you got free?"

He seems surprised. "She was in the car that dropped me at the Parklands."

Jordan looks around at us, prim eyebrow raised. "Who has a circular operating theater lit in green? Nobody...except a UFO. It's *Escape from New York* mashed up with half the UFO movies ever made. The entire operation was a memory revision."

"But what if it's not?" The Brick Slinger asks. "I remember it—I was there."

"You *think* you were," I say. "She was there to get you out of the booth, and there to drop you off, and in between you had an implant at an alien facility as the mayor watched?" I shake my head. "You were revised during that car ride, that's all."

"What do you know?" he snaps.

"Plenty," I say. "And I know you wanted the chip out of your neck by tonight, and guess what? It's out."

He yanks at his bindings when he realizes we're going to leave. Shelby sticks him with another knockout pin and we take off.

Packard calls his force-fields guy from the car. Some highcap I've never met named Robert. Packard congratulates Robert for getting out of the hospital and arranges for him to create a field around the Brick Slinger's boxcar.

I pull out my phone. It's two. I have to be back at our condo by five o'clock.

Jordan laughs some more at the false memory Sophia chose to plant. "You'd think she'd try a little harder to make it seem different from a TV show or a movie."

"I don't see anything funny about Midcity's most dangerous killers thinking they'll die if they don't deliver Packard's severed head."

"It is strange that she'd make it so bizarre," Packard says. "And why put Otto in the new memory? I don't think that was her getting sloppy. I think it was a small rebellion. A clue."

"They believe it; that's the part we should worry about."

"I'll be okay," Packard says.

"Yeah, if you go back to the one place they won't look."

"You must go to Delites," Shelby says. "Our only choice is to leave city or you must go back to Delites."

"I'll do neither," Packard says. "We need to find Sophia. There are other prisons out there, and she's probably in one of them. Let's see what she wanted to tell us."

Jordan says, "I'm going to guess her information pertained to crazed highcap criminals out for your severed head."

"It's a no-brainer that Otto would send people after me. There has to be more that she can tell us. Something useful. We need the rest of the Vindalese document translated—I bet her location's in there." He fingers the hem of my jacket. "And guess who knows a guy who has a contact who knows Vindalese? Simon."

Shelby says, "Simon?"

"We had some of Otto's books looked at once," Packard says. "Do we know where Simon is right now?"

"Tailor," Shelby says. "For outfit. For wedding."

"Call him," he says. And then he catches my eye.

The wedding.

Chapter Twelve

A bell rings as we enter Trinh Tailor, a tiny storefront in the university corridor, just west of the Tangle. The four of us wait at the counter, watching the little door that must lead to the back room. Here in this small space, I'm uncomfortably aware of how badly we must stink of Tanglelands tea. We raised a few eyebrows at the drugstore where we stopped to print out my photos, too.

While we were there, I picked up some sterile bandages and antibiotic ointment that I'm eager to use on Packard's wound. I've noticed he's not using that arm much, and I worry it hurts, which could signal infection.

A dark-haired boy of maybe ten comes out and frowns—at the smell, no doubt—then motions us to follow him down a hall and into a large back room, which is mostly empty except where Simon and Ez stand on side-by-side elevated platforms. I half expect them to react to Packard strolling in, but they don't. Meeting with him all along, I suppose.

Ez wears the lovely black bridesmaid's dress we picked out last month, only now she wears a black silk cape that's trimmed with white fur. The cape is pinned to her dress and she's glowering in a general way—at the room, us, the situation.

Simon wears a cape identical to Ez's, but that's where the similarity ends. His chest underneath the cape is bare, except for two crisscrosses of leather and one chain, allowing for yet another display of his many dragon tattoos. His black pants are shiny as can be, and his boots reach up nearly to his knees. The bruises on his face from the impound-lot fight complete the insane effect.

"What are you supposed to be?" I ask. "King of the freak farm?"

Simon smiles. "I'm your bridesmaid, Justine, and I couldn't be more excited. Ez here agreed to stand in as the model for all the rest of you so we can all have matching capes. Wait until Trinh comes back with my hat."

"Simon told me this was a mandatory fitting," Ez glares at Simon. "It's good I'm here anyway. Or our capes would've been five feet longer."

Shelby laughs. "A bare-chested man standing up at Otto's wedding. I will like that very much."

"I will too." Simon pushes his cape backward, baring his shoulders. "I'm having four of these capes made so we'll all match. Don't worry, Justine, it's fake fur. It'll be a great effect during the horse procession."

"Unless the horses trip over them," I say.

"There's not going to be a procession," Packard grumbles. "It's not going that far."

Simon gives him a look. "Come again?"

A hush falls over the room as an elderly woman in a bright-blue smock brings out a black top hat with white fur around the brim. Trinh. She smiles at me as she hands the hat to Simon, who introduces us. Trinh clasps my hand, telling me how honored she is to play a last-minute role in the mayoral bridal party's couture, and how important it is to her to match everything to the work of my original dressmaker. She also compliments me on my *bold design vision* for Simon's special outfit; nonpraise if I've ever heard it. I thank her, praying she doesn't recognize Packard, who's taken a seat on the couch in the corner, next to Jordan. He's kept his black winter cap on, at least. Not much of a disguise, but it's better than his curly, reddish hair acting as a flashing beacon.

Shelby introduces herself as a member of my bridal party. Trinh apologizes—she has the capes cut out only, not yet sewn. She starts removing the pin-filled cape from Ez, telling us she needs only two hours.

"Take your time," I say.

She looks at me strangely. "You are indeed a calm bride."

"Not at all—don't be fooled." I force a laugh. "Do you mind if we stay to have a quick, private meeting in here? We're meeting a friend. Secret wedding stuff."

"Please, stay as long as you like." She removes Ez's cape, and then Simon's, leaving him wearing just his chest straps, hat, pants, and boots. We decline her offer that the boy bring refreshments.

"Where's your Vindalese guy?" Packard asks Simon as soon as Trinh's gone.

"He's on his way," Simon says. "What's this about stopping the procession?"

"The second she senses danger she needs to jump out, that's all. It's becoming far too dangerous," Packard says.

"Nothing's different," Simon argues.

"Everything's different," he says. "A day ago she wanted to marry him and thought I was a killer. Now she knows *he's* a killer who's set loose the most dangerous people in Midcity." He tells Simon about the highcaps let out of the prisons.

"Let's concentrate on going forward," I say. "Otto and I are leaving to get my dad in a couple of hours, and there's no reason to call that off. We'll bring him back to the condo to have dinner and then to his hotel. I'll keep my eyes open."

Packard huffs out a breath, forehead furrowed. "You've had your eyes open for two months."

"No I haven't. My eyes are open *now*."

"Just in time to be trapped in a car with him for an hour? You're a good liar, but you're not that good."

"Yes I *am* that good. All my life I've been pretending to feel fabulous when I'm freaking out. You think I can't act like I'm having a nice time when I'm not? You think I haven't done worse?"

There's this awkward silence where I'm guessing everyone is taking the time to remember that I had sex with Otto when I thought he was Henji, a super dangerous killer.

"Christ," Packard says.

"It's not going to come to that, but just to illustrate. This is something I can do, and only I can do it. And maybe I'll find something," I say this with a bravado I don't feel. In truth, I'm anxious about being with Otto, and worried about Packard, hunted by the most desperate and dangerous men possible, yet running around in public. I wish we could get out of this tailor shop, out of Midcity.

Jordan raises a finger. "And if Justine gets killed or sealed away forever, you'll feel sad, blah, blah, blah, but later you'll find somebody of similar looks and personality, and she will replace Justine. That's how it always works with people."

Packard and I both glare at Jordan.

Just then, the boy comes in with a man with impossibly shaggy blond hair and blue-tinted aviator glasses. Hank the languages genius. Hank compliments Simon's outfit, and the two of them settle down on the couch with the printouts of my photos. Jordan, Ez, and Shelby gather around them.

Packard pulls me off across the room to a little alcove with a coffee maker and a plate of decorated sugar cubes, plus every color of fake sugar packet known to mankind.

"What are you going to find new in the condo, or on a trip to your dad's? I don't want you taking risks for peanuts."

"We have a day," I tell him. "There's something to find, I know it. Don't forget that e-mail from Fawna. Even Fawna predicted *his downfall*. Fawna predicted *our success.*"

"Fawna also predicted the ground running red. And she didn't say whose blood that was."

"She didn't even say it was blood."

The planes of his face seem harder. "Justine, when a seer uses the phrase 'ground running red,' she's not talking about the carpet."

An excited murmur from the group.

"You can't prevent the world from being dangerous," I say.

He says, "I can *want* to." The wounded intensity of his gaze drills clear into my heart. He takes my hands and squeezes. "I don't want you to leave me again."

I don't know what to say, or really what he means, by my leaving him *again*. I was never really *with* him. But then I realize something: I grew up with a family that loved me, messed up as they were—people who loved me unconditionally. Packard never had that. He's always been alone—fiercely, completely isolated. Fighting for whatever he could get.

A crash of metal and glass from the front. I jump. Packard lets go of my hand and moves stealthily toward the sound. In comes a dapper man, dragging the boy with him, gun to his head. The man wears a tan business suit, and his kinky, black hair is slicked back with so much product, it looks wet. A second man enters, pudgy and pale with bushy, angry eyebrows, and an old yellow chainsaw that also looks angry.

"Vanderhook," Packard says, addressing the dapper man with the boy, who seems too stunned to cry.

"It won't help," Vanderhook says. He means it won't help that Packard has just let us all know that this is Vanderhook, Midcity's most notorious short-term prognosticator. Not everyone would know Vanderhook by sight, but we've all heard of him. He's a thief and a killer who can see ten moves beyond the present. Another one Otto supposedly imprisoned. I don't know what type of highcap the chainsaw man might be, but just to be safe, I skunk my thoughts with a repetitive song: "It's a Small World After All".

He glares at me.

"The other's a telepath," I announce.

"That won't help either," Vanderhook says.

A scream—Trinh stands in the open doorway, a wad of white fur at her feet.

"Stay back!" Vanderhook gestures at the boy. "This one doesn't have to die." He turns to Packard. "You do."

"Hey, we got a disillusionist over there!" The telepath points the chainsaw at Simon. "That one's a disillusionist! Heard it before he started skunking. Wanting to whammy us."

"Disillusionists are a myth." Vanderhook eyes Simon. "Yes? No? Maybe so? It doesn't matter. Either way, this thing ends bloody."

Trinh screams.

"Shut up and get over to the couch!" he yells.

She complies, a look of shock on her face.

"You all stay right there."

The boy whimpers as Vanderhook tightens his grip, staring at Trinh—his grandmother, I'm guessing.

"Trade me for the boy," Packard says. "Let the boy go and I'll come along with you."

"We really only need part of you," Vanderhook says.

"Don't!" I grab Packard's hand, but he pulls away, with a sly sideways glance and walks toward Vanderhook.

"Stop!" Vanderhook says suddenly. "Go to him, not me." Vanderhook nods his head at the chainsaw-wielding telepath, but as soon as Packard changes direction, Vanderhook changes his mind. "Stop! That doesn't work out either." Warily he watches Packard, who waits in front of the platforms where Simon and Ez had stood. "What are you doing?" he barks.

"Standing where you told me to stop," Packard says.

"Everyone stay where they are." Vanderhook says, then he pauses, getting impressions—waves—from the future. I heard a short-term prognosticator explain it that way. "Packard lies down."

Packard kneels.

"All the way."

"Not until you release the boy," Packard says.

"We'll release the boy once we cut your head off."

My fear surges. I think about lunging, but the boy... I consider zinging Vanderhook, but then I decide it's the chainsaw guy I should zing. Maybe go at him from the back. The room is eerily silent, except for my pulse, *whoosh*ing in my ears.

Vanderhook looks over at me. "You make trouble in this scenario. I want you down too."

"What do you mean?" I sidle nearer to Packard.

"No. In the other corner," Vanderhook says. "You can't be by him. You're a highcap or..." he glances at his telepath pal, then back at me. "Doesn't matter. Get over there with the others." Vanderhook tightens his arm around the boy, who cries out.

"Okay, okay." I back off.

How can we win against this guy? He can read the near future, the instant events are set in motion. Whatever I commit to doing, he'll know.

I take my time getting over there. Maybe zinging the guy would have worked—is that what he saw? Fear trumps most weapons.

Over by the couch, Ez holds Trinh, who sobs quietly. Simon, Shelby, and Jordan stand by. Do they have a plan? I don't. Hank keeps reading the Vindalese papers, scribbling notes, like he's in study hall or something. Where does Simon get these people?

"It's a Small World" plays senselessly and somewhat ironically in my mind.

"There's no chip in your neck, you know." I'm stalling, hoping to distract them. "It's a memory revision. A fiction. You've been revised."

"Shut up." Vanderhook says.

"Let the boy go," Packard says. "It's my head you want. Get these people out of here and it'll be just us. You have a chainsaw and a gun. You're in control."

"We don't make it two feet out the door in that scenario. Wait—" Vanderhook pauses, then he jerks his head to the side. "Maybe..." He stops, tilts it a different way, as if he's getting a new wave of information. "You wouldn't," he says to Packard.

Packard waits.

"Stop that! You're forming intentions you don't intend!"

Packard gives him an innocent look that tells me he's anything but innocent.

I gasp as Vanderhook turns the gun to Packard "We can chop off a dead man's head easy as a live one's." But then he tenses and lurches the gun back onto the boy. What did he see? "Stop it!" Vanderhook says. "I know what you're doing!"

"Don't need him dead to chop off the head." The telepath pulls the chainsaw cord. Vanderhook stares mutely at Packard as a throaty roar fills the room. I'm so focused on the chainsaw I don't see Vanderhook push the boy away, but the next thing I know, the boy's stumbling across the floor. Shots boom out, and Vanderhook's a blur heading into the front hall—spooked by whatever he saw. Which leaves his partner holding a chainsaw—it's him and the chainsaw against nine people.

Packard's up with a metal folding chair, and he's stalking toward the man. "Drop the saw!"

Simon has a chair too; he comes at the telepath from the other side, still wearing his top hat and belt-and-chain shirt.

The man pulls the trigger to start up the chainsaw part, making the buzz of the giant, angrily vibrating thing more shrill.

Trinh rushes around the perimeter of the room and pulls the boy into her arms.

Shelby and Ez have crept to the wall behind the chainsaw-wielding telepath. Nobody wants to get close to him. Suddenly the man throws the entire buzzing, shaking behemoth at Packard, narrowly missing him, and spins to run out, crashing right into Shelby. He grabs her hair and flings an arm around her neck, as if to use her for a human shield, backing toward the door.

And then, all at once, his angry face softens. It looks as if he's thought of something disturbing. His shoulders droop—his whole body droops—until he's practically leaning on her. "Fuck it," he says.

She wrenches away from him, triumphant, majestic. "Yes, that is right, fuck it." There's a gleam in her eye. She's glorying.

The man sits cross-legged on the floor. "It doesn't matter anyway."

She zinged him, of course—zinged all her grim hopelessness into him. He picks at the carpet. I have a new respect for Shelby's weaponized grimness—it really is a destabilizing force. Meanwhile, she's free of her darkness for at least an hour, feeling normal for once, or likely, beyond normal. Beyond happy, beyond powerful.

"Let's get out of here," Simon says. "Vanderhook's coming back. He'll keep initiating and testing new attacks until he hits one with a successful future."

"Gimme one more sec," Hank says, scribbling furiously.

Simon turns to Packard. "You really fucked him up. Forming crazy intentions you didn't intend? How *do* you form intentions you don't intend?"

"Oh, I intended them, that's the trick," Packard says. "It takes a massive inner shift—rearranging the packing material of your personality. Hard to hold something like that."

Unless you have the highcap psycho-sight, I suppose.

"Done." Hank slaps the sheaf of papers down next to him on the couch and holds out his hand to Simon. "That'll be three hundred bucks."

Shelby grabs the papers, scans with a pleasant expression. "Anything of Sophia Sidway?"

"In there somewhere," Hank says, counting the money Simon gave him. "There's no word for Sophia in Vindalese, but a phonetic spelling like that showed up. Near the end."

Shelby shuffles through. "Here! With address." She shows it to Packard.

"Good. You and Justine and I can go find Sophia—she may be able to give us something for leverage. Simon, you do some cleanup and, you know, manage things." He nods his head at the far corner where Trinh and the boy huddle. "After that, maybe you three can settle our glum friend in with Mr. Bricks." In the railcar with the Brick Slinger, he means.

Shelby suggests meeting at Mongolian Delites after that.

"Not me," Packard says.

"Otto and I have our rendezvous with Dad," I say.

Packard gives me a look out the corner of his eye. Still not a fan of that plan.

Chapter Thirteen

Packard and I ride in the back seat of Shelby's car on the way to the North Midcity apartment complex where Sophia's imprisoned—according to Hank's translations, anyway. Shelby drives quickly and expertly; we all tend to be better drivers when we're glorying.

I'm glad to finally get the chance to treat Packard's shoulder wound, but I'm not so glad when I peel back his shirt.

"This...this is full of..." I pat the area with an antibacterial pad, then just resort to wiping it. "Sludge."

"Quite some bedside manner."

I don't tell him that this was my positive spin on things, commenting on the sludge aspect instead of the fact that the sludge could be laden with anything from flesh-eating bacteria and E. coli to encephalitis strains, and it has been soaking into his open gash *all this time*. It was good that the field bandage I'd made stopped the bleeding, but that same bandage held the Tanglelands Tea in place. I go through wipe after wipe, patting the gash and thoroughly scrubbing his entire arm and shoulder, as though getting the whole area insanely clean will somehow reverse things. I scrub and scrub. I'm so worried.

"You trying to amputate my bicep with those wipes?"

I put it aside. "No." I grab a new wipe and dip it in some salve. "It's a good thing I got this salve," I say. "This salve is amazing. It will fight anything."

"Excellent." He kisses the top of my head.

Fight anything. I don't say win, but of course Packard doesn't pick up on that; only a hypochondriac would. It's not that I want to deceive him, but it's important that he believe the treatment will work; the placebo effect cannot be overstated in cases like these. At least it's not red or inflamed; that's a good sign, but still, I'm so worried—it's unsettling to think of him as vulnerable. I wrap new gauze around the area, then I press my lips to his pale, firm, chemical-smelling shoulder, just above the bright, white bandage.

I don't want to leave him, either.

I look up to find him watching me; he slides his hand around the back of my head and kisses me. I stretch up to him, dragging my lips against the seam of his until they open, hot and hungry. My heart races as I taste him, melt into him.

His teeth graze my lips like a dark promise, hands sliding secretly under my coat.

Shelby clears her throat. "We are there."

Sophia is imprisoned on the top-floor community room of a mostly vacant 1970s building. A sign on the door says "Closed Until Further Notice". But from the cobwebby condition of the hall and the dust on the party room sign-up sheet, no Closed sign is needed; it was 1994 when it was last reserved. Probably 1993 when it was last cleaned.

I open the door and pass right through the force field. Otto has imprisoned her with low security, like our friends at the fun house.

I could swear Sophia looks happy and relieved when we walk in, but then she shakes it all off, acting all tough girl. "Well, looky what the cat dragged in," she says, standing up unsteadily from a green-and-orange-plaid couch. She strolls toward us with a challenging gaze in her glassy eyes. The woman who invaded my mind, stole my memory.

I beeline to her, grab her lapels, and push her up against the dark-paneled wall. "Did Otto hold my eyes open?" I ask.

"Justine—" Packard says.

"I want to know!"

"He didn't hold your eyes open. I did. Otto held your arms; he held you still."

A queasy feeling comes over me. "And I saw it? I saw him shoot Avery?"

"Seems so," she says. Her breath is boozy, and faint dark lines of mascara drool track down her cheeks. I guess she's been crying, though you wouldn't know it from the proud, smug look she's got on her face now. Even in here, she's wearing one of her crisp, beige safari-looking outfits.

"Did *you* see it?"

"Nah. I came after."

I want more. More than this.

"Hey." A hand on my shoulder. Packard pulls me off and I let him, regarding Sophia with disgust, avoiding her eyes.

She straightens her jacket.

"We need her sane," he says.

"That stench alone is going to drive me crazy," she says. "You guys been down in the Tangerlands again?" She doesn't get the word quite right.

Shelby comes and links her arm in mine, surveying the moth-eaten, mood-lit 1970s-era party room Sophia's imprisoned in. A half-full bottle of brandy stands on the counter. "You deserve worse. However, this step goes in right direction. Is right start."

I give Sophia a hot, hateful look. "You're lucky Shelby's glorying."

"I'm not the only lucky one here." She squints at Packard. "Glad to see you're alive."

Packard nods.

"Gotta say, accommodations on the side of evil were way better." In the new light you can really see her puffy eyes, her red nose; she's definitely been crying. Her proud look can't erase those things. "And you busted the revise. Out of professional curiosity, Justine, was it the quality of the replaced memory, or was it emotional nonalignment?"

Crying or not, I want to slap her. I want her to act more sorry.

"Never mind." She waves her hand, like she's drying nail polish. "Don't tell me. It doesn't matter. I'm done with revision. I deserve this, and worse. I know. God, look at this place. Hey! I need you to get a message to someone. I know you don't owe me—"

"What? What else happened that day on the waterfront?"

Sophia picks up her glass and sips with a pinched look on her face. Maybe if I had to sit in here forever, I'd be drinking too. "You were happy to see me for once, I'll tell you that. You were fighting with Otto when I walked up. Avery dead on the rocks. You told me Otto shot him."

"Then what?"

She swirls the liquid. "I said, *Maybe he shouldn't have had that antihighcap chip implanted in him.*" I feel Shelby tense at this. Sophia looks at her. "I'm not proud of that. I know that following orders isn't a decent excuse."

"Then don't use it," Packard says.

"Do you have any idea what you took?" I snap. "Do you even care?"

"I don't review the memories, my friend, I just revise them. Look..." She sits, clumsily crossing one leg over the other. "I took something from all of you and I'm sorry for it, okay? I really am. I'm telling you straight. Hell, I lost something too. Have you supersleuths detected that I'm stuck in here, likely forever?" She stares into her glass. "Whatever," she adds. I get the feeling she says that to herself a lot.

"I tried to make it right, afterwards," she continues after a bit. "I know that's no decent excuse, but I wanted to warn you. I was starting a new life with somebody, and I left him in a hospital bed especially to go and warn you." She raises her glass. "As you can see, Shelby, I got detained on the way to our fateful meeting. Otto had a telepath checking on me, and he knew I'd turned against his whole..." She waves her other hand to indicate Otto's plan. His vision. His everything, I suppose.

She doesn't seem too sorry, but I tell myself she *tried* to do the right thing and now she's paying for it. I walk over to the window and push aside the avocado curtain, just enough to get a look at the street, in case people followed us, but nothing looks amiss, though I don't know what amiss would look like out here.

"I really would like you to get a message to somebody for me."

"How about Shelby and Simon?" Packard says. "He's got somebody watching them both. Does he know they're with me, or is it just insurance?"

"If he knew they were with you, they'd be in the fun house. You know that's where—"

"We know," Packard says.

Sophia shrugs. "He's wait-and-see about Shelby, but Simon? No-go. He'll put Simon away after the wedding, if only because of the way Simon's always losing whoever's tailing him. But, Justine, you're his blind spot." She seems to have trouble focusing on me. "Oh yeah, you do what no doctor could do; you can make him feel okay when he's..." she flutters her hand around next to her head. "All messed up. You know that? You make him feel A-okay."

"He's not the least bit worried?" Packard asks. "She's not exactly his fiancée of her own free will."

"He sees it as...what?" Sophia takes a thoughtful sip. "Her original free will, I would say. Her original path restored. You remember, Justine, back when you and Otto thought of yourselves as soul mates? Vein-star soul mates?"

Of course I remember it. The excitement of finding each other, being able to confide in each other. We had said something like that.

"But it's not as if she's got total immunity," Packard says. "If he suspects her of betrayal—"

"Yeah, yeah," Sophia says. "*That* wouldn't go well. But you, dude, you've got more heat after you than you think. 'S the day before the big wedding right? You oughta get in your car and drive. *Away.*"

"Why?" I cross my arms. "Because you turned a bunch of guys into killing machines and set them after him? Your stupid *Escape from New York* bit?"

She raises her perfectly shaped brows. "Hey, I tried to warn you all." She squints at Packard. "So you also know, these last hours, the guys will be desperate."

"That creepy operation memory?" I press. "A man's head exploding? How do you even look at yourself in the mirror?"

Sophia sighs. "Oh, righteous, righteous Justine, struggling valiantly to be normal. I don't expect you to understand. Sure, I regret it now, but at the time, it was the mad challenge of it. When you revise, plant something new, the whole key is plausibility—creating a false memory that will weave seamlessly into existing memory. The idea of revising so many with such an extreme tale, and causing them all to focus on a common and utterly outrageous goal—it's never been done. I wasn't even sure if it could be; it was like my own personal Himalayan Mountains or whatever. I could see nothing but the mad challenge of it." She turns to me. "There are some people in life, Justine, when you put a mountain in front of them, they climb it, whereas others just pop a few aspirins and hope it goes away."

"And your mountain was them sawing off Packard's head."

"The head was Otto's idea. Anyway, I figured you'd survive, Sterling. You always do. And, well, Otto was going to have people after you whether I helped or not. I know, I know—" She holds up her hand to forestall any commentary. "Bad excuse. You'll be happy to know that after that...that *orgy* of revision...I was disgusted with myself. *Disgusted!* Barely wanted to be in my own skin. Don't get me wrong, I wasn't happy to revise you, either. But doing all those highcap creeps was the last straw. I did it successfully, scaled my Himalayas, but I was sick inside after. *Enough,* I said. It was my last revise for Otto." Her face is looking pinched again; only this time, she hasn't taken a drink.

"I don't understand," Packard says. "That was your information for Shelby? You risked a meeting with us to warn me to be careful?"

"Not just that. For one, Otto's tracking these guys. The chips in their heads don't exist, but they've got trackers in their shoes, because Otto's planning on rounding them up after the wedding. I thought, if you can tap into that tracking, you can stay safe. Guess that was probably more valuable intelligence last week. But here's this—something big's going to happen at the wedding."

"Does it have anything to do with my severed head?"

"Your head's the pre-party. All I know from bits and pieces is that the wedding is a big public game changer for Otto. You know the Felix Five is trying to get Otto thrown out of office?"

"Everyone knows that," I say.

"They recently got a sympathetic judge. Otto's not supposed to know, but he does. Let's face it, the tide will turn, and Otto knows it. For now, most Midcitians will give up their rights for safety—hell, they spent all last summer hiding in their houses thanks to the Brick Slinger, so a curfew isn't a big deal—who wants to be out with the cannibal sleepwalkers anyway? At least they can walk in the daylight, and there are soldiers at the ball park, in malls, the places that matter to people, and they accept that. And there's the hero worship thing people have for Otto. But eventually it will wear thin. Because, look, he's acting like a dictator." Sophia frowns out the window; for a moment she seems lost inside her train of thought. "He'll lift that curfew after the wedding—I know he plans that. And when the dust settles, there will be a lot less crime. Right now he's using the curfew and police powers to sweep the city, grab baddies of different sorts, highcap and human. He picked up most of you disillusionists too, huh? He's getting the city shipshape for his next phase."

"Why has he not caught cannibals, then?" Shelby asks. "Cannibals, they move so slow, come out at night—"

"Strange, huh?" Sophia says. "There's something up with the cannibals and that Stuart." She twists up her lips. "But here's the thing—after the wedding, Otto thinks nobody will be able to throw him out. Something big happens and he comes out the hero, buys himself another six months of adoration. Slides from there into a safe prosperous city, beloved mayor and first lady, no more crime. New port. Ton of new construction coming."

I squint at a dried-up lava lamp, thinking of all the times Otto assured me the trouble would be over soon.

"A *televised* wedding," Sophia adds. "A live, televised, massively-watched wedding, and everyone who's everyone will be there. The wedding is the turn."

"Except the wedding won't happen," Packard says.

"Unless it has to happen," I say.

Sophia looks from Packard, to me, to Packard. "So, have you figured out yet that he can't be killed, zinged or attacked in any way?"

"Yeah," I say. "Personal force field."

"Like a suit of armor," Sophia says. "Man's unkillable. No way to stop him now. No way to break through his personal force field. *Unless* you had a pair of those antihighcap glasses, of course."

"All destroyed," Shelby says.

"Which brings us to part two of my message." Sophia's smile is catlike. "Or maybe it's part three. I know it's not four." She looks at the ceiling. "Anyway, according to records grabbed in the factory search, there was a pair of those glasses shipped out in some deluxe kit that's still unaccounted for. Otto's PIs have not found the guy with this last pair of glasses, and I'll tell you, they're frantic to—considering Otto's personal force field is rendered null, void, and nugatory if somebody's standing there wearing those glasses. One pair still out there. Some guy named Miles Pinbocker." She sniffs. "Who would name their kid Miles Pinbocker?"

In the silence that follows I catch a glow of recognition in Shelby's eyes. Shelby knows who Miles Pinbocker is.

"If you can find Pinbocker and his glasses and get to Otto, Justine can zing the fuck out of him and he'll cash in these force fields so fast." Sophia snaps. "So fast. Maybe add a dash of grimness, and some of Simon's crazy, too."

"We know how to reboot a man," Packard snaps, and he grills her on the PIs and a few other things about Otto's security operation.

"If you do get the glasses, you can't let Otto get killed," Sophia says. She doesn't want to be in there for eternity, either.

"We've got people trapped too," Packard reminds her. "What's the latest on Fawna?"

"Who's Fawna?"

It turns out Sophia doesn't know Fawna. Not surprising.

After promising her we'll get a message to Robert, who Packard apparently knows, we get out of there and head into the gloomy stairwell to start the ten-story trek down. None of us trusts the elevator in this building.

"You know Pinbocker," Packard says to Shelby once the door shuts. More a statement than a question. So he noticed too.

"Pinbocker is Avery's ninja identity," Shelby says.

"What? It's Avery?" Of course, there's no question Avery is dead. We all saw the body.

"Not Avery, but one of his identities, yes."

Somehow I'm not surprised he created alternate identities.

Shelby grabs a metal banister pole and whirls herself around to the next set of steps. We follow. "He wrote entire book about this, how to build new identity for emergency. *Build Your Ninja Identity Before It's Too Late*, that is title. For *lights-out* scenario. I have book." She whirls around to the next staircase. "We were working on my ninja identity when Otto murdered him."

When Otto murdered him. I'm amazed she can say that so evenly, so factually. "Is a ninja identity different from a false identity?" I ask.

"Oh, yes. False identity is on surface. Ninja identity runs deep. You disappear into new persona. You need all regular identification, of course, driver's license, birth certificate, these things. But, Miles wore different clothes than Avery—jeans and jerseys, with sports team here." She points to her chest. "Miles was bowler, and Avery hated to bowl. We once bought bowling trophy at garage sale for Miles. Miles was from Kentucky. Avery always said, if you wait until you need false identity, is too late to make one. But, Miles, he would want safety too. Miles had some PO Box, and this is where deluxe kit would have been shipped." She grabs the next banister and whirls slowly. "Miles Pinbocker."

"Did Miles have an apartment?" Packard asks.

"No, because he is not real. But his things are somewhere. Book tells how to hide things for your ninja identity, so we must read book. I did not get that far. We had only just ordered false driver's license. For Genika Shogun."

"Genika Shogun?" I ask. "That's your ninja identity name?"

She frowns up at me from the set of steps below. "Avery thought of it."

"It's nice," I say.

We come out of the building, careful as cats. Empty sidewalks run bone dry through dirty snow, past empty parked cars. Packard looks up at the gray sky—I can feel his relief every time we go outside. His need to reconnect with the open sky. To know he's still free.

He and I jump in back of Shelby's car, and Shelby starts it up and pulls out, heading southeast. Now and then she drives around a random block to make sure we're not being followed. I get the sense she's coming off glory hour.

My phone vibrates as we're heading past the railroads. It's Max, the bodyguard. I tell Shelby to flip on the radio to cover the car sound, and then I answer.

Max sounds mad. "You coming down anytime soon here? You and Otto are due to depart from the condo in an hour, and I hear traffic's a holy bitch at the moment."

Max is still outside Shelby's apartment, of course, thinking I'm still inside.

"Crap," I say, thinking fast. "My hair is still wet, in rollers!"

"Are the rollers going to prevent you from driving across town?" Max asks.

"The future first lady isn't driving around in rollers. Just tell Otto I'm running behind."

"How behind?"

"I don't know. It's a bride's prerogative to be running behind on the day before her wedding. I'm indecent and in rollers. Do you want bridezilla in rollers to come out?"

He tells me he doesn't want bridezilla in rollers to come out, and I click off before he can add anything more.

Shelby eyes me in the rearview mirror. "Your hair. If this is the result of rollers..."

I don't need to look in the mirror to know my long brown hair lays limp and flat along my face, and that it's smelly and probably has gunk in it from this morning's jaunt through the Tanglelands. "I'm going to need nine showers."

"And I cannot just drive up and park," Shelby says. "I have one way to sneak back in, and it is not quick."

"Take your time," Packard says. "Most men will cower before your bridezilla bit. Deep down, most men are frightened of a bride. Even their own. You can use that."

"And I'm his blind spot," I say. It hadn't really struck me, the crazy position I'm in, until Sophia had said that. He needs me, and it's making him less observant, less shrewd around me.

"You're his blind spot until you're not," Packard says. "That's what I don't like. We have to find those glasses. We have to stop this today."

"Otto's downfall is coming," I remind him. "The danger comes from his inner circle."

"And the ground will run red," he adds quietly.

"Is there anything that can prevent a prognostication from coming true?" I ask him. "You were messing with Vanderhook. You changed his view of the future."

"Vanderhook was a short-term prognosticator. Short-term prognostications are just the details. Long-term is the destinies. To shift the long-term prognostication, you'd have to shift the very currents of fate."

"What changes the currents of fate?"

"That's the billion dollar question, isn't it?" he says.

"I will kill him," Shelby says from the front seat. "As soon as he releases force fields, I will kill him, and ground will run red."

"Shelby, no." I catch my old friend's brown eyes in the rearview mirror. "No."

"I know I will regret it, Justine. Yet I very much want to. And I think that I will."

"I'll stop you," I say. "We'll get justice for Avery, but not the kind that destroys you in the process."

She looks back at the road. "And you will also stop Packard?"

I furrow my brow. "Packard's not the one—" I'm about to say, *the one who vowed to kill Otto,* but then I look down at the blue chain circling his wrist. It's such a part of him, I never think about it, but I certainly remember the day he put it on. It belonged to his best friend, Diesel, who'd died in one of Otto's makeshift prisons—an abandoned gas station. He'd died, trapped in there without food or water, for the crime of being Packard's best friend. When Packard learned about it, he put on Diesel's bracelet and vowed not to take it off until he strangled Otto with his bare hands.

"Strangulation doesn't make the ground run red," he says. "It means more to me on, Justine."

I touch the chain, his wrist. Remembering how he'd once told me the bracelet serves as a reminder to be vigilant.

"Neither of you are turning into killers," I say.

"Maybe you will kill him," Shelby says.

I don't answer. I don't like all this casual conversation about killing a man, even Otto.

"Keep driving past Delites. I'll wait at Maria's Deli," Packard says. Maria's is the place down the street from the restaurant.

That's why he seemed tense—we're nearing Mongolian Delites.

"Come on," I say. "Mongolian Delites is the safest place on the planet. Shelby will bring the book, and you all can have privacy in the back to study it and make a plan."

"Keep going to Maria's," Packard says.

"Ling will be at Delites," I say to him. Ling is the restaurant manager, and a good friend to us all. "They're not even open for dinner yet. And afterwards you can have her close off the back booth section and get a nap. When was the last time you slept?"

"I'll sleep when this is over."

"Nothing's open at night. All your normal places are being searched. What are you going to do the whole time? You'll have no place to be safe or to sleep. You'll be delirious when we need you most."

"We have to find those glasses tonight," Packard says. "Shelby will bring them to you tonight when you get back with your dad, and you'll zing Otto. We'll start breaking him down so he frees our people. That's the plan."

"It may not be so simple," Shelby says. "Avery would not make these things simple to find. We may need to work tonight and tomorrow both. When things are open. With no curfew."

"We have to get them tonight. Justine—" He looks at me wildly. I know what he's thinking. I can't spend the night with Otto.

"You know how superstitious I am, Packard." I curl my hand around his. "It's bad luck for the bride and groom to spend the night before the wedding together. And especially to see each other the next morning. I'm planning on making a reservation at the Midcity Arms. If you don't get the glasses to me, that's where I'll be tonight."

He looks only marginally relieved.

Shelby stops half a block down from Delites. Even from here, you can see the double doors are plain now. They once had Otto's face on them—his *signature*—Otto with long hair and a beard. That signature image automatically appears near every force field he creates, whether he wants it or not. Now that the restaurant force fields are gone, the door is blank.

"Come on," I say, yanking him out of the car with me. He allows this, allows me to drag him down the sidewalk to the restaurant, but he points down the street toward Maria's.

"No," I say, pulling his winter cap lower over his ears so less of his bright hair is visible. The sidewalk is empty, and nobody is around except Shelby, halfway down the block in the car, but still, best to be safe. "We'll go in together," I say, "and you'll see you can walk out again. Otto's wrong—you *can* rise above your conditioning."

"Sometimes you can't."

"You can do every insane thing, but not go in here? And if this thing doesn't end in a few hours, you'll need somewhere safe to sleep when curfew falls." I take his hand and pull him toward the door.

He stays still as a statue. "I can, but I won't."

I try something new— "I need to know you'll be in there. For when I sneak out of the hotel to come to meet you."

"Don't promise that," he says with ferocious urgency.

"Well, I *am* promising. If this thing's not over, I'll come meet you."

"Don't."

"What?"

He takes a pained breath. "Justine—"

"What?"

He looks helplessly at the sky. "It's what you promised that day. That last day."

The day I lost.

"I promised to meet you?"

He looks down to me, eyes steady as steel. "We were going to go away together. To Mexico. I was on my way out of town when you came and found me, and we talked about everything." He studies my face, like he's seeing it anew.

"Everything?"

"We don't have time for this," he says.

"I don't care," I tell him. "Tell me."

"You knew about what happened all those years ago at the old school. Nobody else ever knew, and you...it was the first time...before that, nobody knew what I'd done except Otto, and he's seen me as a monster ever since—"

"It wasn't your fault, what you did. Nobody would ever blame you for saving yourself!"

"That's what you said. That day. And it was huge to me. And we talked about what I'd done to you. To all of you. I was so sorry. *Am* sorry."

"We talked about all that?"

"That's not even the half."

"Tell me," I demand.

"I can't just tell you. It's the kind of thing that needs to recur. When a person is revised, they're no longer the person who had the experience, they're—"

"Christ, just tell me!" I shake him. "Tell me!"

He takes a breath. "You said you loved me." He drops his hands to my belt, takes hold, pulls me closer. "And I told you that I loved you. So fucking much—those were my words. So fucking much, and it's true. I would tell you a million times more."

My heart bangs in my chest.

He continues, "And you...we..."

"We had *sex?*"

His gaze changes slightly. A *yes.*

"We had sex and I don't *remember?*"

"It was..."

"And I don't remember?"

"I remember enough for both of us," he says. "We came together in every way. I didn't know it was possible...that this..." He's at a loss for words.

I'm in a whirl of emotions—excitement, joy...outrage that I don't remember. Anxiousness that Max is waiting, the clock's ticking. But mostly happiness.

He looks serious suddenly. "In some parts of the world, they don't have a word for snow, because they don't know what it is. I never had a word for this. Love's too trite. It's more than that—just *more.* And I can't lose you again. But here we are. You're going to him and promising to meet me. I can't do this again."

I put my hand to his cheek, feel the grit of new whiskers.

He brings his hand up to mine, wraps his fingers around my fingers. "You left to pack," he says. "We were going to meet. I waited for you."

"*Oh.*" Did he wait into the night? Of course. I can picture his face, eyes searching the street. "It doesn't mean it'll end the same," I say. "Just before, you said a person can't change a prognostication—*except* when something alters the currents of fate. I think the currents of fate are that we'll be together." I'm saying this for him, but I'm saying it a little bit for me. "Think about it—I was revised to believe I saw you kill our friend. And guess what? Even *that* couldn't wreck things. And today you walked into the line of fire of the Brick Slinger, protected by nothing but crazy weirdness, and you survived. God!" I shake him and he winces. I pull back my hand when I realize I touched his arm wound. "Sorry. But, do you know what it was like, loving you like I do, and watching you walk out there like that?"

He looks down at me, gaze keen. "Say it again."

"About the Brick Slinger?"

He tilts his head, all sly annoyance.

"You know it's true," I say. "You've exploited the fact often enough."

"Say it."

When I smile into his eyes, everything is uncomplicated. "I love you." I say it free and clear, like a song in my heart. So *this* is what it feels like, I think, when you say it and mean it. "And I can't believe we had sex and I don't remember!"

"It was..." He's concealing a smile, "...*so* hot."

Just then, something falls into place—"Gumby!"

He tilts his head.

Time is running out. I speak quickly: "When I found my car, Gumby was in the happy mode. Arms up, chest puffed out. I was like, *who did this?*"

"You never put Gumby in the happy mode before."

"I know! But, I must have...after. I probably drove my car right after I saw you. And Gumby was happy that day. Happiest possible Gumby."

He smiles. "Goddamn, I love you," he says.

"Trust in it, then." I pull us gently toward the door. "You'll go in, and it's only for a little while this time. Trust that this is right. You'll study Avery's book with the gang and find clues and make plans; and you'll leave this place with them, and hunt for the glasses, and if they don't turn up right away, you'll come here to rest during curfew."

He shakes his head.

"And I'll come to you tonight."

"You can't promise it."

"I can. As much as I can promise anything. Will you not be here when I come?"

A silence. He looks very young, suddenly. He wants to believe. He looks at the door, then at me. "You'll come to me," he says.

"Yes." I yank one side of the door open, hold it for him. You can see through to the dim inside. Only half the lights are on, since it's not yet open. Wait people rolling silverware at the bar.

He takes his hand from mine, sizing up the entrance. I see it the moment he makes his decision. A minute shift in his posture. And then casually, like it's nothing whatsoever, he walks over the threshold.

I follow, letting the door close quietly behind me.

Inside he turns to face me. "You'll come to me."

"At three or so. When everyone's sleeping."

He takes a deep breath. He won't look around, like if he doesn't acknowledge his surroundings, he won't really be here, but the memories must be assaulting him all the same. The old spicy-sweet curry smells hang thick in the air, and they're playing one of the usual Bollywood soundtracks. The same old Asian and Indian artifacts decorate the walls—masks, swords, ornate mirrors imported from import stores—that used to be our joke. We used to laugh about how nothing was really Mongolian.

"I'm so..." I don't have a word. It seems like anything's possible now. "You've just busted eight long years of conditioning."

"Don't remind me," he whispers.

I take his hand. I want to take a leap of faith too. I want to face down my own demons—not by zinging, but for real.

"We don't open until five." A blonde hostess in a polished ponytail has appeared at the hostess stand. "You'll have to come back in twenty minutes."

"Far-back booth," Packard says, as if in a trance.

"We're not open."

I spot Ling, beelining across from the kitchen. I wave. "Friends," she says. "I got it."

"You'd better show up," he whispers.

I smile. "I'll move the moon if I have to."

Chapter Fourteen

It's a Midcity miracle that it takes me just under an hour to sneak into Shelby's apartment with her, shower the Tanglelands tea off myself, get my long hair half dry and teased and into barrettes so that it looks fussed over, change back into my yellow dress, and speed across town behind Max to show up, breathlessly, in the penthouse foyer.

Otto comes out, kingly as ever in his black dinner jacket. Kingly and impatient. "Where were you?"

"Shelby's," I say. Do I sound too insistent? Too defensive? I look into his eyes, trying to keep my face and mind relaxed.

"All this time on your hair?" He doesn't look convinced, and really, my hair looks like crap. As any woman knows, it's not unusual for hair to look worse after several hours of fussing than when you just flop it up into a binder, but Otto doesn't know that.

"Day o' failed hairdo experiments," I say.

"Are you ready now? Are we ready to go?"

I hold my hands open, a gesture that says, *Yeah, can't you tell?*

He stabs the elevator button. *Where were you?* Why ask that? He knew I was at Shelby's. What if Max went up to Shelby's while we were gone?"

As we step into the elevator, he exchanges glances with Norman the mercenary elevator operator. Okay, something's wrong—I have this intuition that they've had a conversation about me. Norman turns the key. Is this amount of silence weird? It seems so.

"Needless to say," I blather, "I think I won't be using Shelby as my stylist tomorrow after all." I go on to prattle about hairdos.

By the time we're stepping into the lobby, I'm running mental clips of every mafia undercover movie I've ever seen, all those tense scenes where the cop goes around with the murderous mafiosos, sometimes wearing a wire, never entirely sure if they're onto him.

Otto takes my hand and speeds his pace. Why is he in such a hurry? Is he acting weird? "I think you'll be quite surprised by what you find in there," Otto says.

My heart jolts, like an electric shock went through it. What will I find in there? We approach the door. The limo waits just outside.

With a lurch I picture Packard's severed head on the seat. It couldn't be—I just saw him. The world turns fuzzy, and I'm not sure how I'm still walking—my legs feel like concrete.

"What is it that I'll find?" I ask.

"A surprise," Otto says. "If I tell you the surprise, that ruins it, doesn't it?"

Sammy the doorman holds the door for us.

"Hold on." I stop and look in the lobby mirror, pretending to do something to my hair with one hand while Otto pulls gently on the other. "Can't that wait? We're late."

Definitely impatient.

Heart pounding, I yank my hand out of his and stuff some hair into the barrette, glancing through the double doors and out to the sidewalk where Otto's driver, Smitty, waits next to the limo. He holds a bunch of white cloth. I imagine it clamped against my nose and mouth.

But he could have been wiping the windows. Except the cloth wouldn't look so pristinely white. But why chloroform me out here? Why not wait until I'm inside? That's not the most comforting thought, either. My mind goes again to Packard's severed head. My panic torques and rises.

"Justine," Otto places his fingers on the small of my back. "We're late, for God's sake. Your hair is fine." Gently he pushes.

I take a step. Another. I have to commit, or run. I decide to commit. "Okay," I mumble. I accompany Otto through the door, as if in a dream. I'm on the sidewalk with him. I can still run. I get a closer look at what Smitty's holding—it looks like a bunch of white-cloth shower caps. It could be chloroformed stuff, but it doesn't seem likely.

But what's the surprise? I close my eyes, try shaking myself out of it. *There is no actual sign you've been busted!* I tell myself. But I feel Otto's eyes on me.

I steel myself as Smitty pulls open the door.

And then I almost fall over. Everything inside the limo, or at least the back passenger area, is blindingly white. My mind pretzels up with stress and confusion. "You've redecorated the limo?"

Otto laughs. "In a manner of speaking. Come here." He holds out his arms like he wants to pick me up.

"What? You want to carry me over the threshold?"

"Come on."

Warily I go to him. He lifts my arm and places it around his neck, and then he hoists me up. Smitty puts white shower caps over my shoes.

"What are you doing?"

"Give him your purse," Otto says. "It's a known fact that women's shoes are every bit as filthy as the bottoms of their purses.

I hand it over and Smitty encloses it in a white thing and gives it back to me.

"What is this?"

"Don't let your feet touch the ground." Otto sets me down on the limo seat and I and I scoot over. He sits on the side of the seat and puts bonnets over his own shoes before sliding in. Smitty shuts the door.

"Oh my God." I run a finger over the plastic-covered walls, the new white upholstery. Even the floor mats are white. And there's a new vent in the back. "HEPA filter," I whisper.

"That's right," he says.

I widen my eyes, so relieved. Stunned. "You've made this entire back area into a clean room," I say. "This is a mobile clean room."

"That's right." He runs his hand along the white seat between us. "Bacteria-resistant upholstery imported from Japan. I know your dad's reluctant to travel, that it's a big deal for him, and I want him to feel comfortable. Do you think he'll like it?"

I'm speechless. His agitation, his pressuring me, all I could think all this time was *vicious killer*. But he just didn't want to show up late. Otto is a man—a groom—desperate to impress his future father-in-law.

I swallow a lump, feeling so horribly sad. This is the old Otto. It would be so much easier if he'd stayed scary.

A dark look. "You don't think he'll like it—I see it in your eyes. Do you feel he'll be insulted? Is that it?"

"No, he'll love it," I say. "He won't even have to think twice about wearing his hazmat suit or respirator in here. Wow."

"I had his room at the Midcity Arms done the same way," Otto says. "And the church is being cleaned extensively, though with it being a historic property, there is only so much I could do as far as installing—"

I put my finger over his lips. "It's thoughtful. Wonderful. It is a big deal for him to come, and you've made it so much better."

He takes my hand and kisses it, then lets go and leans back contentedly.

I give him a bit of mock anger: "And what's this about women's purses and shoes?"

"More bacteria than a dirty toilet seat, according to the consultant I worked with. Mostly from public restroom floors.

Apparently women put their purses down on the floors next to public toilets."

"Right," I say. "Yuck."

"The germs from your purse are contained, and with this filter, we could drive through a cloud of nerve agent and be protected. Kind of nice."

I place my bonneted purse on the seat across from us. It's not nice. It's insane.

Suddenly we're zooming around the curves of the Tangle. I clutch the handhold, surprised that such a long car can take the hairpin turns, merging at such high speeds, and I'm struck with the crazy contrast of it all: Packard and me and our friends, down there just yesterday, covered in sludge and grime, and now Otto and me riding up here in this sterilized, hyper-clean pod. And down below, there's truth, and up here, it's just one lie piled on another.

"One of these days," Otto grumbles darkly. He means, one of these days he'll get rid of the Tangle.

"Messed up as it is, Midcity's kind of known for it at this point, wouldn't you say? The Tangle's part of our heritage. Our mascot. We can't kill it." I think how it does seem alive sometimes.

"The Tangle's not something to be precious about, it's something to be erased. We should bulldoze and bury it. Forget it was ever there. Getting rid of this monstrosity would make for an impressive welcome mat to new businesses. Of course, I'm sure the Felix Five would find a reason to keep the Tangle. I'll bulldoze it all the same if I so choose."

We shoot off from the Tangle, heading west, leaving Midcity behind. "Good luck," I say.

He smiles his little bow of a smile, eyes calm. "You think I can't?"

Something in the way he says this stops me from the flip answer I was about to give.

He watches my face, like he's enjoying my discomfort. Or is that my paranoid imagination? "Don't underestimate your fiancé, Justine." He raises a finger. "And before I forget, look what La Patisserie sent over." He pulls out his phone and scrolls through his e-mail. "Mmm. We're nearly thirty minutes late." This, like it's my fault. Which it is.

"It'll be fine. Dad won't even notice."

"I hope not." Otto comes to what he's looking for. "Behold." He hands the phone to me. "Ten tiers."

With a silent sigh I look at the photo of our wedding cake, frosted and ready for tomorrow. It's a flourless chocolate cake with chocolate frosting, draped with a white filigree of frosting lace and flowers. "It's gorgeous," I say, trying for a happy tone. "I might have to devour it all on my own."

He gives me a smoldery look, lush smile playing on his lips, the kind that used to put butterflies in my stomach. Now I just feel tense. "I might have to devour *you* all on my own." He takes his phone from me, pockets it, and slides his hand over my thigh.

"Not here," I say, alarmed. "I mean, after you've done all this sanitizing?"

"He won't know."

"I can't. *We* can't." I push his hand off, frowning. "And it's disrespectful to his concerns."

"The threat of germs is all in his mind."

"How can you say that? How can you of all people say that? You hate when people doubt us about vein star."

"That's because there's basis to our fears, but there's no basis to his germ phobia. Germs help build immunities, and there's certainly no pandemic raging at the moment."

"When you fear something, that gives it more power. And it also makes it more powerful because of the negative visualization aspect, so that means he is more susceptible."

"Negative visualization. You only believe that when it's convenient," Otto says.

I cross my arms and sit back with a huff. "I'm not going to argue with you about negative visualization the day before our wedding." I like the way this small spat has taken the idea of sex out of the air. "I don't want people doubting each other, or being disrespectful in any way for our wedding. Everything has to be perfect and beautiful. Like a fairy tale."

He's silent a few beats too long. "Justine," he says finally, "that bridezilla bit may have worked on Max, but it doesn't work on me."

"Excuse me?" I say hotly.

"I know that's what you told Max. It simply won't work on me. You're not a bridezilla type." He watches me, head cocked. "What aren't you telling me?"

"What aren't I telling you?" I echo stupidly. I'm uncomfortably aware that I'm enclosed in a small pod with the most brilliant detective in Midcity history, a man who tends toward paranoia. And he thinks I'm hiding something, which I am. Still, I look at him like he's crazy.

"Please. You have a *tell* when you're holding something back. You make a certain face," he says. "A micro expression."

"A micro expression? Like what?"

"Now what fun would it be if you knew? Come now, my love."

I try to look neutral, but of course, it's too late. I have a micro expression. I scramble for something to say, recalling what Packard said, that deep down, most men are frightened of a bride—even the men who are keen to get married. I straighten up. "Okay, here's the thing. I have always dreamed of the day when I'd walk down the aisle toward the man that I love, wearing a beautiful, amazing, white princess dress, and a veil, with perfect hair and perfect everything. With a train trailing behind me. Pure white." His brows draw together just the tiniest bit. I press on. "I'm not a bridezilla. But do I want my wedding to be perfect? Of course I do! Every girl dreams of this day. You want to know if something is going on? Yes, our wedding is tomorrow and everything is going wrong. There's a curfew out, and dangerous cannibals roam the streets at night. I'm in hairstyle limbo, I have to rearrange the reception place settings, and one of my maids of honor will be wearing a chest full of straps and tattoos, a fur-trimmed cape, and a top hat." Never have I been so thankful for Simon's fashion sense.

His brows draw together more. "Doesn't the bride have some say in these matters?" he asks. "You don't want him up there dressed as some sort of circus ringmaster."

"Like an S&M circus ringmaster? No, I don't," I say. We discuss my taking the hat away from him and hiding it. Putting a button on the cape. Otto still seems suspicious. I continue on to my dinner-seating quandary. I'm feeling so tense, and I really am acting like a bridezilla.

"But more than anything, you're worried about *him*." He raises his brows. His knowing look. "Aren't you?"

My throat seizes up; I'm sure I look like a scared rabbit. And then I realize he's talking about my father. Or is he? I choose to assume he is. "Well, yes," I say. "Not just that he's going to be dressed more appropriately for a radioactive cleanup site than a wedding, but he's never been to Midcity. To him, it's like venturing into a dangerous wasteland. It helps, what you did with his room at the Arms." I swallow here—it's as good as any time to break this to him—"I'll try to have my room moved near to his."

He frowns. "What do you mean, your room?"

"At the Arms. Have you never heard it's bad luck for the bride and groom to spend the night together before the wedding?"

"You're not superstitious."

"I'm a bride, Otto. I don't want to jinx anything. This is what brides *do*. I'm staying at the Arms, and it'll be my base of operations for getting ready. Everything has to be storybook perfect."

He watches me with steady eyes. Does he sense the lie? My tension goes high and shrill, as does my voice. "Is it so wrong to want the next time you see me, after our dinner with Dad, to be the next day when Dad's walking me down the aisle? To have there be a little anticipation? I know I'm not the most regular girl in the world, but I still have certain things about my wedding fixed in my mind. I want it to be perfect!"

His smile has a hawkish quality to it. "You're not superstitious, and you're not into fairytales."

"Today I am." Heart pounding, I turn my face to the window, where run-down developments rise out of the muddy, snowy fields. And what the hell is my tell? "Excuse me if I want it to be perfect."

Nothing on the planet could make this wedding perfect. Then I get this new thought: I could be wearing tatters and standing in the Tanglelands in the midst of cannibal carnage, and things would be perfect if I were marrying Packard.

If I were marrying Packard. I get this sick feeling in my stomach, thinking of him out there, searching for the glasses with all those maniacs after him. So determined, and really, so vulnerable, though he doesn't think so. I only hope he stops when it's curfew; being out after curfew will make things worse. For him, getting caught means death, or at best, eternal imprisonment.

At a gas-station stop, Otto has Smitty buy him a water and a nonaspirin pain reliever. I watch him swallow three of them as we pull back out onto the road.

"You're only supposed to take one or two of those," I scold, trying to sound normal.

"It'll be fine."

"Not if you get liver failure." I don't ask if it's his head.

"I just need to relax the area. It'll be okay." *His head, then.*

"I couldn't even tell," I say, a compliment we sometimes pay each other. At times it can be a point of pride, how well we conceal our freak-outs.

"I can feel them, the force of their will. Railing against their walls."

His prisoners, I think. And just like that, the little bit of sympathy I felt over his headache drains away. I picture Helmut banging on the fun house window. Carter looking so small and drained. I know I should say something comforting like, *It's just the tension of the wedding. Just a stress headache.* But I don't. He's hurting my friends, and it's not wrong that he's suffering for it.

He bows his head, thumbs on his cheekbones, index fingers on his forehead. He stays like that for a long while. He expects me to put an arm around him, maybe rub his back. It would be smart if I did, but I keep thinking of Carter. Vesuvius. Helmut. Enrique. Packard's severed head. Avery dead on the rocks.

"It hurts, Justine."

My silence is getting weird. Grudgingly I hover a hand over his back, and finally force myself to settle it onto him. "I know."

"I feel them more strongly than ever. They're clambering to get out, as if they're physically inside my head. They don't want to be in there, and they never leave me alone. I can't remember the last time I felt peace." A silence, then, "Maybe I never have." He rubs his forehead. "I'll be relieved when tomorrow is over and we can start our life."

I should say something, but I just stare at the top of his beret. I'll be relieved when tomorrow's over too. Unless I end up having to marry him. In spite of how Packard feels, if we can't get the glasses, I *am* going to see this through. An agent on the inside is the best hope for our friends getting free. And if Packard weren't so biased, he'd agree too. He makes a fabulous rebel leader, but he too has blind spots.

"All that tension is getting constrictive, don't you think?" he asks. Meaning, constricting veins in his head.

"Possibly," I say. "We don't know."

He turns to me. I know what he's going to ask, and it sours my stomach. "Will you…"

"Of course." I pat my thigh.

He takes off his beret and settles his head on my lap, eyes closed. I place my fingers over his dark, curly hair and rub in light circles. It's strange, having Otto so trusting and vulnerable to me, like a baby in my lap. Except he's not vulnerable at all, thanks to his personal force field. Hell, even if I wanted to kill him, and had a knife in my hand poised to stab through his eye, I couldn't. Would it even break the eyelid skin? Yet he's suffering horribly. I grit my teeth, hating that I'm comforting him. Even the gentleness with which I rub seems like a lie, like he should be able to feel the anger and revulsion bleeding out of my fingertips.

When did he create his personal field? Was he thinking about me when he did it? Or was it in response to Fawna's prediction? And if so, could developing an awesome new power like that be enough to change the currents of fate?

His eyelids twitch once, twice. Again. There's almost a rhythm to it. I continue with my soothing and hate-loaded massage circles. Then I think of Packard's severed head and I lift my hands up and off Otto's head. I've lost my will even to be fake-kind.

He sits up, brown eyes glittering darkly. "Thank you."

"Sure," I say, feeling nervous about my tell.

He turns his attention out the window, to the frozen fields rushing by. We pass a billboard for a burger joint. A billboard for a skating rink. His silence makes me nervous.

"What thoughts, my love?" I ask. Usually his line.

"Everything," he growls.

"Everything?"

"And I am going to get rid of the Tangle," he says. "I've just decided."

"Otto, seriously, you and every mayor for the last ten years has wanted to knock it down."

He turns to me. "The difference is, I really will."

"People will resist."

"Of course people will resist. It's what people do." He turns to me, seems to look right through me. "People resist what they think they can't live with, but in the end, they come to live with it, even embrace it."

I nod and turn my head away. He's right, of course. Horrifyingly right.

Chapter Fifteen

The best way to describe my father's house is to say that it looks like an old shack that's been buried up to its eyeball-windows, with a fringe of bangs made by a thatched roof. And right next to it stands a big, sturdy structure that looks like a concrete bunker with a garage door on it.

And that's exactly what it is.

And if you'd spent your late-teen years there, as I did, you would know that plague-stricken intruders could break the shack's windows or hack in through the thatched roof and not have a prayer of getting at the safe family in the living quarters that stretch far beneath the earth.

"Don't make a movement to shake his hand unless he offers first," I remind Otto. "He'll offer if he has his gloves on. And don't stare at his outfit. I'll warn you now, he always wears jumpers. Like he's on a 1950s race-car pit crew."

I haven't seen Dad since Christmas, three months ago, for a sad, little TV-dinner celebration. He gave me some awesome computer programs he'd developed, and a hot-pink stethoscope he'd ordered from Singapore. I gave him beautiful boots and an e-reader, and these polyvinyl gloves I had made. They're really thin, and they're dyed to the color of his skin, so that when he shakes hands with somebody, they almost can't tell he's wearing gloves.

Smitty stops the limo in front of the garage. I pull the bonnets off my pumps as the big steel door lurches and lifts, revealing my dad's brown boots, and then his gray zip-up jumper.

And then his smiling face.

I'm more relieved than usual to see him. "Dad!"

"Justine McBean!" My dad has had a bald head ever since I can remember—a pleasing, well-shaped bald head. His brown eyes are crinkly and warm, his ears stick out, and he gets two long, horizontal furrows in his forehead when he smiles, which he's doing now.

He grasps my hand—he has the gloves on—and I half hug him, clothes to clothes.

Otto strolls up. "Mister Jones," he says.

"Call me Carl." Dad grasps Otto's hands with both of his. "Wonderful to finally meet you. I've heard so much about you."

"Likewise," Otto says. "All good."

My dad waves this off. He probably can't imagine my speaking fondly of him. True, there was a time, back in my early twenties, when I railed against him and rejected him quite bitterly. I'm much more understanding about him now, but deep down, I haven't exactly forgiven him for not believing Mom was ill when she said she was ill, and also for being such a freak about germs, and moving us out here after Ben Foley ripped us off. And I suppose there are times I feel angry he never worked up the gumption to visit his own daughter in Midcity all these years; he never even got to see my little apartment. He only goes into Hobart, the neighboring town, where he wears a mask or respirator, depending on his level of germ anxiety. And most of all, I guess I'm angry he can't be like other dads—that he can't just be *normal*. I know that's unfair of me. I'm just as challenged in the normal department as he is.

I suppose you're never quite fair to your family. And I love him anyway.

"Can you stay a minute or two?" he asks. "I've made iced tea. Your driver can join us."

"We'd love to," I say.

Otto nods. "Sounds good. And don't worry about Smitty. He enjoys a chance to game."

We go into the garage, walking between the armored Jeep and the ATV, toward the wall of locked steel cabinets, which I happen to know are full of firearms. I've told Dad that he shouldn't bother hiding the guns and things that might be displayed—his future son-in-law isn't going to arrest him for gun infractions—but he shouldn't go out of his way to open gun cabinets.

In the corner hangs the hazmat exoskeleton, looking like a modern-day suit of armor. The lighter biohazard suits are down below, but the hazmat exoskeleton weighs a good seventy pounds; it's not the kind of thing you want to run up the steps in. Otto goes right to it. "Is this what I think it is?"

My dad smiles. "If you think it's an ambulatory bulletproof biosphere, then yes."

Otto touches it, asks about the material, and Dad explains how the galvanized titanium plates connect, with titanium mesh at the joints. He points out the retractable tree-climbing spikes for the boot-and-hand parts. He tells how he constructed the armor over a standard hazmat suit, and engineered the self-cooling capabilities, and shows Otto the respirator, which fits over your head. It looks like an astronaut's helmet, complete with a glass window to peer out of. Level-four protection with an air exchange. No self-respecting paranoid recluse would settle for anything less.

Otto asks all kinds of questions about battlefield applications of the suit, and its potential use during chemical attack. "This is fantastic," he says at one point. "I wonder how hard it would be to manufacture these on a mass scale."

Seriously?

I turn a baffled gaze to Otto. To my dad. To Otto.

We head into the shack, which is an indoor sprouting and hydroponic operation. Dad loves plants; he'd have been an excellent farmer if he didn't fear dirt so much. Mom planted outdoor gardens every year while we were growing up in the suburbs, and Dad helped with them when he could. Indoor gardens, however, have become his forte.

Before I can stop him, he opens the latch in the low ceiling. Down comes the panel and the small ladder that takes you up the chimney, which is actually a machine-gun turret. I give Dad a look. The machine-gun turret qualifies as hidden and not quite legal, but Otto is impressed.

I feel grateful that I'd prepared Otto ahead of time for some degree of firearms infractions. "It's all defensive," I'd explained to him over coffee last week. "When you're worried about pandemic-level outbreaks, your enemies aren't just germs, but people carrying germs who overrun the countryside looking for shelter, food, and, you know..." I'd shrugged, attempting to keep it all sounding breezy, and not a big deal, "... escape from the crazed hordes. Stuff like that. Plague defense all through history had a military component."

After Otto and Dad tear themselves away from the turret, we go down the stairwell, which, like a normal family's staircase, is lined with family photos. These are mostly of my brother, Jimmy, and me. Otto examines each one, remarking frequently on my adorableness, though in truth, I was an unkempt child, a pimply, teen.

We stop for the longest time when we get to the picture of my mother. "You look just like her," Otto says.

Dad puts a hand on my shoulder. It's our favorite picture of her, taken in the yard of our old house. She's dressed for a party. She forced Dad to be social, to push through his germ phobia. Her hypochondria had nothing to do with germs, of course. You don't get vein-star blowout from germs.

She died of it a year after the photo was taken.

Dad shows Otto the TV room, the periscope ports, the pantry that holds six months of dehydrated food, and the cloak room, which is a euphemism for the place where there are more hazmat and bio-agent-resistant suits, plus a selection of firearms, though I'm happy to see that he's thrown a wool blanket over the grenade-and-sonic-weaponry shelf.

I want to groan when Otto stops in front of the antibacterial spray booth. I remind everyone of the time. "Don't you have tea, Dad? Are you packed?"

"What is this? A shower stall?" Otto asks.

"As a matter of fact, no," Dad begins.

And with that we're there for another ten minutes, and of course Dad wants to give Otto a demo, and Otto is happy to have his clothes, skin, and hair misted with antibacterial vapors.

And then it hits me: *I'm engaged to marry my father.*

My father goes to crazy extremes to defend against tiny germs and organisms, and Otto goes to crazy extremes to guard against larger threats—antihighcap glasses, criminals, sleepwalking zombies, my own free will. Hell, he's even fighting the currents of fate as predicted by Fawna, and apparently, he has more battles in mind.

"None for you?" Dad asks while Otto's closed up in the booth.

"No thanks," I snap, channeling my angry teenager. "I checked the weather and there's no plague forecasted for today."

"Just thought I'd offer, honey."

God, what's wrong with me? "Ignore me," I say. "I'm just stressed."

Dad lowers his voice. "He's a good man."

I look away. We can't have this conversation.

"Is it the turret?"

I shake my head. "Drop it."

"Wow," Otto says, coming out. "That'll hold me for a while, I'd imagine."

I tell Dad how Otto made the entire back of the limo into a mobile clean room. Dad is touched, I can tell. Otto adds that the hotel room got the same treatment, and Dad is in love.

I've always imagined bringing a great guy home to Dad, and having him feel proud of me, and the three of us bonding. This is a perversion of that. We're bonding, but it's all bad.

After Otto tests the periscope and views the computer room, we head up to the kitchen and sit around the little table. Dad has used a tablecloth, something he is typically against on the grounds that tablecloths are unwipable.

"It's cheery here during the day," I say, pointing up at the skylight tube. "You get a good amount of natural light through there."

We sip mint tea from tall glasses.

"Wait until you see Otto's garden." I tell him about the night flowers, and the domed roof. Suddenly Otto has to make a call. "Mayor stuff," he explains. Dad walks him back up top, where he'll get better reception.

I smile suspiciously when he returns without Otto. The best reception is down below; Dad made sure of that. "Why'd you make him go all the way up there?"

"You may be fooling your fiancé," he says, "but you're not fooling me."

"What? They're jitters. No big deal."

"Your old dad isn't stupid. You're full of dread and it's not wedding jitters. It's him."

"That's silly."

"What's up?"

I look in the direction of the stairs. "Nothing's *up*," I say. "Nothing you have to think about."

"Do you love him?"

I can't bring myself to say that I do. "It's nothing to do with that."

He nods, as though he expected this answer. "I haven't been the model father," Dad says. "I taught you all the wrong lessons, none of the right ones. but you've grown into a beautiful, brave young woman in spite of me—"

"Don't," I protest.

He puts up a stern hand. "You've grown to be a beautiful, brave, successful woman and you're getting married and you're worried about his reaction to me. I know that's it. He's a good man for acting impressed."

"Believe me, that wasn't an act, and my being jittery has nothing to do with you."

"You're telling me you haven't been the least bit worried about being married in front of all Midcity's elite and having your old pop giving you away while wearing biohaz gear?"

I smile. "That's not my worry at this point."

"I know that's why you bought me the gloves, so that I wouldn't embarrass you."

"Dad, I got you the gloves so things would be simpler for you."

"I want you to know that I won't be wearing a hazmat suit and respirator or even a surgical mask when I give you away."

I sit up, shocked. It's unthinkable.

"Justine, I want to step up for you. It's time I step up. While I may be covered in antibac and full of Fanarizin when I walk you down the aisle, I want you to know that I will look to the world like any normal father of the bride. I've been building up my immunities. I even visited Hobart in street clothes and no mask the other day."

A flop in my chest, like a trapped sob. It's huge what he's offered, what he's doing. I want not to be lying to him. And suddenly I want him to meet Packard. "That's such a gift." I put my hand over his, tears in my eyes. "I know what it takes."

"It's time for me to act like a father."

"You are amazing. That is amazing." I feel like such a jerk, putting him through all this for a fake wedding—one that, if it happens, could be violent.

"You're not ill, are you?"

"What? No, no—"

"Is it incurable? Are you going to level with your pop or do I have to ask Otto?"

"No! Okay." I get up and check the stairway, close the door. Take a breath. He deserves to know. And he's as good a happiness-faker as I am. "You have to pretend everything is normal. Not a word, got it?"

"What's going on?"

"I'm not marrying Otto." I sit beside him, speak in hushed tones. "It's this whole situation I'm playing along with. It's a *bad* situation, and I hate that you're even involved in it, and I hate lying, that's why I'm telling you. I need you to play along though, okay? Bring whatever gear you want, stay at the hotel, try to have a decent time. I don't care what you wear. I'm hoping this wedding doesn't even happen, but we have to plan for the worst—"

"The *worst*?" A flash of anger. "Are you okay? Are you under duress?"

"No. And he has no idea I'm not one hundred percent with him, so let's keep it that way."

"Why not just break up with him?"

"It's not so simple—this isn't just a quarrel or something, Dad. Otto isn't what he seems. He's a killer, and lots of people are in danger, and we're trying to help them. The best way to do that is from the inside. This thing has to be handled secretly and delicately. It's complicated, but he's holding people against their will…"

"My God, what are you doing in the middle of something like this?"

"Stopping him. Don't worry, we have a way to stop him, but it's not ready yet; so right now, we have to act like everything's normal."

"So we pretend it's going forward until this way to stop him is ready."

"Exactly."

Dad scowls in the direction of the stairway. "He's a man people trust. He's the mayor."

"A mayor who has done terrible things."

"I don't like you in this."

I give him a steely look. "I know I can count on you to act like everything's normal. And tomorrow night, if things haven't worked out, I'll figure out some excuse so you don't have to go to the church. Because, we have intelligence something big might happen there."

"If my girl is going to the church to play a thing out, the least I can do is go too. What will people think if the father of the bride isn't there?"

"Seriously—it could be a very dangerous place. And not from rogue strains of bacteria." I hear a sound and hold up a finger, opening the door to check the stairwell. Empty. I close it. "The ground may well run red, if you know what I mean. He has to be stopped, and it won't be easy, for reasons I can't go into."

"And I'll be there. I'll help."

"I can't drag you into this."

"I'm your father. Wild horses wouldn't keep me away."

"What about horses with head colds?"

He smiles. Crinkly brown eyes. "Even those."

"Seriously, Otto has a small militia, and they'll be present and probably armed. Possibly the only people who get weapons in." This last thought hadn't come to me before, and I don't like it. What if we never find the glasses? What if we can't stop him? What will happen to my imprisoned friends if I dump Otto at the altar? Where does it end?

"You think he's planning a mass hostage situation? You think he's capable of something like that?"

"I don't see what a mass hostage scenario gains him, but you'd be surprised at what he's capable of. I'm surprised."

"Well, honey, *you'd* be surprised at how much automatic weaponry a man can conceal inside a biohazard exoskeleton."

I smile. Is he joking?

He raises an eyebrow. "I do believe it's what all the best-dressed fathers of the bride are wearing."

Shivers run down my spine. "You're not joking."

"Hell no."

I smile wide, pleased with these new possibilities. "You're the best father of the bride ever."

"Can't say it's the wedding I imagined for my McBean. But if it comes to a showdown, I'll have your back."

I feel so relieved suddenly. Not just that my dad, a man who's been preparing all his life to fight armed hordes, will be wearing a gun-concealing, bulletproof suit to my wedding, but just that he's my ally in this. I suppose I have this idea that Dad is especially powerful in ways that others can't understand. Maybe all daughters secretly think that on some level.

Footsteps down the staircase.

He places his gloved hand over mine.

When Otto arrives, Dad announces he's going to finish packing. Ten minutes later, Otto and Smitty are heaving large, heavy cases into the limo's storage trunk. Otto pauses before he shuts it, staring down at Dad's silver case.

Why? Does he think it's odd that Dad brought so much? How much weaponry *did* Dad bring? The stare lasts too long. Is he thinking of opening the case? I feel a wave of alarm. No, he wouldn't.

He watches Dad get into the limo, assessing look on his face. I know that look. Things aren't adding up.

"God, I hope he didn't bring all kinds of backup oxygen," I say, hoping that might explain the weight. "The bellboys are going to be bummed."

"We're transporting oxygen?" Otto peers into the trunk. "That's not entirely safe."

I swallow. I just gave him an excuse to open it. "Hold on, I'll ask."

I stick my head in the door. "Are your cases heavy for a reason? It's not oxygen in there, right?"

Otto comes up beside me.

Dad grins. "Maybe it's the inversion boots with the inversion stand. And the water purifier. It might still have several gallons in there."

I smile scoldingly. "Dad!"

Otto goes around and bangs the trunk shut, and we join Dad in the back seat.

"Inversion boots?"

Dad has a big, long explanation about inversion boots, like he's trying to get Otto to buy a pair. He's fabulous. Cool as a cucumber. He goes on to question Otto on everything from police procedure to Midcity history, as a way to give me space to rest my mind. This also allows me to text Shelby: "Did you find the special bouquet?"

"No."

We stop to drop Dad's luggage with the bellboy at the Midcity Arms, and then we continue to the condo to dine. Dad dons a surgical mask and accompanies us past the knot of photographers out front and on through the lobby. I suspect, with his practice in Hobart, that he could have gone through without the mask, but it's probably a smart move, considering he'll be wearing the full freak-suit if the wedding happens tomorrow.

Kenzo comes out before dinner with a little speech about the origin, freshness and technique of cooking the steak, as well as the sanitizing of the vegetables, not to mention the entire penthouse. Dad even gets his silverware wrapped in plastic. I encourage Otto to tell some of his police stories; they're entertaining, and an excellent way to let Dad see that Otto is not somebody to be taken lightly. Otto is brave and powerful, even when he's being evil.

I keep my phone on vibrate in my dress pocket, longing for news. It's nearly nine. The curfew starts at ten. One more hour to chase down leads.

After dessert, Otto urges Dad to come out to the night garden.

"You'll never see flowers like this, Dad," I chime in.

Otto's phone rings. He pulls it out and scowls at it. What does that mean?

He waves us on ahead.

I hesitate: there's something about the way he scowled at that number I don't like. My stomach feels twisted up. How much more of this can I take?

Dad's watching me. "Shall we?"

"Yes," I say, leading the way out the door. The enclosed deck is cool and vast and dark. I suck in a deep breath.

Dad asks, "Are you okay?"

"Yeah," I say.

"Was there a problem with the cases I brought?"

"I think I'm overreading everything Otto does. Or maybe being paranoid. And you can tell? Crap."

"I can tell, but he doesn't seem to," he says. "He adores you."

"He reads micro-expressions that I don't even know I make."

"You're okay."

"*Micro-expressions,*" I say. We stroll deeper into the garden. I show him the hot tub and the outdoor dining room, and tell him how the top is removed in the summer.

"Regular palace," Dad observes quietly.

"Are you planting outdoors this summer?" I ask him.

"I may," he says. "The upcoming growing season's supposed to be the best in half a century.

"Oh yeah? Did you read that in the *Farmer's Almanac* or something?"

"Just something we've heard. John Rickert's bought double the soybean seeds. The Hensons are getting into tomatoes."

Neighbors. Names from the past. "And you've all gotten this special advanced forecast?"

"No..." He shrugs and looks away. "Sort of."

I smile, amused to see Dad's embarrassment. "This is something you *heard*?"

"Never mind," he says.

"What? Now I really want to know."

He waves his hand, as though it's silly. "I usually don't go in for this kind of thing, but there's a fortune teller walking the Old Arrowhead trail. Girl's been causing a stir up through the farms along the way with her predictions."

The air goes out of me. "A girl walking? A walking fortune teller?"

"Guess you could say that. Strange-looking duck. She predicted a tornado would demolish a dairy barn out in Wentworth, Iowa. Told the farmer the exact time of the collapse a good three days before it happened—in her own woo-woo way. The chime of eight and all that. But three days later, sure enough, a thunderstorm starts rolling in, with a tornado watch—not even a warning, mind you, but just a watch. Well, the fellow thought to move those animals, and sure enough, the barn went down. I was awfully surprised the fellow took heed, but it saved 'em a fortune. Rickert heard it at the feed store from a guy who heard it from his hauler..." Dad goes on to tell about the chain of information.

Could it be Fawna? "Have you met her?"

"Nah. Rickert knows a guy, knows a guy who caught up to her a week later—she told him he'd have a roundworm problem if he planted beets. Sure enough—"

"He sent soil samples to the lab," I say.

He nods. "And they confirmed it. Girl's pretty sure of herself, I'll give her that. Told one guy his field would flood come spring, and he says, *how do I prevent that?* And she says, *If your field is not a field. If a flood is not a flood.*"

"And she's heading east? A prognosticating girl who is heading east?"

He looks surprised. "You heard of her? All the way in Midcity? Though she must be somewhere north of Midcity if she kept walking the trail—could be nearing town."

"You think she's still walking the trail?"

"I'd imagine."

"Walking the trail?" Otto comes up, puts his arm around me. I nearly jump out of my skin. "Is that anything like walking the plank?"

Dad says, "There's this little girl been walking—"

"It's stupid," I cut him off. "It's a Bonnerville thing. A whole long story. This girl...but if you don't know the people involved. Just...hey—" I tug on Otto's lapel, giving him a sly look. "Otto, you have to show Dad your Vernal vinca before it closes its petals."

He regards me strangely. "It's hardly going to close its petals, Justine. Are you thinking of the Zentapha?"

"Right, yeah." Gently, I drag Otto. "I purposely didn't tell Dad the story of the Zentapha so you could."

Otto tells the story, which involves his going to heroic lengths to protect it from the cold during transit.

All the while, I silently marvel, and even freak out a little, over this amazing news. *Fawna is walking the Old Arrowhead trail.* This would explain why Otto's people couldn't find her on the roads or the bike path system.

Many major Native-American trails in the Midwest became wagon roads, and eventually streets, but the Old Arrowhead barely stayed a trail. It runs along a series of dried creeks and rocky outcrops, forming the border of a few farmers' fields, but you have to know what you're looking for to recognize it. As it nears Lake Michigan, it veers north of Midcity, running through suburban developments, where it's pretty much invisible, and then it goes south along the lakeshore for several miles. It's all quite obscure unless you belong to the set of rural or suburban kids who had maps of it from the Historical Society and got into hunting for ancient Indian-warrior arrowheads along it—a set that includes pretty much every kid I grew up with.

Digging for arrowheads was a major pastime for my brother and me—there was a good stretch of the old Arrowhead trail that was accessible to us by bike, and we actually did find a couple of real arrowheads over the years, but mostly the little boxes in our bedrooms grew full of triangular-shaped rocks that, when looked at in a certain way, could be explained as the beginnings of arrowheads, experimental arrowheads, or else arrowheads carved by warriors with poor carving skills.

The other sort of people likely to know the Old Arrowhead trail are those who own cropland or hunting land that it runs through, because you're forever chasing away kids, and grumbling about the little holes they dig.

"Don't you agree?" Otto's speaking to me.

"What?"

"Your father can ride in a limo to the church. He doesn't have to ride a horse."

Dad says, "I can ride if I have my gear on."

"Huh." Otto gives me a look. He knows I don't want Dad in biohazard gear for the wedding.

"I think that sounds good," I smile. "I'm proud of you, Dad, and I want you to be in the procession however you please."

It's true, I think. True and new. I'm proud of him.

Chapter Sixteen

It's like a déjà vu, blading along the Midcity River in the cold night, on the lookout for cannibals, criminals, and cruising cops. Avoiding streetlights for the cover of darkness. But this time, instead of heading to the Tangle, I'm skating toward the prosperous downtown by the lake. When I finally hit the lake path, I turn north, following the Old Arrowhead in the reverse direction that Fawna's supposedly walking it.

The lake path is a little too exposed for my tastes. I crouch and speed when I pass through lit areas, wind biting through my face mask. The fear has built back inside me, an icy hand in my heart. It was so nice those few hours when it was gone, it almost makes me want to cry.

Back in his heavily vented Midcity Arms hotel room, Dad and I had pulled out a map and made a few calls to his gossipy farmer friends, plotting Fawna's known points. We figured out she travels about fifteen miles a day. Apparently, she has a warm sleeping bag, and finds refuge at night in barns and outbuilding ruins, though she's often gone when people go to find her. We'd identified St. Peter's Prairie, a near northern suburb with a strip mall and a industrial park, as Fawna's most likely stopping area tonight.

She'd said in the e-mail that she was bringing Otto the coon hand, that childhood good-luck charm he'd made. Is the coon hand a wedding present? I feel certain she's timing her trek to end at our wedding; it makes sense when you look at her path and progress, and it makes sense on a gut level too. She's Otto's only family, in a sense—his foster sister from way back. Traveling to attend weddings is what out-of-town family does. And big things will happen there.

Unless we can prevent it.

Of course, the Old Arrowhead was erased by the city, but if she continues along the ghost of the path, it takes her within a block of our wedding on our wedding day. Tomorrow.

I aim to find her before that—I have so many questions. I want to know what Otto's planning, and how to avoid the ground running red. Will finding the glasses prevent the ground from running red, or cause it?

Before I left Dad, I got ahold of Shelby. She informed me that they still had not located the glasses—*still not found the special bouquet,* as she put it, but that *there are flower shops open tomorrow.* One flower shop she calls *promising, just outside town.*

Promising, coming from Shelby, is practically a guarantee of success, considering she usually looks at everything in such a negative light. She also let me know they stopped off for an *old-fashioned dinner,* the whole group of them, before going home. I take that to mean they all went to Mongolian Delites, including Packard. I told her that I hope everyone is *minding the curfew.* I'm talking about Packard of course. Shelby told me that *everyone* plans to mind the curfew.

Right before I set off from the hotel, I thought to inspect my skates. Sure enough, underneath the cushion inserts of the right skate, there was a tracker. I pulled it off and threw it disdainfully on the floor, like it was some insignificant piece of trash, though in truth it quite upset me; and I checked the rest of my clothes thoroughly, vowing never to be tracked again.

I pass the port, the northern city limits, and then veer left when I hit the stone crick that marks the inland turn of the Arrowhead Trail. It's not hard to cover several miles on rollerblades in summer, but winter after a snowfall is a different situation. My winter-modified cleatskates grip the icy sidewalks pretty well, but where the snow is piled, I have to trudge.

Finally, I reach the desolate commercial stretch of St. Peter's Prairie. I loop around, checking the scrabbly spaces between buildings, thankful I'm in a suburb where the curfew isn't rigidly enforced. I'm trying to think where I'd stop if I were her; not easy since I know nothing about Fawna, except that she's a weird girl, all alone, and she can see into the future. She's a few years younger than me—twenty-seven, Packard once guessed. And what's her state of mind? Is she angry? Scared? Does she see herself as running away from something or toward something? Nobody has seen her for twenty years, not since she was kidnapped by the Goyces, taken from the boarded-up ruins of Riverside School where she lived with Otto and Packard and the others. Did she really end up in a lab as the rumors suggest? Did the lab keep her prisoner all this time? Is that why we're only hearing of her now?

After an hour, I widen my search area. Since people tend to the familiar, I look out for old cinder-block buildings that seem schoolish. Up and down dark streets I skate, cold and exhausted.

And then it hits me—she would go to the familiar, yes, but it wouldn't be a place *like* the old elementary school, it would *be* the old school. She'd do what anybody returning to their hometown does: she'd go home!

The school is long gone, but I still think that's where she'd go. Back before she was kidnapped, she and Otto and Packard and their little friends had built a decent life there, wild and on their own. It was only after she and the other kids started getting kidnapped that things got grim, and twelve-year-old Packard persuaded eleven-year-old Otto to use his powers to suck the Goyces into the wall. Packard promised Otto he'd take the Goyces to jail, that they'd be given justice, but Packard was lying. And all hell broke loose when Otto discovered the Goyces' bones encased in the crumbling cinder blocks, and realized he'd buried seven men alive. Otto was shaken to the soul, in fact—that's what started the battle between him and Packard. Their fight that day leveled the school. And they're fighting still.

241

It's after one-thirty when I reach the quiet five-story condo building that sits on the old school site. A few lights shine from the upper windows, and in the entrance you can see a doorman behind a desk. I sneak around back to the dark picnic area, avoiding picnic tables.

A walk winds along the shadowy grounds, past a bike rack that holds one ruined, ice-encrusted bike; it continues down to the Midcity River bike trail.

Right at the river's edge, I spot a lone figure on a bench under one of the old-style lamps that line the river. The person faces away from me. Small in stature, all bundled up.

Fawna.

My wheels rattle on the pebbled surface as I approach, but she doesn't move. I go around, and stop; we're eye to eye, or rather eye to eyelid. She's sleeping.

Closed eyelids are practically all I see of her, plus bits of blonde hair sticking out willy-nilly from under her green face mask and scarf. She wears a hodgepodge of layers, but these aren't any normal winter layers—they're weird and vaguely punk rock or postapocalyptic, except instead of being draped with chains and furs, she's draped with bright things. A profusion of colorful ribbons, shiny stuff, and bright fabric shreds hang off her clothes; there are even small toys woven or somehow sewn into the fabric—doll parts and bright plastic dinosaurs. Stuff she picked up on the trail? Pelts of sequined fabric hang from her shoulders like overgrown lapels, and a plastic baggy clumsily stitched onto her sleeve holds two shiny rocks and a marble. A small backpack, equally decorated, sits by her side on the bench.

She's like a feral girl-animal, and I can't stop staring at her. If there was a time to wake a person up, it would be now, but it seems rude.

"Hello, Justine," she says, startling me out of my wits. She opens her eyes—they're big and gray and pretty, and she seems to look right through me.

"Hi," I say.

"Take a load off."

"Oh. Okay." I sit. *Take a load off.* I'm surprised, because it's sort of a normal, albeit outdated, thing to say. "Thanks."

"Well?"

"So you must be Fawna."

She just stares at me, two gray eyes in a green mask.

"I like your outfit," I say.

Her lips are small bumps under the fabric of her face mask. "Right. Liar. I might be done with you already."

"It's not a lie. I like it," I protest, but that's not precisely true. "Well, I like its wild weirdness, but I guess I would never wear it."

She fingers a yellow, plastic flower that's stuck onto her jacket near her shoulder. "Ask your question."

"So, I've heard the ground will run red tomorrow."

"That's not a question."

"Oh, right." I can't think of questions, only requests: *Tell me what will happen. Tell me what to do. Tell me how to save the people I love. Tell me how to not be full of fear.*

I gaze across the river at the Tangle; its higher interchanges, the ones that let cars bypass Midcity, are still open during curfew and cars stream around and around them like fireflies in the dark. "Okay, will the ground run red?"

"I have already seen that. I have already revealed that. Why do you people want me to reveal things twice?"

"I don't know," I say. "Okay, do you have any advice for me?"

"Yeah. I'll tell you the future. My advice is to walk away before I do it."

"I can't."

She says, "I know."

"What kind of advice is that, if you know I can't do it?"

"The kind you asked me for," she whispers. "If you don't have a question, I'm going back to sleep. Big day tomorrow."

"No, wait. Okay, what will happen tomorrow?"

"A question. Alert the marching band." Fawna pulls off her face mask; she's pale and pretty in a delicate, almost frail way, like glass filigree. Her nose is red from the cold, and her pale hair is still trapped in the scarf, making a poof around her ears. She sniffles, staring across the river at the Tangle. "You will fight Henji. You will win. The sun will shine upon your friends again."

Henji. That's what they used to call Otto. "My friends will be free?"

"I see the sun shining upon their heads."

"But that could mean that they're standing inside a prison, with sun coming in a window."

She glares at me. "They are *outside,* with the sun on their heads. Free."

"Okay! Sorry. It's not like you're talking plain."

"That's how I style my prognostication talk. I'm telling you the picture. If you don't like it—"

"No, no, I like it."

She watches me suspiciously, like she doesn't believe I like it.

"It's good. What else? Was there something else?"

"I see Sterling Packard growing old."

"Also with the sun on his head?"

"Yes."

"Good! So, if I go to the wedding and fight Otto—Henji, that is—Packard gets to live to old age, and my friends go free."

She looks annoyed that I'm asking her to repeat herself.

"Okay." My heart pounds. "So, that's good. It sounds positive. Wait, what happens to Otto? You said the ground runs red. Is it his blood?"

"His and yours."

"Mine?"

She gazes dolefully at the river. Dull flashes dancing on inky waves.

"I get hurt?"

"You die. You die with Henji."

I sit up as a cold blast of horror whooshes into me. "What?" The horror settles deep into my bones, heavy as lead. "No," I whisper.

"Sorry."

"No, Fawna. I can't."

She's silent. It's not a question.

"Are you sure?" I ask. "Tomorrow?"

"Technically today."

Right. It's after 2 a.m. My wedding day. My chest flutters like mad. "I don't want to die. I don't even want Otto to die. I just wanted him stopped from what he's doing."

"Well…" she shrugs. *Shrugs.*

"What? So we die? Just like that?"

"Wait." She turns her gaze up to the Tangle. Then, "I see another possibility. Another possibility now opens. Made most likely by my telling you the future. It's another opening."

"Really?" My heart leaps. Another possibility has opened. "What is it?"

"You do not fight Henji at the wedding. He is safe at the wedding."

"Oh, right. I can do that. I can *not* fight him at the wedding. That would get me out of death?"

"Yes."

"Good." Somehow it seems too easy. "Okay, what else happens if I don't fight him at the wedding?"

"Sterling Packard dies."

"Packard dies?"

"If you don't fight Henji at the wedding, Packard dies."

"But if I *do* fight Henji at the wedding, I die, right?"

Her face draws tight with annoyance.

"Excuse me if I want to get these crucial details straight."

"You have them straight. You just don't like them."

"Well...don't you see another way?"

"There are two ways only."

"There has to be another way."

"No, Justine, there *doesn't* have to be another way. You fight Henji at the wedding or you don't fight Henji at the wedding. There's no third possibility."

"I won't accept it."

"I don't like it either, Justine." The Tangle hums in the distance.

A frenetic flutter in my chest. "I don't want to die."

Fawna's silent.

"What about nothing being set in stone? What about free will?"

She turns to me, lips twisted tight under her pretty nose. "Free will? You don't know *anything* about free will. You have two choices. That's a luxury!" She says this urgently. "Some people don't get any choices. You think you're so special that you can't die? You think Sterling Packard is so special that he can't die? Nobody's special. It's just how it is."

I feel sick. Tears fill my eyes. "I'm scared to die."

"I know." She gazes back across the river. "That's what will keep you from fighting Henji."

"No! I have to fight him. Or else it will be Packard's blood."

"Yes."

"No way. There has to be an alternative. Packard and I, we can't just never"— *be together.* I don't bother to finish the sentence.

"Look out there. Look at the highway interchange. Do you see it?"

"The Tangle? Yes, I see the *Tangle*," I snap, sensing a no-win exchange.

"Can you change it? Can you change what you see there?"

"I can if I close my eyes," I say, "or, if I look the other way. Or blur my eyes."

"That's how you would avoid seeing it, but it doesn't change what's out there. It doesn't change what's contained in this moment. The wheels are already turning. Three plus one is already four. You can no more change these outcomes than you can change what's contained in this very moment."

"And that's it."

"Yes."

I give her a hard look. "You can always change the future, because it hasn't happened yet. Everybody knows that."

"From where I'm sitting, it's already happened and it goes one of two ways. These things have already happened." She closes her eyes.

"Nothing's written in stone," I say.

"Actually, lots of things are written in stone."

"Tell me how to change it." Silence. "You changed it by telling me the future. You opened another possibility and made it more likely I won't fight."

"Maybe I was always going to tell you."

"Right...but..." My mind spins in circles as she pulls her face mask back down over her head. The eye holes don't land in the right spot, so that all I can see is rosy cheek flesh showing through; she might as well have a giant sock on her head. She crosses her arms and hunkers down. Closed for business.

I have this impulse to grab her and shake her, tell her that it's not fair.

Her breath steadies.

"I'm in love. Packard and I just found our way back to each other."

Nothing. On her sleeve, a little mass of crystal beads that was probably once an earring flashes. A lump forms in my chest.

After a while, I get up from the bench and skate down the river path.

Nobody's special. Everybody dies.

In my mind I search for ways that she's insane, or wrong. But I keep coming up against her legacy of successful predictions; Dad and I learned of even more while calling around.

I skate on, scoffing, bargaining, railing. I decide I don't believe it. *You can no more change these outcomes than you can change what is contained in this very moment,* she'd said. I ponder *what is contained in this very moment.* I focus on the word *contained,* like there's some secret key there. Can I change what is contained in a moment?

I pass the Midcity Bridge and head into the neighborhoods, pushing my legs against the hard surface, muscle against inertia, like if I skate hard and fast enough, I'll outrun the fate she's seen. The feel of my quads working, even hurting, is a strange comfort.

I can't die. *I can't.* I run through the options. What if I call off the ceremony? What if I tell Packard and we escape together? Or I skate to the condo and confront Otto, or tie him up? But all those options feature my not going to the ceremony, and not fighting Otto. If I don't go to the ceremony and fight Otto, Packard dies.

I can't let Packard die. I can't imagine choosing a world without him. There's just no question.

I must fight Otto at the wedding. I must die.

Decision made.

Tears blur my eyes, and my thoughts whirl in trapped circles, a merry-go-round of grim options.

The idea of fighting Otto at the ceremony suggests that's when they deliver the antihighcap glasses to me—the plan was to fight him whenever I got the glasses. I wish I'd asked about that. But does it matter? I just have to go forward with it. I skate toward Mongolian Delites. My stomach feels like it's full of helium. My old friend, fear. I am going to die.

Screw her—I'll fight to win! I decide this as I pass the next block. Nothing's new here. There was always a risk. And nothing is written in stone. I find myself wishing I'd told Fawna that somebody could drop a bomb on the Tangle—that would change her view, wouldn't it? That would change what's contained in her stupid moment.

Everything familiar looks new. The night air is fresh and cool. The shadows on the building create a magical contrast. If Fawna is right, then this will be the last time I see this street. The last night I see the moon. The last night of my life.

How would I die? Probably blood loss. I'm thinking a bullet to the head, especially if I die *with* Otto, because dying with Otto suggests quick death, and most body wounds are somewhat treatable. I try in vain to stop myself from imagining a bullet cracking through my skull, from deciding it would feel like a hard strike from a tire iron. Would the bullet pass through or lodge in? I imagine the alarming feeling of blood, cascading through my brain. The awful warmth and gurgling I've imagined thousands of times. Except it would be real. Panic thickens in my throat.

This life. My hands. My friends. Packard. My dead body in a cold metal box in the morgue.

I pass a shuttered pasta joint. *Last meal.*

Tears stream down my face and angrily I scrub them off. *Screw it!* I'll fight and I'll win!

Do you think you're so special that you cannot die?

Not tomorrow, I won't. I careen on toward Mongolian Delites.

I love you so fucking much, he told me he'd said. The moment of his saying that to me is lost forever from my memory. What did he look like as he said it? *I love you so fucking much*, I whisper back to him. *So fucking much.*

My pulse pounds so fiercely, I think it might explode out my neck. Who said there's nothing to fear but fear itself? The fear grows like crazy, destabilizing me as I make my way toward the Mongolian Delites neighborhood. I've never stoked up so

Carolyn Crane

much fear in my life. Death is closer, more real than it ever has been. And I can't exactly zing it out now. I need everything I have to attack Otto. I have to make it good.

Then I have a truly horrifying thought—what if I just can't handle this much fear? What if she's right and I don't come through? What if I fall apart? Maybe that's why she said it was becoming more likely I would fail to fight Otto. My fear has made me fall apart before.

I think about something Helmut once said—back when he was a soldier, huddled with his fellow soldiers in the back of an air cargo plane shipping off to the first Iraq war, he told me that he'd known two kinds of fear. The first kind of fear was the fear of being killed in battle. The second kind of fear was in not knowing what kind of man he'd *be* in battle. He'd said that every soldier he knew worried that he'd be the one who falls apart, the one who runs away, instead of the one who bravely fights to the last.

Chapter Seventeen

I reach Mongolian Delites just before 3 a.m. and pause in front of the door, clutching the brass handle. My black mitten glows red from the CLOSED sign.

I have to be the one who fights bravely.

I'll control my fear enough to get to Otto. I'll put on the glasses and zing him, and I'll fight to win. And whatever happens, happens.

I trace the cool curve of the handle with my mitten tip, stomach aquiver, thinking about the olden days when the door was Otto's face, and time was unlimited. Back when I didn't know what it was like to love, and to be loved back.

The door moves toward me. I step aside as it opens. Packard stands inside, outlined by candlelight. His bright smile quickly fades. Of course he notices how much terror I've stoked. "What happened?"

I slip in and walk partway into the empty restaurant. Candles light the perimeter of the dining room, making the white tablecloths glow and the knickknacks on the walls shine. I hear him lock the door. He comes up behind me and pulls me into his arms, kisses the top of my head. "Talk to me."

I pull off my mittens and turn to him. "Just jacked up."

He smells like soap, and he's changed his clothes. Clean, green shirt, faded to nearly white in places, small buttons down the front, and his favorite old jeans. His worn and faded clothes contrast with his fierce energy, his flushed skin, his bright hair. He slides his hands down my arms, and, with intense concentration, he takes the time to fit his fingers in with mine, as though our hands are interlocking pieces that must be perfectly and minutely connected. And then he looks into my eyes, gaze steady.

Slow smile.

"We know where the glasses are," he says. "A storage locker out in Wild's Way. We'll drive out there tomorrow. Shelby's going to pose as Pinbocker's widow—we've got a guy working on identity and death certificates tonight, though we may bribe the operators. I'll take a look and see how to handle them." He'll use his powerful insight, of course. He can see a person's moral edge plain as their nose. "It doesn't open until two on Saturdays," he continues, "but the ceremony isn't until seven-thirty or so. We'll get to you before then. This is going to work, Justine!"

With a look of happiness that borders on silliness, he lowers himself slightly, coming down to my level to catch my gaze. "This is going to work. Once we have the glasses, you can zing him. We'll do a tag team." He squeezes my hands. "This is going to work! It's a little unorthodox, but if you fill him with all this fear you've stoked, and then Shelby and Simon give him grimness and recklessness, that'll destroy his will. He's wound so tightly right now, he's brittle. His breaking point is right there. So close. And the Felix Five are working on the official side of it. Once he's disillusioned, it'll be easy for them to grab the power back."

"You were looking at him? You shouldn't go anywhere near him!"

"I had to assess him." He brushes his thumb across my cheek. "Have you been crying?"

"Hazard of winter skating." I brush my other cheek.

"This will be over soon. And with the amount of fear you have right now? Devastating. I don't know what you've been doing—I didn't know you could stoke so high. You should be careful."

"I will."

"Once that force field goes down, we have him. I feel like we could even get a confession."

I try to picture the sunny outcome he imagines, just to pretend for a while.

"I only wish we knew what he was planning for the ceremony," Packard says. "I don't like not knowing this whole *something big* of his."

"It doesn't matter. It doesn't matter what he's got planned."

"Are you sure you're okay? Is your dad okay?" The tender way he looks at me hurts my heart.

"I'm fine!" I snap. "Just stop, you know, stop!" I turn and hobble away. *Stop loving me. Stop making me love you.* Because what if I fail? What if I'm the coward Fawna saw in her revised prediction? I pull my winter jacket and sweatshirt off and plop down on a chair to wrestle my skates off. My left skate won't come off.

Two brown work boots appear on the plush, patterned rug in front of me. "Let me." He kneels, takes my ankle in his strong, knuckly hand, and begins to undo the lace. "Something's different. What?"

"Don't do your thing on me right now."

"Don't look at you? Don't care? Don't want to help?"

All of the above, I want to say. Obviously I can't let him know what Fawna said. He'd keep me away from that wedding—probably lock me in the broom closet or something so that I couldn't fight Otto. He'd go himself to fight. To die.

"It's almost over," he says.

"I know," I say, voice steady. "It's just this whole thing."

He works at the laces. "A bit much, isn't it?"

I chuckle. *A bit much.* "Yeah," I sigh. "You know what would be nice? Instead of all this about the wedding tomorrow and glasses and zinging, I just wish we were normal for a day. I'd love it if we were sitting here trying to decide whether to go bowling tomorrow, or maybe lounge in bed with coffee and the newspaper instead. Or, thinking about going to a movie. And that was our only problem—what movie to see. We've never had a problem like that."

He loosens the flaps enclosing my foot. "How about if we do that the day after tomorrow?" He takes my ankle, gently pulls off the skate. "What movie should we go to?"

"No."

"Come on," he cajoles, "no movie at all?" He tosses the skate aside and starts on the other. "Everything will be over. Otto will be defeated, fully disillusioned, or almost there. He'll have freed our people, confessed. Henry Felix will be in charge. The curfew will be lifted. We'll be bored. A movie is a great idea."

"There's no movie I want to see."

"There's always a movie to see. We'll look online and find one and we'll go to it. And we'll have popcorn." He looks up at me slyly. "With lots of butter."

I don't answer.

"Or should we get it with no butter?" He waits for me to answer.

I love him so much, I have to look away. "Butter," I whisper.

"Butter then. And Milk Duds?"

Such a simple little thing. It rips up my heart.

"Milk Duds?" he asks again.

I shake my head. "This is stupid."

He has the other skate off. He's peeling off my sock. Damp toes cool in the air. "I hate missing the previews," he says.

Me too, I mouth.

"Where do you like to sit? Front? Middle? Back?"

"Don't."

"I always liked to sit in the back."

"Way back?"

"Very back row," he says. "Don't tell me you're a front sitter."

"Fourth row."

He looks incredulous.

"Your amazing gift doesn't tell you that?" I joke.

"You know it doesn't. And I'm glad, because I want to spend a lifetime finding out things like that." He wraps his warm fingers around my cold toes. "Fourth row. Then that's where we'll sit when we go to the movies. I decree it."

"Oh, you decree it, huh." Tears blur my vision. It's so like him. No compromise. No, *We'll sit in the middle.* Packard makes the big romantic gesture even in this.

He kneels in front of where I sit, rubbing my toes. "I knew you would come," he says. "I needed you to come, and here you are." He kisses my big toe.

His trust feels like a gift I don't quite deserve—what if I flake out? The more time I spend with him, the higher the stakes rise, the more frightened I am that I'll let him down, and the more likely that I will. If Fawna were to look at the future again, right now, would she see only the option where Packard dies?

I pull back from him, sitting straight. "This is stupid. We shouldn't do this. And I don't want to go to the movies anyway." I push back my chair and trudge off to the corner of the darkened bar area where I stop, staring at the empty nut bowl, thinking again about what Helmut said, about not knowing who you'll be under fire until you're there. It's human nature to struggle in the jaws of death, and I'm not just any human. What if my courage fails me when it comes time to zing Otto? It's not such a stretch, considering my level of fear now. I imagine myself passing out at the altar and they rush me to the hospital. Or I fumble with the eyeglasses so much, all crazed with shaking hands, that I can't put them on, and then somebody takes them from me and subdues me and I never get to fight Otto. Or I'm paralyzed at the church door, knowing I'll likely go in and never come out.

My stomach does a flip at the very thought of it.

I trace a circle in the crumb dust at the bottom of the nut bowl. Fear of fear has always been the worst for me. I have to get it under control. I have to get everything under control!

"Tell me," he says, warm breath on my ear.

"Fear of fear." I trace a larger circle in the nut bowl.

"It's not fear, it's power. Think of it as power."

"What if it's too much? Too overwhelming?"

"It's just another zing, Justine. You've done this a hundred times."

Not this, I think.

"Do you have a bad feeling about it? Because you should listen to your instincts—"

"It's not about instincts." I turn to him. "I just want to know, how did you do it? All these past months you stayed in Midcity when you could've been free and safe elsewhere. Or that day you climbed into Otto's penthouse like Robin Hood, knowing there were snipers around. And walking into the line of fire with the Brick Slinger. Especially that. What did you say to yourself, to make yourself do it? Didn't you ever worry you'd collapse into a frightened little ball?"

"Don't do this, Justine. I know what you're doing."

"I'm asking you to tell me. Weren't you ever scared? Scared of being...*less than*?"

He puts a hand on either side of my face. "All the time."

My entire being flares with something I can't name.

"After I hurt so many people with my mistakes back at the little school, and destroyed Otto—I *was* less than. I know how it feels—"

"You were just a boy—"

He presses a finger to my lips. "You can't change what it was to me, the idea that I'd let so many down. I didn't ever want to feel like that again, and it felt safer not to care. I used my power to control people. To control everything. I took what I wanted, and the hell with anyone. That was me, curling into a little ball. So, to answer your question, I have felt like it, and I have done it."

I think back on confident, charismatic Packard, the man I met at Mongolian Delites, the mastermind overlord. A man out only for himself. That was actually a man being safe. I've always imagined his living dangerously. I wonder if he's ever lived as dangerously as he is now.

"You found the strength to stand and fight for what's right. What did you say to yourself?"

"Mmm..." he smiles. "It's not quite so noble as that. Going to the penthouse that afternoon, I needed to see you again. It was stupid and reckless, but I wanted to see you and touch you. I didn't say anything to myself, I just did it. And the Brick Slinger, I couldn't let him get you, or Shelby or Jordan." He kisses me on the nose, on the cheek, the forehead, pulling me closer with each kiss, so that we're chest to chest. "There was no great bravery or nobility in it."

"Don't diminish it."

He puts his forehead to mine. "You're driven by a sense of justice. I just wanted you."

"That's not all it was."

"And you came back. I trusted you would, and you did."

I push him away, overwhelmed, wishing I could trust like that. I shouldn't have come. Seeing him tonight, it's already made everything harder. "This won't work." I back up. "I need to keep my wits about me."

His eyes seem a brighter green against his flushed cheeks. "Who needs wits?"

"Maybe I do." I back up some more and hit the wall.

"You don't need wits. You have good instincts." His voice is husky, and he looks at me with the forward focus of a predator. Or a lover. "Sexy, hot, wonderful, delectable instincts." He comes in closer.

"Oh, God—" I put up my hands to stop him, only to touch his shirt. I bunch up the fabric in my fists. "Goddammit."

He pulls my fists off him, clenching his hands around mine, then, slowly, he opens my right hand and kisses my palm, watching my eyes as he presses it against the paneling above my head. The surface feels cool and smooth against the back of my hand, and my stomach goes quivery.

He's near enough I feel the warmth of his ragged breath on my forehead. He turns to kiss my other palm, and pushes that hand to the wall above my head, so that both my hands are trapped. Then he kisses the silky slip of skin between my elbow and my armpit. Everything is spiraling out of control.

"You okay?" he grates.

I don't know if I'm okay.

He pulls away. "Justine?"

"Do it again. On the other side."

He kisses the tender part of my other arm now. I want him to kiss everywhere tender. I want to open up to him, and cast everything to the wind. To be as undone as my skate laces.

I go up on tiptoes to kiss him. The graze of his lips and the press of his cock make my belly go liquid. He lets go of my hands and slides his fingers down my arms, pushing his hard ridge between my legs, a keen deliciousness, even through my long underwear, jeans, and snow pants. I suck in his tongue, a substitute for his cock—not near enough, but delicious all the same.

I tangle my arms around his waist, needing to keep him pressing specifically in that spot. He's gone on to the buttons of my shirt, feverishly. Soon he's kissing my breast, sending a blunt wave of lust down through me.

"Justine, I want to discover every inch of you!" he says. He has gotten my shirt open and he kneels, nuzzling my bare tummy with his sandpapery face, pushing down my snowpants. I fist my hands in his hair and step out of them.

"Every single inch of you," he adds, enthusiastically. He looks up at me, holding my gaze as he fingers the top button of my fly. I watch him watch me. He snaps it open.

"You've already discovered every inch of me. You remember it just fine. I'm the one who can't remember." Air chills tender inches of bare tummy above the lace of my panties.

"Not really, because, you're not the woman I made love to that day. You're the woman who had that day stolen from her.

Who fought like hell to bust the revise. And this is the first time of forever."

I swallow. I have nothing to say to that.

He pushes down my pants, sliding his warm, rough fingers up and down my hips, like he's learning me.

I grab onto his hair and pull him up for a kiss. I want everything to last. It has to be enough to last. I stiffen up at this thought. God, what am I doing?

He feels my hesitation. "Fall into it. Trust us. *I* trust us," he says. "I trust us enough for both of us."

He trusts us. He believes I won't let him down; it's a gift, this trust of his. It's a gift he's never given anybody else. He's as bare and vulnerable as when he went after the Brick Slinger. I see that now.

"You're amazing," I say.

"Yeah, yeah, yeah." He kisses me, and I get this flash—this feeling memory—of being down in the Tangle and first realizing I'd been revised. I trusted, I jumped, fell into it. I found what I needed.

And it was glorious. Liberating. That's the feeling I have now as he nuzzles the top of my head, sways into me, almost like he's drunk. I move my hand to his cock, touching the outline of him, and he exhales forcefully.

I want him inside me so badly, I feel almost crazy. I move to unbutton his pants. He puts his hand down to help, but I move it away. I just want to do it on my own, to follow that feeling, to fall. His jeans slide easily over his hips; his blue briefs not so easily. I enjoy the silky heaviness of his cock in my hand, and the way his whole being tightens up when I tighten my grip. He nudges my face up, kisses me against warm wall. It's like I'm enclosed in a slice of heaven. It's so easy. Things are sometimes easy.

A crinkle. He's got a condom.

He stops kissing me, out of breath. I let go of him, let him put it on. "Aha, you planned all this," I joke breathily.

"Planned?" He looks up at me, eyes shining feverishly. "Of course."

"Oh, that's a good, good answer," I breathe, pulling him back for a kiss. "Good, good, good." I'm all nonsense. He kisses me, pushing his hands all over me, fingers hot between my legs, and my hands roam all over him—belly, shoulders, neck. His skin is warm. Sweaty in places.

He reaches down to my thigh, the back of my knee, and lifts my leg free of my pants, nuzzling and kissing me, and pushes the fat tip of his cock to my core, and I let my head tip back onto the wall, wanting to take him in, wanting everything.

He pushes into me, deeply, filling me. The world seems to stop in midair. Packard exhales. Packard not in control.

"Again," I say.

He pulls out and presses back into me, and then again, and I open my eyes and find his, and I watch him as he moves, as I move against him. It's like an underground wave is swelling between us, with every slow thrust, every kiss. Then he's out— he slides his hands around my butt and lifts me up.

"Hey!" I laugh as he turns and thumps me down on one of the sturdy Mongolian Delites tables. But he looks serious in the candlelight. He pushes things off it—candle holders and silverware crash to the floor.

I lay back onto the scratchy tablecloth, napkins and sugar packets in my hair, heaven all around me. His cheekbones shine with sweat; red curls around his forehead have grown moist and dark.

I wrap my legs around him. "Come here," I say.

He comes to me, one hand on my belly, one guiding his cock a little ways in. I gasp, wanting more. "Oooh," I say, coaxingly, smiling.

He goes still, watching me, with all his love and trust bared, it seems, and I stop my smiling and coaxing.

Something real is here.

Slowly, he pushes in. He makes this grunt—not quite a cry. The grunt feels like it contains secret things—surrender and pleasure, and also, ancient need, maybe dredged up from his deepest core.

I have this sense that, with this sound, he's baring himself more fully than when he pulled off his clothes. Like I'm hearing the sound of a voice in the wilderness, alone no longer. It breaks my heart and also strengthens me.

"Packard," I say.

He touches my cheek, kisses me. The moment is naked. The way we move together, the way he offers himself up. Trusting me with everything. Trusting us.

It changes something in me, his trust, his gaze, so bare and brave. It scares me a little, and I do something I've never done before: I let it scare me. Fear, suddenly, is not the biggest thing.

And just like that, I know something: I can fight Otto. The fear is still there, but it doesn't matter. The fear of the fear is...gone. So simple, so strange.

New.

His heavy hands slide across my skin. He bends to me and I run my tongue along his neck as he fills me, swells in me. His breath tickles my ear. Everything's out of control, and I just fall into it.

I love him. It's scary and I let it frighten me. Everything's new.

He covers my breast with a heavy, dragging touch, and the swell between us breaks apart, like a powerful wave breaking and crashing through me, phosphorescence at its edges. I cry out as I feel his shudder inside me.

He collapses over me, all heavy goodness. He tries to pull out, but I wrap my legs around him, keep him there locked inside me. I don't want to be apart from him. "Don't go."

"Ever?"

I smile. It's okay. *I can do it.* It's shocking, and a relief. A puff of a laugh escapes me.

"What?"

"Nothing. Just everything. Tomorrow."

He lifts himself onto his elbows. "If you're still worried...your instincts..." he tilts his head. "It doesn't have to be you."

"Oh, it has to be me," I say. "It'll be me." I kiss him on the cheek.

He doesn't reply. Maybe he senses something.

"It has to be me." I will love Packard tonight. And fight Otto tomorrow. And I'll fight like hell not to die with him, but if that's what happens, it happens. Packard trusts me, and I won't let him down. I feel new. "The good guys will win. I believe that with all my heart."

He strokes my hair with both of his hands. "You sound so sure."

"I am," I whisper, pressing my face to his neck, feeling his heart pound on my cheek, luxuriating in the simple feeling of it. "You know why?"

"Why?"

"Because I have wonderful instincts."

I'm sitting sideways in the old back booth with my legs on Packard's lap, smashing my soft-boiled egg over buttered toast. We've had sex three times and have eaten two sumptuous meals—our own little all-night orgy. I learned some odd, new things about him. One, he wants to go to Europe, but he's never ridden in a plane—he's not sure if he can stand the enclosed space now. Two, he can't concentrate when he's wearing socks that are too tight around the ankles—even his gift doesn't work as well. We made some jokes about his Achilles heel, which I found uproariously funny, due in part to exhaustion, and in part to my buzzing core of adrenalin.

"I need you to promise me something," I say.

"I'll promise you anything. If you give me a bite of that." He nods at my plate.

"Just a bite?"

"For now." He smooths his hand along my jeans leg. "For appetizers."

I salt my eggy concoction, then pepper it, schooling myself not to think about the future or anything else, just to feel how much I love him. I sever a soppy square with my fork and float it carefully to his mouth.

He chews and smiles at the same time, which makes me want to kiss him.

"What then?" he asks. "Promise what?"

I gaze out the restaurant window at the dawn light reflecting on the building across the street. Time is running out. I have to be at a special breakfast at 9 a.m. with the Midcity Daughters of Industry.

"If it takes longer than expected to get the antihighcap glasses, and I actually *do* have to show up at the church for the wedding, you can't come in. You can't try to get into the church, okay?"

"We know where the glasses are. We'll get them to you before that. You'll zing him before that, and I'll be there to back you."

"But if it comes to that, to my going to the wedding, I don't want you there. Simon and Shelby will be there, and it will be full of security, too dangerous for you. Can you imagine how distracting it would be? For the job we have to do? It will be up to us at that point."

He eyes me brightly. "Why do I feel so suspicious of this request?"

"Yes or no? If it comes to that, I want you not to be there. Don't you think our odds of success are better if Midcity's number-one fugitive isn't getting arrested or killed in the church aisle? I think it's very logical, don't you?"

"Logic isn't everything."

"And you had your bite, didn't you?" I move onto his lap. "This is the promise I'm requesting." I nestle into him with the sensation that we're two creatures of the same species, the last two on the planet, and we've finally found one another. These moments feel expansive, like they contain everything. Like they're almost enough for a lifetime. Almost.

"Promise," I say.

"I'll promise. Only because it won't come to that."

"Thank you."

We stay mashed together, dallying over breakfast, until I pull myself away from him to go refill my coffee. I should be going.

When I get back Packard is looking serious. "I don't want to be apart anymore, Justine. After all this is over, I want to wake up together. Always be together like this. Not here, of course."

"Let's talk about that after we get through today."

"But where are you going to stay, even tonight? Your old apartment's condemned, and obviously Otto's penthouse isn't an option."

"I can't think that far."

"Then I'll think for both of us. Come stay with me at my place. For good. And tomorrow we'll wake up and have coffee in bed, and we'll go to the movies after that."

I look away. "That's a sweet plan."

"Nothing sweet about it." He moves his hand firmly along my back, and his breath warms my neck. He feels like home. "I want us to share a place together, Justine. And if you don't feel like my home is home enough, we can find somewhere else. Anything together."

A lump forms in my throat. "I would love that."

"Good." He goes serious. "And there's something else I want to ask you. Something else important..."

My core of adrenalin buzzes bright. "Let's get this day behind us first."

"I want to ask you now."

"No Packard." I can't let him ask me.

A glint of humor sparks in his eyes as he figures out what I thought he was going to ask. "Justine, it's that I've never had a pet or anything, but I dream of having a dog. Adopting a rescue dog. A big, loping one. Would you be up for that?"

I straighten. "A dog?"

He grins, like the picture of it makes him happy.

I swallow. "You *should* get a dog," I say. "You have to."

A flash of confusion in his eyes. "I meant *us*. Me and you. Together. How would you feel about a dog? A dog is a lot of commitment."

A lurch of grief. I swallow against it. "I love dogs."

"Well, then," He takes my hands— "Justine, would you have a dog with me? You and me and a dog. Like a family. Maybe we'll have lots of dogs."

I smile a teary smile. "I love dogs," I say. "And I love you."

He frowns. Stills. "What's going on?"

I want to throw myself against him, tell him I don't want to leave him, don't want to die, *that's what's going on.*

His gaze intensifies.

And it's here I pull it out—all my years of acting like nothing's wrong when everything is. Because I have to keep him from playing the hero, being the one killed. I reach down and gather everything I have and I smile. Not just any smile, but a radiant, heartfelt smile. "I just love you like crazy. Is that okay?" I lean in and kiss him softly, sweetly. "And you're not paying attention to the time, but I am. I have to leave. And I don't *want* to."

He smiles back. "We'll get you the glasses. I'll be there when you attack him."

"Unless it's in the church."

Silence. I can see he regrets the promise.

"And we'll win," I say. I extract myself from him and climb out of the booth.

He stands, traces his finger down the side of my cheek. "Until then," he says.

This could be the last time I see him. Certainly the last time I'm alone with him. I close my eyes, drinking in his presence, thinking I ought to say something big and all-encompassing, something that will last him into old age, but he's too smart. He'll know. This will have to be enough now.

So I take his finger, kiss his fingertip, and look into his eyes. "You."

He smiles a big, cockeyed, heartbreaking smile.

Chapter Eighteen

The sun is up over the lake, painting the snow-capped faces of the downtown buildings in pale yellow as I cross the bridge. My emotions roll through a Mobius-like maze from grief over leaving Packard to a *fuck-you-Fawna* defiance to determination to beat the prediction to a strange sense of glory, and even, here and there, to desire just to burn the city down.

And of course, to fear.

And yet...something is different. My fear doesn't feel so suffocating, so all-encompassing. It doesn't feel like my *world* anymore. Because I have a family now—Packard and I are a family, and I feel fierce about protecting him, and just fierce *about* him, like an animal in the wild. And the disillusionists are like our pack. They'll walk in the sun, because no amount of fear will stop me from fighting Otto. And I'll do my damnedest to survive it.

I think about writing Packard a letter, for Shelby to give him just in case I do die, but I hate the thought of some letter about how I want him to go on to live a happy life. It seems maudlin, and also, it strikes me as a stupid and even dangerous thing to ruminate on my death like that—the ultimate in negative visualization.

Just as I hit the promenade, I get an idea for something better than a letter anyway. On the next block I head up to Otto's street, and use my key to sneak into the parking garage. The inside is cold and quiet. I doubt anybody's hanging out in here at this early hour, but I don't want to take the chance, so I stick to the shadows as best I can. Fear hums inside me like crazy.

Let it, I think.

My little car is on the second level. I open the door and get into the driver's seat, rest my hands on the wheel. *Good ol' car.*

Then I take ahold of Gumby's feet and yank him right off the dashboard. I scratch the glue bits off him, and I put his hands up, and even one of his legs, and bend his chest a bit to puff it out, making him look as happy as possible. Happy Gumby. Beyond-happy Gumby. This is my letter to Packard. He gave me peace and freedom I've never known, and his trust, and this excellent feeling of love.

I'll give Gumby to Shelby to give to Packard, with instructions that he has to keep Gumby exactly like this, because that is how things ended up.

The dashboard clock ticks. Here in the closed car, it's like the only sound in the world. Seven forty-five. It's going to be an insane day, even without the predicted fight to the death. I'm tired just thinking of it all, or maybe that's the exhaustion setting in. The Dowagers' luncheon, as Shelby calls it, is at nine-thirty—she's the only one of my bridesmaids going to it. Then I will accompany school children to the Midcity graveyard to honor the dead. Shelby will have to find an excuse to duck out—she needs to get to the storage locker with Packard, but Ez, Simon, and Ally will have to go with me. The school children are to sing songs.

Otto will be with the Midcity Mavens at that time; they're holding an honorary wedding ball game in which Otto is expected to play for an hour. At that point, I'll be in my final fitting for the dress, and then having my hair done. Otto's club, the Merovingian Club, is holding some cigar-and-cocktail event for him during the early evening. Dad is invited too, but he won't go. That's around the time I'm to attend the Midcity Fashionista Club's champagne event where I will give them a sneak peek of my dress, alongside my bridesmaids in their dresses. At seven, I'm to show up at the courthouse steps with Dad for the horseback procession. Dad and I and some Midcity guardsmen will lead it, along with my bridal party, followed by a band, some classic cars carrying dignitaries of the city and other guests, then baton-twirling brigades, more horseback riders. Otto and his groomsmen and best man, Fancher—his detective partner from Otto's time on the police force—will join the parade at the rear, once it begins. In keeping with tradition, I won't even see him for the parade. We will enter the church at seven-thirty. The reception is set for eight-thirty.

I get out of the car, shutting the door softly.

A deep voice. "Hello, Justine."

I jump and spin around. Otto leans on a nearby concrete pillar.

"Otto! What are you doing here?"

"What are *you* doing, skulking around in a parking garage on your wedding day?" Lazily, he pushes off the pillar, comes toward me. "I thought you weren't going on any more secret skates."

I study his face. How much does he know? Does he know I pulled off the tracker? There's something held back in his gaze, as though he's refusing to connect with me.

"I didn't think you were going to track me anymore." I regret saying that the instant it leaves my mouth.

He stops in front of me—too close. This is not the way he usually acts, and not the way he usually looks at me, either— there's a tentativeness, as though he's unsure about me now. I wonder if somehow he's sniffing out Packard, if he *knows*. Men have a kind of canine sense about other men. Maybe he's intuiting the night of sex from my expression—people can do that. Or maybe he's plain old smelling Packard. I'm drenched in Packard on so many levels.

"Where were you?"

"Skating." I try a smile. "Not all of us get to go out and play baseball today, you know. Some of us will be sitting around being endlessly primped over."

He looks away. There's too much contained in the sudden pause. He's not confident of me anymore. I hold tighter to

Gumby, keeping him down by my leg. I don't want Otto to see Gumby.

"How's your father?" he asks suddenly.

My father? "He loves his room."

"Did he sleep well?"

I shrug. Is this a warning question? Should I be worried about Dad? "We'll see when I get back," I say. "I should start getting ready for the Dowagers' breakfast."

"Wait."

"What?"

A pause. Fighting with himself. Then, "What do you have there?"

I smile. Barely convincing, I'm sure. "Huh?"

He tips his eyes down to my hand. "There."

I lift Gumby up by the legs. The way I'm holding him in the space between us, it's like Gumby's a cross I'm using to ward off a vampire.

Otto takes this stricken breath, just staring at Gumby. And then he shifts his gaze to me, with the weirdest expression, like grief. Like it really *is* having a vampire-cross effect on him.

"Justine," he says.

I swallow, give him my best poker face.

He comes to me, pulls me into a hug, and then he kisses me on the forehead. "You are so precious to me. You'll never know."

I pull away after an appropriate time span. He still seems grief-stricken. I give him a curious smile.

"You've made Gumby this way on our wedding day." Otto nods at Gumby. "Happy Gumby. To know this, to see this, it's better than any other gift I could have gotten."

I nearly collapse with relief. I have him back—Gumby assuaged whatever concerns he had.

He says, "After all this work to clear our path…there's not a lot I wouldn't do for you, Justine. Not a lot I wouldn't take on.

And the fact that I've made you this happy..." He thumps his fist onto his heart.

I feel this thump in my heart too. Pity. Sorrow. "Oh, Otto," I say.

The worst thing is, I don't hate him, and I truly don't want him to die. I'm just...*disillusioned* with him. And I can't let him destroy my friends.

"It's all going to be worth it."

"I hope so," I say.

"You were going to bring him? To the wedding?"

"Gumby?" I swallow. Collect myself. "Riding in my bouquet? What would the Fashionista Club say?"

"They would say you're the loveliest bride on the planet."

His smile gives me shivers. He rests his hands lightly on my shoulders. "Everything is clicking into place. Everything is turning out perfectly for this day. Sometimes, Justine, the best laid plans do work out."

I feel a little sick, imagining Packard's severed head. But no, Packard will grow old. I'll make sure of it. Otto regards me thoughtfully. "I wish it were tonight right now, Justine. I wish this day were behind us."

"It will be," I say. "But Otto, it's bad luck to see your bride on the wedding day."

"The hell with luck."

I roll my eyes and give him a quick kiss. "It will be tonight soon."

With that, I skate off from the man who once was my hero, leaving him there in the dark parking garage with all his plans and hopes and dreams. This man I will betray and attack tonight. The man I just might die with.

Outside, the sun is higher, the air crisp and cool, skies endlessly blue. The day seems blandly happy and sure of things, as if it's preparing for the wedding too. The day doesn't know.

I continue down to the Midcity Arms and enter the lavish, chandelier-laden lobby just before eight-twenty. I spy Shelby in the far corner-seating area, ensconced in a velvet couch. She stands and waves and I wave back, then smile at the desk clerks. I move across the floor in a way that hopefully looks like walking, and not skating.

Shelby's wearing a black dress with white polka dots and a black hat, chosen, no doubt, out of some sense of irony. With a knowing look, she watches me approach. I meet her gaze. So much is there in the space between us. My best friend.

"Out all night." She raises one eyebrow. "I trust it was worth it."

I don't even know what to say to that. I just hug her.

She looks at me too long when I finally let her go. "What?"

"Come on," I say.

Up in my hotel room, I set Gumby down on the table and collapse on the couch, unlacing my skates.

Shelby picks him up. "I think that you must have had excellent night. But why remove him from his home?"

I toss my skates on the floor.

"Justine, we have not vanquished Otto yet. However," she raises a finger, "we know where glasses are. In Self-Store Village out by suburb of Wild's Way. Packard told you, no doubt."

"He did."

"So very perfect that Avery would choose Wild's Way. Finding these glasses, being sleuth of Avery's mind, it has made me love him more."

"Wild's Way." I peel off my damp exercise clothes.

"There is new problem now, though," she says.

"It will take longer to get them than you originally thought?"

She looks surprised. "Yes. Your wedding has triggered city to have holiday. Owner of Self-Store Village has gone on overnight fishing cruise. Out on Lake Michigan. We will get glasses, Justine, but we must hire speedboat to track him.

Simon wants to break in, but I do not think that is best way, and I know Packard will agree. I know we will get glasses, Justine—" She tilts her head, twirls Gumby by his arm.

"Don't change him," I say.

"How did you know it would take longer?"

I pull a hotel bathrobe around me. "I saw Fawna."

Shelby's mouth falls open and she stops twirling Gumby. "And?" Gently, she sets Gumby on the table. "And?"

I swallow, unsure where to begin. Her eyes fall back on Gumby. She turns back to me, alarmed.

I give her the story of how Dad's comment led me to find Fawna, and I tell her Fawna's prognostication: if I fight Otto at the ceremony, my friends will walk in the sun again and Packard will grow to old age. But I will die.

"Justine!"

"But if I don't fight Otto at the ceremony, Packard dies. I'm going to do it. Don't try to talk me out of it."

"But, Justine—" Her eyes brim with tears.

"Don't try to talk me out of it."

She sinks to the bed. I sink next to her.

After a long moment, she says, "If I could go back to be shot in place of Avery, I would do so."

"I know," I whisper.

"Not merely that I *would* do so, I would exalt to do so." She purses her lips, stares into nothing. "In both a dark and a bright way, I would exalt to take that death as my own. Do you understand what I mean, Justine?"

"I know exactly what you mean."

She watches me, brown eyes grave. "I do not exalt in *this*, however."

I touch her arm, feel the tears come. "I know."

She shakes her head. Sucks in a breath. "You did not tell Packard, of course."

"Definitely not," I say. "He wants to move in together after this."

"Oh, Justine."

"It was really hard, Shelby. He wanted to talk about the future, and it was horrible. Even the idea of going to the movies tomorrow."

"Packard hates the movies. After being imprisoned, the space is too dark and enclosed for him."

"That's just like him. To go just because I wanted to. To push through it." I smile bitterly. "Well, that's what I'm doing. I worried before that I wouldn't be able to step up to the challenge, but I'm not worried now. Something's different. He trusts me, and I trust myself, but it's not just that"—I pause, trying to put my finger on what feels so different inside of me— "it's like I trust life too. Things seem more solid somehow."

"You have found your feet."

"Yeah, and I'll do this thing and if I die, okay, I'll trust that's how it had to be. But I'll tell you something else—I know Fawna's supposedly so powerful and has this perfect record, and I've made my peace with that. But other times, I think, *Screw it!* You know? I'll make my own future. Nothing is written in stone! I want to step up and save everybody and after that, I want to live with Packard. I want to have dogs together."

Shelby gives me a pitying look. "The bad things are almost always written in stone, Justine. I am sorry..." she shakes her head. "Oh, Justine, I do not exalt in this at all."

I can't help but smile. Of course Shelby would accept Fawna's dark and dire prediction. "On the bright side"—I point at her—"I think I'm going to eat the most fried and potato-ey breakfast possible. And I already had one breakfast. But why not?"

Shelby sniffle-laughs. "Then I will too."

"And, today, after I zing Otto, you're supposed to zing him. You and Simon. You have to follow up right away. We'll make him let everybody go, possibly even confess. Packard thinks he will confess. Jordan will be at the fun house, and she'll call us as soon as they're free."

"Is your zing that will do it."

I don't feel quite as pleased about this as she does. "Packard was very keen on the combo," I say.

Shelby nods. "Otto will have combo. But your fear, that is true weakness for Otto. Your fear is our cannon. And I will make sure that he pays. I will be there with you, like the second in old-fashioned duel. And I will help you get him and make him pay."

"I don't think *making the other guy pay* is what seconds in old-fashioned duels did. Seconds made sure the weapons were in order, and that the rules were followed, and sometimes they fought the other seconds."

"I am different kind of second, for different kind of duel. And he will pay. In tears of agony he will pay."

"You don't need a death on your conscience, Shelby. And our friends don't need it—"

She crosses her arms, clearly insulted. "I know." She doesn't appreciate my reminding her that if Otto dies, our friends are stuck in the fun house forever. But she doesn't seem entirely in control.

I smile. Poke her arm. "I think this is the only wedding in history where the maid of honor considers herself to be just like a second in a duel."

She narrows her eyes. She likes that. "You know, Otto will sense antihighcap glasses. As soon as I bring them into church, he will feel fields weakening."

"But he won't know who has the glasses. And once I put them on, his fields will be completely down."

"You will render him pitiful." Thoughtfully, she touches a finger to her cheek. "Packard must be nowhere near church."

"He promised me he wouldn't go in." I tell her about his promise.

"His promise will not be enough if he believes you are in danger. I will hire somebody to detain him."

"He'll hate you," I say.

"He will hate me already when he finds out I knew what Fawna saw. He will hate me for not telling him, not allowing him to die in your place. He will be right to hate me for that, but you are my best friend."

I take her hand. She allows it. I say, "You have to give him Gumby, from me. Okay?" I pick Gumby up. "Gumby has to stay just like this. This is what Packard gave to me. You tell him that. This happiness. It was all worth it."

She closes her eyes. Her coal-black lashes shine with moisture.

"It'll all work out." I stand. "I have to take a shower."

Shelby settles back in the couch. There's nothing more to say. I look down at the table, at the *Midcity Eagle*. The headlines are all about Stuart the dream invader being captured, and then escaping again. Conspiracy theories abound.

It seems like somebody else's story. Somebody else's newspaper.

The shower is warm, and I let it pound my back and neck and head, washing off all that sex and sweat. It feels like I'm washing off a little bit of life.

Chapter Nineteen

The day passes like a fever dream. I wear my favorite green-wool dress, and I eat an outrageously fattening breakfast with the Daughters of Midcity Industry while they ask me questions about our planned Caribbean honeymoon and discuss the new port.

Shelby trades home décor tips with the women at her end of the table. They think she's joking when she tells them she prefers holes in the walls, so that she can see the lathing and mouse nests, because that is what is really there, so why conceal it? She informs them that she paid extra to get the best view of the Tangle. I can very nearly mouth along with her at this point: "Do I want view of beauty? No! Pfft. I say, do not give me lies."

Afterwards, I bundle up in the hat and coat that go with the wool dress and head out to the sunny, snowy Midcity graveyard with my bridesmaids, minus Shelby. The schoolchildren who meet us there are so fascinated with Simon, so taken with his strange fur coat, not to mention his bruised face, his tattooed chest, and his top hat, that they can barely remember the words of the songs to honor the Midcity dead.

The look of rapt wonderment Simon wears on his face while listening to the song makes the children giggle, and, judging by their facial contortions, has Ally and Ez dangerously close to hysterical laughter.

After that, there's the laying of the flowers and the reading of the names. I don't laugh at any part of this ceremony; I think it's all lovely, and kind of meaningful. And the air is crisp and sweet, and the walks are shoveled so that they're clean and dry;

the snow elsewhere is new enough that it sparkles in the light. Even gnarled, old hickory trees look more glorious than usual, with their craggy, black fingers grasping at the sky. At the top of one of the hillocks I catch sight of the blue, blue lake, and I wonder if Shelby and Packard have caught up to the storage place owner yet. And I wish fervently that it was me on that boat with Packard.

The fitting of the wedding dress goes quickly, since there's really nothing much to fit or alter. Even after that mammoth breakfast, my dress hangs just right; it's a simple, elegant, tulle silk empire-waist dress with tiny straps, winterized by long gloves that stretch clear up over my elbows, and the white faux-fur coat that I'll wear for the horse procession. The seamstress alters the length of the gloves, and there are last minute adjustments to my jeweled tiara. Ez and Ally have tagged along, plus some of my old friends from the dress shop.

I try not to think about what will happen. Unsuccessfully. I can feel my fear building, hot and grating inside of me. Well, there's nothing I can do about it, except not let it stop me. That's my thinking as I sit there with people buzzing around, asking me questions, showing me glittery jewels, and worriedly informing me that Shelby is nowhere to be found.

We do my hair opera-style, piled on top of my head and cascading down in ringlets behind my tiara. Sometimes I wish the wedding were finally on, so that it would all be over with. Other times the clock seems to be moving far too fast.

A big glass of champagne at the Fashionista fashion event does me good. Ally grows increasingly concerned that Shelby hasn't shown, but Simon invents some explanation. I'm thankful, and as soon as we're alone, the only two at our table, I take Simon's hand. "Your friendship means a lot to me," I say. "*You* mean a lot to me."

Simon looks down at my hand and then sends his piercing gaze up into my eyes. His left eye looks more piercing than normal due to the dark bruise around it. "Spill."

"Just that."

"Liar," he says.

"What?"

"This isn't a real wedding. It's just another day at the job. Why would you say something like that?"

"I can't say that? When I'm about to do something dangerous?"

"Don't bluff a bluffer, sister."

I hesitate. The more people I tell, the more real it makes Fawna's prognostication. But he is a good friend, and I tell him what she prognosticated.

And he laughs.

I whisper angrily: "Do contain your grief, Simon."

"Justine, when they tell you that you're screwed, that you've lost everything, that's when the fucking game *begins*. You'll beat the odds. I don't care how stacked they are, there is *always* a way to pull it out of the fire. You have to decide not to accept it. Fuck Fawna and her predictions. If Fawna was standing right here, I'd say that to her face. God, I hate prognosticators." He balls up a cocktail napkin and whips it onto the empty stage. "I hope she shows up at the wedding, so I can tell her she's full of shit right to her face, and laugh at her when both you and Packard pull through." He snorts. "This wedding is really shaping up. After you fight Otto, we should get the schoolchildren in there to serenade you."

"Stop it."

"They can sing you one of their insane songs as you walk out of that church unscathed." Simon smiles, and I just start laughing suddenly, and I can't stop. I'm laughing, but I'm crying a little. Then the makeup woman comes back. She's not laughing.

Things begin to move with heightened speed. My bridal party—still minus Shelby, of course—takes a limo to the courthouse, which is the gathering point for the horseback procession. The parade will stretch about three blocks long, and Otto and his party will join it at the end, once it's going.

Midcitians don't want the groom and bride intermingling any more than I do.

My dad emerges with difficulty from his limo, being that he's decked out in his full hazmat exoskeleton. I introduce him to my friends. By this time they all know, all except Ally, that he's the go-to guy if we end up needing weapons. Who knows if we will? No matter how hard we've hit the grapevines, nobody has been able to figure out what big thing Otto has planned.

Dad asks me if I found *our friend*, meaning Fawna, and I tell him it's all good, all okay, and I smile. I guess that's what I want him to understand—that if I do die, it's all okay. It's not a lie.

People want to hold up the procession to wait for Shelby, but I tell them to go forward, that she'll catch up.

We're matched up with our horses. All of us get our own horses to ride except for Dad, who will be riding along with a stable hand, because there is some fear that his gear will upset the horse. My horse, Mercurious, is white with gray spots. He's strong and gentle. I have to ride with my legs off to the side—sidesaddle, they call it—with the help of a saddle that's adjusted for that sort of thing.

We set off behind the new Midcity Chief of Police, who leads the procession, alongside two of the horse handlers. I ride between Dad and Simon, with Ez and Ally on the outer flanks, and we wave at the people lining the streets. More horse handlers are behind us, followed by the band and classic-car-riding dignitaries and baton-twirling groups, and more, with Otto and his party at the rear, presumably.

My heart pounds like crazy as we clop along down the promenade, and then up the main boulevard. I think Mercurious senses my high anxiety, but he doesn't react; he just clops along. It's what I'm doing, too, just clopping along. I pet his thick, rough mane. "We just go forward," I say to him.

I look over to find Simon scowling. He leans in to whisper, "And kick ass on fate."

And then I look over at my dad. All I can see are his eyes through the face mask, but I have this sense that he's proud, and it means the world to me.

TV and news crews film us as we near the church. I smile and wave. The grand old structure with its soaring peaks and flying buttresses is surrounded by heavily armed guards and police officers, as well as men in their Sunday best who look a lot like guards in their Sunday best. For the thousandth time, I think about Packard out there. It's way after three o'clock, of course, which means he's no longer in danger from the highcaps who were hunting him. When the devices in the backs of their necks don't explode, I suppose they'll assume somebody delivered on Packard's head. Or did a message go out extending their deadline?

We dismount, wave to the cameras, and head up the steps through metal detectors set up discreetly in the grand entrance. My bridal party beeps like crazy, thanks to Dad, but we're given a free pass and ushered to the west side of the church, to an empty, echoey foyer area that's been decorated and cordoned off just for us.

The church. We're here.

Kit, the motherly stage manager for the ceremony, comes in and greets us. It's clear she's been warned that the father of the bride would be wearing a big metal spacesuit, but her lips form a grim line as she assesses Simon's bruised and beat-up face. He flings his cape backward over his bare shoulders to reveal his shirt of leather straps and gives her a smile. She's even more unhappy when we inform her that the maid of honor has not yet arrived. She disappears, presumably to stage-manage a wedding holding pattern. Organ music sounds through the richly paneled walls.

The five of us wait on benches in the foyer as the minutes crawl by. Simon's more sprawled on his, and he requests a bucket of champagne and a bucket of cold sodas from one of the many people coming in and out. He seems a bit out of breath, actually, but then again, he often seems out of breath.

Not like he would ever stoop to exercise or anything. An increasingly unhappy Kit pops in now and then with reports of the audience getting restless. "There are a good number of people who have fallen asleep!" she says. "Half the city council is asleep!"

"The entire city council is here?" I ask.

"Of course."

The Felix Five is here, then. I wonder vaguely if the big thing has to do with them.

Dad is looking hot inside his suit. When somebody finally brings the beverages, I ask people to give our wedding party ten minutes of privacy in our little alcove. I want Dad to take his headgear off for a moment, but we can't let anybody see him do it; that would blow his excuse for wearing it, which is a fear of germs.

When he gets his headpiece detached, I introduce him properly to Simon, Ez, and Ally. I suppose in any other circumstance they might have attitudes about each other, but there's a good feeling here that makes me love everyone.

Simon's produced a deck of cards from somewhere. He's trying to get up a game, of all things.

I put a bottle of cold, bubbly water into Dad's gloved hand, but he doesn't drink it; he just looks at me, his gaze shrewd. "You seem so different, Justine," he says.

"It's a big day," I say, taking a sip of fizzy water. It makes my gloved fingers moist.

"Not just a big day. I don't know how to explain it." He puts the bottle to his forehead. "I was trying to work it out during the procession. You seem more substantial. Like you've got some ballast."

I almost want to cry at my dad's insight, and the approval tucked inside. I hide it by quipping: "Are you calling me fat?"

His smile crinkles the edges of his warm eyes.

Ez announces she has a bad feeling. Simon takes off his top hat and downs another glass of champagne. Maybe *he's* even starting to worry.

But I'm not. "This will all work out," I tell them. It feels good to say it and mean it. It's strange, this new sense of trust I have. I could never reach down and feel certain about important things like this before.

Now there's no question of anything.

A voice from down the hall. "Knock, knock!" It's Kit. She wants to come back in.

"I love you, Dad," I say and he tells me he loves me too, and then he shoves his helmet back on.

Kit announces that she wants us to begin without Shelby. "If she misses the wedding, she'll still get to be at the reception."

Ally agrees. She wants us to start too.

"We'll wait some more," I say.

A few minutes later, my phone vibrates. I reach into my silk bag and pull it out. A message from Shelby. One word: "Start."

I loosen the fingers of my elegant gloves and yank them off. "Let's do it!"

The relief is palpable. Audible, in the case of Kit.

Simon squeezes my hand. Kit sends word to the front and the organ music changes. We move to the entrance as a group, my dad all metallic and mechanical, my bridesmaids in black with matching black capes with fluffy white trim.

Dad and I wait together, just shy of the entrance, as Ally heads down the aisle, followed by Ez, then Simon. Slowly they proceed to the altar and stand across from Otto and his men and wait for me.

I used to say happiness was the absence of something—the absence of darkness, hate, fear. Especially fear. I thought, if I could get rid of my fear, life would be great.

But now, standing at the threshold of the church, my arm hooked in Dad's, the rhythmic hum of his respirator faintly audible over the pipe organ, I see that I was wrong. Happiness isn't about getting rid of my fear. Happiness is when something outshines my fear.

Like my love for Packard—wild and fierce and beating uncontrollably in my heart. And my love for my friends, and for my dad, being so brave, and even for scrappy, beleaguered Midcity. And fear isn't going to stop me from doing this thing.

My pulse races.

I smile over at Dad. Then I take a deep breath and we march down the beige carpet, strewn with white flowers. Slowly we pass between the pews, all trussed up with ribbons, toward the flower-strewn and beribboned altar. My strange wedding party is assembled in front of a gleaming wall of golden organ pipes. Simon stands proudly as my temporary maid of honor in his belts and chains and top hat next to Ez and Ally, who are looking gorgeous in their black gowns. On the other side, Otto's three men wear matching tuxedoes, and probably side arms. And in the center stands Otto, dashing in his red captain's uniform, heavy with medals and insignias. Lights flash and cameras whir as we approach. The music booms triumphantly as we mount the steps.

I come face to face with Otto.

"My love," Otto mouths, holding out both his hands.

The hush takes on strange gravity as I place my hands in his, observing the scene as if from the outside—Otto and I about to marry. I think about how I'd have felt a year ago if I'd known I'd be standing here next to the heroic Otto Sanchez. He's not so heroic, I know that now. He's a man full of dreams and desires just like anyone, but also a man full of fear, and that fear has driven him to do evil things.

Otto smiles into my eyes—a smile I can't return. Is he happy? Does he think he's home free? I feel a little bit sad. And more disillusioned than ever.

And I have to stop him. Where is Shelby? I need those glasses if I'm going to get through his force field to zing him. I don't want him to die; I just need him to make things right. I marvel at how our mutual health fears give us great power to help each other, and great power to hurt each other, too.

The ceremony begins. The pastor recites the wedding prayer, which I barely hear; I'm focused on increasingly loud yelling from outside—the street? The church steps? Has Shelby arrived?

The pastor's wedding lecture is interrupted by pounding from behind me. I twist around to see a guard opening a door that's concealed in the side wall. Shelby, her bridesmaid's dress askew, rushes through and leaps up the steps to my side. Applause sounds out from the pews. I'm still holding Otto's hands, but Shelby clutches my shoulder and whispers in my ear: "He *knows*. Fawna is out there with him—she told him the prediction. He's trying to get in to stop you!" Packard, she means. Packard knows if I fight Otto I'll die. "They are detained, but not for long." She jabs something into my back. *The antihighcap glasses.*

The applause is still going as I pull my right hand from Otto's grip and take the glasses from her. Then I shove them onto my face and turn back to Otto, grabbing his hand again before he can get what's happening. I look into his eyes as I burn the hole between our energy bodies.

He goes ashen. "What are you doing?" The applause dies in a swell of murmurs. The pastor continues, a quizzical look on his face.

With all my strength I grip Otto's fingers, prepared for him to try and yank away, but he seems simply bewildered. I hadn't expected bewildered. "Justine—"

The hole is burnt and I'm in. He could smash the glasses and jump off the altar now and I'd still have him. I open the floodgates between us, waiting for the heat in my fingertips that shows when my fear starts rushing out.

But there's no heat. Nothing comes out.

Crashes from the direction of the front entrance. *Packard, trying to get in and stop me.*

Otto furrows his brow, his face a mask of pain. "What is this, Justine?" he whispers fervently.

"You know what it is." Frantically, I try to stoke up my fear.

The pastor eyes us warningly as he continues on about the sacredness of marriage. I try again and again. I even visualize a photo from one of those fashion-magazine disease articles I so loathe and fear. Why isn't it working? A car alarm sounds from somewhere.

Otto pulls his hands from mine. "Justine—we're a team!" he says under his breath. "Get those glasses off! Talk to me."

"About you killing Avery?" I whisper.

"Packard did that! You saw it."

I grab his arm. "I didn't see it, and you know it." I struggle to call up my fear, but it's lost its aliveness, its *charge.*

The fact that I haven't zinged him yet seems to give him hope. "See?" He grips my arm now and pulls me close. "You can't bear to do it because you love me. Because you can't betray us. We're in this together."

*Thump*s against the far door.

"Here's what's going to happen," I whisper back. "You are going to let Sophia and the disillusionists go." I try to stoke as I talk but my weapon is gone. What will I fight him with?

"I love you."

"No you don't!" I whisper furiously. "You just need me. And I love Packard, and you'll never take that away again. *Ever.*"

Otto regards me with repulsion as a few camera bulbs flash. Then, with a jerk, he shoves me backward, into my bridesmaids; we stumble as a group. Simon holds me up by the upper arm.

"Somebody get those glasses out of this church. Now!" Otto points at me. "Now!"

More camera lights flash as plainclothes police emerge from either side of the altar, and I realize, with horror, that I have not yet fought Otto. If I don't fight Otto at the ceremony, Packard dies. I try to use this terrifying realization to stoke the old fear. Still nothing.

But there's more than one way to fight Otto. I rush at him, haul off, and hit him with my bouquet. He looks stunned. Murmurs and shouts go up from the audience, a sea of camera flashes, but I don't care. I punch him with my other hand as a cop tries to pull me off, but still I fight him—furiously! I'm fighting him at the wedding. Nobody can say otherwise. The prophecy didn't say *how* I would fight him, just that I would fight him.

He grabs my wrist—eyes wide, color high—and he shoves me back into the cop, who clasps my upper arms with an iron grip. They all think I'm crazy, but it's okay because I fought Otto. I fought him at the ceremony. I fulfilled my part of the prophecy.

Otto points at the glasses. "Get those things out of here!"

The pastor retreats. The cop tries to take the glasses, but I grab onto them, hold them tightly. The confusion mounts as the camera flashes multiply.

"Now those glasses really *will* be wiped from the earth," Otto says to Shelby.

With a scream, Shelby launches herself at Otto, flies at him, knocking him backward against a podium. The impact— Otto's head on the sharp corner—is hard. Loud. I gasp.

Otto's hit his head. Really, *really* hard.

A cop yanks her off, but Otto stays down. There's commotion in the audience, banging of people outside trying to get in. The officer finally gets the glasses.

"What have you done?" Otto sits up on his elbow, puts his hand to his hair, comes away with blood. A shout goes up for a doctor.

Otto looks like he's having trouble focusing on his hand; he moves it in, near to his face, then away. "Is there blood?" He looks wildly around. "Somebody turn on the lights!" He can't see. He's gravely injured. His man Fancher grips his shoulder.

Screaming. Something's going on in the pews, but I can't look away from Otto.

"I'm a doctor." A man kneels beside him, tries to calm him. Another doctor comes. I try to twist away from the cop who's holding me. Screams sound out from the pews.

There's fighting down there—guards, guests. People seem to be wrestling on the floor. A gunshot is fired and the screaming loudens.

Dimly, I'm aware of Dad, threatening the cop who has me. He lets me go and joins the fray. At the foot of the stairs two people seem to have piled onto another, the three of them struggling wildly. Then one of them looks up, and there's blood around his mouth.

Cannibals! A shot rings out and the cannibal who stuck his head up flies backward, shot in the head. I scream. The other starts lumbering toward us. It's Henry Felix! A guard knocks Felix out with the butt of his gun. But there are lots of other cannibals—I can tell now from the way they're lumbering around. The cannibals seem to be attacking guests. The guards and cops have left the altar to pull them off the people who are mobbing the doors, which are apparently locked. More sleepwalkers come at us from the side.

Dad's handing a gun to Simon, whipping out a machine gun.

"Try not to kill them, Dad!" I say. "They're sleepwalking!" Even the cops are usually under orders not to shoot to kill the cannibals unless necessary.

With the mobs at the locked door, there's no way to get out, and Packard will never get in now. "I have to get to Packard."

"Stay here," Simon says. "I'll find him. I'll bust him in."

Dad and Simon jump into the sea of mayhem. Dad's slamming his arms at the sleepwalkers, keeping them back, fighting a dozen at once; he's a human battering ram with his impenetrable exoskeleton. Increasingly, you can tell the cannibals by their bloody faces.

A camera flash—some reporters have climbed to the rafters.

No way would Otto have planned this. This is Otto's plan gone wrong, I think. He was probably supposed to do something heroic. Save people from getting hurt. Something heroic against the Felix Five, who are all trying to eat the guests.

More shots. Screams.

Shelby takes my arm; "You have to stay safe."

"Too late now."

She looks alarmed. "You are hit?"

"No, but I fought him, didn't you see?" I pull her toward the fighting. "I have to get to Packard."

"Stay. He could be anywhere now. He knows you are here."

I know she's right, but I have to do something. Fighting rages in the pews. Do one of the cannibals come up here and kill me? Is that how I die? Ally's run off, trying to get out the side door.

I get a glimpse of Otto, lying on his back, hovering his hand in the air. He seems to be waving away the pastor. The pastor retreats.

The doctor comes over to us. "We called for transport, but—" he pauses. "I don't know what the status is between you, but best say your good-byes in the next few minutes."

Gunshots in the pews—I'm shocked to see Ez, pumping a man full of bullets.

"Is Stuart," Shelby announces in a loud whisper. "Must be Stuart."

I look back over at Otto, lying there with just a doctor and a couple of government people, none of them friends. My heart lurches for him, for how frightened he must be, and in a daze, I pull away from Shelby, and I go to him. His companions eye me warily as I kneel down, take his bloody hand. Blood soaks the beige carpet around his head. The ground running red.

"Oh, Otto," I say.

He pulls his hand from mine. "Go away. Leave!"

"Okay," I say. "Okay." I stand, unsure what to do. I'm frightened too.

"Wait, Justine! Come back," Otto says. His eyes are glassy. He doesn't seem to see anything.

"I'm here." I kneel, take up his hand again, but he jerks it away.

"Just tell me—how bad is it?" Even now he needs me to tell him.

"It's bad." I won't lie to him now.

"It's coming true," he mumbles. "The prophecy."

A high-pitched crash. The stained-glass windows have been broken. A rush of light and cold air fills the church. "I know," I say. "Yes."

"Leave me." But then he grabs my hand. "No, wait." He seems angry—angry at me, angry at needing me. His breathing is shallow, and he's white as a ghost, covered in sweat. "It would've been so good. What you ruined. I don't care what she foretold—I had to try..."

As he trails off, I realize something—he could have changed his plan, changed everything. Would that have averted fate? Surely it would have averted this fate, but he went forward, just like me.

"You had to go for it," I say. "We both had to go for it." I touch his forehead with just the pad of my pointer finger, make a soothing line.

His breathing sounds wheezy. Vaguely, I realize the screaming has stopped. There's a deeper *crash* and *crack*, like breaking wood. Shouting.

"All ruined," he says. "It wasn't supposed to be like this."

"I know." I make another soothing finger line. "You've always had a vision for something more. Better. It's something I always loved about you."

"I'm sorry, Justine—" Those familiar, brown eyes don't quite fix on mine anymore. He looks toward my voice.

"You went forward. You had to. It couldn't have been any other way..." I'm speaking to myself as much as him. I cling to his hand, sucked into our familiar and unholy fear-alliance.

The strength with which he grips back surprises me. "I'm scared."

"I know." I swallow against my tears. "So am I."

More commotion. Otto's grip is going slack. His hand slides from mine. "Otto?"

Arms around me. Packard! Bloody, but alive. I turn, throw my arms around him. "Packard!"

Packard's breath gusts out with relief. "Thank God you didn't fight him. Ally told me *Shelby* fought him. You're going to be okay, Justine! I could've never lived with it, you dying. This is the right way, Justine."

"No, wait—it's not."

"Don't argue," he says imperiously, gazing at me fiercely. "I love you more than my life."

"But—"

"There's no time!" He drops to his knees, takes Otto's hand. "Henji!" He pats Otto's cheek. "Henji!"

He thinks I didn't fight Otto, which means, according to the prophecy, Packard will die instead of me.

Otto groans.

"It's okay, old friend," Packard says.

"Go away," Otto wheezes.

"After all these years, you think I can't see you? I know you're more than this."

"Go," Otto says.

"Henji, you have to release the innocent people you still have sealed." He leans in to speak over some new screaming. Shelby's crouched at my other side. Packard goes on. "It's not in you to damn them to that."

Otto says. "You don't know..."

"I know you."

Otto's eyes flutter closed.

Sirens sound. There are crashes. Another gunshot

Packard looks at me, desperation in his eyes. He's envisioning our friends in the fun house for eternity. Packard thinks he's the one prophesied to die any minute, and his concern is for our friends.

"I still feel them, Sterling," Otto says. "After all these years. I always have."

Packard's face is ashen. "The *Goyces*."

Otto nods.

"Forgive me, old friend," Packard says. "You were a good boy. A loving boy. I tricked you into sealing those men in the walls. You didn't know what you were doing—"

"Stop," Otto says weakly. "*I knew.* I knew I was killing them, but I pretended I didn't, because I hated it. I fought you because I hated it."

"What?" Packard's voice sounds hoarse. I don't see Packard's face, but he draws closer in to Otto, like a thirsty man, yearning for water, and this tells me everything. It's huge, this gift that Otto has just given him, this knowledge that killing so many men and ruining Otto isn't all on Packard.

"You knew you were killing them?" he whispers.

More sirens. Wailing and lights. Packard turns to me. An ocean of secret meaning flows between us, and I love him so much, I can barely think straight. "You're not going to die," I say.

He looks at me blankly. He doesn't get it—he's too consumed with this news, that the weight he's carried for so long was a false weight.

Just then, Fawna appears, making her way up the steps like a postapocalyptic bride, all bright scraps and wild, blonde hair.

"I let it be on you," Otto says. "I wanted it to be yours. Forgive me."

"Of course I forgive you," Packard says. "Of course."

"Stop it." Fawna pushes to Otto's other side. "Both of you are ridiculous."

"Fawna?" Otto whispers hoarsely. He can't see her.

"Yes, Henji." Fawna scoots in to cradle Otto's head in her lap. "Oh, Henji, if you hadn't put them in the walls, dozens more children would have died or been taken. Packard, if you hadn't gotten the idea for it, the same. Dozens more. Horribly dead. You argue about who forgives who. The tears of our friends would have filled seven oceans."

There's shooting outside. Medical teams and cops have arrived, but somebody keeps them from us.

Fawna murmurs to Otto how he protected her as best he could, and how he and Packard gave the other children hope.

"Fawna, where were you?" Otto asks. "Are you truly all right? I searched. For years."

Fawna strokes Otto's hair. She's his only real family, I think. "It doesn't matter," she says. "I'm safe now, Henji. Everything is as it should be."

Otto sighs. "Packard—I dissolved the fields. Your people are free."

"Thank you," Packard says. "I knew you would."

Otto squeezes his eyes shut.

He lived to keep Midcity safe, I think. Even killing Avery was a twisted version of that.

Fawna takes Otto's hand and closes something into it. "See what I brought you. The coon hand."

Otto puts the bright, beribboned thing to his cheek. Fawna's whispering to him, telling him he's safe, something about the brightness of his spirit—solemn words, oddly holy.

I pull Packard away—to give them privacy. Us, too. "I have to tell you—"

"You have nothing to tell me."

I look into his eyes, and I find I'm not afraid. I pull him closer. "Listen—"

Another gunshot, like a whomp of lightning in my arm, my chest, throwing me off balance.

"Justine!" Packard clutches me by the arms. "Justine!"

A red stain spreads over my white bodice. "What the hell?" I feel confused. I didn't think I was shot, but dimly I realize I must have been. It seems like magic, the way the blood spreads, so red on the white fabric.

He calls out, "We need help here!"

"I fought him," I say.

"No, *Shelby* fought him!"

"I fought him before she did. And I would again."

His expression changes—*cold fire* is all I can think.

I put my face to his shoulder. I just want him to hold me. I want to stay like this.

"No!" Packard whispers into my hair, arms tight around me.

"It's *okay*."

"No!" His fingers are like pincers on my arm. I feel woozy.

There's activity around me—I try to keep track of it, but I can't. I'm on the floor, unsure how I got there. When I open my eyes, I see faces I don't recognize, but Packard has my hand, I know that.

My eyes feel heavy, and I close them, just for a moment. I hear voices I recognize—Dad. Shelby. People are upset. Arguing. A stab in my arm. Packard is squeezing my hand so hard I think it might break.

Chapter Twenty

I wake up to the muffled sound of voices. Lights so bright, they hurt my eyes, even though they're closed. A voice. "She's coming to."

Packard?

Another voice says *no*. Arguing. I don't understand what they're arguing about. Where am I? Is this a dream? The thinking makes me feel like I need to rest. I should rest. Then I realize I am resting.

The next thing I remember, I feel something cool and wet on my face, my lips, the softest, coolest sensation in the world. Have I died? I open my eyes. The moon is bright in the window.

"Hey." A whisper. "Hey." Packard. He laughs. "Hey!"

I think I smile. I feel a smile inside me, anyway. "Hey." I can barely eke out the word.

"You're okay." He lowers his voice. "Look, you were shot, but you'll be okay. Got it? You'll be okay." It's like a command. As though I won't be okay if he doesn't command it. Imperious, bossy Packard that I love.

I swallow through my sandpapery throat. Everything is floaty. "An elephant might be sitting on my chest," I croak.

Suddenly he's gone.

The next time I wake—an hour later? A day?—Shelby is there. "Hey you," I whisper.

"Hey *you*."

"It didn't come true?" I ask.

"What?"

"Fawna's thing."

She smiles. "Does this look like hell to you?"

"It *is* a hospital."

She snorts.

Two nurses kick her out. They change the bandage on my chest. I learn I was shot by a stray bullet, in the arm and chest both. A large artery was hit, and I lost a lot of blood. I'm hooked to IVs.

I quiz them on my condition, becoming more alert as they work. Soon I'm utilizing my medical knowledge to have a very high-level conversation with them, using words like *suture* instead of *stitches,* and I find out a lot of scary information about my injury. I almost died, but they assure me I'll be okay.

"And there's no reason to worry about vein star," one of them says, apropos of nothing.

So it *is* on my chart! The information that I'm paranoid of vein-star syndrome. I'm about to protest, but then I think, let it be there. Let it be there with the flu shot and broken arms and blood tests and all the rest. That chart is about the past, not the future.

Still, why am I not dead? Why would fate spare me?

They want to know if I want visitors, and I do. There's a commotion at the door. One of the nurses is trying to enforce a rule about two at a time, but Packard's having none of it. The next thing I know, everyone's crowding in: Shelby, Carter, Vesuvius, Simon, Helmut.

Dad wears a surgical mask. I don't blame him; hospitals are the most bacteria-laden environments on the planet.

Packard's hair is mussed, and he looks tired. Happy. "We're going to break you out of here," he says.

I spy Fawna, in her usual outrageous outfit.

"Fawna! I thought I would...you know..." I don't want to say it aloud.

"Die?" Simon snorts. "It didn't come true, Justine, isn't that a shocker?"

Fawna flings a hand at him, like he's an insignificant bug. "It has nothing to do with true or not true." She draws nearer to me, pretty lips parted. "The one for whom the fate was cast was not you."

"Huh?" I ask.

"Fate was made to be fucked with," Simon says. "I think that's what Hello Kitty Visigoth here means."

Fawna crosses her arms, pointedly ignoring Simon. "You yourself changed, Justine. When the one who is to have the destiny changes in a profound way, the psychophysics of that person's fate is forever changed. You transformed so much, so *essentially*, that the fate no longer applied. You are no longer that one."

"Plain as day to *me* she's different," Dad says. "This prophecy, now—I certainly would've liked to have been informed about this prophecy."

"I couldn't zing him," I announce. "I can't zing anymore!"

There's a twinkle in Packard's eye. He gets it. The fear was outshone. "You beat it," he whispers. "And I love you so goddamn much."

Tears mist my vision—happiness, sadness, it's all mixed in. I'm dimly aware of Fawna, saying something else about the psychophysics of fate—"Three plus one is four, unless you change that one into a two. Or that three into a one. Profound and complete transformation of one of the subjects changes the outcome..."

I'm in the hospital for three more days. It takes practically that long to get caught up on the upheaval caused by the wedding.

It turns out that Otto and Stuart the dream invader were indeed working together. Stuart had gotten all of Otto's enemies under dream control, particularly Otto's political enemies. The big plan was for them to attack us *en masse* in front of the cameras during the wedding. Otto had planned to fight them—

quite publicly. He would have won too; Otto's force fields made him invincible. And nothing ruins a politician's credibility like being a sleepwalking cannibal on TV.

But as far as we can tell, Stuart brought in dozens more cannibals than he was supposed to.

According to the coroner's report, Otto died of head trauma, not vein star. Specifically, a shard of skull pierced his brain. His *inner circle* was his skull.

The day after the almost-wedding, Otto's body went missing, and the old pogo-stick-and-stilt factory by the river went up in flames. Packard is convinced it was Fawna who was responsible for that. He believes that she'd somehow gotten Otto's body to the one place he'd ever been happy, and set it ablaze. I'm glad for it.

I find out Shelby was in jail overnight for attacking Otto, but let off on probation as evidence of Otto's link with Stuart and the cannibals emerged, and especially his guilt in Avery's murder.

The papers were full of crazy pictures, some of which even made the national news. The reports that there were sleepwalking cannibals was chalked up to mass hysteria. People say Shelby and I both attacked Otto because we'd just learned that he'd killed Avery. People say that's what she whispered in my ear. The glasses remain unexplained. To most people, anyway.

Packard's there all through it, or at least, he's never far. And I'm getting gourmet meals and very attentive care, and Packard is allowed in the room at all hours; overall, the entire staff seems more interested in earning his approval than in enforcing rules. I call him on it one evening. "Are you using your mastermind powers to run this hospital wing?" I ask accusingly.

Packard smiles, just a little bit evil. "You'd rather have Jell-O?"

"I'd rather have buttered popcorn," I say.

Epilogue

My toes sink into the warm sand of the Midcity public beach. The August breeze whips my sundress around my knees as I look across the bright expanse toward Packard, who waits on the shore in jeans and bare feet and a billowing white shirt. His hair shines like an old penny, and behind him stretches clear, blue sky, and the waves of Lake Michigan, speckled with sun diamonds. All our friends are here, and somewhere, a lone violinist plays a simple little rondo. We wanted everything simple for our wedding. Just simple and easy and free.

I start my bridal stroll, grinning over at my pals—Shelby, Carter, Enrique, Simon, Vesuvius, Helmut, Jay. Cubby's there with his new wife. Francis and Rickie and my old dress shop friends have shown up, too. Professor Teufelsdrock leans on his cane beside them; he's helping to administer a university endowment in Avery's honor. Nobody wants the antihighcap glasses to be manufactured again, but some of Avery's wave theories have proven highly valuable to the physics community. Assisting with the endowment and the students seems to have helped Shelby immensely.

I smile over at Fawna, who is looking as wild and pretty as ever, holding a large picnic basket. She has a little apartment now, and is working with therapists. She promises to tell what happened to her...someday. But she's adjusting, aside from the strange hostility between her and Simon. Apparently the reckless gambler and the prognosticator are natural enemies in the wild.

Dad's in a Hawaiian shirt—he's not even wearing a surgical mask.

Seymour, the mutt Packard and I adopted a few months ago, races around, weaving in and out of the crowd.

Off to the side, telekinetic jugglers decorate the air with colorful balls, flowers, and silver stars.

I beam at Packard as I near him. It's all I can do not to run to him and jump into his arms.

This morning, Packard tied a pristine white bandana around Seymour's shaggy black neck in honor of our beachside wedding, even though there's nothing virginal about our union. We have spent a gloriously unvirginal spring, followed by a totally unvirginal summer, together in our fabulous apartment we picked out.

I reach Packard and take both his hands.

Midcity's new mayor, Henry Felix, starts the ceremony; he insisted on performing it himself. He's quite grateful to us, being that he was one of the cannibals under Stuart's control.

Henry Felix calls for rings. Shelby gives me mine; Simon brings the other to Packard.

Our vows are simple: we'll love each other always.

"I'm so happy and excited," I say.

Packard touches my cheek and kisses me. Henry Felix objects—we're going off script. "You mean we have to kiss *again*?" I ask. Packard gives me a sultry look. I can't wait to be husband and wife.

Finally, the mayor does the you-may-kiss-the-bride line and we enjoy a long, dipping mash of a kiss while everybody applauds.

Later, the picnic blankets are unfurled, and feasting begins. Mayor Felix's assistant hands out the champagne and people do toasts in our honor, which is nice, though a bit embarrassing. Afterwards, Shelby and Simon wander over and plop down on our blanket.

"Too many rainbows," Shelby says. "Always so many rainbows."

Simon snorts and takes a swig out of his champagne bottle.

Shelby says. "I hear your little family is expanding."

I narrow my eyes.

Packard gives me a sly look that makes me want to kiss him, and I do.

As if on cue, because she's always on cue, Fawna walks up with her picnic basket. She sets it down and takes out a scruffy little gray dog. "She was searching for you."

"Aww!" I scratch the little dog's head.

"Thank you, Fawna," Packard says.

"Was she searching for them in the *pound*?" Simon asks.

"Yes," Fawna says. "She has always belonged with them, and sought them in the pound."

Simon rolls his eyes.

Shelby pets the little dog's floppy ears; there's a softness in her face I haven't seen in a long time. I catch Packard's eyes; he sees it too. Suddenly I know she'll be okay. I know we'll all be okay.

I lie back with my head on Packard's stomach, staring up at the blue sky, careful not to look directly into the sun, which shines and shines like crazy, outshining the darkness.

About the Author

Carolyn Crane lives in Minneapolis with her husband and two daring cats.

She works a day job as a freelance advertising writer, and has for years. She's also waited tables at a surprising number of Minneapolis restaurants and bars (though not as many, incidentally, as her writer husband has). She's also been a shop clerk and a plastics factory worker, which she was dismal at (think *I Love Lucy*).

Also, she can relate almost any life experience to one or another Star Trek episodes, and if you invite her to your party, your cheese plate will be in grave danger.

During rare moments when she's not at her computer, she can be found reading in bed, running, helping animals, or eating Mexican food.

Find Carolyn at www.authorcarolyncrane.com, Twitter (@CarolynCrane), Facebook and Goodreads.

It's all about the story...

www.samhainpublishing.com

CPSIA information can be obtained at www.ICGtesting.com
Printed in the USA
BVOW03s0507010514

352137BV00001B/179/P